CRUEL EMPIRE

A.J. FALLOW

—•—

Boston Kings Series

The McTiernan Clan Trilogy

Dark Empire

Saint

Cruel Empire

Brutal Empire

The Moretti Syndicate Trilogy

Deadly Secrets

Deadly Lies

Sinner

Deadly Games

AUTHOR'S NOTE

Cruel Empire is part 2 in the McTiernan Clan Trilogy. It is highly recommended that you read *Dark Empire* (McTiernan Clan #1) and *Saint* (A McTiernan Clan Novella) first, as frequent mentions are made to characters and events. *Cruel Empire* is a dark romantic suspense novel, and it contains content and situations that could be triggering for some readers. This book is explicit and has explicit sexual content. It also contains graphic violence. It is not intended for readers under the age of 18.

The following is a list of potential triggers and explicit/graphic content. This list contains spoilers but is intended to better inform and pre-warn readers.

Graphic violence, blood, injuries, gunshot wounds, depictions of medical procedures, possible medical inaccuracies, infection/illness, death, death of a loved one/death of parents, fear of losing loved ones, pregnancy, childbirth/premature childbirth, smoking, illegal activities (related to mob/mafia lifestyle), gun trafficking, violent interrogation techniques, murder, assult, kidnapping/abduction, discussion of an off-screen r@pe/attempted r@pe, dominance, depression, anxiety, panic attacks, alcohol abuse, foul language, racial/ethnic slurs, sexually explicit scenes.

CHARACTER LIST

The McTiernan Clan

Territory - South Boston - Waterfront to Shawmut

Callum McTiernan: Clan Chief, father to Sloane and Aiden

Connor McTiernan: Warlord, Callum's nephew, married to Cassidy

Aiden McTiernan: Warlord (Deceased)

Sloane McTiernan: Arbiter, bartends at Lady Devine's

Michael Quinn: Former Clan Chief, father to Tommy and Cassidy

Tommy Quinn: Warlord

Cassidy McTiernan (Quinn): Trauma resident at Boston Medical Center, Connor's wife and Tommy's sister

Alfred "Alfie" Doyle: Master-at-Arms, Connor's best friend

Teagan Kelley: Reaper, works with Alfie, mole for Moretti family (deceased)

Dr. Jerome Carter: Chief Trauma Surgeon at Boston Medical Center, Cassidy's boss

The Moretti Family

Territory: North End – Downtown from the Charles Town to Beacon Hill. Ties to the Giordano Family in Providence by blood, Alliance with the Volkov Bratva

Lorenzo Moretti: Don, father to Dominic and Angelo

Viviana Moretti (Giordano): Lorenzo's wife

Salvatore "Sal" Giordano: Consigliere

Isabella Giordano: Sal's wife

Dominic "Dom" Moretti: Underboss

Angelo "Angel" Moretti: Capo

Luca Mariano: Capo, Emilia's best friend

Julian (Jules) Russo: Capo, Sofia's brother and Emilia's cousin

Sofia Russo: Emilia's cousin and Julian's sister

Emilia Russo: Lorenzo's adopted daughter

The Volkov Bratva

Territory: Jamaica Plain to Brookline. Ties to the Sointsevskaya Bratva in Moscow through Uncle Dmitri Volkov

Aleksandr Volkov: Pakhan (leader) of the Volkov Bratva

Misha: Soldat (soldier)

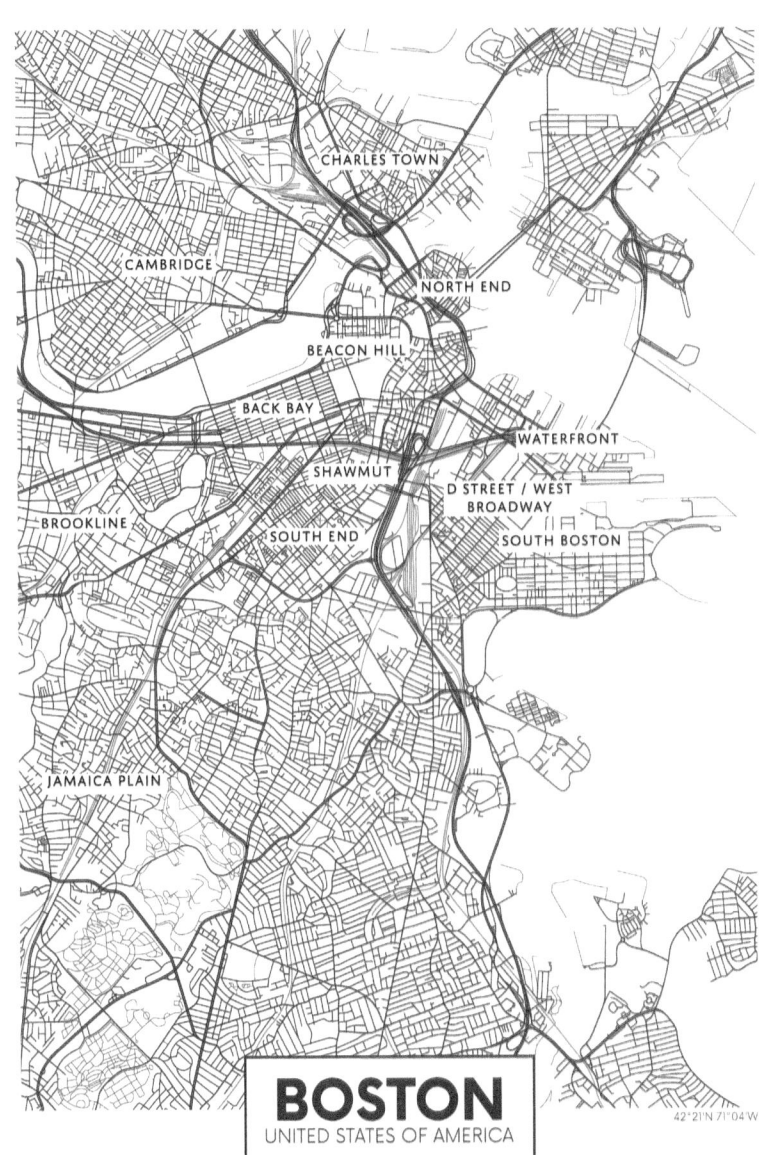

CHARLES TOWN

CAMBRIDGE

NORTH END

BEACON HILL

BACK BAY

WATERFRONT

SHAWMUT

D STREET / WEST
BROADWAY

BROOKLINE

SOUTH END

SOUTH BOSTON

JAMAICA PLAIN

BOSTON
UNITED STATES OF AMERICA

42°21'N 71°04'W

—·—

Playlist

Listen to the playlist on Spotify **HERE**

Rose Tattoo – Dropkick Murphys

No Good – KAELO

Be Mine – The Heavy

Come with Me Now – KONGOS

Fire – Barns Courtney

Delilah – Florence + the Machine

A Quick Death in Texas – Clutch

Supermassive Black Hole – Muse

Zombie – The Cranberries

Demons – Imagine Dragons (Acoustic)

Those Eyes – New West

—·—

Alfie - Now

The alley stank. Overflowing garbage spilled onto the ground, soot and grime creeping up the faded bricks. Layers of filth as old as the city itself. A dead end.

It seemed like a fitting place for this life to end.

Despite the potent surge of adrenaline rocketing through my system, I felt strangely calm. My focus lasered down until I could make out the individual dust motes in the air, each crack in the brick façade. I heard the hum of the flickering sodium lamp high overhead, the slow scuff of shoes against the pavement, the lazy drip, drip, drip of water down the sewer grate ticking down my last few moments like some kind of cosmic clock. The hyper-focus was at once both exhausting and invigorating. My God—this is what Connor must feel like all the time.

My time had been running out for a while now, and when Luca's huge shadow bracketed the end of the alley with Dominic and Angel close behind, I knew it was finally here.

I wasn't going to be walking out of this alley.

"Did you really think you could outrun us?" Angel sneered, stepping closer with an unsettling grin on his face. "You're not so clever now, are you?"

"Enough talking, Angel," Luca snapped, pulling out his gun and aiming it at my chest. "We've got a job to do."

"Luca...please. You don't have to do this." My back pressed against the chain link fence blocking the alley, and my heartrate doubled at the sight of the gun in his hand, unerringly pointed right at me. I raised my hands, palms out like that was all it would take to stop what was about to happen. "Look, I—"

"Angel, you're taking too damn long." Dom raised his gun.

And fired.

The bullet hit my side with the force of a sledgehammer, and I stumbled backward, gasping for air. Every breath I took rasped in my ears, and my vision started to checkerboard.

Fuck, this hurt so much more than the last time I was shot.

My knees buckled, and I collapsed against the chain link fence. My hands fumbled for purchase, rattling the metal links uselessly. I couldn't keep my feet. My knees hit the sidewalk, and I folded onto the concrete.

"I thought I'd save you the trouble," Dom said with a shrug.

Angel whirled on him, eyes blazing. "He was mine!"

"You were taking too long." Dom's gaze slid to mine, a cruel smirk twisting his lips. "Looks like you're not so tough without that behemoth Quinn to back you up, are you Doyle?"

Two pairs of boots stepped into view, and Luca gripped me by the hair and tilted my face up. "You should've known better, Alfie."

"Luca," I said, my voice hoarse. "Please."

"You think you can mess with Emilia, and we won't notice?" He released me and I slid bonelessly to the ground. "I'm doing this for her, you fucking piece of shit."

My pulse pounded unevenly in my ears. "Please..."

"Listen to the shithead cry." Angel leaned down into my wavering field of view. "This has been a long time coming, Irish."

"Let's go, Mariano," Dom said. "Finish him off."

I tried to say something, but I couldn't seem to get enough air. *Emilia.* At least she would be safe, now. That was really all that mattered in the end.

Luca stood and took a step back, aiming the gun directly at my heart. He was standing a few steps in front of Angel and Dom, so I was the only one who saw the regret in his dark eyes, his mouth a grim slash of tension.

"Don't...do this," I gasped. "Think about Emilia."

Luca looked at me, and his face smoothed out into something expressionless and cold. "I am."

He pulled the trigger. The bullet slammed into my chest like a battering ram, dead center. Blood blossomed on my shirtfront, drenching the fabric and pooling quickly on the pavement around me, reflecting the sodium lights overhead like so many stars across its inky surface.

I couldn't feel much, this time. That probably wasn't a good thing. My heart thudded wrongly in my chest, heavy, laboring beats as I tried to drag my arm up to my chest. Angel crouched down in front of me and eyed me like I was some kind of new, interesting species of insect. I unsuccessfully tried to spit a wad of bloody spit on his shoes.

He pressed the muzzle of his gun to my forehead.

"Say goodbye, Alfie."

1

— . —

EMILIA - TWO MONTHS AGO

THE NIGHT AIR WAS heavy with the scent of rain and the distant echo of sirens—a lullaby for the city that had become my battleground. It felt like a lifetime since the pages of my last chapter had closed; pages soaked in the blood of a war between two powerful families, and yet, it was only a few months ago.

I sighed and rested my chin on my hands, letting the familiar sounds and scents of the city wash over me. It was a rare moment of peace and quiet in a world that had become increasingly complex with each passing day. A chance to stop and breathe.

It was strange how the world could seem so quiet while everything around me bustled with life, and yet, in this one moment, it was just me and the city.

And all the secrets we shared.

Six months ago, a scruffy Irishman stumbled through the door of my bookstore with my brothers hot on his heels. A man I'd never seen before in my life, who'd turned my world upside down in a matter of hours. A man who changed me in ways I never might have imagined.

At the time, I didn't know what to call it.

Love? Obsession? Infatuation?

No matter what word I tried to use, it always felt like something more.

Alfie Doyle had wormed his way under my skin and into my heart, until I wasn't sure where I ended and he began. He'd been on the run, chased down by my brothers Dominic and Angelo. Our family had a long-running feud with the Irish mob in South Boston, headed by the McTiernan Clan, which had been made worse when a doctor at Boston Medical Center witnessed a hit by one of our moles. The doctor turned out to be none other than Cassidy Quinn, the daughter of former mob boss, Michael Quinn, and sister to one of their warlords, Tommy. In an effort to protect her from the price my family placed on her head, Michael had her wed Connor McTiernan, nephew of Callum, the current leader of the McTiernan Clan.

Alfie had been bruised and bloody and every bit the scoundrel on the day he slipped through the back door of my bookstore. I'd never forget the look in his eyes. That wild flash of desperation. That challenge. Against my better judgement, I hid him in the back storage closet and lied to my brothers when they asked if I'd seen him, waiting on pins and needles until they relented and left my shop. When I tried to shoo him off, he was playful and charming, seductive and just a bit possessive, an infuriating combination of hot-blooded male ego with the looks of a fallen angel.

But then he kissed me.

I closed my eyes and let my fingers drift up to brush against my lips, remembering.

I'd never felt anything like that. The heat. The rush.

It was like being struck by lightning.

In the weeks that followed, Alfie returned to my bookshop again and again like the love-struck fool that he was, and our secret affair continued. There was something about him. Something dangerous, but tender. Something broken, but steadfast. Something dark, but pure. And, for some reason, he looked at me like I was his saving grace. Like he saw something in me that nobody else did. Something I couldn't even see in myself.

Our Romeo and Juliette love affair burned hot and fast, like a candle lit at both ends, and it was only a matter of time before the bottom dropped out. I shuddered, remembering the sound of the gunshot and the sight of Alfie's blood on my hands. The dark days that followed, and just how close I'd come to losing him.

"Hey," a voice broke through my reflection as I sat on the fire escape above the bookshop, looking down at the darkened alley below. "You've been out here for a while."

"Thinking," I murmured, not turning to face Luca, who had joined me on the rusted metal platform.

"Careful, thoughts are a dangerous neighborhood to wander alone at night."

"Are they?" I asked rhetorically, the corners of my lips twitching into a faint, wry smile.

Luca didn't answer right away, and I was grateful for his silence. My best friend knew better than anyone what kind of dark thoughts kept me up at night.

Although Luca ranked as a made man in the Moretti Crime Family--one of three capos under my brother Dominic's command--Luca's loyalty to me had been proven beyond all measure during the weeks leading up to the explosive showdown at our family compound. It was Luca who had gotten Alfie to safety after he'd been shot by Angel. It was Luca's shoulder I had cried on after finding out the horrible truth about my mother's affair with Lorenzo. My father's murder at Lorenzo's hands, the man who had raised me as an adoptive father. My mother's subsequent suicide. It had been Luca who had agreed to help me betray my own family by smuggling Alfie and Connor into the compound to rescue Cassidy after she'd been abducted by Teagan.

And it was Luca who had kissed me before the gunpowder had even settled.

I knew he'd done so to throw off Angel's suspicion over my involvement, but the kiss had been searing and passionate--it didn't leave me weak in the knees like a kiss from Alfie, but it had been telling all the same. That kiss might have sparked something in another life. Sweet and longing and possessive, tempered by Luca's desperation and the knowledge that it would be the first and the last time he kissed me. Because someone else already held my heart, and Luca knew it.

And he risked it all, our friendship and his heart, in order to give me an alibi for that night.

"All right, kid--talk to me. What's got you tied up in knots?" Luca asked.

"I just...I keep thinking about that night," I replied. "The night Angel and Dominic came looking for me. The night..."

"The night I kissed you," Luca said flatly. "I know."

I nodded. "That night."

"I'm sorry." He leaned forward, resting his arms on his knees and peering out at the glittering city. His dark features were hardened into something impenetrable, and I thought with a sudden pang that I couldn't remember the last time I'd seen him smile.

"Luca..." I trailed off. How could I even begin to put it into words? It felt like there were too many things to say. Too many emotions swirling around inside of me. Too much to untangle. I sighed. "Do you regret it?"

"Kissing you?" he asked, turning to look at me. His dark eyes seemed almost black in the dim light of the alley below us. When I nodded, he turned away again, staring into the darkness. "No."

"No?"

Luca shook his head. "No. I don't regret kissing you, Emilia."

I frowned. "But--"

"Don't. Don't ask questions that you don't want answered," he cut me off with a harsh laugh. He ran a hand through his hair, leaving it tousled. "Emilia...you're my best friend. My oldest friend. The only person in this whole goddamn family that I trust--and I mean truly trust. Except Sofia, maybe, but she's too damn flighty."

I laughed at his spot-on description of my little cousin.

That got a rare smile out of him, but it faltered around the edges. He turned to me, and for a moment, I saw the weight of everything that he carried on his shoulders reflected in those dark eyes. A weariness that mirrored my own. A resigned sadness that was both familiar and heartbreaking.

Luca cleared his throat, and the mask slipped back into place. That stoic, unreadable facade that was heartbreakingly new. "I won't lie to you,

Em. Not even to spare your feelings. I wish things were different, but they aren't. We're not kids anymore. And that night proved that we can't just run around pretending like the world doesn't exist."

I sighed and rested my chin on my knees. Luca reached over and tucked a lock of hair behind my ear. "Alfie Doyle is one lucky son of a bitch."

"Luca..."

He shook his head. "It's okay. Really. I'm fine. I've been fine. It sucks, but it is what it is. I still love you, even though you will never look at me like that. I just need time to get used to the idea, you know? But I promise--we're good. I swear it."

I nodded. "I understand."

"I'll keep your secrets." He smiled faintly. "Always."

And what a secret it was. Alfie and I continued to see each other in secret. Hidden meetings stolen between the pages of my favorite books, furtive kisses and passionate nights together. It was a reckless, stupid, dangerous thing to do, and yet, I couldn't stay away. I was addicted to him, to his touch. To the way he looked at me. The way he made me feel.

Safe.

Loved.

Wanted.

Beautiful.

Things that nobody had ever made me feel before. Things I didn't even know that I wanted.

It was a dangerous game we played, but it was worth it.

Or at least, that's what I told myself.

We had to be careful. Nobody could know about us--if Lorenzo found out, or worse, if Angel figured it out, Alfie would end up with a bullet in his head along with Luca. I couldn't bear to think about the consequences. Too many people knew about us as it was.

"When do you see him again?" Luca asked, interrupting my thoughts.

"Tonight," I replied. "I'm meeting him in an hour."

Luca shook his head, his jaw clenching. "Be careful."

"I always am," I said lightly.

He snorted, but it resolved into a grin. "You were until you met that Irishman."

I shrugged. I couldn't deny that Alfie brought out something reckless in me. Something wild. Something that felt more alive than I'd ever felt before. I didn't care if it was reckless, or foolish, or even dangerous--I just knew that I needed it.

I checked the time on my phone for the millionth time, glancing around the smoky, dark room. The music thumped loudly in time with my heartbeat, making me anxious. My phone was on silent, but every time I glanced at it, the screen lit up to show no new messages.

I took a sip of my drink, the bright citrus mingling on my tongue, trying to ignore the fluttering in my stomach. My fingers drummed a nervous rhythm on the polished wood of the bar as I waited. It was absurd to feel like a virginal schoolgirl on her first date, but it had been this way every time Alfie and I met. One of these times might be our last moments together, and I would never know until it was too late.

My pulse jumped when I felt a hand slip around my waist, and Alfie pressed a kiss to the curve of my neck. "Miss me?"

I shivered, my eyes fluttering closed as he pressed his lips to the sensitive skin below my ear. "You're late."

"You look incredible," he murmured, his voice sending a fresh wave of goosebumps over my skin.

"Thank you." I turned to face him, slipping my arms around his neck. "But you're still late."

Alfie laughed, the sound rumbling against my chest as he pulled me against him. He smelled like spice and smoke and something else, something I couldn't name, but something that was uniquely his. His hair was still damp from the shower, and his eyes were bright as he grinned down at me.

"I'm sorry, things ran long with Tommy, and I wanted to wash up before I came here."

My brow creased. "Is everything all right?"

"Yeah, everything is fine," Alfie replied, kissing the top of my head. "We were just working out some business with Callum, who loves more than anything to hear himself talk. Nothing to worry about."

"Okay," I murmured, forcing myself to relax. Alfie kissed my mouth, my jaw, down my throat, tickling me with his scruff until I giggled.

"There's my girl. Come on, let's dance," Alfie said, tugging on my hand. He pulled me towards the crowded dance floor, the lights flashing and strobing above us as he wrapped his arms around me, his hands resting on my hips.

I smiled up at him and slid my arms around his neck, letting myself relax into the music. Alfie's eyes never left mine, his gaze hungry and possessive, and I loved it. I loved that I made him feel like that. I loved that he wanted me.

The song shifted to something slower, and Alfie pulled me closer, our bodies pressed together as we moved to the music. I ran my fingers through his hair, and he leaned down to press a kiss to my lips, his tongue sliding against mine. I felt the heat of his hands on my body, one hand pressing against the small of my back, the other sliding up to tangle in my hair. I sighed into his kiss, melting against him. The music shifted again, and Alfie pulled back, his breath coming hard and heavy as his eyes darkened with desire.

He kissed me again, searing and desperate, and I could feel the throbbing of my heartbeat between my legs. It was a sweet ache, a yearning, like all of my nerves were centered on one thing--my overwhelming need to have him.

"Let's get out of here," he whispered into my ear, his fingers tracing a slow path along my spine. I nodded, unable to speak. Alfie grinned and took my hand, leading me through the throng of dancers and into the cool autumn night.

We stepped outside, and the cool breeze across my heated skin felt amazing.

Alfie's hand slipped around mine, and he led me down the street to his car parked at the curb. It was a sleek, black town car, and he hurried to open the back door for me. I climbed inside, and he followed, pulling me to him the moment the door closed behind him.

His kisses were hungry and passionate, his fingers digging into my hips as he pulled me onto his lap. He buried his face in my neck, his teeth and tongue marking a trail along my collarbone, his hands roaming the curves of my body.

"You are mine, Emilia," he whispered across my skin. "Do you hear me? Mine."

I let my head fall back, loving the sound of his voice as he said my name. I felt the steel length of him pressed against my center, and I shuddered, knowing how badly he needed me. I leaned back and tugged on the buttons of his shirt, my lips tracing the tattoos inked into his skin.

Alfie groaned, his breath hot against my neck, as he fumbled with the buttons on my dress, peeling it from my shoulders. He stopped, staring at my exposed skin, hunger shining in his eyes. I blushed under the weight of his gaze.

"What?"

"You're so fucking beautiful," he murmured. His hands traced over my body, like he was memorizing every curve. I shivered at the feeling of his touch on my bare skin, and he kissed me again, his lips moving over mine in a way that made me melt.

Alfie kissed a trail down my neck, his scruff scratching in a delicious way that made my toes curl. He trailed kisses along my collarbone, his tongue teasing the sensitive skin, before he captured one of my nipples in his mouth. I gasped as he sucked and nibbled on the stiff peak, my hands tangling in his hair.

I ground my hips against him, and Alfie moaned, the sound vibrating through me. His fingers teased my other nipple, pinching and tugging in a way that sent a jolt of pleasure through my core. He switched his attention to the other side, lavishing my other breast with the same attention. I writhed on his lap, the friction of his jeans against my center driving me wild.

Alfie's hands gripped my hips, holding me in place as he kissed his way down my stomach, his tongue teasing the hollow of my hip bone. I felt him smiling against my skin, and he kissed the inside of my thigh, tracing the lace edge of my panties.

I moaned, my head falling back, as Alfie's lips moved against my center, his tongue teasing my most sensitive spot through the thin fabric. I felt the familiar tightening in my stomach, and I gasped as his teeth tugged on the edge of my panties, pulling them to the side to expose me to his mouth.

His tongue flicked against me, sending another shockwave of pleasure through my core, before he captured me with his lips, sucking and teasing in ways that made my legs shake. He worked me with his mouth, circling and swirling until I was panting and gasping, begging him to let me come.

"Not yet, baby girl."

Alfie's grin was pure sin. He kissed the soft skin of my inner thigh and slowly pulled my soaked panties off, taking a moment to admire my glistening center. He trailed soft kisses up my thigh, making me tremble with need, before sliding a finger inside me.

I gasped as he curled his finger, pressing against the spot deep within me that made me tremble. His thumb circled my clit, and I bit my lip to keep from crying out.

He added another finger, pumping into me slowly, before picking up speed. I rocked my hips against his hand, my breath coming in ragged gasps. Alfie leaned forward his tongue teasing me as he pumped his fingers faster and deeper. I clutched his hair, my eyes squeezed shut as waves of pleasure crashed over me. Alfie growled against me, and the vibration sent me over the edge. I could feel myself climbing towards that delicious precipice, my legs shaking and my breath coming in short gasps, before he slid his fingers out of me and sucked on them, his eyes dancing wickedly. "Tell me what you want."

"Please..." I panted, grinding my hips against him.

"Tell me, baby," he cooed, trailing kisses up my throat, taking my nipple in his mouth and biting playfully. "You know I like it when you beg."

I shivered, the combination of his soft lips and sharp teeth sending lightning through my body. "I need you."

"Yeah, I know. But where do you need me, beautiful girl?" His hands kneaded my ass, rocking me against his thick erection, the friction of it making me tremble with want.

"Inside me," I whimpered, my voice breaking.

Alfie chuckled, his fingers gripping my hips to hold me steady as he unzipped his jeans. I took advantage of his distraction and lavished attention on his inked chest, teasing and stroking his nipples and drawing a sharp curse from him. He swore again as I ground my hips against him, and I smirked into his skin.

He fisted the hair at the nape of my neck, tilting my head back and kissing me with a savage hunger that left me breathless. Alfie lifted my hips, positioning himself against my entrance, and I sank down onto him, moaning as he filled me.

I gasped as he thrust into me, his grip on my hips bruising as he pulled me down onto him, his cock stretching and filling me in all the best ways. I dug my nails into his shoulders, my head falling back as he drove into me, hitting that perfect spot deep within me with every stroke. Alfie growled and buried his face in my neck, his breath hot against my skin, as he pounded into me.

I was getting close, that familiar tension building in my core as he slammed into me, his rhythm erratic and frantic. Alfie slipped his hand between us, his fingers rubbing my clit as he fucked me, sending me hurtling towards that sweet release. I cried out as I came, my orgasm washing over me in waves, my body clenching around him. Alfie groaned, burying his face in my neck as he followed me down into the abyss, shuddering as he spilled inside me.

I collapsed against him, my head resting on his shoulder as we caught our breath. Alfie kissed my temple, his arms wrapping around me and holding me close. I smiled, tracing the lines of his tattoos with my fingertips. Beneath my fingers his heart still hammered a frantic rhythm against his ribs, echoing mine. Alfie tilted my chin up, his lips finding mine in a tender kiss that made my toes curl. He stroked my cheek, his expression soft and vulnerable in a way that made my heart ache.

"Love you," he murmured.

I kissed him softly. "Love you more."

Alfie held me close, his fingers playing with my hair as we basked in the afterglow. My thoughts drifted, and I sighed, trying to hold on to my contentment. Alfie kissed the top of my head.

"Hey," he said, his voice rough and warm. "What's the sigh for?"

I shrugged. "I just...I wish we didn't have to hide."

Alfie sighed, and I heard the pain in the sound. "It's not always going to be like this. I promise."

"You seem so sure."

He pulled back and looked at me, uncharacteristically serious. "You deserve better than this. You deserve to love who you want--"

"I love you."

"I know you do," he grinned, a flash of white in the darkened interior of his car. "And I love you more than anything, beautiful girl. But you deserve a life that's not secret and hidden and full of lies. You deserve a life where you don't have to constantly be afraid. And I am going to give that to you, if it's the last thing I do."

Despite the warmth his words inspired, I shivered at the conviction in Alfie's voice. I didn't want to think about last things and ultimatums. He must have sensed my unease, because he kissed me, slow and sweet and full of promises, and I melted into him, letting myself believe that this was a beginning and not an ending.

2

— • —

CONNOR

THE WORLD HAD A way of putting me in my place, and it always seemed to happen just as I thought I was invincible. The taste of victory still lingered on my lips as I stared out at the rolling waves crashing against the shore. Each surge of water mirrored the unbidden emotions that threatened to consume me.

It was bittersweet, this feeling of victory.

I had won. Cassidy was safe.

Teagan was dead.

So why did it still feel like I was fracturing into pieces?

The salt air whipped around me, stinging my eyes as I stared out at the ocean. The sun was just starting to rise, painting the sky in hues of gold and pink that seemed too bright for my mood. I inhaled deeply, letting the scent of seaweed and brine fill my lungs. It was a familiar smell--one that reminded me of childhood summers spent running across the sand, chasing Aiden and Tommy as we pretended to be pirates or spies or soldiers.

Those days seemed like another lifetime ago. Another version of myself. One that was carefree and lighthearted, without a single scar.

But that boy was gone, and the man that was left behind carried scars that went deeper than skin. Scars that ached with a dull, persistent pain that never quite went away.

Scars that were my penance for failing to protect those I loved.

First, my parents, and then Aiden.

Cassidy.

It was my burden to carry--the knowledge that I wasn't enough, would never be enough, to keep the people I cared about from getting hurt. To keep the people I loved from being broken. I was very careful never to let Cassidy see the weight I carried like a lodestone around my neck. She carried enough scars of her own.

Scars from Teagan's clever, wicked blade. Scars from her desperate escape from her prison. Even more scars, deeper than flesh and bone, invisible and cut into her very soul. I felt my heart falter and crumble every time I imagined what she must have gone through in that basement--and that's all I could do. Imagine. Because Cassidy refused to say a word about her abduction, not to a therapist, and not to me.

That one stung the most.

She said she didn't blame me, but how could she not? I blamed myself. It hadn't quite been rape, the doctor had told me, but my God, did that make it any better? Cassidy was my heart and my soul, the strongest person I knew and the woman who somehow accepted me and loved me back despite everything I was, and this is how I repaid her.

Teagan had taken something from her that day, and I was powerless to give it back.

So, day by day, I watched her belly grow with the baby I'd put inside her as I tried to hold onto the tattered edges of our life and maintain some semblance of normalcy.

Our child. Just one more thing she hadn't had any say in.

I couldn't make the fear or pain go away, no matter how much I wanted to. All I could do was stand helplessly on the sidelines as Cassidy pushed herself too hard, refusing to acknowledge that what happened had hurt her in the first place. I'd watched as her nightmares worsened, watched as she barely ate a thing, watched as the woman I loved broke before my eyes, and yet, I couldn't do a thing about it. The more I pushed her, the more she drew away from me.

This was my own personal purgatory.

"That's enough brooding, Heathcliff!" Sloane called out, jogging down the beach towards me. I turned to face her, not bothering to put a smile on my face. I had little patience for small talk these days.

"What are you doing here?" I asked. "Wait--where's Cass?"

Sloane shoved a hand into my chest, stopping me as I started for the stairs up to the house. "Woah there. First, Cassidy is in the sunroom, manically typing away on her computer. And before you ask, Tommy drove up with me and is with her now, and yes, he made sure she ate something, and yes, she was warm enough. She also scowled at Tommy and called him a dirty word in Gaelic. Tommy says she's been hanging around you too long, but I thoroughly enjoyed it."

The knot of tension in my chest eased a bit. "And the second thing?"

Sloane crossed her arms over her chest as she came to a stop next to me. "Callum called a meeting. Apparently, things are heating up with Lorenzo."

I sighed. "Of course they are."

Sloane frowned, studying me closely. "You look like shit."

"Thanks," I replied dryly. "I'd return the sentiment, but you look fantastic as always."

"I know I do." Sloane pulled me into a hug. I stiffened for only a moment before I forced myself to relax. Sloane was a tactile person, and I knew it was more for her benefit than mine.

"How are you holding up?" she asked, pulling back to search my face.

"Fine."

"Bullshit."

I shrugged, turning to stare back out at the ocean. The waves rolled in, one after another, each crest crashing against the shore with a vengeance. A muscle ticked in my jaw, a sure sign that I was worked up over something, and I knew Sloane saw it, too. She reached out and grabbed my arm, forcing me to look at her.

"Connor...talk to me," she said, her voice softer than I expected. Sloane studied me for a long moment, and I could tell she was choosing her words carefully. "How are things with you two? We haven't really talked since..."

She trailed off, and I saw the uncertainty written across her face.

"Between us? Good, as long as I don't ask how she's feeling or why she barely eats or what's keeping her up at night." I glared out at the waves. "And it's not like I don't know. It's not like I don't know that bastard is haunting her day in and day out, that she's in pain. She just...she won't talk about it. Not to me, not to anyone."

I scrubbed a hand over my face, exhaustion seeping into my bones. I felt stretched thin, like a rubber band about to snap, and I knew she saw it. "I can't help her, Sloane. This is all my fault. She won't let me help her, and it is ripping me apart."

Sloane was quiet for a moment, her fingers tightening on my arm. "What happened wasn't your fault. There was nothing you could have done to prevent it."

I didn't want to hear that. Empty platitudes. Her pity made it worse.

I pulled free from her grasp. "I'm going up to the house. Callum will be here soon."

"Connor, don't--"

I strode back up the beach towards the sprawling estate, leaving Sloane behind. I knew she meant well, but I didn't want to hear it. I couldn't bear to listen to anyone try and make excuses for my failures. Cassidy was my responsibility. My wife. The mother of my child. And I had failed to protect her in the worst possible way. That was my cross to bear.

Tommy and Cassidy were in the living room, a sunny, oak-paneled room with floor-to-ceiling windows that overlooked the ocean. A Steinway Concert Grand stood resolutely in the corner, its keys gathering dust. I'd played for Cassidy a couple times since we'd arrived, but it didn't seem to bring her pleasure like it used to. Nothing did.

I would burn South Boston down to the ground for one of her smiles.

Tommy looked wildly out of place in his jeans and fauxhawk amidst the tasteful furnishings and seascapes on the walls, a delicate China teacup balanced in one massive hand that displayed carefully inked scrollwork across the knuckles--Fuil agus Onóir.

He glanced up as I entered the room, but didn't move from the couch next to Cassidy, who was typing away on her laptop, a stack of notebooks and papers scattered across the coffee table. She'd gotten quite adept at typing one-handed, since her left arm was still encased in a heavy plaster cast. Months of physical therapy still awaited her, and even if she regained full use of her arm, returning to her residency was still questionable. One more thing she refused to talk about.

I studied my wife as she worked, taking in the dark circles under her eyes, the tension in her shoulders, the way she absently chewed on her lower lip as she concentrated. She'd lost weight, too much weight, I thought, and the dark gray sweater she wore hung off her frame. Her belly had begun to swell and round as our child grew, but even the rosy glow of pregnancy couldn't hide the ever-present weariness that seemed an integral part of her now. My heart twisted painfully in my ribs as I watched her work, and I hated myself for selfishly wishing she would look up and smile at me. Even just once. Just like before.

Tommy caught me staring at Cassidy's belly, and he set his china cup down on the coffee table. "You need to get some proper coffee mugs, man. I feel like I'm at a goddamn garden party with this shit."

A smile twitched at the corner of my mouth. "Blame Callum, not me. I just live here."

"I thought you would've remedied the situation by now, Cass." Sloane leaned in the doorway. "Where's your usual soup bowl-sized mug of joe?"

"I gave it up," Cass said without looking up. "It's bad for the baby."

So's stress, I thought.

Cassidy reached for the cup of herbal tea she'd been drinking instead of coffee, but her fingers were shaking. She fumbled the handle, and the cup fell off the table and shattered on the floor. She flinched at the sound.

Tommy was already on his feet as I took a step towards her, but she shook her head violently. "It's okay. I've got it."

I stopped, feeling useless, watching as she stooped to gather up the broken pieces of the teacup. Sloane brought a dustpan in from the kitchen and helped her clean up the rest. The surge of jealousy that briefly flared when Cass let her help made me feel even lower that I already did.

I ran a hand through my hair, frustration eating away at me.

"I'm out," Tommy muttered, stalking over to me. He jerked his head towards the hallway, and I followed him out of the living room.

We walked in silence until we reached the library--a grandiose name for a cozy little study with bookshelves lining three walls and a fireplace dominating the fourth. Tommy closed the door behind me, walked over to the built-in bar, and poured himself a whiskey out of a crystal decanter. He tossed it back in one shot.

"Damn, that's good stuff. Why don't we stock this at Lady D's?" He frowned at the decanter and poured himself another whiskey. It didn't escape my notice that he didn't offer me one. Tommy dropped into one of the leather wingback chairs. "Talk to me, brother."

"About what?"

"Don't play dumb with me." Tommy fixed me with a knowing look. "You're beating yourself up over something that isn't your fault."

"Isn't it?" I countered bitterly.

Tommy shook his head. "No. No, it fucking isn't. You think I don't blame myself for what happened to Cassidy? You think Alfie doesn't feel responsible for dragging Emilia into his mess? We both did everything we could to find her--everything short of burning Boston to the ground. And that's exactly what Lorenzo wants."

"It wasn't enough." I clenched my hands into fists, my nails digging into my palms. "I wasn't enough. I promised I'd keep her safe."

Tommy slammed his glass down. "Stop wallowing, McTiernan. Get your shit together. Your wife needs you to be strong, whether you believe it or not. So suck it up and help me figure out how we're gonna rain hellfire down on Lorenzo Moretti."

"I'm not wallowing," I snapped, annoyed at his tone. Tommy had always been a loose cannon, but lately, he was teetering dangerously close to a full-blown explosion. "I just--"

Tommy narrowed his eyes. "If you say you just want Cassidy to be happy one more goddamn time, I swear to Christ I'll punch you in the mouth."

I glared at him. "Fine. What do you want me to say?"

"That you're pissed! That you want blood! That you wanna rip Lorenzo Moretti limb from fucking limb for what he allowed. For what he orchestrated. For what Teagan did to Cassidy. Jesus, Con--you're acting like a kicked puppy, and it's pissing me off."

Tommy downed another whiskey. "You may be married to Cass, but she's still my goddamn sister. Do you think it's any easier for me to see her like this? You think I don't want to make this all go away for her?

Of course, I do. But I also know my sister, and Cassidy has never done anything until she's good and ready for it. Push her, she'll push back. And you slouching around like a moody teenager ain't helping anybody."

I blinked. "I do not slouch."

"Sure you don't," Tommy said as he reached for the decanter.

"Think you've had enough?"

"Don't tell me what to do."

"Tommy--"

"Shut up." Tommy poured another two fingers of whiskey. "Just...shut up. Don't act like you're better than me, McTiernan. You think I don't know what you're doing?"

I raised an eyebrow. "Do enlighten me."

"Punishing yourself." Tommy slammed the decanter down with a thud that made me wince. "It's always been your MO, ever since Aiden died. You blame yourself for not being able to save him, so you beat yourself up--take all the guilt and the pain and the shame and pile it onto your shoulders like you're Atlas or some shit. Well, it's not helping. And it's not fair to Cassidy."

I opened my mouth to argue, but Tommy cut me off with a glare. "You wanna be a martyr, fine. Be my guest. But leave Cass out of it. And for fucks sake, get your head back in the game. Callum needs you, and Alfie and I are getting pretty damn tired of having to do everything ourselves."

He was right. If I was feeling particularly self-pitying, I'd admit to myself that Tommy's words hurt. It wasn't that they lacked validity; no, his honesty was exactly what I needed to pull my head out of my own ass, as he so eloquently put it. Anything would be better than hovering in this perpetual state of limbo. And who knew--without me hovering over her like a mother hen, maybe Cass could start to heal too.

I sighed, scrubbing a hand over my face. "Sorry. You're right."

"I usually am."

"So modest, too."

He stood up and clapped me on the shoulder, a little harder than necessary. "Come on, Callum should be here soon."

3

— · —

ALFIE

"THAT IS THE LAST time I'm riding with you, Doyle," Callum grumbled as he hauled himself from my car. "You drive too damned fast."

"Don't ever ride with Tommy, then," I said dryly.

"I already learned that particular lesson." Callum glared at Tommy's car across the drive, a midnight blue Challenger with a 6.4L V8 HEMI that he'd inexplicably named Diana. Tommy was a damn terror in that car.

The summer air held a hint of crispness, a reminder that fall was just around the corner. The scent of blooming flowers hung heavy in the air, but it was tainted by the undeniable weight of something darker. I followed Callum up the gravel path, the sound of my polished shoes crunching against the stones beneath my feet. Like Callum, I wore a tailored three-piece suit, but a Glock rested snugly in my shoulder holster; with Teagan the turncoat dead and Connor temporarily out of the picture, I had added a few extra duties to my already overloaded plate, and it was playing hell on my wardrobe.

"Somebody get me a damned drink," Callum declared as we entered the foyer. "Alfie took about a decade off my life on the drive up."

"Hold your horses, old man." Sloane appeared at Callum's elbow with a tumbler of Knappogue Single Malt, her dancing eyes softening her sarcasm. Callum grunted his thanks and took a long swallow from the glass, his expression immediately relaxing. Tommy strolled in from the library, a bottle of expensive whiskey clutched in one massive hand. He smirked as Callum drained the last of his drink and handed him the open bottle.

The sight of Tommy with a bottle in his hand was becoming more and more commonplace, and I wondered how much longer Callum was going to ignore it. Everybody had their own way of dealing with trauma, I guess. For all his tough-guy act, it was clear that the fallout from his sister's abduction was eating Tommy alive. I didn't envy him.

Tommy jerked his head towards the sunroom. "Cassidy's in there working on whatever the fuck it is she's writing. Connor's in the library."

Tommy met my eye with a slightly glazed but weighted stare which I assumed had something to do with Connor's state of mind. I hadn't seen him since he brought Cass up here to the summer house, and if Tommy looked as rough as he did, I could only imagine how Connor was going to be.

I left the rest of them in the foyer and walked down the hall to the library. Connor was leaning against the windowpane, staring out at the ocean beyond. It looked like he had slept in his clothes. His normally immaculate appearance was slightly rumpled, and there were dark circles under his eyes. Beneath the couple day's worth of beard scruff his skin had taken on a sallow cast, like someone who'd been sick for a while.

Damn. I should've come up here to check on him sooner.

"Hey, brother," I said quietly.

Connor turned to face me, and I winced inwardly. Yeah, he was definitely looking rough. His gaze drifted over me, and he frowned. "When did you get a suit?"

I shrugged. "About the same time I got a desk job."

"You look ridiculous." Connor smiled faintly, but it didn't reach his eyes. "It's good to see you, mate."

I clasped his extended hand, pulling him into a tight hug. Connor stiffened for only a moment before he relaxed into it, and I thumped him hard on the back. "Good to see you too, man. Sorry I haven't made it up here until now."

"It's okay. You've been busy." Connor released me and stepped back. He ran a hand through his hair, the movement betraying his frayed nerves. It wasn't like him to have a tell like that. Except for people who knew him, it was usually almost impossible to guess at what was going on behind that icy blue stare. The man was a sphynx and seeing him like this was shocking.

"How is everything?" he asked.

I shrugged. "As good as can be expected."

"That bad, huh?"

"It could be worse." I tilted my head. "How's Cassidy?"

From down the hall, I heard Callum's booming voice carrying through the house. Connor glanced towards the door, his jaw clenching. "She's ...hanging in there. As best she can."

"And you?"

"I'm fine," he snapped. "Tommy and Sloane are already up my ass with that head shrinking shit, don't you start too."

I held up my hands placatingly. Connor was touchy as hell, which was unusual for him. He must really be stressed. "All right, all right. No head shrinking. But...if you wanna talk--"

"I don't." Connor brushed past me. "Come on, Callum will want to get started soon."

I followed him back down the hallway. As we passed the sunroom, I saw Cassidy and Sloane sitting together on the couch. Cassidy looked up as we passed, and our gazes met for a split second before she dropped her eyes back to her computer screen. She looked exhausted and painfully thin despite the telling roundness of her belly. I didn't envy Connor right now. Cassidy was going to be a handful for the foreseeable future, especially since she refused to let anyone help her. I knew all too well about the stubborn streak of iron that ran through the Quinn siblings--Tommy alone was proof of that.

We joined the others in the dining room, where Callum sat at the head of the table with Tommy and Grady flanking him. He glanced up as we entered, and I knew by the crease between his brows that he had noticed Connor's disheveled appearance. "Take a seat," Callum said.

Connor settled into a chair across from Tommy, and I took the one next to him. Callum steepled his fingers in front of him, his expression grave. "Now listen up. It's been a hell of a month for everyone, but a few things have come to my attention that can't be ignored any longer. Alfie?"

Callum nodded in my direction, and I cleared my throat. "Right. So as you know, Lorenzo's intelligence has been compromised with Teagan

Kelley's death. He's been scrambling to patch holes in his network, but we've managed to infiltrate quite a bit of his operations since the mole's demise. Unfortunately, it seems that Lorenzo's brutality has increased in lieu of information, and several of our local businesses have suffered. We've also received reports of retaliation attacks, some of which have been...rather extreme."

"Extreme how?" Connor asked.

"Street level brutality," I said. "Beatings, robberies, assaults--all increasing at a fairly alarming rate. We think Lorenzo is trying to send a message by targeting small businesses that aren't directly tied to the Clan."

Tommy scowled. "He's cutting our legs out from under us. Stir things up enough in our own backyard, and our people begin to doubt our protection. My guys have been working their asses off, trying to keep things level, but for every fire we put out, two more pop up."

"It's a losing battle," I agreed. "Callum's given me leave to bring more men into the fold, but--"

"We need you back, Connor," Callum interrupted. His tone brokered no argument. "You belong at my side. It's time to put this shit with Cassidy behind us and focus on the business."

Connor stiffened in his chair. "This shit, as you so eloquently put it, nearly killed my wife, Callum. She's pregnant, for fuck's sake--"

"And she's still alive because of you!" Callum thundered. "Cassidy is safe, and she's healing. You've done your duty, and now it's time to come back to work."

Tension thickened in the air to choking proportions. I expected Tommy to explode, to rally to his sister's defense, but he just tossed back the last of his whiskey in a single gulp. Connor bristled, his anger palpable. I felt the icy rage radiating off him in waves. "Cassidy--"

Callum slammed his hand on the table. "Is not your priority, boyo! This is war, Connor--Lorenzo Moretti wants us gone, and he's not playing around anymore. We need you here--Tommy needs you here. You're my fucking left hand, and I need you sharp. Remember what happened the last time you shirked your responsibilities."

It was a low blow, one I physically felt on Connor's behalf. Connor was only nineteen when his cousin Aiden, Callum's son, had agreed to take Connor's place on a weapons drop so that Connor could attend his college finals. The drop went south, and Aiden had taken a bullet to the gut. He bled out in Tommy's arms.

Connor's jaw ticked, but he nodded in agreement.

"Good," Callum said. "Go on, Doyle."

Sometimes, I really hated my job.

"Police activity is at an all-time high," I continued. "Between gang violence and Lorenzo's overtures, we're struggling to keep our noses clean."

Tommy glowered into his empty glass and set it heavily on the table. "Moretti's been greasing palms all across Southie. It's getting hard to know who to trust."

"We trust no one, except the people in this room," I said. "Teagan proved that point."

Even as I said it, I felt a twinge of guilt. Tommy looked right at me, his watery gaze hardening. He and Connor were the only ones who knew about my secret affair with Emilia, and although he hadn't said anything to Callum, he'd made it plain that he thought I was a fool. I swallowed thickly, averting my eyes from his accusatory stare.

I cleared my throat. "There's also been a spike in ODs, mostly heroin. Lorenzo has been flooding the streets with it. The Feds are swarming, trying to shut down the supply chain, but Moretti knows how to keep his nose clean. We need to prepare for potential blow-back."

Connor rubbed the bridge of his nose. "What about our distribution?"

"Business as usual, for now. Moretti hasn't targeted any of our major holdings yet, but that could change at any moment. We need to be ready to move if necessary."

Tommy snorted. "Move where? Half the city belongs to Moretti."

"Not true," Callum said. "We have a stronghold in Jamaica Plain--"

"That's a joke," Tommy snapped.

Aleksandr Volkov was the new Pakhan of the Russian Bratva in Boston. He had ties to the Sointsevskaya in Moscow through his uncle, Dmitri, who headed up New York's Bratva contingent. They were ruthless and cunning, and they'd carved out a sizeable chunk of Boston for themselves over the years despite maintaining a fragile neutrality with the Irish and Italians. The incident that had gotten Aiden killed was one of the few flare ups we'd had with the Russians. How that had gotten solved was still a mystery to me, but Callum refused to talk about it, and no one dared ask him.

Callum leaned back in his chair. "Volkov won't be a problem."

"His father wasn't, but I'm not sure Aleksandr is going to honor any handshake agreement you made with his old man, Callum," Tommy said. It was ballsy, calling the boss out like that, but Tommy had always been able to get away with saying pretty much anything he wanted to Callum.

"Moretti used Russians to run intel on Cassidy," Connor admitted. "One took a shot at her."

"Shit," I muttered.

Callum pursed his lips. "Aleksandr knows better than to cross me--his uncle Dmitri would never forgive him."

"We can't fight a battle on two fronts," I said. "We've got the manpower to go up against Moretti, but not Volkov too. Let the Russians be."

Connor was looking at me like I'd sprouted another head. "When did you get so analytical?"

Since you left, I thought. Not that I blamed him in the least. If that had been Emilia, I would've lost my mind. And by the looks of things, Connor was already halfway there.

Callum eyed me thoughtfully. "Alfie's right. We focus on Moretti. He's the immediate threat. Volkov is the lesser of two evils, and I doubt he'll cause trouble unless provoked. But be careful all the same--don't go poking bears. Tommy, I want you to tighten security around the bars, make sure we're on top of everything. Connor, you're back with me. Alfie, I want you on Lorenzo. Intel only, nothing rash. I don't need any more surprises."

4

— · —

CASSIDY

THE WAVES ROLLED IN lazily, foamy whitecaps lapping gently at the shore. Gulls called overhead, and the breeze was warm against my face as I walked down the path towards town. The sun peeked through a cluster of clouds, and I tipped my face up towards it. I felt the tension in my shoulders ease, just a little bit, as I soaked in the sunlight.

I wrapped my arms around myself, my right hand cradling my swollen belly. It had become an almost subconscious gesture, and I was surprised at the upwelling of maternal affection that the little baby bump elicited. Motherhood had been some distant unquantifiable, something that happened to other people. It sure wasn't something I had envisioned for my immediate future, especially given the nature of my marriage. It seemed like Connor and I had barely gotten to know one another, and now, soon, we would be parents.

It scared me. God, it terrified me. I had no idea how to be a mother. My own had been taken from me before I'd reached womanhood, before we'd really had a chance to have all those essential conversations I assumed one had with their mother. I could tell Connor was just as lost as I was--he'd lost his parents around the same age as me--but instead of bringing us together, somehow my pregnancy just served as another crack in the every-widening chasm between us.

"Earth to Cassidy. Are you even listening to me?" Sloane walked beside me along the beach, her body placed strategically between me and the road. Her presence was a comfort, as always, but I knew she was the only reason Connor was letting me out of his sight. The gun strapped to the small of her back emphasized that fact.

I sighed. "Sorry. I'm listening."

"No, you're not." Sloane shook her head. "What's going on in that crazy mind of yours, girl?"

I shrugged and wiggled my toes in the sand. I'd kicked off my sandals as soon as we reached the beach, and I carried them in one hand. "Nothing, really. It's nice out here--peaceful."

Sloane looped her arm through mine. "Talk to me."

"There's nothing to talk about," I hedged. "Connor and I are fine."

Sloane snorted. "Don't give me that shit. You and I both know you're anything but fine. Talk to me."

I chewed my lower lip, considering. Sloane had been there for me through the worst of it. She deserved some honesty, at the very least. I took a deep breath. "I'm just...I'm scared I'm losing Connor."

Sloane frowned. "What makes you say that?"

"He's pulling away from me," I admitted. "Or maybe I'm pushing him away, I don't know. All I do know is that we barely speak, he spends half the night hovering over me when I sleep, and I can't help but feel like he hates himself for what happened to me--"

"If it's one thing Connor does well, its beating himself up over some-thing outside his control," Sloane sighed.

"Tell me about it." I grimaced. "It's killing me, Sloane. Seeing him like this. Knowing that I'm the reason for it."

"It's not your fault."

"Isn't it? All he's done since day one is try to protect me, and all I've done is push back. Now I'm pregnant and he feels trapped, and--"

Sloane stopped walking, grabbing my hand to halt me as well. "Now you listen to me, Cassidy Quinn. Connor McTiernan loves you. He loves you more than anyone or anything in this entire goddamn world, and nothing you can do is ever going to change that."

I opened my mouth to protest, but Sloane squeezed my hand so hard it hurt. "He'll pull out of this. He always does."

I wished I shared her optimism. Still, I appreciated the sentiment. Sloane and I had grown close over the last few months, and I valued her opinion--even if it wasn't particularly realistic.

Sloane saw my hand curl protectively around my abdomen, and her expression softened. "The little guy or girl moving around yet?"

"It's too soon," I shook my head. "You usually can't feel the baby moving until around week 16."

"Ah." Sloane fell silent for a moment as we walked. Then, "Do you want a boy or a girl?"

I shrugged. "Honestly, I don't know. I don't even know what Connor wants...or if he even wants..."

The baby. I trailed off. I couldn't bring myself to finish the sentence.

Sloane's grip on my arm tightened, and she gave me a slight shake. "Hey, none of that. Connor loves you. And he loves this baby, even if he doesn't know how to show it yet. Give him time."

We'd reached the cafe. It was small and cutely decorated, the tables and chairs spilling out onto the sidewalk. Sloane and I sat down at one near the beach. A waitress came out with a couple menus, but Sloane waved them away. "Coffee for me, thanks."

The waitress smiled and nodded, then turned to me expectantly. "Decaf, please," I sighed.

I hated decaf coffee.

The waitress scurried off to the kitchen, and Sloane leaned back in her chair. The wind ruffled her dark hair, and she squinted against the sun. She was wearing a tank top, and I saw the edge of a tattoo peeking out from beneath the sleeve.

I gestured towards it. "When did you get that?"

Sloane adjusted her arm, and I saw the curling tail of a dragon disappearing underneath the hem of her shirt.. "A couple months ago. Alfie introduced me to his artist on the Cape. Mine decided to go backpacking through India. Lucky bitch."

I cocked an eyebrow. "Getaway on the Cape for two...how did that go?"

But instead of answering my question, Sloane gave me a sharp look. "He's in love with someone else, Cassidy."

"Alfie, in love?" I frowned. "I thought he wasn't the serious type."

Sloane shrugged. "He's not. Doesn't stop him from falling head over heels, though."

"Who's the lucky girl?"

Sloane pursed her lips. "I don't know. I think Tommy does, though--has Connor said anything?"

Just before Teagan had revealed himself to be the mole by abducting me, Connor had confided in me that he suspected Alfie. The case against his best friend was alarmingly solid--missed assignments, going off-radar for days at a time, Alfie's usual happy-go-lucky attitude replaced with preoccupied angst. As much as it had gutted him, Connor had confronted him over it, and just like that, the rift between them had been smoothed over. When I asked him about it, Connor had cryptically replied that love will make a man do stupid things.

I shook my head. "Connor hasn't said much of anything lately."

"Tommy neither."

I plucked at the menu, choosing my words carefully. "Do you hang out with Tommy much?"

She snorted. "If, by hang out, you mean I serve him at the bar, then yes. We've got a standing date every night at five."

"I think it might be more than just that, Sloane."

"You mean more than keeping him in a constant supply of alcohol?"

"I've seen the way he looks at you."

"Again, that's the alcohol."

I rolled my eyes. "I'm not the only one who thinks Tommy has a thing for you."

"You are confusing love with the male tendency to hump anything with two legs and a heartbeat when plied with copious amounts of liquor. Tommy definitely falls into that category. I've seen the kinds of women he goes out with." Sloane crossed her arms over her chest. "We're just friends, Cassidy, and sometimes we're not even that. Thank you for the gossip, but you can consider my love life firmly off the table."

The waitress returned with our coffees, setting them on the table with a friendly smile. Sloane dropped several creamers into hers, stirring absently. I blew across the surface of my cup, frowning thoughtfully. Alfie, Sloane, and Tommy. What a strange little love triangle that was turning out to be. I wondered idly who the lucky lady was. Alfie was handsome, charming, funny--a total catch. Not that Sloane wasn't gorgeous, but she was the opposite of Alfie in almost every way; where Alfie was outgoing and friendly, Sloane was brash and sarcastic. Where Alfie was light and airy, Sloane was dark and edgy. And Tommy...well, Tommy was a different story altogether. Honestly, Sloane was more like Tommy than anyone else. Maybe that was why they butted heads so often.

I wished there was something I could do. Alfie seemed happy, but Sloane and Tommy were clearly miserable. Hell, maybe it might even take my mind off things for a while. A distraction at the very least. The thought of shifting everyone's focus off me for a little while was too good to pass up, and I resolved right then and there to do something about it.

Looks like I had a little matchmaking work to do.

Teagan Kelley's eyes lingered on the cuffs, on the bruises that had been raised there and the ragged, torn flesh from where I'd struggled against them. Then down my face, over my heaving chest and then lower, his lips tugging into a faint smile as I shuddered and squeezed my legs together.

"You know, Cassidy," he said softly, "when I first saw you, you were nothing more than feisty bitch that needed to be put down. And what a fucking chore that turned out to be, eh? Shit, the sheer manpower Moretti threw at you, trying to end your miserable life--you would have made it so goddamn easy for us if it weren't for your brother and besotted fool of a husband trying to keep you alive. I just couldn't understand what all the fuss was about."

He leaned closer, the chair creaking ominously. "I'll admit, I got a bit obsessed. I followed you. Watched you. I saw how the great Connor McTiernan fawned all over you. A hard bastard with ice in his veins, reduced to a simpering love-struck fool all over a pair of tits with a savior complex. A cold-hearted cunt who normally wouldn't give the likes of him the time of day." He cocked his head. "Now that I have you though, I get it."

My heart was hammering, my body thrumming with each panicked beat as he got up and sat on the edge of the bed. He could see me trembling, eyes blown in fear, but I wasn't about to give him the satisfaction of a verbal response. Teagan leaned over, laughing cruelly when I recoiled from his touch.

Yet the cuffs held me fast, and I shuddered as his finger lightly brushed my jaw. Softly, almost tenderly, making my skin crawl. I jerked my head away from him.

Suddenly, Teagan grabbed my jaw and squeezed. Hard. Turning my head and forcing me to look at him.

"Yes, you're a pretty little thing, aren't you?" Unbidden, tears rose in my eyes as the pain in my jaw increased. "Feisty. Innocent. Sweet. Heart of

pure fucking gold, but you've got claws. Is that what turns Connor on? Is it the way you fight back, or is it your innocence? Well, you ain't gonna be so innocent when I get through with you..."

I gasped awake. Heart pounding and shirt sticking to my sweat-covered body, I instinctively ran my hand over the round firmness of my belly, a grounding mechanism as I struggled to come back to myself. Clutching at the sheets. Slowing my breathing. Reminding myself that I was safe in my bedroom and not back in that basement.

God, I couldn't even sleep without thinking about him.

I shuddered as bile rose in my throat. I closed my eyes as I gagged, swallowing convulsively until it passed.

I could feel his hands on me. Smell him, even. I knew it wasn't real, in some deep seeded, rational part of my brain, but knowing that only made me angrier. Even in death, Teagan haunted me. Taunted me. His ghost was a constant presence, lingering in the shadows of my subconscious like a monster under the bed.

It was over. Done. Nothing had even really happened--I had gotten out in time. Connor had come for me, he saved me before Teagan coul d...

I shook my head. It could have been so much worse. So many people had suffered worse.

I should be able to get over this.

I rolled onto my side, wincing as my arm ached sharply. It was healing, slowly but surely, and I was finally able to sleep without pain killers, but sometimes I still had pains that caught me off guard. It had been weeks since I'd been released from the hospital. Nearly two months since the attack. My broken bones had healed, and the cuts and bruises had all faded. The only evidence left now was the cast on my left arm, a daily reminder of what had happened.

If it weren't for that, maybe I could just forget it ever happened. Maybe then the nightmares would stop.

But that was a lie, and deep down, I knew it. The pain never stopped. Both real and perceived, I felt it, flaring across my skin and pounding in my head. Dull phantom pains that flared, even now as I lay in bed next to my husband. Still there, even though the damage had all but healed.

The sun crept across the floor through the gauzy curtains, casting long shadows across the room. I glanced at the clock on the nightstand, sighing when I saw that it was barely past six o'clock. I looked over at the man sleeping next to me. And thankfully, he was still sleeping. Neither of us had been getting much sleep lately--my nightmares had been a nearly daily occurrence, and I was afraid any sleeping aids might affect the baby. As a result, Connor only slept in fits and starts, checking on me every few hours and remaining in a constant state of alertness in case I needed him.

I hated it. I absolutely hated what I was doing to him. The fact that he hadn't woken right now was more a sign of his level of exhaustion that anything else, and it killed me to see how much worry and guilt he was carrying. So much that even the famous Connor McTiernan stoicism couldn't contain it all.

I watched Connor's chest rise and fall in a slow, steady rhythm, his muscular chest bare and covered in a light dusting of dark hair. Even in sleep, he was unconsciously turned towards me, laying on his side with his arms loose and open in case I needed him. Even in sleep, he looked worried, a little crease formed between his dark brows and his lips tugged into a frown. It broke my heart.

Slowly, so he wouldn't wake, I snuggled into his arms, sighing in relief as they tightened around me. I felt the rough scrape of his chin as his face turned into my neck, the warmth of his breath on my skin. Connor made a soft noise as he shifted in his sleep, pulling me tighter against him.

God, I loved this man. And I hated myself for worrying him like this.

I hated the constant feeling of being on edge, hypersensitive to every noise, every movement. Weak. Even here in a place that had become a second home to us, I still didn't feel quite safe anymore. Not unless I was in Connor's arms. Yet every day, I felt him slip a little further through my fingers.

I pressed my hand to Connor's chest and lay still, listening to his slow, even breathing and trying to focus on the steady cadence of his heart. Trying to shut my brain off, if only for a little while. Just so I could get some sleep.

"Cass?"

A soft and hesitant voice filled my ear, rich with the Irish brogue he'd never quite gotten rid of. Connor tenderly brushed his fingers down my shoulder, each touch filled with so much love and affection it nearly broke my heart, and I closed my eyes against the tears that threatened.

Connor made a noise in the back of his throat. "Are you here with me, mo chroí?"

He knew better than to ask if I was okay. If I wanted to talk about it. I'd been shutting him out for so long. I hated myself for it, but I was afraid to open that box of horrors and let him see what a complete mess I was. How completely and utterly broken. To relive it voluntarily, to show him the degradations that had been done to me and just how thoroughly tainted I was now. Things he hadn't been able to prevent, and things I knew with utter certainty he blamed himself for as if he had been the one to do them. I couldn't do that to him.

"I'm okay," I lied. "I think I'm going to get up and read for a bit."

Connor's arm tightened around me as I tried to pull away. "Please stay. I'm worried you're not getting enough sleep. Just lay here for a bit with me, love, maybe you'll start to feel tired."

I forced a smile as I looked up at him. "I slept plenty. Besides, you need your sleep--"

"I don't care about me," Connor murmured, his calloused fingertips gentle against my cheek. "I worry about you, about our babe growing inside you. Please, Cass. Stay with me."

I swallowed thickly. I felt myself weakening, and I knew Connor sensed it. I felt something within me starting to crack. It terrified me. I needed to get out of that bed and away from him before I became a bawling mess, because once I started, I was afraid I'd never stop.

"Cass--"

"I need to pee." I practically scrambled out of bed, my feet hitting the floor with a thud. Connor sat up as I darted into the bathroom, closing the door behind me and leaning back against it, my breath coming in shallow gasps. I slid down the door until I was sitting on the cool tile floor, drawing my knees to my chest and wrapping my arms around them. Tears pooled in my eyes, but I blinked them away. I refused to cry.

I heard the bed creak as Connor got up, the slow pad of his bare feet across the hardwood floor and the quiet thud as he rested his forehead against the doorframe.

"Cassidy? Love, please open the door."

I swallowed thickly, resting my forehead on my knees. "Just give me a minute."

"Are you sick? Is it--" Connor cut himself off abruptly, and I imagined his jaw clenching in frustration. "Is it the baby?"

Connor's conversational depth regarding the baby was strictly limited to how it was affecting my health. Somehow, I had the feeling it was something he was blaming himself for too.

"No," I said. "Connor, I'm fine. I just...I'm going to take a shower."

The old Connor would have kicked down the door by now. Demanded I open it. But this Connor--the Connor I had reduced to a shadow of himself by pushing him away--was resigned. Defeated. He sighed quietly. "Put down towels on the floor, and make sure you hold onto the handrails when you get into the shower. I'll be right out here if you need anything."

Connor was terrified I'd fall in the shower, and it was a testament to his exhaustion that he didn't insist on helping me this time. He treated me like I was made of blown glass ever since the hospital.

I listened as Connor padded back to bed, and I sat on the cold bathroom floor until I was certain he had fallen back asleep. Only then did I get up, turning the shower on full blast and stripping off my clothes. I might as well start my day.

Connor was nowhere to be found when I went into the kitchen, but Tommy was there. He was sitting at the table nursing a cup of coffee, looking like death warmed over. I eyed him curiously as he took another sip. Tommy usually wasn't a drinker--he had a hell of a temper and Callum always kept him busy enough that he didn't have time to let it get the best of him. But lately, a moderately plastered or hungover Tommy was becoming a regular sight around here.

My lips thinned in anger. I was sick and tired of everyone treating me like I was going to break, while they were breaking themselves in the process.

"You look like shit," I said crisply. Tommy grunted in response. I turned away from him, opening the fridge to grab eggs and milk. I set them both on the counter, then reached into the cabinet for a pan, making a whole lot more noise than I needed too.

Tommy winced. "Jesus, do you have to bang around like that? It's like, four in the morning."

"It's six thirty, and to some people, this is a perfectly respectable time to get up."

"Not me."

"Why don't you go to bed, then?"

Tommy held his head in his hands like it was about to fracture. "Couldn't sleep."

You and me both.

I cracked a half dozen eggs into the pan, and Tommy eyed me warily. "What are you doing?"

"It's called breakfast." I poured a splash of milk over the eggs, stirring them around with a spatula. "When was the last time you ingested something that wasn't 80 proof?"

Tommy scowled. "None of your business."

"Suit yourself." I grabbed plates out of the cabinet, dishing out a couple servings of eggs. I sat down across from Tommy with my plate, digging into my meal. Tommy stared at me for several minutes before growling and tugging his plate closer. He sniffed the eggs dubiously like an animal, took a hesitant bite, then proceeded to wolf them down in record time.

I watched my big brother, noting the dark circles under his eyes. He looked more rumpled than usual, and he'd lost weight. I was suddenly struck by how much older he looked--Tommy was only a few years older than me, but lately, he looked like he'd aged ten years. Lines of stress bracketed his mouth, and there was a hollowness in his eyes that scared me. I wondered idly if I looked similar.

"You should try to get some sleep after this," I said gently.

Tommy pushed his empty plate back. "So should you. A woman in your condition needs to be resting more."

It was the closest he'd come to mentioning the pregnancy, but it still hit a nerve. "My condition? This isn't the eighteen hundreds, Tommy. I'm not made of glass."

"I didn't mean--it's not just..." Tommy clenched his jaw. "You went through a lot, Cass. Everything changed in a single night for you. You need to deal with it."

I glared at him mulishly. "I am dealing with it."

Tommy snorted. "Yeah, you seem to be handling things really well. Connor too."

"Pot, kettle," I snapped. "Or is homeless wino your new look?"

Tommy bristled. "Fuck off."

"Go to bed, Tommy." I got up, taking both of our plates to the sink. I scrubbed them furiously before putting them into the dishwasher. The anger was flowing freely now, fueling my movements as I cleaned the counters. Anything to keep myself from snapping at him.

"Cassidy--" Tommy stood up, gripping the counter for balance. He must have been more drunk than I thought--Tommy had incredible stamina. "I'm sorry. I just...I don't know what to do anymore."

His admission startled me. Tommy was rarely honest about his feelings, especially with me. He hated to show weakness.

I softened. "Tommy...come here."

Tommy crossed the room slowly, his movements cautious and his expression guarded. I pulled him into a hug, resting my head against his chest. After a moment, I felt his arms circle me. Tommy squeezed me tightly, resting his chin atop my head. I was reminded once again how much older he was now--I used to be able to tuck my head under his chin when I was younger. Now Tommy dwarfed me, all broad shoulders and muscular bulk. His embrace used to be comforting and familiar, but now it was different. Colder. I was no longer the little sister he felt obligated to protect--now I was fragile cargo he feared breaking.

"Dad's not doing great," he said roughly.

"Oh, Tommy." I hugged him tighter. While my dad and I still hadn't quite mended everything between us, Michael and Tommy were incredibly close. Tommy idolized our father, and I knew losing him would gut Tommy like nothing else. "I'm so sorry. What do the doctors say?"

"He's going downhill...fast. I know Connor won't leave you alone, but maybe you could come home for a few days? I know Dad would want to see you. Maybe it would be good to get your mind off things up here."

"I don't know, Tommy."

"I think it's a grand idea." Connor stepped into the kitchen. He was freshly showered, wearing a pair of jeans and a white V-neck t-shirt that showed off the powerful muscles of his chest. Even now, I felt a faint stirring of desire low in my belly that had nothing to do with my condition.

"You've been cooped up here for weeks. A change of scenery might be good for you and the babe." Connor leaned against the counter. His face was impassive as usual, but I sensed the faint undertone of hopefulness in his voice.

"Connor..."

"It's settled then. Pack your bags. Sloane and Alfie will accompany you. I'll call Michael today and let him know to expect us."

Us. As in Connor was coming too.

I felt a thrill of excitement. "Really? You're coming with me?"

Connor nodded. "I've got to get back to work."

The brief spark of elation I'd felt fizzled out as quickly as it had come. Of course. Connor wasn't coming because he wanted to spend time with me. He was coming because he didn't trust me to be safe. And work always won out over me.

Connor must have seen the hurt in my eyes, because his expression softened. "But I want to be with you, Cass. I miss you."

Tommy was carefully studying the marble countertop. I glanced at him before holding Connor's gaze. "I'm right here, Connor. I haven't gone anywhere."

5

—·—

EMILIA

"IT'S TIME TO MAKE those bastards pay," Sal Giordano's voice growled through the closed door. "McTiernan thinks he can move in on our territory? I'll mount his head on my wall."

"He's right," Dominic added. "It's time we struck back hard. I want to send them a message they won't forget."

I pressed my ear to the oiled wood, straining to hear. My heart hammered as I listened. Lorenzo and Sal were meeting with all the capos in Lorenzo's office across the hall, and the sound carried easily through the thick paneling. I heard the scrape of a chair against the hardwood, and then Lorenzo spoke.

"And just how do you plan on doing that?" His voice was icy. "Do you know where Connor McTiernan is? No, you don't. Neither do I. All I know is that he has disappeared off the face of the earth with his pregnant little wife, and he has left his men to fend for themselves while he goes off gallivanting across the country."

Sofia's brother Julian spoke up. "He'll have to come back eventually--"

"Eventually is not good enough!" Angel interrupted. "We need to strike now--"

"If we do that, we'll tip our hand," Julian interjected. "He'll be prepared, and the next time we attack, he'll be ready for us. We need to keep our powder dry, be patient. Let him think we're too stupid to try anything until he gets complacent. Then we strike."

Lorenzo snorted. "You're not the only one with a plan. It's time to show the McTiernans once and for all who runs Boston."

My blood ran cold. I knew Lorenzo wasn't above violence--I'd seen him order hits myself, even if I never actually witnessed the executions. But this was different. He was planning a war.

"Just give the order, boss, and I'll take care of it," Dante said. Of course he would, the soulless brute. I didn't come into contact with the notorious hitman often, but when it did, it curdled my blood.

Lorenzo chuckled darkly. "Not yet. I have... bigger plans for the McTiernans. But keep an eye on them. Report back anything suspicious."

Dante grunted in assent. My nails bit into my palms. What was Lorenzo planning?

"And you, Jules," Lorenzo said. "Make sure our people are ready. When the time comes, I want the McTiernans wiped out, down to the last child."

I sucked in a sharp breath, panic flooding my veins. He couldn't mean that. But I knew in my gut Lorenzo was capable of anything.

Luca spoke up hesitantly. "Boss, that seems...extreme."

"Are you questioning me?" Lorenzo's voice turned icy.

"No, of course not," Luca said quickly. "I just think we should proceed with caution."

"Caution?" Lorenzo scoffed. "The time for caution is over. The Mc-Tiernans have challenged me for the last time. Now, go. And remember, not a word of this to anyone. Capisce?"

Muffled affirmatives came from the men. I heard them rise from their chairs, the scrape of wood against the floor. I turned and sprinted down the hall, my heart pounding.

"Emilia, what are you doing here?" Sofia was coming out of her bedroom. She was wearing a pretty black dress, her dark hair tied up in a bun and her hazel eyes lined with dark eyeliner.

It was true that I hadn't been around the mansion as much lately; sometimes, just being there made my skin crawl. Other than sleeping in the bedroom my adoptive father had given me for appearances sake, I spent every moment I could at my bookstore, because it felt like I was that much closer to freedom. And that much further away from Lorenzo and his sons.

"Looking for you." I grabbed her arm and tugged her back into her room, closing the door behind us. "Where are you going?"

"Out for a bit." Sofia frowned at me, tugging her arm out of my grip. "What's got your panties in a twist?"

I chewed my lower lip nervously. I knew I couldn't tell Sofia about what I'd overheard. For all his level-headedness, her brother Julian was one of Lorenzo's most loyal capos. She already kept my secret about Alfie. I couldn't put her in that position again. I glanced towards the door.

"What is it, Emilia?"

"Nothing," I sighed. "It's nothing. I'll tell you later. Have fun tonight, okay?"

Sofia's frown deepened, but she didn't argue. I gave her a weak smile before darting out of her room. I felt her eyes on me as I practically sprinted down the hallway.

I wasn't really sure where I was going, or what I was doing. My mind was spinning in a thousand different directions. All I knew was that I needed to get out of that house. I needed air. I needed...Alfie.

That evening, I was stocking shelves in my bookstore when I heard the front door chime. "We're closed," I called out, emerging from the office. Then I saw who it was and froze in my tracks.

Angel Moretti leaned against the counter, all predatory grace and arrogance. My stomach knotted at the sight of him. Trouble. Nothing but trouble.

He pushed away from the counter and stalked toward me, a sly smile curving his lips. "Hello, carina. Did you miss me?"

I folded my arms over my chest and lifted my chin. "What do you want, Angel?"

"Aren't you going to invite me in?" He stopped directly in front of me, crowding into my space. "I came all this way to see you."

"The store is closed. You should leave." I struggled not to recoil from his proximity. His cologne was cloying and choking.

"There's the welcome I was hoping for." Angel tsked. "Aren't you happy to see family?"

"We're not family," I said through gritted teeth.

"Oh, but we are. And we could be so much more." His hand came up to caress my cheek. I knocked it away, but he only chuckled. "Playing hard to get, I see. I like that in a woman. But you'll come around, Emilia. You'll realize we're meant to be together."

"I'll never be with you," I spat. Revulsion churned in my stomach at his touch, his words. "Now get out before I call the police."

Angel's eyes darkened. He grabbed my arm in a bruising grip. "You'll regret that." He shoved me away, stalking toward the door. But he paused on the threshold, glancing over his shoulder. "This isn't over. You belong to me, Emilia. I always get what I want."

I flinched as the door slammed behind him. I sank down against the counter, trembling from head to toe. I clutched the sleeve of my blouse with a shaking hand. Angel had ripped it, the force of his fingers grabbing it nearly tearing the delicate fabric. He'd left bruises on my skin, an ugly greenish yellow along the inside of my bicep. I winced as I touched the tender flesh. I didn't know what Angel's game was, but he was becoming a nuisance, and a constant presence in the house that I was increasingly desperate to leave. And I knew he wasn't giving up. Every visit of his was more possessive and overt than the last.

I sat there for a long moment, forcing my anxiety and fear down deep inside me. After taking several shaky breaths, I stood, wincing as my shoulder cracked and twinged. Angel wasn't the type to make empty threats. I'd made a dangerous enemy tonight.

An enemy who wouldn't stop until he possessed me. Body and soul.

I shuddered at the thought of belonging to Angel. He was a monster. Cold. Lacking mercy or conscience. I knew exactly the sort of things he would do to me. Use me. The beatings I would suffer, if I were ever foolish enough to disobey him. The things he'd have me do. The unwanted attention and unwanted sexual advances he'd already tried to inflict. The way my face burned at the sound of his voice. The thought of his cold brown eyes roaming my body. The things I'd have to do to stay alive. It wasn't just the power Lorenzo held over me that scared me, it was the promise of more torment to come. Angel would be far worse.

Angel always got what he wanted.

My phone buzzed in my pocket, startling me from my troubled thoughts. I fished it out with trembling fingers, heart leaping at the name on the screen. I pressed it to my ear. "Hey," I breathed.

"Em, did I catch you at a bad time?" His voice was a balm, soothing my frayed nerves. "You sound upset."

"I just..." I grimaced, unsure whether to tell him the truth. He knew all too well how Angel felt about me. If he even thought Angel had gotten too fresh with me...a soft noise of concern sounded through the line.

"Are you sure everything is okay?"

"No. I'm not, Alfie."

There was a pause on the line.

"What happened?"

"It's nothing." I didn't want to worry him. But I couldn't hide the truth, not from Alfie. He'd see right through me. "Angel paid me a visit."

"That bastard," Alfie growled. "Did he hurt you? Threaten you?"

"I'm fine. He just...unsettled me."

"I'm coming over."

"Alfie, no. It's too dangerous." If Lorenzo or his men saw Alfie at my place, there'd be hell to pay.

"I'll risk it." His voice was as firm as steel. No room for negotiation. I closed my eyes at the sound of it, drawing comfort from his unwavering stubbornness. No matter what, Alfie would be there for me. No questions asked.

"Please," I whispered.

"I'll be there in ten minutes. If he shows his face, or if there's any sign of trouble, you call me."

I sighed. The line went dead before I could protest further. Once Alfie made up his mind about something, there was no changing it. It was one of the things I loved most about him. I put the "closed" sign on the door and turned off the lights, resigning myself to waiting patiently for him.

I busied myself making a cup of tea while I waited, nerves coiling tighter with each passing minute. Finally a knock rattled my front door. I flew to open it, and Alfie swept me into his arms without a word. My breath left me in a whoosh as I crashed into his chest. He held me tightly, and I clung to him, burying my face in his soft white T-shirt and taking a deep breath.

He held me close, burying his face in my hair. "Tell me he didn't hurt you, Em."

"I'm fine," I murmured into his shirt. Alfie let out a sigh of relief, pulling me tighter to him. "He tore the fabric, but that's about it."

Alfie's eyes ignited with anger. "That fucking bastard, I'll kill him--"

"Stop. It's fine." I stroked his stubbled cheek, desperate to calm him down. His face was tight with concern, his hands tense and firm against my waist.

"It's not fine," he murmured, pressing his forehead to mine. He exhaled slowly, trying to reign in his temper. "Jesus, Emilia. Just promise me you won't go anywhere alone with him. You can't trust him."

"I don't," I said quickly. "I have to keep the peace, though, Alfie. Lorenzo has gotten so suspicious. Of everyone. I don't think he trusts anyone anymore."

I could sense the resistance in his body. His hands had moved from my waist up to my shoulders, firmly squeezing as his head bowed. I cupped his cheek in my hand and he leaned into my touch. "I hate this."

"I know."

"I hate not knowing where you are. If you're safe." Alfie gently pried me away to study my face, brushing a stray tear from my cheek. His sea glass eyes were stormy, haunted. "I'm not a violent man, but I'd...I'd kill every last one of them if it meant making you safe."

"No. No more violence. It'll only make the situation worse." I cupped his face, forcing his gaze to mine. "Promise me. No killing."

"I can't promise that. Not where your safety is concerned."

My eyes drifted closed as his hand brushed across my lower back, the heat of his touch burning through the thin fabric of my blouse. I leaned forward, and my mouth connected with his. Alfie stiffened briefly, then buried his hands in my hair and deepened the kiss. With practiced ease, Alfie slid his hand beneath my blouse, his fingers tracing delicate patterns along my spine. I arched into his touch, my nails digging into his shoulders as I fought to keep my composure. As much as I craved this intimacy, I couldn't forget what had brought us here.

"Alfie, wait," I panted, breaking away from his searing kisses. "I need to tell you something important."

He paused, concern darkening his eyes. "What is it?"

I took his hands in mine. "Lorenzo is planning revenge against the McTiernans. I overheard him talking to the capos about it."

"Shit," Alfie muttered, his grip on me tightening. "Did you hear any specifics? What's he planning?"

"I couldn't make out everything," I admitted, my voice trembling. "But it's clear that he's determined to make the McTiernans pay for what happened this summer. He's going to wipe them out. He said...he said he'd make sure every last one of them dies."

"He can try."

"Alfie, I'm scared," I admitted. "He's planning a war."

Alfie swore under his breath. "It's alright, sweetheart. Callum knows what he's doing. We'll be ready when the time comes."

"You need to warn him. Right away. It sounded like Lorenzo has a plan, but he hasn't shared it with anyone yet. You need to prepare."

"I will." Alfie leaned forward, pressing his lips to my forehead again. His hands slid down to cup my cheeks. I don't think I'd ever seen him so serious. "I don't want you eavesdropping anymore. It's too dangerous."

"But if I can help--"

His hands tightened just to the point of being painful. "I'm serious, Emilia. No more. Promise me."

"I promise." I placed my hands on top of his, stroking the back of his knuckles until they relaxed. I hated seeing him so worried. And even though I promised not to get involved anymore, I knew I would do anything to help keep the man I loved safe.

"Good girl." His mouth met mine, softly and sweetly. "Now come on. Let's go out somewhere. I can't leave my girl all alone, not after what happened tonight."

I nodded. For now, I would follow his lead. But I wouldn't stay idly by while Lorenzo went through with his plan. Somehow, someway, I'd find a way to put an end to this.

I had to.

6

EMILIA

THE PULSING BASS POUNDED in my chest as Alfie and I stepped into the crowded nightclub. Strobe lights flashed hypnotically over the sea of writhing bodies on the dance floor. The dimly lit room was packed with writhing bodies, a sea of sweat and lust. I could feel the anticipation in the air, thick like the very smoke that clouded the space. People moved with abandon, dancing and grinding on each other. Men and women alike were scattered around the room, engaged in various levels of debauchery. Most of them seemed to be focused on two things: finding someone to fuck and getting as high as possible.

"Quite the place, isn't it?" Alfie shouted over the music, his voice barely audible as he leaned in close to me. His dark red curls fell into his eyes, and I couldn't help but notice how they contrasted beautifully with his inked skin. He looked devilishly handsome in his black Henley and dark wash jeans, his muscular arms bare except for the tattoos. It was no wonder women fawned all over him.

But this man only had eyes for me. And I didn't intend to share.

I nodded, smiling faintly as I surveyed the room. I couldn't deny that the atmosphere was intoxicating. Alfie was watching me intently, his gaze heated as it traveled over me. I tugged self-consciously at my dress. It was short, skimming the tops of my thighs and showing off my legs. Sofia had picked it out for me, and it fit snugly over my hips, accentuating my curves and plunging low in the back. My long dark hair was loose, cascading down my back in soft waves. Alfie had practically swallowed his tongue when he first saw me tonight, and I couldn't help but feel a little thrill at the way he still stared at me like he wanted to devour me whole.

"Come on, let's dance," Alfie suggested, his emerald eyes locked onto mine. The intensity of his gaze sent shivers down my spine.

As we moved to the crowded dance floor, our bodies began to sway to the rhythm, a primal connection pulling us closer. Our relationship might have been a secret, but it felt impossible to ignore the magnetic pull between us. "You're quite the dancer," I teased, trying to keep my voice light despite the mounting tension.

"Only when I have the right partner," he replied smoothly, a playful grin tugging at the corners of his lips. I rolled my eyes at his flirtation, but I couldn't deny the effect he had on me.

I grinned as Alfie's hands rested on my hips, drawing me against his firm body. My hands came up to caress his strong shoulders as he buried his face in my neck. His full lips pressed against my bare skin, and I closed my eyes as he followed the curve of my neck up to my jaw. My whole body quivered as his hands began to explore, gliding down to the edge of my dress to stroke the bare skin beneath.

It was still shocking to me that Alfie was interested in a "nobody" like me, given his extreme beauty and boyish charm. The way he made me feel when he was near me was electrifying. For so long, I'd wondered what it would feel like to be touched like this, adored and worshiped. Desired. Now that the opportunity was here, I wasn't sure I'd be able to live without it.

But the reminder of what awaited me back home made my chest hurt. Our bodies continued to move in sync, the heat between us palpable. I glanced around nervously, hoping that no one would recognize us or suspect the dangerous game we were playing. It was exhilarating but terrifying all the same.

"Relax, Emilia," Alfie whispered into my ear, his warm breath sending a shiver down my spine. "We're just two people enjoying a night out."

He turned me to face him, pulling me closer to his body. As if I could forget that I was pressed tightly against a man that should be forbidden, completely indecent for me to want as much as I did. Any woman that found herself in this situation would likely wish herself lucky. So why was I filled with dread over what could happen?

"There's so much I want to do with you," Alfie murmured, his voice low and husky. "So many places I want to take you, explore you, hold you. Everything about you is pure temptation. And I don't know if I can resist."

I blushed, unable to meet his eyes. Alfie's hands were resting on my hips, his thumbs caressing my skin in a slow, sensual pattern. It was maddening, the way he always seemed to know just how to touch me. He knew exactly what he was doing, and it was driving me crazy.

His fingers brushed against the bare skin on my back, leaving goose-bumps in their wake. The heat between us was almost unbearable as he leaned in close, his lips brushing against my ear.

"We've got all night, sweetheart. I'm going to take you apart. Piece..." he bit my earlobe, smoothing the spot over with a sensual swipe of his tongue. "by piece."

I could only whimper as his hands trailed down my spine, coming to rest on the small of my back while my heart pounded in time with the bass.

Alfie grinned at me wickedly. "Let's get a drink."

I nodded, allowing him to lead me through the crowd toward the bar. It was so crowded that it was hard to make out the bartender. Alfie had to shout to be heard over the music, ordering me a gin and tonic, and himself a double shot of whiskey.

I watched with interest as the bartender mixed a few colorful concoctions, catching and distilling the essences. I found that I was enjoying myself immensely. Alfie's closeness was intoxicating. He smelled delicious, his scent reminding me of summertime in a bottle. The thrumming in my body hummed with a single constant line that felt like he was a magnet, and the closer he was to me, the more I was pulled toward him, like two poles of a magnet were attracted to each other. There was no escape from his pull, not that I wanted to try. I took a deep breath, savoring the moment.

Which was good, because the moment ended approximately 2 seconds later.

"Alfie?" a feminine voice called from behind us. Alfie and I both turned to look, and my stomach immediately began to sink.

The raven-haired goddess standing behind us had legs for days in a tiny black leather skirt, a faded band tee, and mean-looking doc martins. Alfie tensed. "Sloane. Hey."

"What the hell are you doing here?" Sloane said, flashing him a megawatt smile. My stomach dropped as she went in for a hug. "I thought you were with Connor tonight."

"He uh...Callum needed him, so I decided to come here instead."

"Huh," Sloane eyed me thoughtfully before turning her attention back to Alfie. Her eyes flashed dangerously, instantly cooling several degrees, and I felt my face heat. I recognized the name Sloane as one of the inner members of the McTiernan Clan, but I couldn't quite place her. It was clear that she thought of me as some kind of threat, though.

Had she and Alfie been a thing?

Sloane was still eyeballing me. "Who's your friend?"

"Oh, this is...um..."

"Emma. Emma Jones," I lied, scraping together the most confident smile I could muster and holding out my hand. "You must be Sloane. Alfie's told me so much about you."

"Has he now?" Sloane glanced from Alfie to me.

"Only the bad things," Alfie laughed, trying to diffuse the palatable tension in the air. His hand moved in lazy, soothing circles at the small of my back. Whether it was meant to be reassuring or merely possessive, I couldn't tell, and his steady touch did little to calm my rapidly firing nerves.

After an endless moment, Sloane shook my hand. It was warm and the grip was just shy of too firm. "Well, Alfie hasn't said a thing about you. But, then again, he usually doesn't bother mentioning his flings."

Flings. Well.

My face burned as I withdrew my hand from hers. I didn't know what was worse--Sloane's apparent dislike of me, or her obvious belief that Alfie and I were just that, some one-night stand. The thought stung, and I stepped away from Alfie, desperate to put a little distance between us. Alfie looked uncomfortable, a tightness to his expression as he took a sip of his drink.

"Hey! I remember you." A clearly intoxicated voice cut through the music and the tension the same time a big bull of a man cut through the crowd on a bee line towards us. Alfie stiffened next to me, and I had less than a second to prepare myself before he pulled both me and Alfie into a great bear hug, one beefy arm laid heavily across our shoulders.

"Jesus, Tommy." Alfie staggered and scowled up at the newcomer.

Vaguely, I remembered Tommy from the night of the raid. Tommy and Connor had arrived alongside Alfie as I snuck them in the back entrance to the family compound so that they could rescue Connor's wife, Cassidy. The mission had ultimately been a success, but I remembered Tommy loudly voicing his displeasure at having to trust Luca and me. Foul-mouthed, explosive, and with looks that would put the fear of god into anyone with sense, he was the scariest man I'd ever seen in my life.

And right now, it looked like he was about three sheets to the wind.

"What's your name again, darling? Em...Emily..."

"Emma," I blurted.

He pointed a finger gun at me. "That's the one. Sloane, Emma here isn't just any old fling, she's the one. She's Alfie's girl. The one that got him into so much trouble this summer."

Sloane had paled about two shades, and I felt like I wasn't that much farther behind her. Alfie spluttered and nearly choked on his drink.

But Tommy kept on talking. "Head over heels, he is. I've never seen him quite like this over a girl, to be honest. You must be a keeper."

Alfie set down his drink. "Alright, Tommy--"

"Sloane is too, but she won't dance with me," Tommy lamented. "First time she agreed to come out, and--"

"And I think we're going to be going," Alfie grabbed my hand and led me away. He shot Tommy a murderous look over his shoulder. I waved weakly at Tommy as he and Sloane disappeared in the throng of bodies. "Nice to meet you," I called out faintly.

Out of the frying pan and into the fire.

We threaded our way through the mass of people dancing, and I fell in step beside him. His hand was warm around mine, and he held on tight as if he were afraid I'd slip away. I was feeling strangely unmoored, like the ground had shifted beneath my feet. Part of me wanted to find a secluded corner and cry while the rest wanted to punch someone. So many emotions were coursing through my body that it made me feel like I was coming unglued. Maybe it was just the adrenaline.

I pulled him to a stop in the middle of the dance floor. Alfie frowned, but I placed a hand on his chest and stopped him. "So, are you going to explain what the hell just happened?" I asked, raising my voice to be heard over the music. "Because I'm not sure I understand how we went from you touching me to you trying to avoid me."

Alfie sighed. "Look, Sloane's a complicated situation, okay?"

"She's your ex-girlfriend, right?" I crossed my arms over my chest, trying to hide the hurt that I felt. Alfie hadn't mentioned any ex-girlfriends when we first met, and I suddenly found myself wondering what else he'd been keeping from me.

"No! It's nothing like that."

"Really? Because it sure looked like that back there." I felt a twinge of jealousy and tried to suppress it. Alfie had a history, and I knew that. But seeing Sloane with him made me realize just how much of his life I wasn't privy to. And how much I wanted to know.

Alfie raked a hand through his hair. "Look, Sloane's important to me, but I swear, there's nothing going on between us. She's just a friend."

"You could have fooled me," I muttered.

"Emilia..." Alfie's voice was filled with anguish. "Please believe me. You're the only one I want, okay? It's just..."

His voice trailed off as he caught a glimpse of something over my shoulder, and his expression hardened. "You've got to be fucking kidding me."

I turned to look, and my stomach dropped. Dominic and Angel had just walked into the club.

"Of all the--come on." Alfie grabbed my hand and began dragging me off the dance floor, his grip firm but not painful. I glanced back over my shoulder and saw Angel spot me, his eyes narrowing as he locked onto me. I ducked my head and followed Alfie blindly through the crowd.

"Where are we going?" I asked, but Alfie ignored me. He continued to pull me along, his jaw clenched and his eyes hard. The thick crowd slowly parted for him, but he remained focused, staring straight ahead. I was barely able to keep pace with him as we wound our way through the throng. The music was deafening, the base vibrating the floors and walls. Finally, we made it to the exit.

Only to stop suddenly as Angel stepped into our path.

"Well, well, well," he purred, his eyes gleaming as he took in my appearance. "Fancy running into you here, Emilia. Looks like the good two shoes likes to have a bit of fun after all. Daddy would not approve. But I do. In fact, come with me and I'll show you exactly how much I approve."

He went to grab my arm but Alfie snarled, stepping in front of me. "Stay away from her."

Angel's gaze slid lazily to Alfie, like he was nothing more consequential than a pesky fly, when they widened in recognition. "You."

Alfie pulled me firmly behind him. Just then, Dom strolled up behind Angel with two beers clasped in his hands, stopping comically short as he registered the situation in front of him.

"Look who we have here," Angel spat. "It's that Irish fucker we were chasing that day near Emilia's. Looks like our girl here's got a little secret."

Dom's eyes narrowed. He set the beers on the bar, one by one. It was clear that this was about to come to a violent, bloody head.

Alfie stood tall, not backing down. "Get out of our way."

Angel smirked. "You know, I've been looking for you ever since that day in the alley. You must have some brass fucking balls, Irish. I'll look forward to cutting them off before I gut you like the greasy mick lowlife you are."

"Angel, please," I begged. "I'll come with you, just leave him alone."

Angel shook his head, eyes never leaving Alfie. "It's too late for that, carina. Now move. I'll deal with you later."

I stared at him, defiant and angry. Angel had never scared me before, but now, there was something menacing in his gaze. Something dark and dangerous that made my stomach churn.

Suddenly, Alfie lunged at Angel, tackling him to the floor. The two of them rolled around for a moment, fists flying. Angel landed a lucky blow, and Alfie grunted as the hit connected with his jaw. Angel scrambled to his feet, and Alfie did the same, wiping away the blood that dripped from his nose. His lip was split and bruised. I wanted to look away, but I couldn't tear my eyes from the fight.

It was brutal. Nothing like the clean, choreographed fights you see on tv. Alfie and Angel punched and bit and clawed at each other, grappling on the ground like animals. Angel landed several hard punches to Alfie's ribs. Alfie kneed him in the groin. They pulled hair and snarled, a wild fury I'd never seen lit behind Alfie's emerald eyes. He was fighting for me, but instead of pride, I only felt a sickening of churn adrenaline and fear.

Angel was bleeding heavily, and his eye was quickly swelling shut. His lip was split, and he had a gash on his temple where he had connected with a nearby table. They were starting to attract the bouncer's attention, now, and I prayed for some sort of intervention. But they weren't paying any attention to me as I backed away from the brawl and into the crowd of onlookers. Angel swayed on his feet and shoved Alfie, knocking him back.

And into Dom, who grabbed Alfie by the hair and pulled his head backwards into his knee.

The music and the crowd was so loud, but I still heard the sickening crack of bone on bone as Alfie's skull connected with Dom's kneecap, and he dropped like a stone. I screamed. Dom kicked Alfie's body twice, winding up for a murderous stomp to his ribs when I pushed through the crowd, throwing my body between the two men.

Only to be swept off my feet a second later by a giant.

Tommy surged forward into the fight, knocking me out of the way with a swing of his arm that somehow cradled me safely to the side and deposited me on my feet. He stepped into the fight and immediately went after Dom.

It was like watching a prizefighter pick apart a novice boxer, watching Tommy pummel Dom. His movements were precise and calculated, and it was clear that he'd done this before. He dodged and weaved, throwing punches that connected with their intended targets. Slowly, he pushed them away from Alfie's body on the floor. Angel was a bloody mess, but he still tried to wade into the fight. But he was no match for Tommy.

Tommy landed several blows to Dom's ribs, and Dom winced, doubling over. Behind Tommy, Angel had picked himself up off the floor. He weaved drunkenly for a moment, then threw a wild punch at the side of Tommy's head.

"Tommy—watch out!" Sloane threw herself into the fight, meaning to knock Angel off Tommy, but she distracted him, instead.

The blow clipped Tommy on the ear. Cursing loudly, he shoved Angel away. "Damnit, Sloane—"

His words were cut off as Sloane threw a punch at Angel, and he stiff-armed her out of the way just as Dom staggered back onto his feet. "Sloane, go!"

Tommy delivered a swift uppercut to Dom's chin, sending him sprawling. Angel finally got in a good shot, punching Tommy squarely in the nose. Tommy growled and swung his elbow back, catching Angel in the face. Blood spurted. I struggled to get back to Alfie, but I was knocked aside again, this time by a bouncer that had been called over to break up the fight.

"Move it, lady," he growled, shoving me back with his meaty hands.

I stood helplessly by as the bouncer strode up to Tommy, but Tommy only held up his hands, palms raised. "Hey, man. They started it."

"I don't care. You're out of here. All of you," the bouncer snapped, grabbing Angel by the collar of his shirt and yanking him to his feet. Dom unsteadily slipped Angel's limp arm over his shoulder. He glared at me, or, at least, he tried to with the one eye of his that wasn't glued shut. "Come, Emilia."

"No."

The steel in his gaze didn't waver, but some of the anger leached out. Unlike Angel, Dom knew when to check his temper. He took a step towards me. "Come with us now, Emilia, and this can still be salvaged. If you don't, there's nothing I can do to protect you." He paused. "Or anyone else you care about back home."

The threat was implicit, but I got the message. Lorenzo would take it out on Sofia if I didn't go with them now. I had no choice. My mind was racing as I tried to figure out a way out of this situation, but it was no use. I had no choice but to follow them.

I let my eyes sweep the floor, and they fell on Alfie's body lying motionless on the ground. Tommy and Sloane were bent over him.

"He'll be fine, he's got a hard head, this one." Tommy said, looking up at me with a steady gaze that was a lot more sober than I thought he'd been. "You gonna be okay, sweetheart?"

The words were said casually enough, but the hard concern in his eyes told me that he'd have no problem starting the fight back up on behalf if I chose to go with the McTiernans instead. But nothing would come of that but more blood. I nodded numbly. "Just get him to a doctor."

Sloane's eyes darted to where Dom and Angel waited, and then back to me. "Be careful."

I swallowed against the lump in my throat and followed Dom and Angel out of the club. As I left Alfie behind, I knew that my world had just changed forever. And nothing would ever be the same.

7

CASSIDY

I COULD HEAR THEM arguing beyond the closed bedroom door.

"Do you have any idea what time it is?" Connor said in sleepy irritation.

"No idea," Tommy said. "Does it matter?"

"It matters when my wife needs every ounce of sleep she can get. What happened?"

"Long story. Can I put him on the couch? He's getting heavy."

Alfie's slurred voice grunted indignantly. "M'not heavy..."

Tommy's voice was a bit farther away now, probably because he was moving through the penthouse. "You are when I've been carting your stupid ass halfway across Boston." Another grunt, then Tommy sighed like a long-suffering older brother. "He's sauced and concussed. We wanted Cassidy to have a look at him."

"At *both* of you," Sloane added.

"Absolutely not." Connor's voice was firm. "I'm not waking her up. Cass doesn't need this stress. She needs sleep."

"But--"

"I'm not bringing her into this. Not again. I know where her kit is, I can handle this."

Yeah, I like was going to let that happen. I sat up with a groan, rubbing my eyes. The bedroom was dark and empty, but I heard Connor, Tommy and Sloane still bickering through the closed door. I threw on my robe and went to see what the fuss was all about.

Connor looked up when I entered the living room, his expression softening as our eyes met. I smiled tiredly at him. "Hey, what's going on?"

"Nothing, love. Go back to bed," he said, moving towards me. "I've got this."

I sidestepped him. "And you got your medical degree from where?"

He gave me an exasperated look. "Cass--"

"Let me help, Connor." I placed my hand on his arm and looked up at him. "It's fine."

He shook his head stubbornly. "Not in your condition."

"She's not made of glass, Connor," Tommy said. "Let her help."

"Stay out of this."

"Please, Connor." I wasn't above begging. I knew he would do anything for me, and I needed this. I needed to feel useful again. "Let me help."

Connor looked torn, but he finally relented. "Fine. But you're going back to bed after this."

"Deal."

The scene that awaited me was a mess. Alfie was slumped on the couch, looking worse for wear. His nose was bloody, his lip was split, and there was a nasty-looking bruise blooming across his jaw. By the way he was holding himself, I could tell his ribs were either bruised or broken.

Tommy was in just as bad shape, sporting a black eye and a split lip of his own.

I sat on the couch and opened my kit. "All right, boys. What happened?"

"Alfie got into a fight at the club," Sloane tattled.

I raised an eyebrow at Alfie. "Really? That's the last thing I'd expect out of you."

Alfie started to answer, but Tommy beat him to it. "Dominic and Angelo Moretti were there, and they saw Alfie here out with his little girlfriend."

He gave Connor a weighted look, but I didn't understand. "What am I missing here? Who's his girlfriend?"

"Emilia Moretti." Tommy said.

"Wait, I thought her name was Emma? She said her name was Emma Jones." Sloane rounded on Tommy. "I thought you couldn't remember her name at the bar."

"I didn't, Sloane." Tommy tiredly scrubbed a hand down his face, wincing as he hit a sore spot. "I remembered quickly enough when tweedle dee and tweedle dumb showed up. Alfie is dating Emilia Moretti."

"Russo," Alfie slurred tiredly, like he'd had to make that distinction before. "She's his adopted daughter."

"Like that matters," Sloane huffed. I caught her eye, looking at her for the first time. She looked...upset. Hurt. She looked away, crossing her arms over her chest.

Everything clicked into place. Alfie's secret girlfriend, the sneaking around, the fallout this summer with Connor. Sloane's hurt feelings.

I looked up at Connor, but he was staring out the window, arms crossed over his chest and face carefully blank as he calculated the fallout. He already knew about Emilia. I could tell.

He knew, but he hadn't told me.

I pursed my lips and Alfie hissed as I probed a deep bruise along his ribcage. "Sorry."

"...'s alright, Doc," Alfie mumbled. "Where...where's Emilia?"

"He took a pretty good knock to the back of the head," Tommy said. "He was out for a couple minutes."

I found the knot along the base of Alfie's skull, and he sucked in a breath as I probed the area cautiously. Blows to the occipital were especially dangerous--it didn't take much to cause some serious damage. Alfie seemed pretty out of it, though it was hard to tell how much of that was from the head injury and how much was from the drink.

"Well, you don't seem to have any obvious fractures," I said. I reached for a penlight. "Hold still."

"M'fine," Alfie muttered. "Where's Emilia?"

"Tommy, help me out here." I gestured to Alfie. Tommy grabbed Alfie by the jaw and held his head steady while I shone the light into his eyes.

"I'm fine, stop," Alfie said, trying to bat away the light. Both his pupils evenly reacted to the light, so I clicked it off.

Tommy kept a heavy palm on Alfie's shoulder to hold him still while I cleaned the cuts on his face. "Emilia went home, brother."

"Home...You let those bastards take her?" Alfie shoved to his feet and got in Tommy's face. I'd been around enough of Tommy's fights to know when to get out of the way, but before I could lever myself to my feet,

Connor swooped me out of the way and carefully deposited me on the other side of the sofa. He got ahold of Alfie and shoved him back down on the couch.

"Sit down," he growled. Alfie struggled against him for a moment, but Connor shoved him down again, hard. "You'll not be starting that shite around my wife."

"Emilia's in danger--"

"And I said sit the fuck down, or I'll knock you out again myself. She's not my problem, she's yours. You knew exactly who she was when you started seeing her, and you did it anyway. Don't expect me to feel sorry for you now."

"They'll hurt her."

Connor's thunderous expression didn't change. "This mess is on you, mate. It's not my responsibility to clean it up."

"Jesus, Connor. I didn't ask for this!"

"You should have known better. This is exactly what I warned you about when you started seeing her."

"Connor, we have to do something," I interjected. "We can't just leave her there."

"She's not my concern, Cass. You are."

"But she's my concern," Alfie said.

"The Clan should be your concern," Connor retorted. "You've already put it at risk once before. I'm not going to let you do it again."

"I'm not going to abandon her. I love her!"

Silence descended, cloyingly thick. Sloane blanched, and she turned on her heel and left the room. Tommy went after her. "Sloane, wait."

Alfie stared up at Connor defiantly as I packed away my med kit. I heard raised voices in the other room, Tommy and Sloane arguing through the closed door. So much for my matchmaking efforts.

"You will not see her again," Connor said, his voice deadly calm. "I forbid it."

Alfie launched to his feet again. "Who the fuck do you think you are--"

"Your warlord, you fucking numpty--"

"Connor, stop."

He pointed in my direction without even looking at me. "Stay out of this, Cass."

"You're being cruel."

Connor finally turned and looked at me. His eyes were the same, cold, unfeeling things they'd been when I'd first met him. Ice on the edge of a rocky shoreline. I knew, deep down, that this is how he reacted when he was scared and losing control, but it still hurt.

Tommy entered the room looking gutted. Whatever had transpired between him and Sloane hadn't gone well. His lip was still bleeding, so I grabbed a wad of gauze from my med kit and gently pressed it to the corner of his mouth. Tommy's gaze slid to mine, softening, and he took the gauze from me. "Thanks."

"Look at you," Connor said. "Pregnant, still recovering, running on next to no sleep, and you're mopping up our blood. By God, I'm not going to have this."

He grabbed me by the arm, gentle but firm, and led me to the couch, forcing me to sit. I glared at him as he knelt in front of me. "I'm fine, Connor. I want to help."

"You've helped enough."

"You're smothering me."

His jaw tightened. "What further care do the two idiots need?"

"Hey, in my defense, Alfie started it," Tommy growled. "I finished it."

Connor stood and squared off with Tommy. He was three inches shorter than my brother, but his cold fury cut the height difference down to nothing. "You wanted me back in the fold? Well, here I am. And you better believe things are going to be changing around here. I am not having this come into my home yet again and place my family at risk, all because you decided to play with fire. The only reason I haven't gone to Callum about this is because of what you did to protect Cassidy. But things change. This stops now."

Tommy shook his head, a bitter smile tugging at his lips. "You've been playing pretend for so long that you've forgotten what it means to be a Clan man. You forget that we're your family too. And right now, that includes Emilia. We don't abandon family."

Connor stared at him in silence, his eyes hard. I'd never seen him look like this before. So cold, so distant.

Tommy took a deep breath and turned to look at Alfie. "You good?"

Alfie nodded.

"Good. Because we've got some things to talk about, and I don't think we should be doing it here." He looked at Connor, and then at me. He scooped a hand under Alfie's arm. "Come on, up you get."

"He's got a concussion, wake him up every couple hours," I said. "Call me if there are any problems. And keep that ice pack on your eye, Tommy, for at least 20 minutes."

Tommy nodded. "Will do, sis."

Alfie looked at Connor as Tommy helped him to his feet, but he didn't say anything. Probably a good idea on his part. Connor watched them leave, then he folded me into his arms. "I'm sorry, love."

The sentiment was there, but my husband wasn't. He'd withdrawn into that distant place where I couldn't reach him, his armor snapping firmly into place once again. The same armor he wore when he first met me, that icy exterior that he used to protect himself from the world. I buried my face in his chest and tried to melt my way through to his heart. "You're upset."

He pulled back and placed a gentle kiss on my forehead. "Not with you. Never with you."

"Why didn't you tell me about Emilia?"

"You know why." Connor tucked a strand of hair behind my ear and grazed his fingers down my cheek, thawing just a little. "I want to insulate you from this world. I have to."

"I'm not sure if you can."

It was the wrong thing to say. Connor stiffened and pulled away. He picked up my med pack and stowed it back underneath the bathroom vanity where it belonged. It wasn't until he grabbed his jacket and car keys that I realized that he was leaving.

"Don't go. Stay here with me." I placed my hand on his shoulder, but it slid down his back as he turned.

"I have work to do, Cass, and you need to rest. I'll be back soon, I promise."

Connor kissed me on the cheek, a quick, chaste thing, and then he was gone. I watched him leave, the sound of the door closing echoing through the empty penthouse. The quiet that settled in the room was suffocating. I was alone again, with nothing but my thoughts for company.

It was all too much, and I slumped down on the couch, tears pricking at my eyes. I felt like I was losing my husband all over again, and I didn't know how to fix it. My hand soothed over my baby bump.

"It's going to be okay," I whispered, not sure if I was trying to reassure the child growing in my belly, or me.

8

CONNOR

THUNDER RUMBLED OVERHEAD. I stared out the window, watching the rain streak down the penthouse window in rivulets. The lights of the city were dimmed by the deluge, and I felt oddly alone. For once, the stormy weather matched my mood perfectly.

I blew a ring of smoke into the carved glass in my hand, letting the smoke infuse the bourbon. It was one of Callum's cigars, and it wasn't half bad. I didn't smoke often, certainly not around Cassidy and the baby, but my office was the one place I could go if I needed something more to settle my nerves. I wasn't used to this kind of tension, not with the people I cared about, and the longer it went on, the more I felt like I was losing my mind.

And tonight was a bad night for it.

I took a deep drag of the cigar, blowing the smoke out into the room as I exhaled. The acrid smell filled my senses, and I closed my eyes for a moment, trying to quiet the noise in the back of my head. Black and red. Scratching. Clawing its way out.

The ice cubes in my glass clicked together as I lifted the bourbon to my lips, and I took a long, slow swallow. The liquor warmed a trail down the center of my body, right past that aching void in my chest. The place where my heart had once been. The place where Cassidy reached in and taken it for herself, filling in the cracks with her love and saving me in the process.

The place where it felt like I was slowly losing her all over again.

A month had passed since Tommy and Alfie's fight in the bar. A month of grim tension and avoided conversations, of blood and smoke and one mistake after another.

A month of me trying to hold together a shattered world.

Moretti was at the root of it all, of course. They'd been pushing us hard lately, and we'd been pushed back just as hard. We were hemorrhaging money, losing ground, losing men. They attacked our people, our legitimate business fronts, our supply routes and partners. Things were getting bad, and there was no end in sight. I'd done what I could to mitigate the damage, but it was getting harder to keep the Clan intact.

Tommy and I held a fragile truce. He continued to drink and vent his feelings loudly and often, and I continued to steer the Clan with an iron grip. Alfie and I barely spoke. As far as I knew, he'd ceased communications with Callum on pain of death. Going to Callum had been his idea, not mine, and it had backfired spectacularly in his face.

I should have stopped him. I should have known better, but I was angry.

Alfie was a fool. He'd lost his head over Emilia, and he'd put the Clan at risk in the process. He was a loose cannon, and I didn't know how to rein him in. He'd become reckless, his temper flaring at every turn. He was a liability, and I had to find a way to control him.

But I was only one man. I couldn't be everywhere at once, and there was only so much I could do.

I drained my glass and set it aside. My cell phone buzzed, and I reached for it without thinking. The caller ID read unknown number.

I frowned. Unknown numbers usually meant one thing. Trouble.

I thumbed the answer button and lifted the phone to my ear. "McTiernan."

"Well, if it isn't the prodigal son." The voice was unfamiliar, but I knew the accent. Moretti.

I sat up straighter in my chair. "What do you want?"

"Straight to the point, eh? No pleasantries for an old friend?"

"You're not my friend, Dominic," I growled. "And if you call me again, I'll make sure you regret it."

He laughed. "So touchy. But I don't think you will. Because I'm calling about your wife."

The blood in my veins turned to ice. I gripped the phone tighter, my knuckles turning white. "What about her?"

"She's pretty. I can see why you like her. But she's not really your type, is she?"

"Stay away from my family," I spat.

"Or what? You'll let Alfie loose on me? I welcome the chance to put that little shit in the ground. You have no idea what's happening in your own house, McTiernan."

I stood, moving towards the door. "What the fuck does that mean?"

"It means that you're losing. And soon, there will be nothing left for you to lose."

"I swear to god, Dominic--"

"No, you listen to me. The McTiernans are nothing more than a bunch of lowlife gangsters, and you are their puppet. A fucking joke. Lorenzo is going to rip you apart and you know it. It's only a matter of time. I've got a message from him for you."

"Oh yeah?" I stopped, one hand on the doorframe. "What's that?"

"You'll be seeing us soon. Who knows, maybe I'll even pay a visit to your pretty young wife. Angel's got his eye on Emilia, but your boy Teagan told me a few things about Cassidy when he had a little taste of her. Sweet as a peach. It's too bad she's all swollen with your brat, *mammalucco*, but I'm sure we can make things work."

"You're dead."

The call disconnected. I slammed my phone on the desk. It didn't help. I was angry, so fucking angry that I couldn't breathe. My hands shook. I grabbed my glass and hurled it across the room, watching it shatter into a thousand tiny pieces. I knew that little asswipe was baiting me, but that still didn't stop the red haze creeping across my vision.

Cass. They were threatening her. And there was nothing I could do to protect her.

The office door opened. "Connor?"

Cassidy stood in the doorway, her hair sleep tousled and her robe wrapped around her growing belly. She looked tired, dark circles under her eyes. "Did something break?"

"I dropped my drink. Don't come in here, there's glass all over the place."

Cassidy stared at me, her eyes searching. I tried to school my features, but she'd always been able to see past the mask. It was a gift of hers.

She crossed the room, closing the distance between us. "You're upset."

"I'm fine," I lied.

She placed a gentle hand on my arm. "Connor, talk to me. Please."

I looked at her, my heart thumping heavily against my sternum. This woman was my world, and there was nothing I wouldn't do to protect her. "It's nothing, love. Let's go to bed."

Cassidy sighed and dropped her hand. She wasn't happy, but she knew not to push. "All right."

I followed her to the bedroom. She crawled back under the covers, and I lay next to her, wishing I could pull her against my body and hold her close. I missed her. I missed her so much that I thought it would drive me mad. But I couldn't. Not like this.

We lay in silence, the rain pattering against the window. I couldn't sleep. Truth be told, I was still seething inside, my mind whirring with half formed plans and contingencies. I had to protect Cassidy, and I would do whatever it took to make it happen. Even at the cost of my own life, if that's what it took.

"Connor?"

I turned towards her and forced my voice to stay level. "Hmm?"

"I'm sorry."

"For what?"

"For whatever you're dealing with right now. For whatever it is you can't tell me. Just know that I love you, and no matter what happens, we'll face it together."

I reached for her, my hand sliding down her arm, wanting to hold her hand, but instead I found the cast on her wrist. Something inside me fractured and bled. "I love you too, Cass. You don't ever need to question that. I will always love you."

The silence lay heavily between us, broken only by the rain and our soft breaths in the sprawling opulence of the penthouse. Cassidy fidgeted, rolling from one side to another, trying to find a comfortable spot. "Are you all right?" I asked.

She started to sit up, more of a roll now that her belly was getting bigger. "Just a cramp or something. I can't seem to get comfortable. It's all right, I'll stretch out on the couch, I promise, I just--"

She gasped, her face visibly paling. I must still have a heart, because I'm sure it stopped. "Cass?"

"I'm okay," she said shakily. "I just sat up wrong."

But it wasn't okay. Because she didn't sit back down, she stayed sitting up, her face contorted with pain. "It's okay, I'm fine. *I'm fine*," she said, trying to convince herself as much as me.

I grabbed her hand, pulling it into mine, holding it tightly. I was no doctor, but I knew enough about pregnancies to know that this was bad. She was shaking. Her face was ashen.

"Cass, you're not okay," I said, trying to keep the fear out of my voice. I let go of her hand and reached for my cell phone. "We're going to the hospital."

"No, please."

"Then I'm calling Jerome. Non-negotiable, love." My heart was pounding so hard I felt it rattling my entire body, but my hands were steady as I helped ease her back onto her side. I tucked a pillow between her knees and another under her head. "It's going to be okay, Cass. Just breathe."

This time, there was no stopping the tears that slipped by, each one another pinprick into my already shattered heart as they trickled down her cheeks. She clutched at my arm, the cast on her wrist rough and foreign. The cast she'd gotten because of me. "Please don't leave me."

I pressed my lips against her forehead and closed my eyes. "Never."

<hr />

I sat outside the master suite of my home while Dr. Jerome Carter examined my wife, and I tried to pretend that my world wasn't crashing down around me. He was my wife's close friend and mentor, the Chief Trauma Surgeon at Boston Medical Center and someone who was privy to the true nature of my line of work and Cassidy's involvement in it. I trusted him with both our lives, but I still felt like I was back in that awful waiting room again. Waiting to hear if Cassidy was alive or dead. I knew it probably wasn't as dire as all that--God, I hoped not--but it still felt like that moment all over again.

I should have done more. Maybe I pushed her too hard. Maybe I didn't push her hard enough. She was working too hard, burying everything down and I just let it happen. This was my fault.

My fault.

"Mr. McTiernan?"

My head shot up. Jerome was standing just outside the door. I hadn't even heard it open.

"How is she?"

"She's resting, which is exactly what she needs right now. She had some cramping and light spotting—"

I was confused. "Spotting?"

"Bleeding. Very light."

I felt my face drain of color. That sounded serious. Really fucking serious. There didn't seem to be enough air in the room. "But she's okay?"

Jerome placed a hand on my shoulder to steady me. "It happens occasionally during the second trimester. I brought a portable ultrasound with me and verified everything, but the baby looks just fine. He or she is even starting to move, which is a great sign this early."

I closed my eyes and took a deep breath, trying to calm the storm raging inside. . "You said this happens sometimes? That it's normal?"

He hesitated. "Not exactly normal, but it's not uncommon. I'll continue to monitor her and we'll push her appointments with the OBGYN up to every two weeks, but the baby looks to be doing just fine. It's Cassidy I'm worried about."

I gave him a sharp look. "What do you mean?"

"Her blood pressure was significantly elevated, which is a concern during pregnancy. I won't go into all the details, but it's something that we need to keep a close eye on. I'd like to get a full workup on her and I want to start her on some blood pressure medication and prenatal supplements. She should have been taking those already. I'm also going to refer her to a friend of mine, a psychiatrist that specializes in PTSD."

I stared at him. "I don't understand. This isn't PTSD, this is a physical reaction."

"The mind is just as much a part of the body as anything else. There are no simple solutions when it comes to mental health, but it's an area that is very important to me, and I've seen some great results from using a combination of therapies. You know what's happening with her, and I know she's been through hell, but it's important to remember that you have to care for the mind as well as the body."

My face and hands felt numb. I knew Cassidy had therapy appointments she was supposed to be going to, but she had said she didn't want to talk to a stranger, and I hadn't pushed. I thought that it was just a matter of time, that she would come to terms with what happened to her and that she would open up to me. Or somebody. Anybody.

"I tried." The lie was weak and sour in my mouth. I hadn't tried nearly enough, but I was at the end of my wits. "I've tried to get her to talk to her therapist, but she won't talk to anyone about it. Not even me. It's like she's trying to pretend it didn't even happen."

"Avoidance and denial is a common response to trauma," Jerome said gently, "and, given her personality, I'm not surprised."

"She's afraid of her own weakness. I know she's struggling, I just don't know what to do or how to help her."

He nodded. "I understand you not wanting to push her, but right now, this is jeopardizing the health of both Cassidy and the baby. Things need to change if we're going to continue with a healthy pregnancy."

I looked at him. "Is she going to lose the baby?"

"I don't believe so, no. But I won't lie to you, Connor. If things continue this way, it is a concern. Right now, Cassidy needs stability and peace more than anything, and the most important thing you can do for her is to be there for her."

"I can do that," I said, straightening my shoulders.

"Good. Now, she's exhausted and her blood pressure is still elevated, so I'm going to have to insist that she remain on bed rest for a few days. No more working, no more stress. I've told her everything I'm going to tell you, and although she wasn't happy about it, I think she's finally listening."

Jerome's phone rang, and he pulled it out of his pocket with an apologetic look. "Excuse me, I need to take this. Go check on her, I'll be right back."

I didn't need to be told twice. I moved quickly into the bedroom and shut the door behind me. Cassidy was sitting up in bed, the covers pulled up to her waist, looking pale and small against the stark white linens. She was chewing relentlessly at her bottom lip, the skin starting to tear.

"Hey," I said softly. "How are you feeling?"

"Okay." It was barely whispered and not very convincing.

I crawled into bed with her. I kept my movements slow, telegraphing my intentions, but when I put my arms around her she positively melted into my side, holding onto me like I was the last thing tethering me to reality.

She was shaking.

"Shhh...it's okay," I murmured into her sweet strawberry blond hair. "Just let go, mo chroí. I'll catch you."

It started slowly at first. A little hiccup, a small hint of wetness on the collar of my shirt. All the anger and pain and fear she'd held back, swelling up and cresting like a mammoth tidal wave, building in momentum and velocity until she finally let go, until it swept us both over the edge.

Huge, wracking sobs that threatened to shake her apart. Each one heavier than the last, until they gathered into a heart-wrenching scream that was muffled against my shoulder, but it still cut like a knife to the heart. I clenched my jaw and held her tightly, terrified at the strength of the demons she'd kept hidden for so long.

You did this to her. You chose to love her and bring her into this darkness, and now you've nearly lost her to it. You don't deserve her.

A deep, animalistic noise escaped my lips, and I gripped her tighter, shutting out that voice in my head. I hated myself for how much I'd failed her, but I would never--could never--let her go. I loved her too much and I was far too selfish.

Gradually, she quieted, breathing heavily. My hold never loosening, I cradled her in my arms as I slid us down between the sheets. I pulled them up over both of our shoulders, and she shifted to get comfortable, tucking herself against me.

Her hand landed on my chest and her fingers splayed over my heart. It was beating out a harsh rhythm, still thrumming with adrenaline and fear. Something trickled across the bridge of my nose and she brushed it away. Tears. I hadn't realized I'd been crying.

In the wake of that release, the air felt lighter somehow. Cassidy moved her hand up to cup my face, blinking tiredly, her eyes rimmed with red. "I'm so sorry."

"Don't." I petted her hair, smoothing away the last few residual tears. "You have absolutely nothing to be sorry about. You're so strong and you're so brave. You're the bravest person I know." I held her gaze, silently pleading with her. "But you don't have to carry this alone."

"I know." Her lips trembled. "I need to talk about it. What happened. I don't want to, but I think I need to."

I gently rested my forehead against hers. "Whenever you're ready, I'm here. I'm right here with you."

She smiled. It was faint, barely even there, but it was filled with so much warmth and love that it nearly broke what was left of my heart, and I found myself falling in love with her all over again.

Her eyes were growing heavy, and she snuggled against my chest. "I'm so tired."

"I know, sweetheart. Go ahead and sleep, you need it. I'm right here with you. I won't let go."

***

One week later, I was waiting for Cassidy outside her therapist's office when my phone rang. I glanced at the screen. Callum.

I thumbed the answer button and brought it to my ear. "Yeah?"

"Where are you?"

"I'm taking Cassidy to her appointment. Why? What's wrong?"

Callum grunted. "I need you to come down to the pub. We've got a problem."

"What kind of problem?"

"Teagan."

I paused, confused. That bastard hadn't been a problem since I'd nearly taken him apart with my bare hands, and I'd put him in the ground again if I could. "I thought I took care of that."

"You did, but Moretti kept the leftovers. Teagan Kelley's body just washed up in the Harbor wearing a Chelsea Smile."

"What?" That...made no sense. The Chelsea Smile, also known as the Glasgow Smile or the Glasgow Grin, originated in Scotland in the late twenties. It was a particularly gruesome form of torture in which the victim's cheeks would be slashed clean through from mouth to ear on either side. But why Teag's body surfaced with those kind of marks after all these months was beyond me. Steamin' Jesus, the smell must have been horrendous.

"It's a fucking message. One the cops are going to figure it out and pin it on us."

The therapist's door opened, and Cassidy came out. She looked drained but lighter, somehow, even smiling at me as she saw me, but one look at the phone in my hand and the look on my face, and she stilled. I held up a hand to stay her. "That makes no sense. That's a Scot's calling card, not Irish."

Callum laughed, but it held no humor. "You think those cops are going to care?"

He was right. The police were going to see a dead McTiernan man with a very specific signature, and they were going to jump to conclusions. "It's been months. Why now?"

"Who knows, but apparently they kept the bastard on ice. I told you there'd be problems from this, Connor. I told you to wait for fucking backup. Get your ass back here. We've got work to do."

I disconnected the call. I couldn't deal with this right now. "Cassidy..."

"I know, you have to go." She tucked her hair behind her ear, trying to smile. "It's okay, Connor. I understand."

I pulled her into a hug, and she relaxed against my chest. "I'll be home soon. I promise. Will you be all right until then?"

She nodded. "Yes. And when you do come home...I'm ready to talk. About everything."

"You're sure?"

"Yes. And no." Her smile broke me and made me all over again. "But I'll be okay as long as you're there."

I pressed a kiss against her forehead. "I'll be there."

9

— • —

ALFIE

THE LIGHTS OF THE dimly lit room cast eerie shadows on the faces of the McTiernan Clan, gathered for an urgent meeting to discuss our escalating issues with the police. I felt the tension in the air, as thick and suffocating as the smoke from the cigarettes burning between the fingers of my fellow clan members. The anxiety weighed heavily on all of us, but we had to figure out a way to protect ourselves and maintain control over South Boston. We'd never recover if we lost what we'd worked so hard for.

Connor sat at Callum's right hand, Tommy at his left, the rest of the men spread around the table. It was clear, ever since his return, that Connor was being groomed to take over some day. I wasn't sure how he felt about that. We hadn't spoken any more than strictly necessary since the fight at the club.

It was a grim reminder of just how many things had changed over the last few months.

"So far they've just been hanging around the neighborhood," Callum was saying. "A couple of unmarked cars, just sitting there with their lights off. Not really doing anything."

"For now," Tommy growled. "It's only a matter of time before they pin Teagan on us."

"How the hell did this happen?"

"Fuckin' Moretti."

"We should just take them all out!"

"We can't touch them, are you mad? The police would be all over us like flies on shit."

"They're already all over us, they've got us by the bollocks!"

"Enough." Callum raised a hand. "I'll handle the cops. Like I always fucking do."

He leveled a watery glare in Connor's direction, and I felt a stab of anger. It wasn't fair to blame this latest stunt on him. I would've done nothing less if Emilia was the one who had been taken. I'd been with Connor the night we rescued Cassidy, and the man had been as cool as I'd ever seen him. No one would've guessed Moretti would stoop to this.

"Cops aside, we've got other issues," Tommy said. "Moretti's guys have been messing with Skip. So far just a bit of petty vandalism, but we need to nip this in the bud."

That was an understatement. Tom O'Reilly, aka The Skipper, owned an aging convenience store a couple blocks down from Lady D's. He'd been around since Callum had been just starting out in the business, and nearly everyone considered Skip and his wife Mary to be family.

"What kind of vandalism?"

"Stuff's been stolen. Smashed. They egged the store."

Callum frowned. "Why hasn't he said anything?"

"He didn't want to cause trouble."

"Sounds about right. Pay for the damages, post a few guys up, permanent. Draw lots about it or something, because you know Mary will be feeding whoever's watching the store until they can't eat another bite."

Tommy smirked. "Will do."

"It's just a temporary fix. We need to come up with something more concrete, or this will keep coming back to haunt us."

The room erupted into heated debate once more. It felt like we were going in circles, and my impatience got the best of me. My mind began to wander, thinking about Emilia and how much I needed her presence to calm the storm inside me. Even in the darkest moments, she brought light into my life, and I knew I had to prioritize my relationship with her amidst the chaos surrounding us.

Contrary to what I'd been ordered to do by both Connor and Callum, I continued to see Emilia. How could I not? It was like asking my lungs not to breathe or my heart not to beat. She was as much a part of me as anything else, and I would never be whole without her. I had no regrets, not when it came to her.

Even if it meant directly disobeying the Clan.

Thankfully, somehow, nothing had come of the fight at the club. Angel and Dom continued to keep Emilia's secret, although that didn't inspire as much confidence in me as it did in Emilia. They were up to something. We hadn't heard the last of this.

But, Emilia worried about Sofia, and at least Luca was there to watch over her somewhat. I didn't trust the big ape as far as I could throw him, but I trusted Emilia.

So, we met in secret in the vacant apartment in the building next to the bookshop. Angel and Dom watched Emilia too closely for her to leave, so I came to her like I did when we first met, stealing down the alley at night like a thief, a single black rose in my hand. It might have been corny to anyone else, but they made her smile. And right now, I would pay anything for just one more of her smiles.

One day, I wouldn't have to steal her smiles away like a thief. One day, every single one would belong to me.

One day, when I got us both out of this life.

I was already making plans. We'd have to go off the grid, disappear entirely. I had a place, a cabin up north that I'd inherited from my grand-parents. It was remote, tucked away deep in the woods. I hadn't been there since I was a kid, but I knew it would be safe. And I'd do whatever it took to protect Emilia, including giving up my identity entirely.

She was worth it. She was everything.

And I would do whatever it took to keep her safe, even if it meant defying the entire Clan.

Suddenly, Connor slammed his palm on the table, startling me back to reality. "We're getting nowhere like this! We all know what's at stake here – our lives, our families, everything we've built. Let's stop talking in circles and focus on what needs to be done."

I saw the fire in his eyes as he took charge, the fierceness that made him a force to be reckoned with. As much as I admired his strength, I couldn't help but notice how it seemed to consume him, leaving little room for anything else.

"Connor," Tommy interjected, his voice laced with frustration. "Have you even considered what all this is doing to Cassidy? You can't just keep throwing yourself into danger and expect her to be fine with it. I know I said you need to come back to work, but Jesus Christ."

"Stay out of my personal life," Connor growled, his jaw clenched so tight I saw the muscles straining beneath his skin. His knuckles were white against the broken table, and I knew that any second now, he would snap.

"Your personal life affects all of us," Tommy shot back, undeterred. "Cassidy's part of this family too, and she deserves better than to be left alone every night wondering if her husband will come home alive!"

"Look, I'm doing everything I can to keep us safe and protect our interests. I'm doing everything I can to keep her safe and to keep this family together, and you have no right to question my methods!"

Tommy shook his head. "It's not about your methods, it's about your priorities. And I'm not the only one who thinks so. Right, Alf?"

All eyes turned to me, and I shifted uncomfortably in my seat. "Let it go, Tommy. It's not the place for it."

"Damn right," Callum said gruffly. "We've got other things to worry about, boys, and now isn't the time to be fighting amongst ourselves. So let it go. We're not going to solve anything like this."

The tension in the room was palpable as the men around the table resumed their discussion. I understood Tommy's frustration, and I couldn't blame him for it, but I also knew that Connor was doing his best to hold things together.

"Hey man, I'm sorry." Tommy's voice was low as he leaned in close to me. "I didn't mean to put you in the middle of it like that, but someone had to say something."

"It's okay," I said, trying to reassure him. "You're just looking out for your sister. I get it."

Tommy nodded, but he still looked troubled. "Yeah, well, I hope he does too. I love Connor like a brother, but I think he's forgetting what's really important."

I thought back to my secret meetings with Emilia, the stolen moments when we were able to lose ourselves in each other, and I felt a sharp pang of guilt. I knew exactly how Connor felt, and I couldn't deny the hypocrisy of what I was doing.

But I couldn't bring myself to regret it. Not when it came to Emilia.

"I've got to run," I said, pretending to check my phone. "I'll catch up with you later."

"Alfie..."

I ignored him and left the meeting early, en route to the only place I called home anymore and the woman I loved. I didn't want to deal with Tommy's questions or the weight of my own conscience. I'd never been a liar before, not to my family.

Until now. Until her.

And I didn't care. I'd do anything for her.

Emilia was worth it.

10

— · —

CASSIDY

OUTSIDE ON THE PENTHOUSE'S terrace, the air was cold but the sun was warm. It seeped into my pores, warming me from the inside in a way I hadn't felt since before I was taken. Behind closed eyelids, the world was a soft technicolor of reds, pinks, and golds, and I sighed, drawing it in as a shield before I dove back down into the harsher depths of reality.

The patio door slid open behind me.

"Cass? Love?"

"I'm here," I answered.

Connor's familiar footsteps sounded on the cobblestone, his hand gently caressing my shoulder. "Aren't you cold?"

Eyes still closed, I tilted my face up towards the sun. "Not really. The sun feels good. It's going to start snowing soon, probably one of the last days we'll get to sit out here."

Connor clicked his tongue and draped a blanket over me anyway, carefully tucking the edges under my legs before sitting down. I leaned into him as he wrapped his arm around me, one large, warm hand laid protectively over my belly.

"How are you feeling?" he asked.

"Better," I answered truthfully. Last week's scare had been a wake-up call, and I was done trying to hide my pain from him. "How did your thing go?"

"It was...unpleasant, but nothing I can't handle."

"Do you want to talk about it?"

Connor shook his head. "I'd rather not, if it's all the same to you."

I nodded, leaning my head on his shoulder. "Okay."

We sat in silence for a while, simply enjoying the closeness and the warmth of each other's company.

"How did your appointment go? You don't have to tell me if you don't want," Connor added quickly. He swallowed visibly and fiddled with the corner of the blanket. He was nervous. "I just want to make sure you're doing okay. I know I haven't been there like I should have."

"Hey, stop that." I grabbed his hand, pressing my lips to his knuckles. "You're doing everything you can. I know how much pressure you're under, and I'm so proud of you. I've always known what this life is like, and I knew what I was getting into when I agreed to marry you."

His lips twitched up into a humorless grin. "I think that's putting it pretty mildly, don't you think?"

"Probably." I grinned back. "But you're not exactly the one who started all of this, you know. The Moretti Family has always been at odds with the McTiernans, and we both know they're the ones who really need to pay for what they've done. Not you."

Guilt was written on his face, as it had been ever since he'd rescued me from that basement. I would give anything to erase that worry, and to ease the heavy, heavy burden I knew he carried. Talking to the therapist had been the first step--a scary but necessary first step towards recovery.

But, as it turned out, talking about what happened with a complete stranger was easier than I had expected it to be. It had been messy. It had been ugly. But in the wake of all that release, I felt just a little bit lighter.

The therapist, a sturdy older woman named Dr Baumgardner—she insisted on being called Ginny--hadn't said much at all. Verbally, at least. But she had listened. Waiting patiently as I took my time. As I spoke, the feeling was something akin to drawing poison from my soul, the words tumbling out in an incoherent, jumbled mess.

Together, we had begun to help me sort through this mess. It was uncomfortable, at first, to be sitting on the other side of the table--to be the one unburdening myself to someone else rather than the other way round. But it also felt strangely like relief, letting someone else help share the weight of my trauma.

It was time to let Connor help me share that weight as well.

"I know I don't have to talk about it Connor, but I want to," I said, interlacing my fingers with his. "We agreed—no more secrets between us. No more lies. I don't want this thing to sitting heavily between us, something we have to keep dancing around. Teagan Kelley has hurt us enough. He doesn't get to keep hurting us now."

Just saying his name sent a thrill of fear and revulsion down my spine. Connor felt me stiffen, and he held me a little tighter, his lips rubbing against my temple soothingly. Deep within my belly I felt a little flutter, almost sensed rather than felt, and I smiled softly.

"They movin' around in there?" Connor asked with a little smile of his own. His hand pressed a little firmer against my belly, and I knew he was wishing he could feel it too.

I nodded. "More and more every day, it seems. They're strong."

"Just like their mum."

He said it softly, but that didn't lessen the intensity of his words or the meaning behind them. The way he was looking at me—just when I didn't think I could love him any more than I already did, he had to go and look at me like that, like I was his entire world. His beginning and his end. His angel.

"Do you remember that night in Maine, the last night we were there?" I asked. "The night you first told me you wanted me?"

Connor's eyes never wavered from mine. "I remember all of it."

"I said that you couldn't possibly feel that way. That you didn't know anything about me." I smiled faintly, remembering. "But even then, you knew me better than I knew myself. You said that I was a strong woman, but the thing I feared more than anything was my own vulnerability."

I laughed bitterly. "You were right. But I didn't want to hear it then, and until now, I didn't want to believe it. I learned from a very young age to wear that armor and never let them see how much it hurt, but that fear was always there. And there, in that room...with him...I was afraid. I was helpless. More vulnerable than I'd ever been in my entire life, and that's what terrified me the most. It broke me."

Connor made a little sound in the back of his throat, but I pushed on. There was no stopping it now.

"Then, after...I was afraid to show you how broken I was. How much it affected me. How much I was hurting. I didn't want you to see how vulnerable I am now." I shook my head. "When I think back to that room, I feel terror, but I also feel my weakness. My shame. I feel dirty—tainted—and I didn't want you to see that. I thought that if I could just lock it all away, then it would lessen over time. But all I was doing was hurting us both."

Connor looked away, swallowing hard. I reached for his face, pulling him back towards me.

"Hey," I said softly. "Look at me, Connor. I'm not done yet."

He shook his head. "You were dealing with it the only way you knew how. Nobody can predict how they handle this kind of thing. I saw what you were doing—I knew it, but I didn't do a thing to stop it. I should've pushed more."

"Since when have you ever been able to make me do anything I didn't want to do?" I smiled at him, but it held little humor.

"Fair point."

Connor's hand lay open in my lap, and I traced the lifeline on his palm with my good hand. For the longest time I didn't say anything, turning his hand over and memorizing every scar, every callus. The same hands that brought me warmth and love were also the hands that had taken my attacker apart, and although those scars were long since healed, the ghost of them remained for us both.

I started talking. Haltingly at first, each word physically costing me effort to bring forth. Down into that pit once again, except this time I was dragging him with me. Letting him see.

Connor didn't say a word, but then again, he didn't have to. I tried not to pay attention to his reactions, but I felt him stiffen, heard his breathing accelerate into harsh, deep breaths as he struggled not to lose it. His hand was wrapped around mine in a grip so firm it would have hurt if it hadn't been for the underlying gentleness, instead providing an anchor point I could ground myself to.

And I needed it as we finally came to the meat of the story. What had actually happened in that basement. What Teagan had said, what he had done. The degradations and the violations, still just as fresh and angry and raw as ever.

It came in fits and starts, shudders and gasps, and I kept my face resolutely turned away from Connor. I couldn't bear to look at him. Not while I sat there and bared my soul to him, showing him just how thoroughly I had been defiled.

"When he left me alone the second time," I whispered, "that's when I broke. He'd already done...enough, and when he came back I knew he'd do more...worse than he'd already done. I-I knew he was going to kill me. He told me that I was bait, and that he'd make you watch before he killed you, t-too."

I wasn't sure at what point I had started crying, but the tears ran freely now. Connor pulled me into his arms and I curled into his side. I was trembling.

"I was panicking. Giving up. I-I don't even know how long I was down there, I just...I was out of my mind...about to pass out...s-so much pain...so s-scared, and I..." I drifted off, lost in my own head.

...cuffs...the cuffs. I can't get out...hurts so bad. I'm trapped and exposed and he's coming back. He's coming back and he's going to take from me he's going to kill me he's going to kill Connor and it—

Two warm hands appeared on either side of my face, gently tilting my head up so I could see him. Two impossibly blue eyes, clouded with grey. Reflecting every tortured, stormy emotion that was threatening to pull me under.

Connor brushed his thumb along my cheekbone, catching my tears and smoothing them away. "It's not real, love. He can't hurt you anymore. You aren't in that room anymore. You're here. You're safe. I've got you."

Gradually, my breathing slowed and the world resolved back into itself. Sharpening as the shadows fell away, and I looked around in a daze before setting back on Connor. HIs eyes were red rimmed and liquid with misery and a deep smoldering anger, but they were the same eyes that had given me strength when I had none left. The same face, the same voice that had calmed me at the height of my panic.

"How did you do that?"

"Do what?"

I didn't answer him right away, looking down at the blanket in confusion. "You were there...with me. In the room. You were there."

Connor frowned and tucked a wayward strand of hair behind my ear. "What do you mean?"

"I could hear your voice," I told him, desperate to make him understand, "as clear as if you'd been standing next to me. Calming me. Telling me what to do, how to escape. The handcuffs, the room, how to...how to stop Teagan when he came to k-kill me. You told me what to do. You saved me."

Connor choked back a sob, realizing what I was saying. "You saved yourself, love. I...I was almost too late."

"You weren't, though. You told me what to do, kept me calm. You killed him, and you got me out."

In the wake of all that unbottling, I felt drained, but calmer, somehow. "Ginny--Dr. Baumgardner--called it dissociating. She said that in the face of all that trauma I created a safe place in my head, that it was my subconscious telling me what to do."

I looked at him, trying to convey how important it was that he understood this.

"But it spoke with your voice. I got myself out, but it was you who guided me. You're my safe place, Connor. You."

A deep, animalistic noise vibrated in his chest, and Connor clutched me to him, holding me so tight I could barely breathe. But I didn't care. I needed his closeness, needed to feel his body against mine and his warmth seeping into my skin. He buried his face in my hair, lips grazing my neck, his breath coming in short, uneven gasps. His body was rigid but his shoulders heaved with silent sobs as he murmured tortured apologies and sweet declarations of his love in a broken mixture of English and Gaelic.

And I let him. I let him take my pain and my fears, completely surrendering that last little bit of myself to him that I had been holding back. In a way, letting go and letting him carry me felt like a final weight had been lifted, and I could finally breathe again.

There was no way to know how much time had passed as we sat there, wrapped up in each other and the enormity of everything that had happened. I could have stayed there forever, tucked away safe in our own little world. The sun dipped below the rooftops as we held each other, hearts raw and flayed open. The sky darkened and the late autumn chill began to set in, but we still refused to move, locked in each other's embrace and silent save for Connor's quiet reassurances.

11

— · —

EMILIA

I SIGHED AND BURROWED beneath the covers, tucking myself closer
to the source of heat at my side. Ghostly residuals of pleasure hummed
through my veins, sweet radiant curls of warmth from his lips and hands
caressing over my bare skin. I yawned happily, shifting my head until I
could see his face.

Alfie stared at me across the pillow, the sunlight peeking through
half-drawn curtains to cast a golden glow on his hair, igniting the dark
auburn curls into a fiery halo. His breath was warm against the nape
of my neck, his arm a secure band around my waist. He shifted, a lazy,
wicked smile curling the corners of his lips as his leg curled over mine,
and he tugged me closer into his body, surrounding me with the warmth
of his love and the protection of his arms.

"You're beautiful, you know that?"

I smiled, running my fingers through the tousled hair at his temples.
"You say that a lot."

His smile widened. "It's true."

My fingers found the curl that perpetually fell into his eyes, pushing
it back affectionately. "Did I ever tell you how much I love your hair?" I
asked, letting the springy locks twine around my fingers.

Alfie hummed, a deep, rumbling sound. "Tell me again. Or, better yet, show me."

I smiled appreciatively and tugged gently on the unruly locks, just enough to make him growl and pull me tighter against his chest.

"Oh," I breathed. "Like this?" I brushed the hair away from the shell of his ear, pressing a trail of featherlight kisses along his jawline. My tongue flicked out to trace along the sensitive skin sheltering the pulse beating in his throat, and Alfie moaned, his grip tightening.

"God, woman." His voice was a deep rumble in his chest, vibrating against my body.

I trailed my lips up his neck, over his chin, and along the corner of his mouth until I finally captured his lips with mine. Alfie groaned and melted into me, his tongue sliding against mine with a need that matched my own. My fingers tangled in his hair, pulling him closer, deeper, and he shifted until he was lying fully on top of me, his weight pinning me down, surrounding me.

I wrapped my legs around him, reveling in the feel of his skin against mine. He was so warm, so solid, and I never wanted to let go. Alfie's hand slid up my thigh, sending shivers of pleasure through my body as I pushed my hips against his. He laughed, a carefree, darkly musical sound as he gently took both my hands and pinned them above my head at the wrists.

"What's the hurry, sweetheart?"

"Need you." I tried to kiss him, but he pulled back, something devious glinting in his sea glass eyes.

"I'm right here."

But he wasn't always here. Our time together had been decimated, shortened to only whatever minutes and seconds we could scrape together, usually with the help of Sofia and Luca. They were covering for us right now, in fact--Sofia was down in the bookshop, covering my customers, and Luca was out with Angel and Dom. The plan was for him to text Sofia if they started heading in the bookstore's direction.

Alfie and I were on a makeshift pallet bed in the vacant apartment next door. There was no heat, water, or electricity, but since we were only able to meet during the day, we made do with open blinds and a mound of blankets to take the chill out of the autumn air. It was a bit cramped and rough, but it was a sanctuary of sorts. The only one we had.

The setup had actually been Sofia's idea, her romanticism casting us as a kind of Romeo and Juliette love story. I only hoped ours turned out better than theirs did.

Luca was less enthusiastic. He'd accepted Alfie's presence in my life with resigned stoicism, but he insisted on helping even though I knew he thought it was a mistake. He didn't say anything directly, but I caught the worried glances he sent my way when he thought I wasn't looking, and it broke my heart.

Angel and Dom had been quiet--for them--ever since the fight at the club. As far as I knew, they hadn't said a thing to Lorenzo, and it seemed like they were content to hold this piece of information over my head and just watch me. For now. I couldn't help feeling like a pawn being moved around a chess board.

Alfie seemed oblivious to it all, focused on the little bit of stolen time we had together. His lips trailed along my collarbone, his tongue flicking out to taste me. "You're thinking too much."

He shifted his weight to one side, supporting himself on an elbow as he continued to explore the lines and curves of my body. My skin prickled in response to his touch, tiny shivers of pleasure radiating out from his fingers as they danced across my skin.

"Turn that brain off in that pretty little head of yours, Emilia. It's not time for thinking." He nuzzled the soft shell of my ear, his breath warm and soft as he murmured against my skin . "Just feel."

He caught my earlobe between his teeth and bit down lightly to prove his point. I gasped, my body arching into him, and Alfie chuckled wickedly, moving to press light kisses along my jaw. His fingers intertwined with mine, clasping them above my head as he covered my body with his, skin to skin, lips to lips, heart to heart.

"Let me love you," Alfie pleaded between kisses, his fingers trailing down my spine, igniting a trail of fire in their wake. I nodded, my breath hitching at the passion in his voice.

What followed was an unhurried, tender exploration, intimacy beyond measure as he slowly and deliberately took me apart with his kiss. Nothing more than his mouth against mine, teasing, coaxing, breaking down my walls while the solid constant of his weight and warmth grounded me. The strong, steady beat of his heart thrumming against my breasts as he drew out my soul and devoured it whole.

After, we lay drifting between conversations and comfortable silences, the kind of quiet that spoke volumes. Our kisses were slow, each one a promise, a silent oath that we belonged to each other—even if the world might say otherwise.

"I could stay here forever," he sighed, his hand stroking along my back as I lay draped across his chest.

I smiled into his skin. "Me too."

"Emilia," he said suddenly, his gaze serious, "no matter what happens, I will always love you. You know that, right?"

I sat up, looking at him. "Why do you say it like that?"

"Like what?"

"Like we're saying goodbye." I heard the tremble in my own voice and swallowed hard. "Why do I feel like you're trying to say goodbye?"

Alfie shook his head, his expression grim. "I'm not trying to say good-bye, love. I'm just making sure you know that I love you. No matter what happens."

I wanted to believe him, I did. But there was something in his voice that made me uneasy, a coldness that hadn't been there before. He'd been different since the fight at the club. Quieter, more introspective. I knew he was struggling with the decision to disobey Connor and Callum, but I also knew that he couldn't bear the thought of losing me.

"I know," I promised, pressing my lips to his, sealing the vow between us. It was a moment of pure connection, of shared dreams and whispered confessions.

"Remember that I'm yours," he continued, his hands framing my face, "and you're mine. No family feud or bloody past can change that."

"Alfie, I—" But I couldn't finish. The weight of our reality pressed in, threatening to shatter our bubble of tranquility.

"Shh," he soothed, his kiss cutting off my fears. "For now, just this. Us. Nothing else matters."

It wasn't true, of course, but for the moment I let myself believe it. The future, whatever it may hold, could wait. Right now, all I wanted to do was lose myself in his arms and pretend that there was nothing else but us.

Alfie was quiet for so long, I thought he'd fallen asleep. His breathing deepened, fingers going still over the spot they'd been caressing over my collarbone. I shifted, trying to see his face, but his arm tightened, holding me in place.

"If you could go anywhere in the world, where would it be?" he asked softly. "If you could leave it all behind, go someplace no one knows you or your past, and money is not an obstacle. Where would you want to go?"

I didn't have to think twice. "Daufuskie Island."

"Gesundheit."

"No, you ass, Daufuskie Island in South Carolina."

"You sure had that one on deck." I felt him smile against my skin. "Tell me about Daufuskie Island."

I smiled, thinking back to the few precious memories I had of my parents and our time there. "It's a little island off the coast of South Carolina. It used to be a resort, but my parents rented a beach house there when I was little and we'd spend the summer there every year. It's private, secluded--really the perfect place to get away from it all.

"I remember we'd go down to the beach every morning and build sandcastles, collect seashells and driftwood. Spanish moss would filter the sunlight onto the sand, creating these little dapples of light that looked like liquid gold. The water was warm and clear, and we'd swim in the surf for hours until my mom would call us in for dinner.

"At night, we'd sit out on the porch and watch the fireflies dance in the dunes, drinking lemonade and listening to the waves crashing on the shore. It was so peaceful, so calm...I've never felt anything like it."

"It sounds perfect." Alfie's voice was a low murmur, almost as if he were afraid to break the spell. He shifted, rolling me onto my back and propping himself up on his elbows. His hair was mussed from the bed, and I reached up to smooth it back, tracing the strong lines of his face with my fingertips.

"What about you?" I asked. "If you could go anywhere in the world, where would it be?"

He kissed the soft skin above my naval. "Anywhere you are. As long as you're with me, I don't care where I am."

"That's not an answer."

"It's the best one I can give you," he said, sobering slightly. "You know how I grew up. Vacations weren't really in the cards for me, unless it was to the McTiernans' summer house in Maine. And that hold very different kinds of memories for me. Good, but nothing like yours."

"I'm sorry."

Alfie shrugged. "Don't be. I can't change my past, but I can create a new future. With you."

He kissed me, his lips moving against mine with a tenderness that stole my breath away. I wrapped my arms around his neck, pulling him closer, needing to feel his skin against mine. Alfie complied, his hands skimming along my body, lighting fires wherever they touched.

"I'm going to take you there some day," he murmured against my lips, "to that island paradise of yours."

"You are?" I smiled, still half-dazed from his kiss.

"Mmhmm." He trailed kisses along my jaw and down my throat, his teeth grazing my collarbone. "And when we get there, I'll make love to you on the beach beneath the stars."

"Just like this?" My hands ran down the planes of his back, my fingernails barely grazing his skin.

Alfie shivered. "Just like this." His voice was a low growl in my ear. "We'll leave everything behind, and I'll spend every day for the rest of my life making you happy. It's all I want."

The sweetness of the moment was almost too much to bear. This far off fantasy that we were writing together, a storybook ending to a treacherous, tenuous romance. An ending that was probably too good to be true.

Alfie must have read the doubt in my eyes, because he pulled back slightly, his gaze intent. "I'm serious, Emilia. I want to take you there."

"I know, Alfie, it's just--"

"As my wife."

My heart stopped. "W-what?"

Alfie smiled, but it held an uncertainty that I had never seen before. He took my hand, threading his fingers through mine. "I mean it, Emilia. I want to marry you. I don't know when or how, but I promise you that we'll figure something out. I want to take you away from all of this and make you feel safe. I love you, and I want to spend the rest of my life with you."

I couldn't speak. I could barely breathe. My heart was beating a frantic staccato against my ribs, my mind racing to keep up with what was happening.

"Emilia?" Alfie's voice was hesitant, almost nervous. "Did I...say something wrong?"

I shook my head, blinking back tears. "No, it's just...you've just taken me by surprise."

His smile faded. "Oh. I, uh, I'm sorry, I didn't mean--"

I cut him off with a kiss, pouring all of my love into it. The tension drained from his body, and he gathered me close, his kiss deepening. We were both breathless when we finally pulled apart.

"Is that a yes?" he asked, his voice low and rough with emotion.

I smiled, feeling like my heart might burst from happiness. "Yes."

"Come here, then." He rolled away from me, plucking at the blanket. I watched, bemused, as he pulled a long strand of navy thread free, and started looping it between his fingers. "I know it's not much, and I promise when I get you a real one, it will be the biggest and most beautiful diamond you can find," he said. "But for now, I need you to understand what I'm asking. What this means to me."

I nodded, too choked up to speak.

Alfie tenderly took my left hand in his and wrapped the thread around my ring finger. His hands were shaking as he tied a knot and slid it down, the makeshift ring coming to rest snugly against my skin. "This is my promise. I'm yours, and you're mine, no matter what happens."

"No matter what," I echoed. "I love you, Alfie."

12

CONNOR

DR. WHITTLEY MANEUVERED THE ultrasound, and the rapid sound of a fetal heartbeat filled the room.

I smiled and pressed my lips against Cassidy's forehead. Our child. New life. Something we created together, and it never failed to amaze me. Listening to our baby's heartbeat, watching them on the monitor, moving and twisting away from the doctor's prodding. They were growing every day, and soon enough we would be able to meet them in person.

Life was so tenuous and fleeting, and part of my job entailed taking it away from others. But creating it? In Cassidy's belly, right where we had made it together, with love? This was just one more way I had been blessed, and it was almost hard to believe it was true. A miracle.

"There's the head...and the heart...the curve of the spine right there..." Dr. Whittley smiled. "They've got their hands in front of their face, it looks like they're sucking their thumb."

My heart swelled at the slow smile that illuminated Cassidy's face, memorizing it in a mental picture I could keep forever. She was going to be such a good mother.

That fragile vulnerability was still there, tempered by that fiery strength and something new. She held her head a little higher. The shame and degradation of what she had gone through slowly disappearing, and I hated that it would never truly go away. That stain would always exist, but she would shine that much brighter to the world with it. I wanted that light, and I saw it already starting to peek out in little things. Small actions. Like sleeping the entire night through without a single nightmare. Or agreeing to speak with a therapist.

She had a glow about her. Life blooming inside of her, and it made her more beautiful than I ever could have imagined.

The baby shifted, kicking again. Cassidy grimaced, rubbing her belly. "That one hurt."

"They've gotten stronger," I said.

"You don't say?" Her voice dripped with sarcasm, but the grin on her face belied the teasing tone.

Dr. Whitley made a few measurements. "Okay, so...baby's right on schedule, looking pretty big at twenty weeks, really healthy."

Cassidy blew out a breath. "Thank God for that."

Dr. Whitley nodded. "We'll get you scheduled for another appointment at twenty-four weeks, but otherwise, everything looks great.

I heaved an internal sigh of relief. I had been on edge ever since finding out Cassidy was pregnant, and especially since the scare a couple weeks ago.

I laughed to myself. The cold, hard man that refused to let fear rule him--I could still become that man when I needed to, but I was softer now. I had something—two somethings, in fact—to lose now, and the fear of losing them was just as fresh as ever. It was a wonder I didn't have an ulcer yet.

"So...do you want to know what the gender is?" The doctor was suppressing a smile that suggested she already knew.

Cassidy looked up at me, asking, but I saw in her eyes that she wanted to know. I answered the doctor, and we both waited in breathless anticipation.

"Well...by the looks of things," Dr. Whitley said as she highlighted a spot on the monitor, "I'd say congratulations, it's a boy."

A son. *A son.*

To be honest, I hadn't cared whether it was a boy or a girl, and I knew Cassidy felt the same way. But now, knowing...it made it all the more real. It was sooner than either of us had imagined, but for better or worse, I was going to be a father.

We were having a son.

I found myself incapable of speaking, swallowing against the heavy lump in my throat as I looked down at my beautiful wife, smiling up at me with luminous joy.

"A boy," she whispered.

Tears began to gather in the corners of her eyes, and I bent down to kiss them away. Cassidy wrapped her arms around my neck, pulling me closer until she could bury her face in the crook of my neck. I couldn't suppress a smile as she kissed me, my heart so full it felt fit to burst. The kiss was slow and sweet, with a fiery passionate undertone that hadn't been there since before she'd been taken. It sent my pulse skyrocketing, and I felt just a little dizzy when we finally parted.

God, I loved her.

Cassidy smiled, her cheeks flushed a dewy pink, and I brushed a stray hair out of her face. She leaned into my touch, closing her eyes and letting out a contented sigh. I sat back, watching as she chatted with the doctor about what to expect. How had my life come to this—this happiness? This satisfaction and this feeling of completeness?

I thought back to the day we met again in the trauma bay of Boston Medical Center, never knowing that our lives, paths that had crossed before in another life, were charted on a collision course that would end with us here. After all we had been through. Hopelessly in love and expecting our first child.

It was enough to take my breath away.

Cassidy's laugh broke me from my reverie, and I focused on her, unable to keep a smile from spreading across my face. I was sure I looked like an idiot, but I didn't care.

I couldn't believe my luck.

As Cassidy spoke with Dr. Whitley, I took a moment to admire the subtle changes in her body as it continued to prepare to bring our child into the world. Her breasts were fuller, more sensitive and tender. Her belly was rounder, her hips and ass a bit fuller, and I found myself attracted to her in new and exciting ways. Her hair was thicker, her skin radiant and luminous. It was as if her body was preparing for the changes that were about to happen, and she was blooming as a result.

She was absolutely stunning.

Dr. Whitley finished her exam, and Cassidy reached for my hand. I took it and laced our fingers together, giving hers a gentle squeeze. "How do you feel?"

"Excited. Nervous. It almost seems...too good to be true."

I bent down and kissed her forehead. "I know what you mean."

Cassidy smiled up at me, and my heart stuttered. It was amazing how one look from her could send my blood racing and my heart pounding, how it could turn me into a bumbling idiot and make me forget everything but her.

It was amazing how much she could love me, despite my flaws. Despite my mistakes.

Later that night, I was still watching her as we prepared dinner together. Cassidy was giddy and full of energy that had yet been unprecedented in our marriage, something that I attributed to the baby more than anything else.

Yet I knew it wasn't just that. The therapy was really helping. Cass was healing, moving on, and especially after today, I finally felt like maybe everything was going to be all right.

For someone who'd been so adverse to it in the beginning, Cassidy actually looked forward to her appointments now. The weight of what she'd been trying to carry all by herself was shocking. What she had told me that day on the terrace had crushed me, and it hurt even more knowing that she'd been struggling with it alone.

Yes, she still had nightmares. She still occasionally lapsed into periods of silence and depression, retreating far within herself. But I was there. Her family and her friends were there, and she had a good, solid support system to help pull her out of the pit when the darkness started to overtake her.

And most importantly of all, she was letting me help her.

It was better, now. It still didn't come easy for her, but it still came. She answered my questions truthfully and didn't hide when she was hurting anymore. That final bridge had been crossed, that final bit of trust relinquished, and although it wasn't much, it did help to ease some of the guilt I still carried.

Not the anger, though. That was definitely still there, raw and festering with each day Lorenzo Moretti continued to draw breath.

"Earth to Connor—you okay?"

I silently cursed myself for getting so wrapped up in my own head. Cassidy was watching me, her tone light but her face concerned as she looked at the spatula I was holding in a death grip, knuckles white. I wondered how long she'd been standing there.

"Right as rain," I lied.

"You know, I can tell when you're lying," she said. "Something's been on your mind ever since this morning."

I pulled her gently backwards into my chest, encircling her with my arms and resting them against her growing belly. Just underneath the skin, a tiny body moved against my hand, and I smiled.

This, this right here...this is all that matters.

"My priorities," I began, "are not what they used to be. I don't want to be that man anymore. I have everything I need or want, right here, and I refuse to do anything to jeopardize it. I almost lost you once, and I won't take that chance again."

"Connor...it wasn't your fault."

I smiled thinly and said nothing.

"You're angry," she observed, "and you feel guilty—you still do."

"I do. I'm sorry, it's not something I can just let go of. When I think about what he did to you...when I think about what could have happened...I wanna kill him all over again. I want to..."

I swallowed back my anger before it could flare out of control. "The man who did it may be dead, but there is still the man who gave the order. And sometimes I wish I could be there when they kill him. I wish it could be me who pulls that trigger."

My face heated with something suspiciously close to shame. I had told her a lot of things about my past, but I had never talked so blatantly about the killing someone before, never been so open about wanting to be that man again. The one she had hated and feared when we first met.

"I want to be a good man for you, Cass. One you deserve. I don't want to be that person anymore."

She turned and cupped my face in her hands. The cast was gone from her left arm, but I still felt how it trembled with weakness, and the anger flared again.

"Wanting it doesn't make you a bad person. I understand your anger. You don't have to be ashamed of it. You are a good man, Connor Mc-Tiernan." She wrapped her arms around me. "I love you."

"I love you too, Cass. I'd do anything for you."

"Anything?"

"Anything."

She pulled back so she could look me dead in the eye. "Then lay down your guilt. None of this is your fault."

But it is. It is. Even now, I can't protect you the way I want to. I can't end this.

But I didn't say that. Instead, I brushed my fingers lightly over the scar along her temple.

"Okay," I whispered.

13

———— • ————

Cassidy

I sat on the edge of the bed and chewed the end of my thumbnail. It wasn't precisely a dream that had woken me. More of a feeling—slow suffocation, the cloying stench of blood and fear. The freefall of panic had set in, so convincing I could actually feel the cold metal of the handcuffs against my flesh.

I rubbed at my left wrist. It was throbbing. Even in the darkness, I could see the ugly puckered flesh, the trembling when I tried to make a fist.

"Sweetheart?"

Movement on the bed behind me, and I felt the heat from Connor's body as he hovered near. Even now, he was still sometimes afraid I didn't want to be touched—I knew it was because he thought it might trigger me, but the thought was laughable. As if his gentle hands could ever be mistaken for that monster's.

I leaned into him and felt his lips brush my hair. "Just a bad night. My wrist was hurting again. It felt like…"

The words died out, and I sighed in relief as he took my hand in his, ghosting his fingers over the scars tenderly.

"Does this help?"

I nodded, and he massaged a little deeper, banishing the phantom pain along with the demons. Bringing my hand to his lips, Connor lightly kissed the scars there, and I felt something stir. I murmured his name as warmth bloomed low, something that had lain dormant until now.

His touch was fire itself, and I was ready to come in out of the cold.

Connor's breath hitched as my lips grazed against the soft spot below his ear, trailing down the long muscles of his throat. He stuttered and gasped. "Cass. Wh-what are you doing?"

"Please," I breathed. "I need you. I just need to feel you. Please."

Hands firmly grasped my shoulders. "Are you sure? Won't it—I don't want to hurt you."

His concern was warranted, and I understood his hesitation. It was something I had asked myself as my desire for him had begun to bloom again over the past few weeks. Part of it was the pregnancy hormones, I knew. Dr. Whittley had warned me of that much.

The other part was the fact that I missed the physical side of our relationship. I missed him, and I hated that the shadow of my abduction still hovered in the wings.

My shoulders fell, and I crawled into his lap. "I want this. I want to try. I don't know if it'll be too much, but if it is, I'll stop you. I miss you Connor, I miss us."

Connor exhaled sharply. "I miss you too. God—I miss you so much, I—you'll tell me? If it's too much?"

I reached up to touch his face, tracing the familiar lines with my fingertips. I felt the tension in him, the restraint as he struggled to control himself. He leaned into my touch, his eyes slipping closed as he savored the contact.

"I promise."

Connor nodded his acceptance, his hands sliding up my shoulders to cradle my cheek in his palm, his breath warm across my skin as he slowly kissed my forehead, my eyelids. The tip of my nose and my chin and down the line of my jaw before nuzzling his way back up where his mouth slotted generously against mine.

Each touch was feather light, but I still felt the ghost of each kiss linger on. I was aflame as he worshipped me, banishing every speck of darkness from my soul as he moved down my body, cradling me gently but firmly in his arms. Grounding me and tethering me to reality.

Clothing was slowly and deliberately shed. It was a rediscovering of sorts, and not one to be taken too lightly or too quickly. We had been lost and drifting for so long—too long. But he was there, holding me in his arms and guiding us home.

Connor pressed a kiss to my collarbone, then to the valley between my breasts where my heart beat a furious tattoo. His hands traveled gently along my skin, leaving trails of goosebumps in their wake. Teasing my nipples into taut peaks. Murmuring against my skin, a chant spoken into my skin as if he could infuse the words into my body.

"Mo chroí. Mo chroí...Is breá liom tú."

I caught his chin and tilted his face up to mine. "You never told me what that means. Mo chroí."

"My heart." He pressed my hand flat to his chest where I could feel it beating swiftly against my palm. "Because although it gives me life, this heart belongs to you. And it will always be so, until it gives its last beat."

Slowly, I kissed along his jawline. "And the rest?"

"Is breá liom tú." His pulse quickened as I nipped at the tender skin there, and he inhaled sharply. "I love you."

I hummed. "Is breá liom tú, Connor."

He shuddered, burying his face in my shoulder. Lips moved down the column of my throat, my collarbone, and down my breasts. When he finally captured my nipple, I cried out as his tongue swirled around it, sending liquid heat straight through to my core. He grinned and murmured against my flesh, kissing his way over the soft round curves of my belly.

"Say it again," he pleaded. "I like my words on your tongue."

I gasped as his lips passed over my hip bone and down my leg. "Is breá liom tú, Connor—please--"

Gently, he smoothed his palms over my thighs, warming the skin. Not demanding, asking. I parted my legs, granting him the permission that had been simmering. God, how I'd missed him. How I'd wanted this. His lips inched their way across my inner thigh, my nerves a firework with each kiss. He hovered a moment and nipped playfully at the tender skin. "Say it again, mo chroí."

"Is breá ah--"

I arched beneath him as his tongue found me, parting me gently before coaxing a slow circle around the most sensitive parts. Connor hummed, a deep, animalistic purr of satisfaction that reverberated straight through to my core. His name fell from my lips again and again, with each swirl of his tongue, each tease and delicate nibble. His breath came in harsh, uneven pants, his movements more determined as I writhed, waves of pleasure unraveling me.

I wove my hands in his hair, pulling him up to meet me. "I need to feel you, Connor. Please."

He brushed his lips over mine, stealing my breath as his need met my own. He was gentle, rolling me carefully on top until I was straddling him. His cock rested heavily against my belly, tip glistening with need. But he lay still, gripping my hips and tenderly brushing his thumbs against my skin.

"Ride me, love," he said. "Take your pleasure from me."

His words fell away to a soft guttural curse as I took him in hand and guided him into place. We both gasped as he slid home inside me, and I felt my eyes begin to burn. Connor clicked his tongue and began to pull away, distressed by my unshed tears until I shook my head and captured his mouth with mine.

When we began to move together it was different. A little fumbling and awkward at first, but with the breathless anticipation of lovers re-united. The way we fit together was different now, my body changed, both by the scars I carried on my body and the life I carried within it.

There was some pain, the slight creep of dark memories. But there was safety and familiarity and above all, love, and I held on to that with every ounce of strength I possessed.

It was love in its purest form. A slow and gentle pace, both out of deference to my fragility and an attempt to regain what had been temporarily lost. It was raw and earnest, a coupling so different from any I'd experienced, but as the heat built up towards a fever pitch, I felt it singe away the edges of the darkness, burning it away as I surrendered willingly to it.

Strong hands gripped my hips, and Connor cried out as he came. I fell into the chasm with him, riding the cresting wave of my release as it carried me away and all I could do was feel. Hold on.

It was only after we'd finished that I realized I was shaking, tears streaming freely down my face. Blissfully, I floated, and I felt Connor desperately tilt my face towards him.

"Love--are you here with me? Are you all right?"

I was wholly consumed with him. His touch, his scent was everywhere, and I boldly kissed him, savoring the taste of him as I smiled against his lips. I was undone, the heavy weight lifted from my shoulders, and temporary as though it might be, when I answered him, I answered truthfully.

"I'm okay, Connor. I...I think I'm going to be okay. We're going to be okay."

———

One week later, I was less sure of the sentiments I'd whispered to Connor in the middle of the night.

The Skipper and Mary O'Reilly's bodies had been found three days ago. They'd been arranged in one of our warehouses in the shipyard in a gruesome tableau, each with a Chelsea Grin. The correlations were obvious but ironclad, and the police were now circling South Boston like vultures.

The Clan was devastated. Many considered the O'Reilly's to be family, and the neighborhood had taken a decidedly cold view on the organized crime present as a result. Connor was gone most nights, now, working late to put out fires that sprang up faster than he could extinguish them.

The fact that Tommy had been the last person seen with them made matters even worse.

The police had questioned Tommy, of course, and Callum had managed to get them to back off. But that wasn't a lasting solution. Plainclothes detectives and unmarked cruisers were becoming a common sight around the neighborhood. We were being watched.

The inactivity was wearing at Tommy. As per Callum's orders, he continued to put his face out there, such as it was, to lend a sense of normalcy to the neighborhood, but he was strictly on the bench as far as the Clan was concerned. To say he was struggling would be an understatement. He spent most of his time down at the gym and here with me in Connor's absence, but he was drinking more, a surly and temperamental constant presence in my life.

"You know," I said to Tommy one evening, "I can't help but wonder if you're using this as a way to avoid Sloane."

Tommy slammed his beer down and glared at me, but the effect was somewhat diminished by the fact that he was wearing a pair of fuzzy pink slippers and a bathrobe. He had a bit of a five-o'clock shadow going on and his faux haws was looking decidedly wilted. "What the hell are you talking about?"

Carol, my physical therapist who had heard more than her fair share of our bickering over the past few weeks, studiously kept her head down. I grimaced as I finished another set of reps. "It's not that I don't love you hanging out here every night, but you've got a perfectly nice bar you could be drinking at right down the street. Nice slippers, by the way."

"They're comfortable. It's not my fault the only color they had left was pink." Tommy flexed his toes and scowled at them. "I'm secure in my manhood."

I would hope so, with Tommy's physique. But the joke died on my lips as I noticed how red his eyes were. "Are you all right?"

"Just peachy." He reached for his beer. "You know, I wouldn't have to come here every night if your husband would just let me back in the fucking ring. I need to fight, Cass. I need to hit something. I feel like I'm going out of my mind."

I glanced over at Carol. She wasn't privy to my less-than-legal lifestyle, and we kept to code while she was around. "You should talk to Sloane. She's a great listener."

Tommy snorted. "She's made it clear she's heard about as much from me as she'd care to."

"What does that mean?"

"Means I took your advice, little sis, and she shot me down." His lips twisted in a wry grin. "I am firmly in the friend zone."

"Oh, Tommy...I'm sorry. I know how much you like her."

He shrugged. "It's fine. I'm not good relationship material anyway. It's probably for the best."

I shook my head, sighing. Tommy's emotions had always been a bit of a roller coaster, and ever since the abduction, they had taken a sharp turn for the worse.

"You're a good man," I told him. "Any woman would be lucky to have you."

"I'm not exactly boyfriend material right now." Tommy rubbed a hand across his face. "And with everything that's going on..."

"That doesn't matter. Sloane cares about you."

"Sloane tolerates me. There's a difference." He took a swig of his beer. "It's better this way. Trust me."

I frowned, but before I could respond, Connor walked through the door. He looked exhausted, but when he saw me, a slow smile spread across his face. It never failed to send butterflies fluttering in my stomach, and I smiled back, my heart skipping a beat.

"Hi," I said.

"Hi yourself." He pressed a kiss to my forehead. "How's your PT going? Are you making progress?"

"She's doing great," Carol said. "We've got one more set to go, and we're done for the day. How does that feel, Cassidy?"

I grit my teeth against the dull ache, pulling against the contraption on my left hand, rubber bands fighting the movement as they closed my hand into a fist. "Okay. Good, I guess."

She held my wrist slightly to stabilize it, feeling the movement of the bones and ligaments. I felt both Connor and Tommy's eyes on me, physically oppressive with their gravity. Maybe we should have done this in another room.

"You're doing great," she observed, "You have already regained a lot of mobility—more than Jerome originally estimated. I can tell you've been keeping up on the exercises."

"Tommy pushes me almost as hard as you do. You should think about hiring him as a side act for your 'Carol Beckett's Traveling House of Pain.'"

From his position on the couch, Tommy saluted us both with his beer bottle. "I aim to please."

Carol grinned. "I might just take you up on that. I can charge a premium if he's shirtless. But for now, let's call it a night. I'll see you tomorrow?"

"Yep. Bright and early." I shook out my hand as the therapist left, trying to stretch out the kinks that had settled deep into the muscles.

Connor appeared at my side, taking my hand in his. He gently massaged my knuckles and wrist, easing the tension that had gathered there. I sighed and leaned into him, savoring his warmth. He dropped a kiss to the crown of my head and wrapped his arms around me, resting his chin on my shoulder.

"Well, I'll take that as my cue to leave." Tommy stood, stretching. "Mind if I crash in one of the guest bedrooms?"

Connor rolled his eyes. "From what I hear, you've got a very nice apartment all to yourself--"

"Go ahead, Tommy," I interrupted.

"Thanks, sis. Besides, my apartment is clear across Southie." He pulled the robe around his shoulders, belting it with a great show of dignity. "And I need my beauty sleep."

Tommy clapped Connor on the shoulder on his way out, pink fuzzy slippers slapping on the marble tile.

Connor snorted, shaking his head. "I love him, but I swear to God, sometimes I just want to kill him."

"He's lonely. And cooped up."

"He's a pain in the arse."

"I'm serious, Connor." I turned to face him. I worry about him. He's not coping well with the whole...situation."

Connor hummed but didn't respond. I felt his agitation in the way his body tensed against mine.

"How was work today?"

"Let's not talk about that now." His hands moved to the base of my neck working at a kink there, and the stress lines at the corners of his eyes smoothed out as he worked at the knotted muscles with a laser focus. "Right now I just want to focus on you."

Connor took me by the hand and led me down the hall to the bathroom. A turn of the gilded hot water handle, and steam rose from the porcelain clawfoot tub. Two strong hands massaged at my shoulder blades and down my back, his touch melting away the tension and feeling positively sinful. A low, obscene moan was the only answer I could give him.

"Christ, love, you make any more noises like that..." Connor's breath fanned across the back of my neck, and he nipped at the soft spot just below my ear.

"Eww—Connor, I'm all sweaty and gross," I giggled, a little embarrassed despite how much he was turning me on.

"You," he said, kissing my neck again, "are maybe a little sweaty, but you are far from gross. You're gorgeous...breathtaking...stunning..."

My breath hitched as he continued down, pausing where my neck met my shoulder. A long, lingering kiss there, and he gently turned me to face him.

"You've always been beautiful to me, Cass. Always. Inside and out, only now...now it's like you're glowing. Full of stardust and moonbeams, just bursting out of you, like there's just too much beauty and strength to contain in a single human body."

Oh, Connor.

I pressed my lips against his, unable to put what I was feeling into words. It was a sweet, gentle kiss, full of love and longing. Gently, I pulled him further into the bathroom. Looking down at the bathtub pointedly, I slowly began to unbutton his shirt. "Join me?"

As if I would honestly need to ask. Connor was still as submissive and hesitant as he'd been during my recovery, but his eyes darkened with want as he let me undress him.

Tie, shirt, and trousers fell to the floor in a heap next to my own clothes. As much as I desired him, I still turned slightly to the side, hands trying to shield him from a body I had yet to become comfortable with in the light of day.

Connor clucked at me. "No, Cass, don't hide from me. I want to see every inch of you."

He gently took my hands in his, ever so careful of my healing wrist. Pulling them and me towards his own body.

"Let me show you how beautiful you are."

Wet, open-mouthed kisses trailed across my shoulder, my collarbone. Pausing at the hollow of my throat, enticing a low moan as he continued down between the valley of my breasts. Worshiping with every touch, every caress, not shying away from the still-fading scars or the new, softer curves my body had adopted.

I yelped and giggled as he suddenly picked me up, his lips never leaving mine as he cradled my body protectively against his and stepped into the bath. Connor pulled me back against his chest, and I melted bonelessly into him.

"Tilt your head back, love."

Connor cupped a hand over my eyes as he wet my hair, working the shampoo in with just enough pressure to loosen any remaining tension I had and to elicit another low moan. Never had I even considered that the simple act of washing my hair could be so intimate.

"Is breá liom tú, mo chroí, mo ghrá." Words whispered in my ear, some I was starting to understand. The important ones, at least.

"Is breá liom tú, Connor."

The smile when he heard those words from my lips could light my way through the most devastating darkness, and I captured it and held it in my heart. Where I once forged my own armor, it was now stripped away, again and again by the man before me. I was finally at peace with it. In its place was a new light, bright and shining. It warmed and protected me, something I could hold onto when I felt my strength fail. Because Connor was that light. He was everything.

Which was why, curled into the shelter of his arms in that bathtub, I made a vow. Time was slipping through my fingers, moving pieces snapping into place in the shadows far beyond my control. Wearing him down, pulling him from me despite our reforged bond. I wasn't about to let him go. I would do anything to keep him here with me.

I would not lose Connor to this life.

14

---·---

EMILIA

I WORE ALFIE'S MAKESHIFT ring for the next two weeks. It helped me get through a period of increasing unrest as Lorenzo's temper grew shorter and his demands more unreasonable. He had always been a ruthless man, but now he was becoming unhinged. I did my best to stay out of his way, as I had ever since finding out about his treacherous past with my mother and the betrayal and murder of my father. The day would come when I would confront him for his past crimes, but for now, it was best to steer clear of him.

Angel was another matter. He was smug--more than he usually was, that is--and always seemed to be watching me. I'd moved Alfie's ring to my pinkie finger to keep it hidden from him, but I felt like he knew it was there anyway. Like he was just waiting for me to slip up. I caught him staring at me more than once, but he never said anything. Just watched.

I felt like the world was holding its breath, waiting for something to happen. It was a tense, uneasy feeling that refused to go away, and I found myself constantly on edge, looking over my shoulder and second guessing everything I did. Sofia and Luca were worried too, I could tell, but they were as powerless as I was.

Then the day came that changed everything.

"Emilia. My office. Now."

My blood ran cold at the sound of his voice. Lorenzo sounded angry, but he always sounded angry lately. It was the way his tone held a hint of something else, something I couldn't quite name that had my stomach clenching in knots.

"What does he want?" Sofia asked, a frown marring her features. We were just about to leave for the bookstore.

"I don't know," I admitted, "but I have a bad feeling about it."

Sofia grabbed my hand, squeezing it tightly. "I'll go with you."

"No," I said quickly. "It's okay, Sof. I'll be fine. Besides, you need to cover for me at the shop."

"But--"

"I'll be fine," I repeated. "Don't worry. It's probably nothing."

But it wasn't. I should have known better than to think I could avoid the inevitable forever. As I walked into his office, I felt the walls closing in on me.

"Sit down, Emilia." Lorenzo gestured to the chair across from his desk. His face was impassive, but there was a glint in his eyes that never failed to send chills down my spine.

"You're looking well," he said, leaning back in his chair. "Positively glowing."

"Th-thank you."

"Is there something I should know about?" he asked casually.

His eyes narrowed, and I swallowed hard. "I don't know what you're talking about, Uncle."

Lorenzo steepled his fingers together, his gaze never wavering from my face. "Are you sure about that?"

I didn't say anything. I couldn't. My mind was racing, trying to think of something to say. My stomach twisted into tighter knots as the silence lengthened.

Lorenzo finally broke it. "There have been some rumors about you, Emilia. Rumors that I would like to dismiss as idle gossip, but the Moretti Family takes such things very seriously. Especially when they concern the family name."

My heart was beating so loud, I could hear it in my ears. I didn't dare speak.

He leaned forward, his gaze boring into mine. "I know you're seeing that Irish boy. Alfie Doyle."

I started to open my mouth, but he cut me off.

"Do not deny it." His voice was ice cold, the words clipped and precise. "Your eyes tell the truth anyway. They always have."

I didn't say anything, but it didn't matter. Lorenzo knew he was right. I was terrified, and the fear was written all over my face.

"I should have known," he said, shaking his head. "You've always been a difficult girl. Headstrong. Defiant. Just like your father."

His gaze slid down to my left hand, resting on my lap, and I resisted the urge to hide it. I felt naked, exposed under his scrutiny, but I forced myself to hold my ground. I refused to cower before him.

Lorenzo's gaze traveled back to my face, a sly smile twisting his lips. "The ring is a nice touch, though. A bit crude, perhaps, but I can't help but admire the sentiment behind it."

He stood and moved around the desk, coming to stand in front of me. His cologne, heavy and cloying, turned my stomach. He reached out and brushed a strand of hair away from my face, his fingertips lingering against my skin.

"Such a pretty girl," he murmured. "I've always thought so. Eyes just like your mother's."

His eyes held a predatory gleam that made my skin crawl. I clenched my hands into fists, fighting the urge to recoil from his touch.

"I'd take you for my own," he continued, "but it would be unseemly. Besides, Viviana would never allow it. She's not the kind of woman who likes to share, as you know. But there are ways around that."

"What are you talking about?" I struggled to keep my voice even, but it broke embarrassingly.

Lorenzo chuckled, a low, menacing sound. "You're not as naïve as you appear, Emilia. Surely you must have considered this."

I stared at him, uncomprehending.

"An engagement," he clarified, a smirk twisting his lips. "It's the perfect solution. You will marry my son Angelo, and then we can put this unfortunate situation with the Irish boy behind us."

"You can't do that!" I protested, my voice rising. "I'm not a piece of property. You can't just marry me off to someone I don't want."

Lorenzo's hand lashed out, catching me across the cheek. My head snapped to the side from the force of the blow, and I bit back a cry of pain.

"You will do as I say," he hissed. His grip tightened on my chin, his fingers digging painfully into my jaw. "I am the head of this family, and you will obey me. Do you understand?"

I swallowed hard, my eyes stinging with tears.

"Say it."

"I-I understand."

He released me, and I slumped back in my chair, my hand pressed to my throbbing cheek. Lorenzo straightened his tie and smoothed his hair, his anger suddenly evaporated. He was all smiles once more.

"Good. I'm glad we understand each other. Angelo will be so pleased. He's always wanted you, you know." His tone turned dark, and his gaze locked onto my ring finger, the blue thread glinting in the light. "And you needn't worry about your Irishman. You won't be seeing him again. I have placed a price on his head, and I'm afraid it's quite substantial. He won't make it through the week."

My blood ran cold. "Why are you doing this?"

Lorenzo smiled, but there was no warmth in it. "Family, Emilia. First, last, and always. You're a Moretti. It's time you started acting like one. You're dismissed."

I walked out of the office on wooden legs. Numb. Heartbroken, my world shattered at my feet, yet I still somehow propelled myself down the hall...

...and straight into Angel.

"Well, well, carina," he taunted. "Looks like you've heard the good news."

I shoved past him, desperate to get away from his smug face. Angel grabbed my arm, pulling me to a stop. "Hey, where are you going in such a hurry? Aren't you happy, carina? We're getting married."

I whirled on him, wrenching my arm from his grasp. "I will never marry you, Angel. Never."

"You don't have a choice, Emilia. You're a Moretti, and you will do as you are told, just like a good little wife." His expression darkened, and he stepped towards me, his voice low and dangerous. "On your back, on your knees, your belly full with what I give you. What pretty little babies we're going to make."

I pulled free from his grasp. "You're insane."

"Baby, you haven't seen anything, yet."

He made another move towards me, but I backed away. Right into Dom.

His fingers tightened around my arms hard enough to leave bruises. "Try to run, and I'll kill you myself."

I froze, the fight draining out of me. I was trapped. Angel laughed, a cruel, taunting sound, and he reached out to cup my face with his hand. "Don't worry, Emilia. Maybe I'll make you a wedding present out of the Irishman's head."

"What's going on?" Luca appeared in the doorway, taking in the scene. His gaze traveled from my tear-streaked face to Angel's hand mark on my cheek. His eyes narrowed imperceptivity, but he kept his tone light. "Somebody want to clue me in?"

Angel released me and moved to stand beside his brother, his hand clapping Luca on the shoulder. "We were just talking about the wedding."

Luca arched an eyebrow. "Wedding?"

"Mine," Angel said with a smirk. "To Emilia here."

Luca looked at me, his expression unreadable. "Is that right?"

I didn't say anything, just stared at him. My heart was hammering in my chest, and I was desperate to get away from them. Angel's hands were still on my arms, and he tightened his grip, pulling me closer to him.

"Lorenzo has given me his blessing," he said smugly. "And he's placed a price on her little boyfriend's head."

Luca's eyes narrowed. "You mean the Irish mobster she's been fucking behind everyone's backs."

"The same one, fratello. I'll take personal pleasure in slitting his throat from ear to ear."

"You'll have to beat me to it," Luca growled. "He's got it coming after what happened this summer."

Luca's voice was enough to terrify me, but I knew it was an act. A slight tensing of his frame, a fleeting shift in his eyes from Angel to me, quick as a butterfly but I saw it. He was doing what he had to, keeping up appearances in front of his fellow soldiers.

"You need to learn to share, Luca." Angel gave him a condescending pat on the back. "I know you've always had a thing for Emilia, but she's mine now. So's the Irishman."

"He's got a name," I snapped.

Angel laughed, his grip on me tightening. "Yeah, well, there won't be much of anything left once I'm finished with him. Take her up to her room for me, will you Luca? I'm going hunting."

Luca's hands were firm yet gentle as he took my arms, guiding me past Angel. Up the stairs, down the hallway to the bedroom that Lorenzo had made for me all those years ago when he'd taken me in, the bedroom that was now to become my prison. Luca led me inside, set me on the bed, and locked the door firmly behind him.

He knelt between my knees and took my hands in his. "What can I do?"

My mouth opened and closed. I blinked numbly.

Luca's gaze traveled to my cheek, his expression darkening. "He hit you?"

I nodded, not trusting myself to speak.

Luca swore softly. He reached up as if to sooth his fingers over my bruised cheekbone, but he pulled away at the last moment. Standing suddenly, he walked into the bathroom. I heard the water run, and he emerged moments later with an ice-cold washcloth in his hand. Gently, he pressed it to my cheek, his touch as soft as a butterfly's wings.

"Keep this on it." His voice was a low murmur, his eyes fixed on my cheek. "It'll help with the swelling."

He looked miserable, his face drawn and pale, his jaw clenched. I reached up, touching the back of his hand with my fingertips as my eyes started to burn. "Thank you, Luca."

He sighed, his gaze lifting to meet mine. "I'm sorry, Emilia. I'm so sorry."

I shook my head. "It's not your fault."

Luca swallowed hard, his hand tightening on the cloth. "I'm going to get you out of here, I promise. I just...I need to find a way. I need time."

"I don't have time," I said, the first tears starting to fall. "They're going to kill him, Luca."

Luca pulled me into his arms, his hands rubbing circles on my back. "Shh, I know, Emilia. I know. We're going to figure this out. Do you have your phone on you?"

I shook my head. I'd left it downstairs. They'd have taken it by now.

"I'll get you a burner," Luca said, "but you're going to have to hide it. I'll find Alfie and tell him what's going on. We'll figure something out. Just...just stay calm, okay? And whatever you do, don't try to run. Promise me."

I nodded, my heart sinking.

"I'll come back tonight after Lorenzo's gone to bed. You'll be able to talk to him soon."

"What if they catch you?"

"They won't. I'm too careful for that." Luca smiled, but it didn't reach his eyes. He leaned forward, brushing his lips against my forehead in a tender kiss. "I'll be back soon, I promise."

He slipped out of the room, closing the door softly behind him and locking it from the outside.

15

ALFIE

"I'D JUST LIKE TO go on record here--I don't like this one bit."

Connor ignored my grumbling and pulled into the parking garage where we'd be meeting with the Russians to work out a gun deal. "Duly noted."

"You know what they say about making deals with the devil."

"I'll be sure to ask Lucifer himself when I see him."

"You're not funny, Con. "I rolled my eyes. "I mean, that's not bad for your grumpy ass, but time and place, man. Time and place."

Connor ignored me, as usual. "For the last time, Alfie, you're overreacting. We've got three different exit strategies, and there are two backup teams on standby just in case anything goes wrong."

"We're dealing with the fucking Russians," I muttered. "Of course something is going to go wrong."

I was nervous. More than a little. The Russians were a new, unknown element, and they had a reputation for being ruthless, brutal, and playing both sides. Callum wanted us to put out some feelers and see if there was any truth to the rumors of their connection to the Morettis. It was a dangerous game, and I was not happy to be tagging along on this particular adventure.

Tommy was out of the game for the foreseeable future. Through no fault of his own--just bad timing, if you asked me, but that meant yours truly was going to be stepping up to the plate to cover the gaps. In other words, I was going to have to learn to play nicely with the other children.

I glanced over at Connor, who was still ignoring me. His face was set in an impassive mask, but his hands tightened on the steering wheel. He still hadn't forgiven me for the pushback I've given him over Emilia. Not that I'd apologized, of course.

I sighed and leaned back in my seat, watching the streets pass by through the window. The sky was overcast, heavy clouds hanging low over the city, and it looked like rain. Again. The air was cool and damp, and I could feel the beginnings of a headache starting to throb behind my eyes.

My thoughts began to drift, as they invariably did, to Emilia. She was never not on my mind. Lately, though, those thoughts had included Spanish moss and sunshine, lazy waves and warm breezes. Emilia lying next to me on a blanket, her dark curls spread out over the sand, her lips curved in a carefree smile. Our whole future before us, away from the violence and secrecy and fear.

It was a pretty picture. One I'd be more than happy to make a reality. But it would never happen if we couldn't get out of South Boston.

"We're here."

Connor's voice snapped me out of my thoughts, and I sat up, peering out the window.

The parking garage was dark and deserted. The fluorescent lights cast a sickly, yellow glow over everything, and I felt my hackles rise. There were no other cars on this level, just a few stacks of crates and some abandoned trash.

Connor turned off the engine and got out of the car, his movements careful and precise. I followed suit, taking in our surroundings. We were on the third level of the parking garage. Not ideal. The height would make it that much more difficult if we needed a fast getaway, and that much easier for snipers to pick us off if Aleksandr decided to double cross us.

Connor caught my eye and nodded, his hand resting casually on the gun in his shoulder holster. He didn't look worried, but then, Connor never looked worried. It was one of his most irritating qualities. I leaned on the trunk and lit a cigarette as I watched the perimeter, and Connor pulled out his phone, seemingly absorbed in the text he was sending. I wasn't fooled. He'd probably already scanned the entire place and knew exactly where every camera, fire escape, and blind spot was.

We didn't have to wait long. Two shadows peeled off from the wall, and then two more, footsteps echoing loudly in the cavernous space. Smart. If I'd wanted to start a shootout, I'd have done the same thing, try to surround us before we even knew we were outnumbered.

Connor's eyes narrowed, his expression unreadable. "That's close enough."

The men stopped about ten feet away, their faces hidden in the shadows. One of them stepped forward, his hands raised in a placating gesture.

"We mean you no harm," he said, his accent surprisingly light. "We just want to talk."

"We can talk just fine from here," Connor replied.

The tactic was more than just about keeping our distance. It also triangulated the Russians' position with the two shooters we'd stationed at the top of the ramp, just in case things went south.

"As you wish," the Russian shrugged. "Although, it's a bit redundant at this point, don't you think? Your men in the shadows and mine, everyone point their guns at each other...this is no way to conduct business. Come, now. As a show of good faith, I'll call my men off, and you can pull the two shooters you've stationed at the top of the ramp."

Shit. The man turned and muttered something in Russian, and two men emerged from the shadows, raising their hands to the side of their heads in mock surrender. They grinned at us, and Connor's jaw ticked.

"What do you say, Mr..."

"McTiernan. Connor McTiernan. And your name?"

"Misha. Just Misha."

"All right, Just Misha. I'll call my men off. But if you think I don't realize you've still got mates sighting down their barrels at us, you're a damn sight denser than I thought."

I watched the exchange with all the morbid interest of someone watching a ping pong match played with hand grenades. But to my surprise, the Russian just threw his head back and laughed.

"I like you, Connor McTiernan. I was told that you do not share your Uncle Callum's sense of humor, but I see I was misinformed. Come. Let's talk like civilized men."

The deal went down smoother than I expected. Connor was all business, his usual stony demeanor giving nothing away. Misha was charming and confident, and they seemed to reach a mutually agreeable arrangement. I stayed in the shadows, keeping quiet for once as money and weapons changed hands.

"It's been a pleasure doing business with you," Misha said. "I hope this will be the first of many mutually beneficial deals between our families."

Connor nodded, his face impassive. "I hope so. I'd hate to find out you were playing both sides, Misha. We tend to take it personally when people try to fuck us over."

"I would expect no less. But I assure you, Aleksandr Volkov is a man of his word."

"He had better be, because those shots your men took at my wife over the summer haven't been forgotten. Or forgiven."

Misha's dark eyes widened, but he recovered quickly. "Your wife? You are a lucky man, Connor McTiernan."

"I'm well aware," Connor said stonily. "And I protect what's mine."

"I don't doubt it. That cannot be an easy job. One hears things in our line of work." Misha turned to leave but held up a finger, turning back at the last moment. "Guard your wife carefully, tovarich. I'm not the one you should be worried about."

Connor raised an eyebrow. "Is that a threat?"

"No, just a warning. The Moretti Crime Family isn't known for playing nice, even with their allies."

"And Volkov is?"

Misha shrugged in that distinctly European way of his. "Volkov is a businessman. His interests come first. But he also knows which way the wind is blowing, and if he has to burn a few bridges to get ahead, he will. But I'm sure you know all about that, don't you, Mr. McTiernan?"

I didn't like the way he was looking at Connor, like he was trying to get inside his head, like he knew something we didn't.

Connor's jaw ticked, but he didn't say anything. He didn't have to. Misha had already turned and walked away, his footsteps echoing through the empty parking garage.

Back at Lady D's, I nursed my lukewarm beer alone. The Pats were playing on tv, but I wasn't really paying attention. My thoughts were too scattered.

I'd spent the last hour in my head, trying to make sense of Misha's warning about the Morettis. Was he talking about Emilia? What did he know about our relationship? Did the Russians have spies in their ranks, or had he learned about it some other way? And what about his cryptic comment about Connor's wife?

I ran a hand over my face. I had a headache, and it felt like I hadn't slept in days. My nerves were shot, and I couldn't seem to sit still. I checked my phone for what felt like the hundredth time, but there were no messages from Emilia. Just like there hadn't been any for the past few days. She'd gone radio silent, and it was driving me crazy. I hated not being able to talk to her, not knowing how she was doing, or what Lorenzo was up to.

I took a sip of my beer, but it hit my stomach like a stone. For a guy who'd grown up surrounded by men who I was honored to call my brothers, I felt utterly alone for the first time in my life. Tommy was lying low for the time being, and Connor had understandably gone home to Cassidy after our rendezvous with the enigmatic Misha. I couldn't blame him. He'd been a wreck ever since she'd been abducted. If she was my girl, I'd be the same. Hell, I was the same when Emilia was in danger.

That just left me and Sloane and the wide expanse of oak bar between us.

"Hey."

I looked up and saw Sloane standing next to me, her expression unreadable. "Hey."

She bit her lip, a nervous gesture I'd seen her do a thousand times before. "Look, I know I've been an ass lately, but I just wanted to say that...well, I'm sorry. I shouldn't have taken out my anger on you. It wasn't fair."

"It's fine. I get it. I'm sorry for how things ended up between us, too. Cassidy, uh...filled me in on things." I shrugged. "I didn't mean to hurt you, I swear."

Sloane sighed. "I know. And for what it's worth, I'm happy for you guys. I hope it works out."

"Me too," I said softly.

Sloane hesitated for a moment, then turned and walked away. I watched her go, a twinge of sadness tugging at my heart. We'd been friends for years, and I'd always cared for her in the way you care about a friend, but now that I knew she'd had feelings for me all along, I felt even worse for not seeing it sooner.

I finished my beer and headed outside, the fresh air doing little to clear my head. I felt restless and on edge, the same way I'd been feeling for days.

Ever since Emilia had gone silent. I leaned against the wall, a cigarette dangling from my lips as I pulled out my phone again. No new messages. I resisted the urge to throw it against the brick wall.

I took a drag of my cigarette, the smoke burning my lungs in a familiar, comforting way. I closed my eyes for a moment, trying to get my emotions under control. I was getting worked up for no reason. Emilia was probably just busy at the bookstore. Or she was hanging out with Sofia or Luca.

I knew I was rationalizing, but I couldn't help it. I needed something to cling to, even if it was just a fragile thread of hope.

I finished my cigarette and threw it on the ground, grinding it out under my boot. I was about to go back inside when I heard a noise coming from the alley, a low, tapping noise. I froze, my hand automatically going to the gun strapped beneath my shoulder.

Tap, tap, tap.

It was deliberate, sounding like a brick being tapped against a downspout. Too regular to be natural.

Keeping my gun pointed down the alley, I eased my way towards the sound, moving silently, my back pressed against the wall, but I stopped before I left the safety of the sidewalk. I wasn't foolish enough to go walking into an ambush. I strained my ears, listening for any sign of movement, but all I could hear was my own heartbeat thudding in my ears.

"Doyle."

I almost jumped out of my skin at the sound of the whispered voice. I swung around, my gun raised, but my finger froze on the trigger when I saw who it was.

"Jesus fucking Christ, Luca," I hissed. "Are you trying to get yourself shot?"

"Well, I'd prefer to go home without any new holes, but I didn't know how else to get your attention."

I lowered my gun, my heart still pounding. "What the fuck are you doing here? Did something happen? Is Emilia--"

"Easy, lover-boy. Emilia is safe--for now, at least." Luca looked uneasily at the street, where the light from Lady D's sign reflected off the wet pavement. "Is there somewhere else we can talk? I don't really want to have this conversation on the McTiernan Clan's back doorstep."

I nodded, tucking my gun back into its holster. "Yeah, come on. My apartment's just around the corner."

We walked in silence, Luca keeping his head down, hands shoved in his pockets. It was strange seeing him like this, so on edge and wary. The big man usually carried himself with a swagger that only came from knowing you could back up the attitude with your fists. Or a gun. Or whatever weapon you felt like using that day. But tonight, he seemed subdued, his usual bravado gone.

I led him to my building, a gentrified factory loft converted into trendy one- and two-bedroom apartments a few blocks away from Lady D's. I unlocked the door and ushered him inside. The place was fastidious-ly clean as always, but I still moved restlessly through the apartment, tidying up things that didn't need to be tidied. I guess it gave my hands something to do, because my mind was working overtime imagining all the different disasters that could possibly prompt Luca to risk his neck to deliver me a message in the heart of Irish territory.

"You want a drink?" I asked, brandishing a bottle of Bushmills 12 Year at him like a shield.

"Yeah."

I poured two glasses and handed him one. Luca took a long sip, eyed the glass with something like surprise, and drained it. I refilled it.

"Thanks." He cleared his throat. "Look, I know this is gonna be hard to hear, but I'm gonna need you to stay calm until I'm through."

"This sounds promising," I said dryly.

"Lorenzo is forcing Emilia to marry Angel."

I blinked. "What?"

"Angel is going to marry Emilia." Luca repeated. "Lorenzo found out about the two of you. My guess is that Angel or Dom told him. He's got Emilia locked in her room at the compound. There is no way I can get her out right now."

I stared at him, my heart kicking into overdrive as the full implications set in. "Is she okay?"

"She's scared, but she's holding it together." Luca's jaw tightened. "Lorenzo's got a price on your head, Doyle. That's why I came to you. To warn you."

I swore. "How much?"

"Enough."

I paced back and forth, my mind racing. I had to get to Emilia, but how? Lorenzo had her locked up tight. I couldn't go after her directly, not with a bounty on my head. I'd be dead before I even made it through the front gate. I needed a plan, a way to get her out without putting her in any more danger.

"I need to see her," I said finally.

Luca shook his head. "It's too dangerous. Lorenzo has eyes everywhere, and Angel is fucking gleeful at the thought of taking you out. He'll be gunning for you, Doyle. You can't afford to take that risk."

"I don't care. I need to see Emilia. I need to talk to her."

"Talk, I can do." He held up a burner phone. "I came prepared."

He tossed it to me, and I caught it. It was cheap, but it would work. "Thanks."

There were only two numbers programmed. "The first one's her's," Luca explained. "Angel took her phone. The second number is mine. I have a feeling you're going to need it. I know it's not much, right now, but it's the best I can do."

Once again, he was going to help us. The impact of Luca's sacrifice was not lost on me. I closed my hand around the phone. "It's enough. Thank you, Luca."

"I'm not doing it for you," he snapped. "I'm doing it for her."

I didn't say anything, but I felt my respect for him growing. I might not like the guy, but I knew he cared for her, and that was enough for me.

Luca's jaw tightened, and he looked away, his voice suddenly gruff. "Look, I'm not asking for anything from you. I just want her to be happy. And if that means helping the two of you be together, then that's what I'm gonna do. But you gotta promise me something."

"What?"

"You gotta promise me that you're gonna take care of her. That you are going to give her the life she deserves. I know what we are, what we do. Emilia deserves better than that."

"I know that."

Luca hesitated, looking for all the world like he wanted to say something else, but he shook his head. "Then you've got to be the man she deserves. The better man."

The silence stretched between us, and I read something in his face, something I never expected to see from him. Vulnerability. His eyes were hard, but I saw something else, an unspoken fear.

"You love her," I said quietly. "Don't you."

Luca's mouth twisted. He looked away, but not before I saw the raw pain in his eyes. "Doesn't matter. She chose you. Are you going to call her, or what?"

I nodded and turned away, letting him have his moment. I dialed her number. It rang once, twice, three times. On the fourth ring, she answered.

"Alfie." Her voice was a breathless whisper, bordering on hysteria.

"Emilia, I'm here. It's okay."

"I'm scared."

"I know, sweetheart. I know. Have they hurt you? Are you--"

"I'm okay. They've just got me locked in my room. Alfie...Lorenzo put a price on your head. You need to be careful."

"I'm always careful. You know me," I said, injecting as much bravado as I could muster. "Don't worry about me. I'm going to get you out of there, I promise."

"No. You can't come after me. Lorenzo will kill you. Angel will--"

The phone creaked dangerously in my hand. "I'm not going to let them hurt you. I'll figure something out."

"Alfie, please. I'm begging you. Don't do anything stupid, okay?"

I closed my eyes. She sounded so scared, and it tore my heart out. "It's going to be all right, Emilia. I've got Luca here, and he's got enough common sense for the both of us."

"That's not funny." She sniffled. "I can't lose you."

"You won't. I promise. I'm coming for you, Emilia, and I'm going to take you where Angel and Lorenzo won't ever be able to touch you. We're going, together, and we're going to stand together with our toes in the sand on your island beach and I'm going to love you for the rest of my life, do you hear me? I am not letting you go. Not now, not ever. You're mine, Emilia."

A possessive, instinctual growl started building in my chest as I spoke, and I knew my words weren't just for Emilia's benefit, they were for Luca's as well. I wasn't sure if they'd registered or not, but the burly Italian was paying far more attention to my LP collection than it warranted.

"Alfie..." Her voice broke. "I love you."

"I love you, too." I closed my eyes, fighting back the emotions threatening to choke me. "I have to go now. I'm coming for you, sweetheart, just sit tight."

"How? There's guards at my door, and the compound is surrounded."

I looked up at Luca. "I've got a plan. But first, we're going to need a little help."

16

— . —

CASSIDY

ON NOVEMBER 12TH, SPENCER Halliwell's body was pulled out of the Charles River wearing a Chelsea Grin. Ordinarily, such a discovery on the heels of three other murders with the same MO would be cause enough for public outcry, but the fact that Halliwell was a special agent for the Immigration and Nationalization Service was enough to spark a media frenzy.

The fact that Agent Halliwell had once launched a personally motivated investigation into my husband was cause of even more concern.

"The sins of my past, come back to haunt me," Connor murmured as he ended Callum's phone call.

I gripped his shoulder, and he covered my hand with his. "Do you think this is Moretti's work?"

"Undoubtedly."

"What do we do?"

He shrugged me off and walked into the kitchen. "Don't worry about it. I'll handle it."

I watched him stalk to the bathroom, my unease growing. "Connor, wait. Maybe I can help."

"No, you don't need to be involved in this."

"But I want to--."

"Cassidy." Connor stopped and turned to face me. "I know you want to help, but this isn't something you need to be worried about. I can handle it."

Wrapping my cardigan tighter around myself, I went to him. He stood at the sink, bracing his hands on the counter, head bowed. I put my arms around him from behind, pressing my cheek between his shoulder blades.

"Talk to me," I whispered. "Let me help you."

He tensed, then gently removed my arms. When he faced me, his expression was shuttered. "You need to rest. Stress isn't good for the baby." He touched my stomach lightly before turning away. "I'll handle this. Trust me."

"I do trust you," I said softly. "But I'm worried about you. This is serious, Connor. Your life could be in danger."

"I know that." He sighed. "Look, I'm not trying to be an arse, but this is my problem to deal with. Not yours. You have enough on your plate right now, and you're carrying our child. I'm not going to let anything happen to either of you."

His words were meant to be reassuring, but they only served to ignite my temper. "I don't need you to protect me, Connor. I'm not some fragile flower that you have to shield from the big, bad world. I would have thought I'd have proven that to you by now."

"I know you're not fragile. But this is different."

I bristled. "How? How is it different?"

"It just is. You're pregnant, Cassidy. I can't risk you or the baby. And I'm not going to argue with you about this. The answer is no."

I stared at him in disbelief. "Don't shut me out like this. We're supposed to be partners."

He whirled on me then, his eyes blazing. "You want to be my partner? Then do as I say and let me protect you." He gripped my shoulders tightly. "You have no idea what I'm capable of, what I'll do to keep you and our child safe."

I held his fiery gaze unflinchingly. "I'm not afraid of you, or the darkness inside you. But I am afraid of losing you to it."

His eyes flashed, and his grip on me tightened. Then he seemed to catch himself. He closed his eyes and released me, taking a step back. I felt his control return, as if a cold wind had blown through the kitchen.

He looked at me then, his expression impassive. Cold. "I'm not going to lose myself. I'm going to do what needs to be done. I have to. For you. For the baby. For our family."

"I know you want to protect us, but I can help--"

"No, Cassidy. You can't."

The finality in his voice stopped me cold.

"Connor, please..."

He turned away from me, his back rigid. "I don't want you involved in this. I won't say anything more on the matter."

I stood there, stunned. My chest felt tight, and there was an ache in my throat that threatened to choke me. "I can't sit back and pretend that everything is fine when it clearly isn't."

"Damn it, Cassidy," he snapped, his icy exterior cracking as anger flashed through his eyes. "I told you I would handle it. You don't need to worry about this."

"Of course I'm going to worry!" I shot back, rising from my seat. "You're my husband, and we have a baby on the way. How can you expect me not to be concerned?"

"Because I need to protect you both!" the undisguised fury in his voice made me flinch. "Do you have any idea how much stress you've been under lately? Your blood pressure is through the roof. You almost lost the baby once, and that night took years off my life. All I could see is you lying in a hospital bed again, fighting for your life."

Connor's voice broke, and I realized he was talking about the abduction. "I held you in my arms the entire way to the hospital, Cass. There was so much blood. You were barely there, I could feel you...you were slipping away, and there was nothing I could do. I can't go through that again....I can't..."

My eyes stung at the raw pain in his voice, and I reached for him, cupping his face in my hands. "Come here."

He closed his eyes, leaning into my touch. Tension radiated off him, and I wrapped my arms around him, resting my cheek against his chest. I could feel his heart racing beneath my cheek, and I closed my eyes, letting the sound anchor me. We stood there like that for a long moment, just holding each other. Connor swore and ran a hand over his face. "I'm sorry. I didn't mean to raise my voice. But you need to understand that I will do anything to protect you, no matter the cost. And I need you to let me."

"Protect us by shutting us out?" My voice wavered as tears pricked at my eyes. "That's not fair, Connor. I love you, and I want to help you through this."

Connor's face shuttered, erasing the vulnerability that had been there a moment before. "Sometimes, love means letting go. Please, just trust that I can handle this. You need to rest and focus on our baby."

He looked at me then, a slight hint of uncertainty in his eyes. As if he was afraid that I might actually refuse.

The silence stretched out between us, and I searched his face for any sign of the warmth and tenderness I had known him to possess, but all I saw was grim determination. And my own fear, reflected back at me.

I let out a shaky breath and nodded. "Okay."

Relief flashed across his face, but it was quickly replaced with a look of fierce resolve. "Good. Now, come on. I'll walk you up to the bedroom."

I let him take me by the hand and lead me up the stairs, his grip firm but gentle. Once inside, he helped me out of my clothes and into my favorite pajamas, and then tucked me into bed.

"Get some sleep." He pressed a kiss to my forehead. "I'll be back in a little while."

"Where are you going?" I asked, surprised.

"Lady D's. Callum needs me."

I sighed. "Okay. Just be careful, please."

"I always am." He kissed me again, and then he was gone.

The moment the door clicked shut behind Connor, I picked up my phone and dialed Jerome's number. I knew I shouldn't be meddling, but

I couldn't help it. I'd spent most of my career trying to find loopholes in the system, and this was no different.

Jerome answered on the second ring.

"Hey Cassidy, what's up?"

"I need a favor. Do you know who's handling the autopsy on Agent Halliwell?" I asked.

"Who?"

"Agent Spencer Halliwell. He was found in the Charles River earlier today."

There was a pause. "Do I want to know what this is about?"

"Probably not. But I need to know who's handling the autopsy."

"Why?"

"Connor knows him, and he's worried that some...friends might want to interfere. I want to make sure that doesn't happen."

Jerome sighed. "Cassidy..."

"Please," I said. "I wouldn't ask if it wasn't important. Connor could be in danger."

"Fine. I'll let you know what I find out, but if Halliwell was a Fed, then they've probably got their own people working the case." Another pause. "As a matter of fact, I have seen a lot more suits hanging around here than there usually are."

"That's good, right? That means they're taking it seriously. But listen--I also need a copy of the postmortem. Do you think you could get me a copy of the full autopsy report when it's done?"

Jerome sighed. "I'm not supposed to do that, Cassidy."

"I know, but please. Connor's life could depend on it."

Jerome was silent for a long moment, and I practically felt his resolve wavering. "The things I do for you, Cassidy McTiernan."

"Thank you," I breathed, relief flooding through me. "You don't know how much this means to me."

"Yeah, yeah," he grumbled. "Just don't tell anyone about this, okay? I could lose my job."

"I won't tell a soul. I promise."

"Good. Now, get some rest. And try to stay out of trouble, okay?"

I smiled. "No promises. Thanks, Jerome."

I ended the call and placed my hand on my stomach, feeling the reassuring flutter of life beneath my palm. Connor had made me promise to stay out of it, I couldn't just sit idly by and watch our world crumble around us. I refused to be a helpless bystander as my husband faced insurmountable odds, even if it meant breaking my promise to him. I would gather as much information as possible, working discreetly behind the scenes to ensure that we were one step ahead of the Italians and the police. And when the time came, I would be ready to fight for my family with every ounce of strength I possessed.

A sudden knock at the door made me jump. I wasn't expecting anyone and I immediately tensed. There was another knock, followed by a muffled voice.

"Cassidy? You in there?"

I peered through the peephole and was surprised to see Alfie standing on the other side. I quickly opened the door.

"Alfie? What are you doing here?" I asked in surprise.

He gave me a weak smile. "Hey. Sorry to just show up but I didn't know where else to go."

I ushered him inside, scanning the hall behind him before closing and locking the door. His usually mischievous eyes were dulled with fatigue and worry, hair disheveled. He looked drawn and tired, but resolute, like a man about to face down a firing squad. "What's going on? Does Connor know you're here?"

Alfie shook his head, running a hand through his unruly curls. "No. I needed to talk to you. Alone."

"What's wrong?"

"I need your help. Emilia is in danger."

I frowned. "What kind of danger? I thought she was safe at her bookstore."

Alfie's jaw clenched, his hands curling into fists. He started pacing. "That bastard Lorenzo is marrying Emilia off to Angel—Angelo Moretti, his youngest son. He's a real piece of work, Cassidy. Abusive, narcissistic, manipulative...He'll hurt her, I know he will. I can't let this happen."

"Wait a minute," I said, holding up a hand. "How do you even know this? And why are you going behind Connor's back?"

Alfie stopped pacing and turned to face me, his eyes flashing. "Because Connor won't listen. He's too caught up in his own shit--and I get that, but this is my Emilia we're talking about. I have to do something. And, he might have forbid me to see her after the fight at the club a couple months ago," he added sheepishly.

I closed my eyes, pinching the bridge of my nose. This was the last thing we needed right now, but my heart ached for him. I knew how much he loved Emilia.

"Okay," I said slowly, trying to process everything. "So you're going to break into the Moretti compound, or what? Where are you getting your information from?"

He hesitated for a moment before answering. "Luca. He's one of Lorenzo's capos, but he's been Emilia's best friend since they were kids. He knows all about us. He's told me that Lorenzo has her locked in her room, and he's placed a price on my head. I'm going to get her out, whatever it takes, but I can't do it alone. The Moretti's will kill me on sight if they find me. I love her, Cassidy. I'd do anything to keep her safe, even if it mean going against Connor. I didn't know where else to turn. Even with Luca's help, there isn't much we can do without raising suspicion."

I stared at him for a moment, torn between loyalty to Connor and empathy for Alfie. I knew all too well the feeling of wanting to protect someone you love, but I also knew how dangerous the Moretti Crime family could be.

"Okay," I said finally. "I'll help you. But we need a plan. We can't just figure this out as we go along. It's too risky."

Relief washed over his face. "I have a plan, but it's going to involve a few people, and we don't have much time. Can I trust you with this, Cassidy?"

"Of course." I gave him a wry smile. "I've kept plenty of secrets in my time."

Even from my husband.

"What do you need me to do?"

Alfie took a deep breath and held it, like he already knew I wasn't going to like what he was about to say. "I need you to help us fake our deaths."

"That's a bit dramatic, don't you think?"

"Angel won't stop until I'm dead." His lips twisted in a wry grin. "And Lorenzo will never let Emilia leave. He's got some kind of...sick fixation with her. This is our only shot at freedom. If Lorenzo thinks I'm dead, the bounty dies with me. And if Emilia 'dies' before the wedding..."

"He can't force her to marry Angel," I finished. It might work, but the timing would have to be perfect.

"There are a few more moving parts to this, which I've mostly got covered" Alfie said, a worried frown creasing his forehead. "But what I really need your help with are the technical details."

This was sounding worse by the second. "I'm afraid to ask."

"Can you fake a gunshot wound? Enough to make it look fatal?"

I stared at him. "You're not serious."

"I really wish I wasn't."

I sat back, thinking. At the right distance, with a clean shot, a gunshot wound could be faked. Especially if the person shooting knew what they were doing. We'd have to use real blood, of course, but that was easy enough to obtain. A bulletproof vest with a strike plate to minimize damage, and of course Alfie would have to be one hell of an actor...

"It might work," I said hesitantly, "If you know someone who can shoot accurately enough."

At this, Alfie's signature smirk returned. "Actually, I do," he said wryly. "In fact, I know someone who would probably relish the opportunity to shoot me."

"Who?" I asked.

"Luca."

"You mean the guy who also works for Moretti?" I stared at him dubiously. "Better you than me."

Alfie sat on the sofa next to me. "I may not be Luca's favorite person, but he'd do anything for Emilia. God knows he's had enough opportunities to kill me already, but he's still helping us out, even though it means risking his own neck. I trust him."

"Alright," I said, allowing myself a small smile. "So, we fake a gunshot wound, make it look like you're dead... what about Emilia?"

"I...don't know." Alfie's voice trailed off. "It would have to be done right under their noses. It's going to have to be convincing, much more than mine."

At what point did my life become something out of a crime drama? Faked deaths? Secret romances? Forced marriages? I shook my head and forced myself to focus.

Alfie saw me concentrating and got up to make coffee. I watched him move around the kitchen, reflecting on what I knew about his whirlwind, forbidden romance with Emilia. Then, suddenly it hit me, and I smiled, unable to ignore the irony that we could save Emilia with a scheme inspired by a tragic love story. I looked at Alfie, his face a mix of fear and determination, and decided our best chance lay in the realm of fiction.

And I knew just the thing.

"Alright. For Emilia, I think we can take a page out of Romeo and Juliet," I said, watching as Alfie's eyebrows raised in surprise. "There's a substance called Tetrodotoxin, found in the livers of puffer fish. We had a case at the hospital a year ago, acute Tetrodotoxin poisoning caused by consuming undercooked fugu, a Japanese dish made from puffer fish. At the correct dose, it can cause paralysis and decreased respiration and vasomotor response."

"Meaning..."

"Meaning that her heart rate and blood pressure will drop so low, she'll appear dead," I said quickly.

Alfie blanched. "Poison her? No, that's too dangerous."

I shook my head. "It can be reversed. We can administer a timed injection of atropine and 2-PAM Cl to reverse the effects. Her body should be able to process the rest of the toxin, and I can work with Jerome to handle Emilia once her 'body' is brought to the morgue."

Alfie rubbed the back of his neck, clearly wrestling with the decision. "Cassidy, I don't want to place Emilia in any more danger than she already is. What if something goes wrong?"

"It won't." I took his hands in mine and gave him a reassuring squeeze. "I would never do anything to put Emilia in harm's way. You have my word."

Alfie looked at me for a long moment before nodding slowly. "Alright. But you better be damn sure this will work."

"It will. There are a few things to be ironed out, but this will work." I frowned as I thought of something else. "Do you think Luca will be willing to give Emilia the injections? It will have to be timed down to the minute."

The hand he pushed through his unruly curls shook slightly, but he met my eyes. "Will he like it? No. But he'll do it. And on that note, there's something else I have to ask of you, but you're not going to like it, either. Don't tell Connor about this plan. At least not until it's done. The fewer people who know, the better."

I hesitated, torn between my loyalty to my husband and the need to protect my friends. But as I looked into Alfie's pleading eyes, I knew he was right. Connor had enough on his plate right now, and adding more stress would only make things worse.

"Alright," I agreed reluctantly. "I won't say anything, but I'm going to tell him as soon as we've pulled it off. Even if it isn't real, thinking he's lost you is going to crush him. That's something he doesn't deserve, Alfie."

Alfie nodded, and I could see the guilt written on his face. "I know. But this is the only way to keep her safe."

I sighed. "I understand. Just...be careful, okay? You and Emilia are family now. I can't lose you both."

"I will. And thank you, Cassidy. For everything." Alfie wrapped me in a tight hug, his voice cracking. "You have no idea what this means to me."

I squeezed him back. "You're welcome."

He stepped back, looking at me with a mix of relief and gratitude. I walked him to the door, my own anxieties swirling despite my resolve.

As he left, I closed the door behind him and leaned against it, heart pounding. I knew I was taking a massive risk by keeping secrets from Connor, but I couldn't stand idly by while Emilia suffered at the hands of Angel. She deserved better, and if there was even the slightest chance that I could help save her, then I had to take it. I'd given my word not to worry Connor unnecessarily. But if he asked me outright, could I lie to him? For Emilia and Alfie's sake, I prayed I wouldn't have to find out.

The moment the door clicked shut, I pulled out my phone and dialed my old boss's number.

"Jerome," I said as soon as he picked up. "I need another favor."

17

— • —

ALFIE

OF ALL THE DEATHS we were supposed to fake tonight, Tommy Quinn
was the one who actually might end up eating a bullet. From me.

Tommy sat on the stool next to me at Lady D's, pontificating on the
finer points of the upcoming Pats-Ravens game. It was clear he hadn't
quite gotten over the sting of losing the last Super Bowl to the Giants,
and he was determined to convince me that the Patriots would avenge
their defeat in the coming weeks. Like I actually gave a shit about football. Or anything right now other than what was supposed to be going
down in an alley in the North End in just under an hour.

The dim lights of Lady D's whined above me as I leaned against the
bar, nursing a glass of whiskey I didn't really want but was sipping on for
appearances sake. It churned in my gut like gasoline. The bar was packed
for a Tuesday, and as luck would have it, Tommy had cornered me and
obliterated my attempt to calm my nerves before the big event.

I was a second away from faking my death right here at the bar and
having done with it.

I really couldn't blame him, though. Tommy had been forced to lay
low for days, and he was going a bit stir-crazy. It said a lot about the state
of the Clan that Callum had pulled him back into active rotation. A very

small part of me felt guilty for abandoning Connor and Tommy at a time like this, but they would be able to handle it without me. They always did. They never really needed me much, anyway.

I tossed back the last of my whiskey and motioned to Slone for a refill. Tommy was rambling on about some chick he'd banged last weekend, but I wasn't really listening. My knee bounced under the table as I checked my watch again. The bulletproof vest was hot as hell under my jacket, and the straps holding the blood bag in place dug into my skin.

"...I'm telling you, man," Tommy was saying. "This girl had legs for days, and the things she could do with them... You should have seen--"

"Can I get you something else, Tommy? An Uber, maybe?" Sloane leaned on the edge of the bar. She did not look pleased. There had been some kind of falling out between the two of them, and Tommy was apparently overcompensating by acting like a complete dick.

"No, but I will take another one of these." Tommy held up his glass. "And you can hold the side of sarcasm. Jealousy isn't really a good look on you, sweetheart."

Sloane rolled her eyes and moved down the bar.

"Come on, Tommy. Quit being a jackass," I grumbled.

Tommy looked at me in surprise, clearly taken aback by my tone. "What crawled up your ass and died?"

"Nothing."

"Right." Tommy snorted and took a sip of his whiskey. "Anyway, like I was saying..."

I tuned him out again, my thoughts returning to Emilia. Cassidy and I had been planning this for days now, working out every detail until it was flawless. But I still couldn't help but worry about something going wrong. About something happening to Emilia. Or worse, Connor finding out what we were doing and blowing the whole thing to hell.

Tonight, Emilia was supposed to take the toxin once Luca returned to the compound. The idea was to make it look like she had been so distraught over Luca killing me that she took her own life. Luca already had the two injector pens that would reverse the toxin's effects. It had taken a lot of convincing to get him to agree to that part, but he'd finally caved, saying he wouldn't trust anyone else with Emilia's life. I had no doubt that he wouldn't. Luca was smart, he had spent most of his life protecting Emilia, and if there was anyone who had a vested interest in keeping her safe, it was him.

I had no doubt that Luca would do his part, but the plan still had to go perfectly. There was no room for error.

"...and then I told her, 'Baby, you're crazy if you think I'm wearing a rubber. If you can't take the heat, get out of the kitchen,' and she--"

"Oh, for fuck's sake, Tommy," I exploded, standing up from the stool. "Can't you shut the fuck up for five minutes? Jesus Christ, I don't give two shits about your sex life!"

Tommy stared at me, stunned. Shit. I hurriedly stood. "I've got to go."

He grabbed my arm. "What's going on with you tonight? You've been acting strange all week. What the hell is going on?"

I tried to shrug him off. "It's nothing."

"Bullshit. We've been friends too long for me to buy that."

"It's just work," I lied, taking a sip of my whiskey. "I'm meeting Grady tonight, there's a problem with one of our shipments. Connor wants me to take a look."

"You could have said something earlier." Tommy's frown deepened. "I'll go with you. You shouldn't be going alone."

I shook my head. "No, it's fine. It's just some paperwork stuff, I don't want to drag you into it. Besides, you're supposed to be laying low."

"Tell me about it," he grumbled. He slammed his empty glass down. "Fine, go. But you owe me a drink when you get back."

"I'll buy you two," I said, feeling even lower. In a few hours, he'd think I was dead. I gripped his shoulder, trying to impart as much of my love for him as I could. "Thanks for always having my back, Tom."

Tommy rolled his eyes and pushed me away. "Yeah, whatever. Get out of here, before I change my mind and chain you to a barstool."

———————

The cold night air did little to alleviate the sweat pooling beneath my jacket. Its bulkiness hid my bulletproof vest, but the blood packs taped to my chest made my skin itch like I'd been rolling in poison ivy. The white tee underneath was ready to showcase the fake blood, adding to the illusion.

I got off the subway two stops away from Emilia's bookstore, deciding to walk the rest of the way. Despite being waylaid by Tommy, I was a little early.

I typed out a quick message to Emilia, one that left me feeling more vulnerable than any bullet ever could.

I typed quickly, my thumb hovering over the send button before continuing.

Emilia. I can't go another moment without telling you how much you mean to me. You've become my everything, and I would do anything to keep you safe. I love you with piece of my soul, and I need you to know that, no matter what happens tonight.

My breath hitched as I hit send, sealing my confession in a digital envelope and sending it off into the ether. It felt like a weight had been lifted from my chest, but the gnawing anxiety remained.

I stuffed my phone into my pocket and continued walking. The streets were quiet, save for a few groups of tourists who were out late exploring the city. They were laughing and taking pictures of the famous landmarks, blissfully unaware of the danger lurking in the shadows.

As I walked, I thought back to the first time I had seen Emilia. It felt like a lifetime ago, but it had only been a few months since that fateful night at the bookstore. She had been so beautiful, so vibrant, so full of life, and I had been instantly captivated by her. Her wit, her intelligence, her passion for reading. For life. She had been like a breath of fresh air after years of breathing in the stale smoke of the Irish mob.

She had been everything I had ever wanted, and now that I had her, I couldn't bear the thought of losing her.

As I rounded the corner to the bookstore, I spotted Luca's black sedan parked a few spots down. My phone buzzed in my pocket, Emilia's answer to my text, but I didn't have time to look at it.

I took a deep breath and squared my shoulders. This was it. There was no turning back now.

I steeled myself and began to walk toward the bookstore, gun sitting heavily in its holster at my side. The entrance to the alley behind Emilia's bookshop was dimly lit, shadows clinging to the brick walls, but it was one I knew like the back of my hand. My boots echoed loudly with every step, and my heart pounded against the vest so hard I thought it might burst from my chest.

As I entered the alley, the sound of footsteps behind me made me tense. Glancing at a nearby windowfront, I caught sight of their reflections – Luca, Angel, and Dom – and my blood ran cold. This was really happening. I forced myself to keep walking, my legs moving on autopilot. I heard them drawing closer, and I braced myself, ready to run.

I took a deep breath, squaring my shoulders. No going back now. Tonight, blood would be shed, and nothing would ever be the same.

"Well, well," Angel's mocking voice cut through the silence. "The rat emerges from his hole."

I ran.

Luca and I had prepared the route ahead of time, planning for every contingency. A cut to the left, then another left, and the alley would dead end in a chain link fence. Free of bystanders and providing some insulation from the cops, the perfect backdrop to our little scene.

I hoped.

Blood roared in my ears as I forced myself to run, my feet pounding on the pavement as I ducked into another alley. Luca was right behind me, his breath ragged as he chased me down. I could hear Angel and Dom laughing, taunting me, but I didn't let it slow me down. I had to get to the end of this alley to make this look as convincing as possible.

As I reached the end of the alley, I skidded to a halt. The fence was right where Luca had said it would be, and I took a deep breath, steeling myself for what was about to happen.

"End of the line, Doyle!" Luca shouted as I skidded to a stop, my back pressed against the cold chain link. The dead-end loomed before us like an omen, the dimly lit street beyond mocking our futile attempt to escape fate.

"Seems that way," I replied, trying to keep my voice steady. I locked eyes with Luca and squared my shoulders, ensuring that he'd have a clean shot.

The alley stank. Overflowing garbage spilled onto the ground, soot and grime creeping up the faded bricks. Layers of filth as old as the city itself. A dead end.

It seemed like a fitting place for this life to end.

Despite the potent surge of adrenaline rocketing through my system, I felt strangely calm. My focus lasered down until I could make out the individual dust motes in the air, each crack in the brick façade. I heard the hum of the flickering sodium lamp high overhead, the slow scuff of shoes against the pavement, the slow drip, drip, drip of water down the sewer grate ticking down my last few moments like some kind of cosmic clock. The hyper-focus was at once both exhausting and invigorating. My God—this is what Connor must feel like all the time.

My time had been running out for a while now, and when Luca's huge shadow bracketed the end of the alley with Dominic and Angel close behind, I knew it was finally here.

I wasn't going to be walking out of this alley.

"Did you really think you could outrun us?" Angel sneered, stepping closer with an unsettling grin on his face. "You're not so clever now, are you?"

"Enough talking, Angel," Luca snapped, pulling out his gun and aiming it at my chest. His dark eyes betrayed the slightest hint of apprehension, but he masked it well enough that only I could see it. "We've got a job to do."

"Luca...please. You don't have to do this." My back pressed against the chain link fence blocking the alley, and my heartrate doubled at the sight of the gun in his hand, unerringly pointed right at me. I raised my hands, palms out like that was all it would take to stop what was about to happen. "Look, I—"

"Angel, you're taking too damn long." Dom raised his gun.

And fired.

The bullet hit my side with the force of a sledgehammer, and I stumbled backward, gasping for air. Every breath I took rasped in my ears, and my vision started to checkerboard.

Fuck, this hurt so much more than the last time I was shot.

My knees buckled, and I collapsed against the chain link fence. My hands fumbled for purchase, rattling the metal links uselessly. I couldn't keep my feet. My knees hit the sidewalk, and I folded onto the concrete. This wasn't part of the plan.

I looked down at my chest. Shit. The bastard hadn't even managed to hit the blood bag.

My vision swam as I struggled for breath. The Kevlar had absorbed most of the impact, but the bullet had still cracked a rib. I sucked in a ragged gasp, forcing myself to stay conscious.

"I thought I'd save you the trouble," Dom said with a shrug.

Angel whirled on him, eyes blazing. "He was mine!"

"You were taking too long." Dom's gaze slid to mine, a cruel smirk twisting his lips. "Looks like you're not so tough without that behemoth Quinn to back you up, are you Doyle?"

Two pairs of boots stepped into view, and Luca gripped me by the hair and tilted my face up. "You should've known better, Alfie."

"Luca," I said, my voice hoarse. "Please."

"You think you can mess with Emilia, and we won't notice?" He released me and I slid bonelessly to the ground. "I'm doing this for her, you fucking piece of shit."

My heart pounded unevenly in my ears. "Please..."

"Listen to the shithead cry." Angel leaned down into my wavering field of view. "This has been a long time coming, Irish."

"Let's go, Mariano," Dom said. "Finish him off."

I tried to say something, but I couldn't seem to get enough air. *Emilia.* At least she would be safe, now. That was really all that mattered in the end.

Luca stood and took a step back, aiming the gun directly at my heart. He was standing a few steps in front of Angel and Dom, so I was the only one who could see the regret in his dark eyes, his mouth a grim slash of tension.

"Don't...do this," I gasped. "Think about Emilia."

Luca looked at me, and his face smoothed out into something expressionless and cold. "I am."

He pulled the trigger. The bullet slammed into my chest like a battering ram, dead center. My teeth clacked together so hard, I bit my tongue. Blood blossomed on my shirtfront, drenching the fabric and pooling quickly on the pavement around me, reflecting the sodium lights overhead like so many stars across its inky surface.

I couldn't feel much, this time. That probably wasn't a good thing. My heart thudded wrongly in my chest, heavy, laboring beats as I tried to drag my arm up to my chest. Angel crouched down in front of me and eyed me like I was some kind of new, interesting species of insect. I unsuccessfully tried to spit a wad of bloody spit on his shoes.

He pressed the muzzle of his gun to my forehead.

"Say goodbye, Alfie."

Over the ringing in my ears, I heard sirens in the distance. Getting closer. Luca heard them too, and he tugged on Angel's arm, his face white with shock. "Enough, Angel. He's done. We need to go."

"Get off me!" Angel growled, shoving Luca back. Pressed his gun to my temple.

"No!" Luca grabbed the gun. It went off, the sound deafening at close quarters, spraying gravel into my face.

"Alfie!"

I blinked my eyes, convinced I was hallucinating this nightmare as Connor skidded to a halt at the mouth of the alley, his eyes wide with horror at the scene before him. Tommy was right on his heels.

They both pulled their guns and fired on the Italians.

Everything happened real fast after that.

Angel shoved Luca away and scrambled for cover. Dom returned fire, forcing Connor and Tommy back while the sirens screamed closer and closer. Blood sprayed. Curses echoed. Luca's head snapped back and he dropped like a stone.

Shit. Shit. Shit.

I tried to get up, tried to reach for my gun--hell, I tried to drag my ass out of the line of fire, but I couldn't seem to make my limbs move. I was still teetering on the edge of breathless consciousness when Tommy grabbed me by the collar and hauled me behind a dumpster. I was vaguely aware of him shouting something at me, but his words were lost to the sluggish pulse in my ears.

As fast as things were moving before, time now slowed to a crawl. The cops were nearly on us. From beneath the dumpster, I saw Luca's side profile, masked in blood. I couldn't tell if he was still breathing.

Angel and Dom ran, leaving him behind. I weakly tried to sit up, but Connor's knees hit the pavement next to me, and he pushed me back down.

"Stop, Alfie. *Stop.* Just lie still." His hands shook as they tore my shirt open. "Stay with me, okay? Just..."

I weakly batted his hands out of the way, but Connor had already rocked back on his heels, staring at the blood bags taped to the Kevlar vest. "You..."

While Connor's face performed some intense emotional gymnastics that ranged from shock to relief to rage, Tommy hauled him to his feet.

The bigger man's hand was pressed to his side, stemming blood from a wound on his hip.

"We don't have time for this," he grunted. "Alfie, I'm glad you're not dead, but when we get back to Lady D's, I'm gonna kill you."

"Fair," I wheezed, wincing at the shift in my chest. Definitely broke some ribs.

Tommy wasn't too gentle yanking me to my feet, but the pain momentarily took a backseat to the urgency of our situation. Flashing red and blue lights ricochetted crazily off the alley. I tried to turn back to the spot where Luca's body lay, but Connor shoved me forward.

"We have to go," Connor insisted, nodding toward the door to a business behind me. "We don't have time to check on him."

"But--"

"Move your ass, Doyle."

I was half-dragged through the unlocked door by Connor as two squad cars bracketed the alley. Cops poured out, guns already drawn. The last thing I saw before the door slammed shut was one of them kneeling over Luca's unmoving form, checking for a pulse.

18

CONNOR

THE BACK ROOM AT Lady D's was a testament to every vice that had ever plagued South Boston. The dim lightbulb hanging from the ceiling cast a sallow glow over mismatched sofas, each one a witness to its own multitude of sins. Dark stains that could've been blood—or worse—decorated the faded upholstery. The wood paneling on the walls bore scratches and dings, relics of brawls past. It was like stepping into a noir film set designed by someone with a penchant for melancholy and the macabre. Usually, this place buzzed with the illicit whispers of lovers or the scheming of criminals, but tonight it served a more desperate purpose: a makeshift surgery for the battered and the bleeding.

I dragged Alfie through the door, his boots scraping along the floorboards, and dumped him onto the nearest sofa. Tommy eased himself onto the couch opposite, pressing a hand to the bullet graze in his side. Blood seeped through his fingers, staining the upholstery beneath him a deeper shade of red.

"You alright?" I asked.

Tommy waved me off dismissively. "It's just a graze. Stop fussin'."

I raised an eyebrow. "You're bleeding all over the couch."

"Fuck the couch. You've sprung a leak too, by the way."

"Am I?" I muttered distractedly, and looked down. I frowned at the torn fabric of my sleeve, the red stain spreading wider than I'd realized. In the chaos, the sting from being grazed barely registered. Now, as the adrenaline began to wane, the pain sharpened, intensifying with each beat of my heart.

"I'll live," I muttered, pressing my hand against the wound, trying to staunch the flow. As I assessed the damage, my thoughts swirled—a volatile mix of relief, betrayal, and fury directed at Alfie. He had a lot of explaining to do.

I turned my attention to Alfie, who was wheezing through what were likely a few broken ribs. Blood had saturated his shirt to the point of being almost completely unrecognizable as white, and the hospital grade blood bag taped to the center of his chest had a neat round hole dead center.

When I turned into that alley and saw Alfie laid out on the ground...all that blood...I thought I had lost him.

It was Aiden all over again. My parents. Cassidy. Just another person I loved--more than my friend, a brother in every way that mattered--just another person I cared about that I hadn't been able to save.

Confusion, at first, when I saw the vest and what was taped to it. I wasn't sure what I was looking at. Disbelief. Shock. Then a feeling of relief palpable enough to leave me lightheaded and trembling. He was alive.

Then the rage came, cold and swift. My old friend.

I wanted to throttle him. Wanted to grab him by the collar and shake some sense into him. Wanted to scream until my voice gave out. Wanted to punch him in his beautiful, stupid face.

I stalked over to Alfie and started pulling the blood-soaked Kevlar from his chest, the spent blood bags flapping comically as I loosened the vest's Velcro.

"You had better start explaining yourself," I growled. "And you better do it fast, or I swear to Christ, Alfie--"

He tried to pull himself up, grimacing with pain, the tattoos on his arms stretching and distorting with the effort. "Connor, I'm sorry. I didn't--"

"Didn't what? Think?" I threw the empty blood bags on the floor. "What the hell is this, anyway? What were you doing so far north?"

"I..." he trailed off, his eyes flicking over to Tommy.

"Don't you dare look at him like you don't know what you did," I snapped. "You went behind my back, Alfie. Didn't you? You were going to see that girl."

"It's not what you think. I didn't meant to..." Alfie closed his eyes and cursed softly. "You weren't supposed to be there."

Tommy looked up from where he was cautiously poking at the gouge in his side. "Well, it was a good thing that we were, brother, because you looked like you were a half second away from getting your head blown off. Who were those ass clowns, anyway?"

"Dominic and Angelo Moretti," Alfie said tiredly.

"The guys from the club?"

Alfie nodded.

"What about the third one," I asked, remembering the big guy who had gone down with what looked like a shot to the head. Alfie had seemed pretty upset about him. "Who is he to you?"

Christ, this was like last summer all over again. Alfie on one side of the line and me on the other, and I had a feeling that Emilia Russo was the dividing line.

"He's...no one." Alfie looked away, his jaw working furiously. "He's just another piece of shit Italian, that's all."

"Bullshit."

"You won't understand."

"Then make me understand. Because this looks an awful lot like you went behind my back. Like you were trying to fake your death in order to be with a girl that Callum expressly forbid you to see again. Make me understand, Alfie. Make me understand why you'd risk it all—for what? For some girl?"

"Emilia is not just some girl!" Alfie shouted, his face contorted in anger. "She is everything to me! I love her, Connor, and I will not let Callum keep us apart!"

There was a tense silence, broken only by the sound of our ragged breathing.

"I thought we were family." My voice was barely above a whisper.

"We are," Alfie said, his voice cracking. "But so is Emilia."

"She's not even part of our family," I shouted, my hands balling into fists at my sides. "She's the daughter of the enemy, for Christ's sake! She's gotten us in more trouble than we've ever been, and you're too blinded by your feelings for her to see it!"

"I love her, dammit!" Alfie shouted, holding my gaze with a fierce intensity. "Emilia is in danger. Lorenzo has her locked up in a room right now, and every second she's in that bastards grasp I am dying just a little bit more. This life is killing us, Connor, and I refuse to lose her to it. I'm going to get her out of this life."

"Get her out?" I scoffed. "And what? Play house while the rest of us bleed for this clan?"

"I love her!"

"Love?" I barked out a harsh laugh, unable to contain my disbelief. "You've known her for what, a few months? And now you're willing to risk everything for her?"

"Sometimes that's all it takes," Alfie shot back, his jaw clenched. "And if you cared about Cassidy half as much as I care about Emilia, maybe you'd understand!"

"Watch your mouth!" I snarled, the mention of my wife's name igniting a fire inside me. "Don't you dare bring her into this mess!"

"Maybe I would if you actually gave a damn about her!" Alfie shouted, finally finding his footing and rising from the sofa. "Instead of dragging her down with you!"

That hurt. The truth often does.

His words struck like a slap, cold and sharp. The room spun, the edges tinged with a red haze as I felt something primal surge within me. Love, loyalty, and a dark, seething rage mixed into a toxic cocktail that threatened to spill over.

"Dragging her down?" I echoed, my voice low and dangerous. "You think you know anything about sacrifice? About what I'd do for Cassidy?"

"Enough to see she deserves better," Alfie shot back.

Deserves better. The phrase echoed mockingly in my head. Probably because it was the truth.

"The truth hurts, doesn't it, McTiernan?" Alfie said stonily.

My fist connected with his mouth before either of us fully registered what was happening.

Alfie stumbled back, blood pouring from his split lip. I lunged for him, but Tommy was suddenly in between us, shoving us apart.

"Jesus, Connor!" Tommy's voice cut through the tension as he staggered over, his hand still pressed to his side. "Leave him alone, damn it!"

He grabbed my arm, trying to pull me away from Alfie who lay gasping on the ground, blood starting to trickle from his split lip. I shrugged Tommy off, the force of it causing him to stagger back, his face ashen as he fell to one knee.

"Fuck," he cursed under his breath, his hand clenching tighter against his side. But before I could even consider helping him, the door burst open.

Cassidy rushing into the room, her eyes wide with concern, followed closely by Sloane and Callum. They took in the scene: Alfie lying on the floor rubbing his jaw, me standing over him with my fists still clenched, and Tommy struggling to remain upright.

"What the fuck is going on here?" Callum growled, his gaze landing on first Tommy, then me, then Alfie. "Are you fucking kidding me right now?"

Cassidy knelt down next to Alfie. "Let me take a look at you," she said, her voice gentle but firm as she began assessing his wounds. I watched, feeling my chest tighten with a mix of frustration and jealousy.

"Stay out of this, Cass," I warned.

But she didn't so much as glance my way, her hands already moving with practiced ease. As she peeled back the vest to reveal the blood packs taped to his chest, the pieces started to fall into place.

Cassidy had known about this whole damn thing from the start.

Somehow, that betrayal cut even deeper.

"Two fractured ribs and some pretty nasty bruising," Cassidy muttered, feeling along his ribcage. "You're lucky it wasn't worse."

"You're telling me," Alfie said, probably remembering that Angel had been about to shoot him in the head when we'd shown up.

I'd saved his ass. Again.

And he'd repaid me by going behind my back and faking his own death.

Callum calmly walked over to the desk, pulled out a bottle, and poured himself a drink. "Somebody had better start explaining right fucking now--"

"You know, out of everyone, you're the one who surprised me the most," I interrupted acidly, glaring at the back of Cassidy's head as she moved on to Tommy.

She didn't miss a beat, helping Tommy to sit and pulling up his shirt to examine the still weeping gouge in his side. "Surprised by what, Connor?"

"That you'd help stage this...this circus act," I spat the words out, tasting the bitterness of betrayal on my tongue.

Cassidy finally looked up at me, her green eyes meeting mine with a steadiness that stung. "Someone has to keep you all alive." Her voice was steady, resolute, but I heard the undercurrent of pain in it.

"Even if it meant lying to me?" My heart thrashed against my ribs, a wild thing caged by her deception.

"Even then," she whispered, turning her attention back to Tommy, her hands moving deftly over his wound.

It was then I understood the depth of her involvement. She wasn't just an accessory; she was the architect of this whole fucking thing.

From the floor, Cassidy ignored me. She rummaged in her medical bag and calmly pulled out a suture kit. Her blatant indifference cut through me like a knife.

"I can't believe you," I said, my voice cold. "You went behind my back. You could have gotten yourself killed, and you *lied* to me!"

"It's not like I had a choice," she snapped, turning back to me. "You would've never agreed to it. Besides, I was just helping Alfie stage a little show. Not like I was taking a bullet for him or anything."

"I can't believe you," I repeated, unable to articulate the maelstrom of emotions swirling inside me. I took a deep breath, trying to rein in my temper. "So, what? You thought it was okay to lie to me, to risk your life, because you were 'just helping' Alfie?"

"Yes," she replied evenly, her eyes never leaving mine. "And I'd do it again. Alfie's my friend, and he loves Emilia. He's been miserable these last few weeks, and I wasn't about to let you stand in the way of him being happy."

I shook my head in disbelief. "You don't get to decide that," I said, my voice low and dangerous. "You don't get to put yourself in danger, to put your life on the line, for someone else's happiness."

"Oh, but you do?"

"That's different."

"How?"

Sloane's hand settled on my shoulder. "She's got a point, Connor. You do the same thing."

"Stay out of this, Sloane," I warned.

"No," she shot back. "I'm not going to sit here and listen to you try to bully Cassidy into submission. If you want to get angry at her for doing something you would have done in a heartbeat, then be mad at her, but don't try to play the moral high ground card. You're no saint, Connor. Not by a longshot. So what if she went behind your back to help Alfie? At least she did something. And it worked, didn't it? Alfie's alive, Emilia will be safe, and the Morettis won't be breathing down our necks anymore. It's a win, Connor. Try to see it that way."

I shook my head, her words echoing in my ears. "It's not that simple."

"You're the one who made it complicated, Connor." Cassidy didn't even look up from where she threaded a needle with surgical precision. "We should discuss this later. Now is not the time."

"Seems like it's never the right time." My fury burned hotter, but her indifference was a wet blanket smothering it into frustration.

"Connor, ease up," Alfie coughed from his propped position on the sofa, his eyes glassy with pain.

"About time you to spoke up," Sloane glared at Alfie. "You're the one that got us in this goddamn mess."

The room descended into chaos as everyone tried to talk over each other.

"Shut the fuck up, all of you." It was Tommy, using the wall to push himself to his feet, swaying slightly with the effort. His face was pale, a stark contrast to the deep red blooming on his shirt. "This isn't helping."

"Tommy—" Cassidy started, but he held up a hand, silencing her.

"Stop. Just stop," he slurred, his words carrying the weight of command despite his condition. "You think this is what any of us need right now?"

The room fell into a tense silence, punctuated only by the ragged sound of breathing and the distant siren calls outside Lady D's. Tommy's eyes met mine, and something in his gaze punched through the haze of my rage. He was right. We were family—a fucked-up, bloodied family—and we were tearing ourselves apart.

Tommy leaned against the wall, steadying himself as he glared at each of us in turn. "You know what family is?" he started, his voice low but cutting through the tension like a serrated blade. "It's the biggest pain in the ass you'll ever know, but it's also the one thing you'd lay down your life for without thinking twice."

I watched him, my own anger simmering on a back burner, as Tommy's words sliced through the room. His hand was pressed to his side, blood seeping between his fingers, but his eyes were fierce, alive with a fire that demanded attention.

"Look at us," he continued, voice growing louder, "fighting each other when we should be fighting the world that wants us dead. We're so busy trying to prove who's the biggest martyr that we've forgotten we're on the same damn side."

I shifted uncomfortably, knowing his words held truth. We were all so wrapped up in our own battles that we'd forgotten the war.

"I ought to knock your heads together until you get it." He took an unsteady step forward, his gaze sweeping over us. "There are bigger things at stake than our egos, bigger enemies than the ones we're making of each other."

"Tommy—" Alfie tried to interject, but Tommy wasn't having any of it.

"Save it, Alfie. I'm tired of this shit." His voice cracked, not from weakness, but from exasperation. "I'm going upstairs to take a goddamn nap because my side is killing me, and you lot are giving me a fucking headache."

Without another word, he grabbed the bottle of whiskey from Callum's hand, the liquid sloshing inside as he stomped out of the room.

We stood there, silent as ghosts, watching the door swing shut behind him. The echo of his steps fading away jarred me into reflection. It was Tommy—the man we'd often dismissed as an unstable, incendiary drunk—who had just shown us what true leadership looked like.

"Christ," Sloane muttered, breaking the silence.

"Didn't see that coming," Callum added, rubbing the back of his neck.

"Neither did I," I admitted, feeling the sting of shame for underestimating Tommy. Out of all of us, it was he who had the balls to call it like it was—to remind us of the bond that held us together even as we seemed hellbent on tearing it apart.

In that moment, I realized that maybe Tommy's brand of chaos was exactly what we needed to unite us again.

Cassidy let out a soft huff and got to her feet, gathering the medical supplies. She gave Alfie a gentle pat on the shoulder. "I'll be back to check on you in a bit."

She swept out of the room, giving me a pointed look as she went, and I followed her out into the main room. Sloane and Callum hung back, and I didn't hear what they said, but Callum's laugh echoed behind us as the door swung shut.

The empty hush of the closed bar seemed almost startling after the charged atmosphere of the back room. The dim light cast long shadows over the furniture, giving the place a dusty, haunted look. I found Cassidy behind the bar, her movements deliberate as she poured cranberry juice into a glass with mechanical precision.

Without looking up, she set out a second glass for me, reaching for a bottle of whiskey that gleamed amber under the muted lighting. She poured a generous measure, the sound of the liquid hitting the glass oddly soothing amidst the chaos of my thoughts. I took the offered glass and sat down on one of the bar stools, letting the silence stretch between us. I took a sip of the whiskey, the burn familiar and comforting as it slid down my throat.

"Let me see your arm." Her voice was low and calm, breaking the silence without shattering it. I looked up to find her leaning against the bar, her eyes fixed on me.

I unbuttoned my shirt, stripped it off, and tossed it on the bar top. Cassidy reached across the bar, gently cradling my arm and turning it to get a better look at the wound. Her touch was feather-light, and it sent a jolt of electricity racing along my skin.

"Just a graze," she said, her voice soft and sure. "It doesn't look too bad. Does it hurt?"

"I'll survive," I said, the ache in my arm heating my blood as her fingers skated over my skin. "If you're not the death of me first."

Cassidy raised an eyebrow, a smirk tugging at her lips. "I think you're doing a pretty good job of that yourself."

I exhaled a frustrated sigh, the weight of the day's events crashing over me like a wave. "How did you know we were here, anyway?"

"Tommy called me. He said you needed me."

The simplicity and tenderness of her statement hit me harder than any bullet could. "I always need you," I whispered, the words rumbling from deep in my chest.

"I'm still mad at you," she said, her eyes shooting daggers at me.

"I know. I'm sorry."

Cassidy didn't answer at first, intent upon cleaning the graze on my arm and carefully bandaging it. The care she took with me made my heart contract. When I finally risked a glance at her face, I found her biting her lip as if weighing my apology in her mind.

"We need boundaries," Cassidy said, brushing a lock of hair from her face, her eyes not leaving mine. "You can't keep doing this—shutting me out one minute and pulling me back the next. It's not fair to either of us."

"Fair?" I scoffed, my grip tightening on the glass of whiskey. "You think any of this is about being fair?"

"Maybe not," she conceded, her fingers tracing the rim of her own glass absentmindedly, "but it's about surviving, isn't it? About not losing each other in this... madness."

Her words struck a chord, resonating with a fear that had been gnawing at me—a fear I'd kept buried beneath layers of bravado and control. I looked away, ashamed of the vulnerability I felt rising within me.

"Cass, I—" My voice broke, and I took a swig of whiskey, hoping it would fortify the walls I felt crumbling. "I'm terrified of losing you. Losing any of you."

"Connor." There was a softness in Cassidy's voice that made me meet her eyes again. "We're in this together, remember? You don't have to carry it all on your own."

"Damn it, Cass, it's not just about carrying it," I growled, setting the glass down harder than necessary. "It's watching the people I love walk into danger over and over again, knowing one day they might not walk back out."

"Then trust us," she implored, reaching across the bar to lay a hand over mine. "Trust me. We know the risks, but we do it because we believe in something greater—each other, this family."

"Even when the family seems hellbent on self-destruction?" I challenged, wanting to pull away from her touch but finding myself rooted to the spot.

"Especially then," Cassidy affirmed, squeezing my hand before letting go. "Because that's when we need each other most, Connor. That's when we fight hardest—to save ourselves, to save each other."

"God, Cass," I muttered, suddenly feeling the heaviness of the night bearing down on me. "When did you get so smart?"

"Somewhere between saying 'I do' to an Irish warlord and stitching up gunshot wounds in a backroom," she quipped, a ghost of a smile flickering on her lips.

Despite the knot of guilt in my chest, her dry humor never failed to touch me. I let out a hollow chuckle, the absurdity of the situation hitting me. I realized it wasn't just the weight of the clan and our enemies bearing down on me; it was the weight of my fears and insecurities.

I reached for her, my fingers trailing through her hair, thumb resting at the nape of her neck. "I know I'm a bastard and a fool, and I don't deserve you. But I can't lose you, Cassidy. You're the best thing in my life, the only thing that makes sense in this madness. Stay with me. We'll figure the rest out together, I swear it. Just please, don't go."

For a long moment Cassidy was silent. Then she touched my cheek, brushing away the tears I hadn't realized were falling.

"You stupid man," she whispered. A smile crept across her lips, softening the bruise. "As if I could ever leave you."

I surged to my feet and kissed her hungrily, my mouth heavy against hers. It felt like an apology—for the violence, the secrets, the mess we were making of our relationship. Cassidy responded with a fierceness that surprised me, her arms wrapping around my neck as she melted against me.

Fuck. I was hopeless. This woman could bring me to my knees with a single kiss.

I scooped her off her feet and deposited her on the bar, my mouth never leaving hers as she wrapped her legs around my hips, the curve of her belly fitting perfectly between us. We broke apart for a moment, and my eyes searched her face, drinking in the sight of her swollen lips and wide, pupil-blown eyes.

"Cassidy, I—" I started, but she silenced me with a finger on my lips.

"Don't," she breathed, her lips curved into a crooked smile. "Just...show me. Show me, Connor."

I slipped my hand beneath her shirt, skating over the soft swell of her belly to cup her breast. Cassidy arched into my touch, pressing herself into me. The fierce swell of protectiveness and desire that flooded through me threatened to overwhelm me, but I knew this was what we both needed.

"I'll show you," I murmured, gently tugging her earlobe between my teeth. "Because this is my promise—to you, to our child, and to our family. No more fighting. No more secrets."

I kissed her gently this time, as if to seal the vow, feeling her trembling in my arms. Cassidy leaned back on her elbows, the curve of her belly accentuated by the thin fabric of her shirt. Christ, she was a sight. Gorgeous. Perfect.

And I would never be enough to deserve her.

I pressed a trail of kisses down her throat, following the curve of her breasts as I pulled her shirt over her head and flung it away. My hands slid over her body, thumbs grazing her pink, pert nipples. Cassidy sighed and arched her back, closing her eyes as I unbuttoned her jeans. In the dark, on the bar top, it was we fumbled, breathless and awkward, giggling at the circumstances and challenges her pregnant form presented.

She helped as I finally got the damn things over her rounded hips. I breathed out an incredulous laugh and peeled the panties off with them.

"I need you. Now."

I looked up to find her staring at me, her eyes bright and shining. A wild, insane desire to claim her flickered in my core. To carve out space for us amongst all the violence and chaos. To remind her that, no matter what, she was mine.

Always.

When I entered her, it was like coming home. Her heat enveloped me, drawing me deeper. The world fell away. There was no war. No violence. No fear. Only us.

For once, I was not bound to anything but her.

I claimed her with my body, my thrusts gentle but firm, taking my time to convey to her everything I couldn't put into words. Cassidy responded with a fervor that incised and propelled me further, her nails carving into my shoulders and leaving half-moon crescents in their wake.

I pressed my face to her throat, breathing her in as she trembled beneath me. Cradled me in her warmth, the building sweetness riding the line between pleasure and pain when I felt her come apart in my arms. Her fingers tangled in my hair, tugging with delicious pressure, and I felt my own release wash over me with a suddenness that nearly killed me.

God damn.

We lay there for a moment, hearts hammering in perfect rhythm, trying to catch our breath. Finally, Cassidy broke the silence with a soft yawn, her fingers combing lazily through my hair.

I looked at the clock and winced at the time. "All right, love, down you get. It's way past your bedtime."

"I'm not tired. Besides, this is all your fault, not mine." She tried for a scowl as I helped her down off the bar, but she looked too damn cute for it to really pack any punch. Then she laughed as I carefully dressed her in her clothes, fussing and clucking over her. "I'm not a child, you know--are you going to put me to bed like one?"

I chuckled. "Oh, I realize you're not a child. But I will be putting you to bed tonight."

Cassidy stuck her tongue out at me, and I zipped her jacket up to her throat, my smile turning wicked.

"I didn't say anything about sleeping, though."

19

EMILIA

MY ROOM WAS EXACTLY twenty-one paces by twenty-one, and I must have walked hundreds of miles since I'd been locked up. I was surprised I hadn't worn a groove in the floor.

Something was going on. I heard the sounds of raised voices, doors slamming. Someone was running down the hall.

I pressed my ear to the door. At first I thought it was Angel, but then I realized it was Dominic. His voice, usually so controlled and calm, was shaking with barely controlled rage.

Oh, God. What had happened?

I ran to the window and peered down. The front gates were open, and there was a line of black Escalades pulling in. My stomach clenched, a cold terror gripping my heart.

Dominic's voice rose again, his words indistinguishable through the door, but I could hear the fury in his tone. I felt sick with worry. If something had happened to Alfie...

With trembling hands, I pulled out my phone and scrolled to the last text message I'd received from him.

Emilia. I can't go another moment without telling you how much you mean to me. You've become my everything, and I would do anything to keep you safe. I love you with piece of my soul, and I need you to know that, no matter what happens tonight.

My heart skipped a beat, then began to race. I read the message again, my mind spinning as I tried to make sense of it. What had he meant by 'no matter what happens tonight'? Had something gone wrong?

My own response had gone unanswered. It had been over an hour since I sent it.

Tears pricked at my eyes as I clutched my phone to my chest. I prayed to God that whatever was happening, Alfie would come through it unharmed.

Alfie's plan had terrified me, but I had to admit, there was a certain poetic justice about it. A simplistic irony. He was willing to risk every-thing—his family, his life, even his own identity—for the woman he loved. And now, as I paced my prison, I found myself wishing I could be as brave as him.

I'm not sure I could have agreed to it if it hadn't been for Luca. He wasn't any more pleased about the plan than I was, but his hands had been steady and his mouth set in grim determination when he handed me the loaded syringe.

"I will be with you every step of the way," he'd promised. "I just wish it hadn't come to this."

"So do I," I'd murmured, my fingers closing around the syringe. It felt coldly clinical. Death delivered in a tiny glass tube.

"The Irish doctor says it won't hurt. It'll feel like falling asleep. Noth-ing more."

I shoved the syringe in my pocket to hide the way my hands trembled. "And after?"

Luca briefly showed me two more small tubes before he palmed them, tucking them safely back in his pocket. "When they're done with you, I'll be there. You'll wake up safe and sound."

"You swear it?"

His eyes had softened and he had reached for me, his hand cupping my cheek. "I swear it. Everything is going to work out. You'll see."

Metal scraped at my door, and a key turned in the lock. I scrambled to tuck the syringe beneath my mattress just as the door opened.

"Sofia!" I yanked her into the room, and the door swung shut behind us. "What's going on down there?"

Beneath her tan, Sofia was white as a sheet. "I-I'm not really sure. Angel and Dom are saying the Irish gunned them down."

"What?"

Her hands fluttered near her face, and she sat heavily on my bed. "There's so much yelling downstairs. I can't really tell what happened, but Dominic's been shot in the shoulder, Angel is stomping around, bleeding everywhere from who knows what, and Lorenzo started barking orders. They called the doctor for Dom...something about the cops, oh, Em, what's happening?"

I felt the blood drain from my face. Alfie. He'd told me he was going to fake his death tonight. Had something gone wrong? I took Sofia's hand in mine, squeezing gently. I had to be calm for us both. "Tell me everything you heard."

"Dom said they were checking on your bookstore, you know, since you haven't been able to...to work," she began, picking at the hem of her tee. "He said that three Irishmen jumped them in the alley behind the bookstore and just started shooting. On Moretti Territory. Lorenzo is--I've never seen him like this."

Sofia winced as I gripped her hand, hard. "Did they recognize the three Irishmen? Was Alfie--"

"He was there, he--Oh God, Emilia." Sofia's voice shook. "He got shot. Luca...he..."

Even though the blood ran from my face at Emilia's words, they were expected just as long as..."

"...he shot Alfie!" She hiccupped, her eyes brimming with tears. "Luca shot him. Right in the heart. Angel was laughing about it, he's saying Alfie's...he's..."

I pulled her into my arms, my heart fluttering so fast I thought it would take flight right out of my chest. "Are you sure Luca was the one who shot him?"

"I'm positive," she cried, burying her face against my shoulder. "Angel wouldn't have told Lorenzo if he hadn't been sure. But why would Luca do that? *Why?* He knows who Alfie is to you."

She sat up suddenly and wiped her eyes with shaking hands. Then she looked at me. "Oh, God. You're in shock. I'm so sorry Emilia, I didn't mean to just...tell you like that."

"No, it's okay," I reassured her, even though I could barely hear my own voice over the roar of blood in my ears. "Where's Luca? I need to talk to him."

Sofia stilled.

"Sof," I said as gently as I could, even though I felt like my whole world was collapsing around me. "Where's Luca?"

"He...he didn't come back with the others."

I had to swallow twice to get the words out. "Why?"

"Luca was shot, too. Angel and Dom left him behind."

I stared at her, unable to comprehend what she was saying. My mind reeled with the implications. Luca was my lifeline in this, my tie to Alfie, who wasn't answering his phone.

If Luca was dead, then...

No. I couldn't allow myself to think that way. Not until I knew for sure.

Sofia squeezed my hand, her eyes wide with worry. "Em, are you okay? What can I do?"

"We need to find out if Luca is still alive." I took a deep breath, steeling myself against the panic rising inside me. "We need to find him."

"Julian's already on it," she said. "That's what most of the shouting was about downstairs. Sal sent Julian to the hospitals to find him, Dom said he was too badly injured to be in police custody."

I lurched to my feet. "All right. All right. That's...that's good. Let's just wait. Julian will find Luca, and we'll figure out what happened."

But Sofia's next words pierced through my fragile façade, sending my heart plummeting. "Footsteps," she whispered, paling. "Someone's coming."

The key turned in the lock, and the door swung open. Angel stood there, a smirk twisting his face into a cruel mask. He was still wearing his bloodied clothes, and his hair was matted with sweat.

"Aww, I guess I won't be the one to deliver the bad news, then."

I stood on shaky legs, my fingers curling into fists at my sides. "Get. Out."

"You're forgetting your place again, carina." He stopped in front of me, smirking. "A shame about your friend Luca. And that Irish scum you were screwing, what was his name again? Alfie?" Angel tsked. "Tragic."

"Fuck you."

Angel's hand lashed out, grabbing me by the throat. "Careful now," he warned, his eyes darkening. "Wouldn't want anything to happen to the little one, now would we?"

I glared at him, my blood boiling with hatred and fear. I wanted nothing more than to drive my knee straight into his balls and watch him crumple to the ground in pain. "Go, Sofia. Leave us."

Sofia gave me a pleading look, but I shook my head. "I'll be fine. Go find Julian."

Angel's grip on my neck tightened, and I shuddered as he ran a finger down my cheek. "Such a sad, pretty little thing you are. And so very, very alone."

"I'm not afraid of you," I lied, heart hammering.

"You should be," Angel whispered, his breath hot against my face. "Because there's no one left to protect you now."

With a final squeeze of my neck, he released me, and I staggered back, gasping for air. My hands flew to my throat, my fingers probing the tender flesh.

Angel laughed, a cold, empty sound that sent chills down my spine. "Run along now, little dove. You have a wedding to prepare for."

He slammed the door shut behind him, and I sank to the floor, my knees trembling with fear and rage. I'd never felt so helpless in my life. Alfie wasn't answering his phone, Luca might be dead, and now I was left at the mercy of a monster who wanted nothing more than to watch me suffer.

I pulled the syringe out from where I'd tucked it under the mattress and stared at it, the sharp tip glinting in the dim light. I knew what it would do. I knew the peace that it could bring. But as much as I wanted to end the pain, to escape this nightmare, I couldn't bring myself to do it. Not yet.

I needed answers.

And then, I would make Angel pay.

20

— · —

CASSIDY

"WELL, MRS. MCTIERNAN, I do hope you feel thoroughly fucked." Connor tucked me into his side beneath the covers, stifling a yawn. "Because I think another go might just kill me."

I smiled, lightly running my fingers along the ridges of his abdomen, felling them quiver beneath my touch. "Well, then. I'd have to revive you just so you could ravish me all over again. Don't worry, I know CPR."

Connor grinned against my throat, his teeth a white flash in the darkness. "I might take you up on that. I think there's a couple positions we haven't tried yet."

"Those might have to wait until after," I said, running my hand over my ever-growing stomach. "Your little one seems to be playing football at my ribs."

He spread his hand across the swell of my stomach and felt the accompanying kick. Something happened to his face, just then. Something sweet and tender, full of wonder and joy, and I wished I could bottle that expression and keep it.

"That's right," he said, his voice soft and serious, as he pressed a kiss to my abdomen. "It's your Da. Listen to me, you don't want to torture your Mum too much. She's a fierce little thing when she's irritated. "

I ruffled his hair and tugged on it. "You're one to talk."

Connor levered himself over me, strong, muscular arms bracketing my body as he trailed kisses up my belly. "Well, you're stuck with me now."

My heart throbbed at the tenderness in his expression, and I couldn't resist leaning up to kiss his lips. When I drew back, he held my gaze for a long moment, his eyes flicking back and forth between mine.

"I'm sorry about today. At Lady D's," he said finally, his voice catching with emotion. "Everything happened so fucking fast...the blood and gunshots...Alfie was dying, and then he wasn't...I didn't know whether to hug the bastard or punch him in the face."

"Looks like you did both those things."

A smile flickered across his face and then died. "And when I saw you standing there after all that, ready to clean up our mess...again..." he shook his head. "I took it out on you, and it wasn't fair. I should have kept a tighter leash on my temper."

"I forgive you," I whispered, brushing a lock of hair away from his face. "Just promise me you'll never shut me out like that again. Because you can't, Connor. I won't be left wondering and worrying from the sidelines, with my heart and stomach twisted up in knots."

"I'll try." His eyes searched mine, burning with an intensity that made my blood heat. "I swear it. The truth is, I'm not half so strong without you, Cassidy. I don't know how many times I have to say it, but I will if you need me to. All the time, every day. I need you with me, love. I--"

I pressed a finger to his lips, stopping the flow of words. "Shh. I know."

I dragged his mouth down to mine and kissed him hungrily, drinking in the taste of him. When we finally broke apart, breathless and panting,

Connor groaned and rolled off me, his eyes fixed on the ceiling. "I have got about a million things to do today, but I'm not sure if I've got the willpower to get out of this bed if you keep kissing me like that, lass."

"Let's start with a shower, then." I nudged him. "I bet there's still room for two, even with my perpetual plus one."

Connor laughed and threw back the covers. "Well, when you put it like that..."

The water felt luxurious on my tired body as I stepped under the spray. Connor stepped in behind me and slid his arms around my waist, his head dipping to kiss the sensitive spot behind my ear. I let myself soak in the warmth and comfort of being in Connor's arms, my breath coming in contented sighs.

"Careful there, love," Connor warned, his voice rumbling against my back. "You might not want to encourage me. My willpower is already hanging by a thread."

"I thought you said you had a million things to do."

"You come first."

The next several minutes were a delicious muddle of hands, kisses, and slick soap. I never did get properly cleaned, but with Connor's skin sliding against mine, the water cascading over us, it hardly mattered.

A sharp knock on the door jarred us out of the pleasured haze we had sunk into as a voice filtered through the closed door. "Hey, uh...boss?"

Connor groaned. "What is it, Grady?"

"I think you're gonna want to come out here."

"Can it wait?"

"Not really, no."

Connor cursed under his breath and quickly wrapped a towel around his waist. Grady was Callum's runner, so whatever it is was most likely important. He went over to the door and opened it a crack. There was a brief exchange, then the door shut again and Connor was back, his voice flat and businesslike.

"Finish your shower, love, I'll be right back."

I ducked my head out of the shower. Connor was pulling on his sweatpants, his damp hair dripping down his chest.

"What's going on?" I asked.

"It won't take long."

He was gone before I realized that he hadn't answered my question.

I finished my shower as quickly as I could and toweled off, listening to the tense, muffled voices down the hall.

"...warrant to search the place..."

"You run their badges?"

"They're legit. I made 'em wait while I called the precinct. They weren't too happy about that..."

I slipped into the bedroom and quickly dressed. I was just about to leave when Connor walked in, his face grim. He took one look at me and what was wearing—clothes a bit more formal than what I would wear for a normal Saturday morning at home—and his shoulders fell.

"How much did you hear?" he asked.

"Enough. Cops are on their way up?"

He nodded. "Two detectives from Beacon Hill, Grady says they have a warrant to search the place."

A warrant. That meant this wasn't just a social call, they actually thought they had some evidence. Enough to convince a judge of, at least.

"I don't like it, Connor."

"I don't either, love, but they're here, so we'll deal with it."

Connor ran his hands soothingly up and down my arms. The lines of worry were still etched on his face, but those blue eyes were cold and hardened. Like glacier ice.

"It's gonna be okay, Cass," he said. "I've dealt with this kind of thing before. Just let me do most of the talking, okay? We've gotta play this thing carefully."

"I know."

A knock at the door, and he took my hand, leading me out into the living room.

Grady was already gathered there with the detectives, his face pinched and his anger palatable. Connor, however, looked like he'd been carved out of stone as he appraised the two men standing in the doorway.

"Detectives Monroe and Channing, Mr. McTiernan," the taller one said. He thrust a paper towards Connor, offering it up instead of his hand by way of greeting. "We've got a warrant to search the place, and we'll be needing to ask you two some questions."

I bristled inwardly at his tone—confrontational and itching for a fight. Connor must have sensed my anger, because he squeezed my hand once in warning as Grady took the paper and looked it over.

"It's like they say, boss," he said quietly, eyes narrowed at Monroe.

Connor nodded. "May I ask what this is about?"

Channing left, headed towards the office with Grady right on his heels. Monroe gestured to the couch, a ploy to maintain control of the situation. "Why don't we have a seat."

"Very gracious of you to offer me a seat in my own home," Connor said icily. "I'll stand, thank you."

Monroe narrowed his eyes. "We're investigating the murder of Teagan Kelley, and your name just keeps coming up. We've got several witnesses that saw you in the Beacon Hill area the day he went missing, and several more that saw you checking in to Boston Medical Center later that day."

"Missing? I thought you said he was dead."

"He is. We found the body."

Zero reaction from Connor. I could feel his pulse through our clasped hands, just as slow and steady as if he was discussing financial reports instead of murder.

"Teagan Kelley's body was in a pretty awful state when we found him. It looks like somebody went to a lot of trouble to make sure he was dead." Monroe continued, undaunted. "He was beaten to death before they carved his face up like a Thanksgiving Turkey. That's a lot of rage."

He flipped open a report and read from it. "The ME called it a 'Glasgow Smile.' That's a calling card for a particular organization here in South Boston, one that you seem to be affiliated with."

"It sounds a lot like you're accusing me of something, detectives, so I won't be saying anything without my lawyer."

Monroe shrugged. "Play it your way, Mr. McTiernan—we can either do this here or down at the station." The detective eyed me up and down. "But we'll be needing to talk to both of you."

Now there was a little flare of anger. "My wife has nothing to do with this."

"I beg to differ—witnesses place her at the scene as well."

"She's not going anywhere, not in her condition. You don't have probable cause. No judge would allow that."

Monroe merely shrugged, and switched tactics. "The security officers at the hospital that day mentioned there was quite a bit of blood, Mr. McTiernan. You were practically covered in it."

"My wife was bleeding."

"And why was that?"

"That's private medical information, and I'm not required to give that to you without a court order. Your warrant doesn't cover it."

"We can get it amended."

"Then do so."

The rapid-fire volley was making my head spin, and I was not nearly as controlled in my anger as Connor. After everything we'd gone through, everything we both had gone through, they were looking to place the murder of my attacker on Connor's shoulders and make him pay for it.

Monroe was watching me carefully. "Is there something wrong, Mrs. McTiernan? You look upset."

I clenched my jaw. Connor could be as coolly collected as he liked, but my anger—and my hormones—were flaring.

"I'm pregnant, I'm tired, and my feet hurt, and there are two cops currently sitting in my living room, grilling my husband," I snapped. "Exactly how should I look right now?"

Connor held up his hand just as Grady came back into the room with the other detective. "Look—I already told you I'm not speaking without my lawyer present, and this is borderline harassment. My wife's health is fragile, and you're upsetting her."

"Then you can tell your lawyer to meet us down at the precinct. Let's go."

Channing moved to my side, and Connor drew me behind him immediately. For a long moment, everyone seemed to freeze, the tension sitting heavy in the air and threatening to crush me. I wasn't really sure what was happening—it seemed like there was a second conversation being held by the four men, one I wasn't privy to.

A muscle ticked in Connor's jaw. "You don't need to talk to my wife. She had nothing to do with it."

"And how is that?"

A long pause, and Connor spoke.

"Because I killed him. I killed Teagan Kelley."

My heart stopped. What was he doing?

None of this made sense. Why was he doing this? Even Grady looked shocked, his eyes wide and mouth slack as he watched Connor release my hand and step towards the detectives.

"Boss..." Grady said quietly, but Connor put his hand up, halting him in place.

Monroe's eyes slid between the three of us, unsure of whether this was some kind of act, perhaps even a trap. "You're admitting that you killed Teagan Kelley in cold blood?"

"He had it coming. Now, unless you want to arrest me, I'm done answering questions until we get to the station," Connor said, his voice firm and serious. "But my wife stays here."

Again, they looked at each other, seemingly taken off guard by the turn of events. Finally, Monroe reached towards his belt and pulled out his cuffs.

"Connor McTiernan, you are under arrest for the murder of Teagan Kelley."

I stared in disbelief as the door to the Penthouse swung closed. The door through which Connor had just been led, handcuffed and flanked by two detectives.

The silence was deafening.

I stood there, frozen to the spot, my mind blank and my face numb as I tried to process the events of the past thirty minutes. Dimly, I could hear Grady cursing in the background. He was saying something to me, but I paid him no mind.

"You don't need to talk to my wife, she had nothing to do with it."

"...I killed him. I killed Teagan Kelley."

"Connor McTiernan, you are under arrest for the murder of Teagan Kelley."

I could still hear his reassurances ringing in my ears, his voice steady and his tone sure, but underneath lurked something desperate and afraid.

"I love you, Cass...No matter what happens, never forget that. I love you both so much."

My lips were still tingling from that final, crushing kiss, the one that said more than all of Connor's last words did.

Something was very, very wrong, and I had a pretty good idea what.

Grady was guiding me to the sofa as if I were made of porcelain, so badly chipped and cracked that one more nudge would shatter me into a thousand pieces. I let him—I understood his concern—but I felt anything but fragile in that moment.

I felt incensed. I felt alive. I felt angry. After everything we had gone through, everything we had now, the future that we had both dreamed about—it was not meant to end like this.

And like hell was I going to allow it to.

Grady was still talking. "Everything's going to be okay, Mrs. McTiernan. I'm getting Cohen on the phone right now, we're going to take care of this. Don't you worry—"

"Grady, for fuck's sake, call me Cassidy. And put your phone away. There's nothing Cohen can do. Connor doesn't need a lawyer, he needs his brothers."

Grady just stared at me, jaw slack.

I took several deep breaths, calming myself. "They were dirty cops, Grady. They're working for Moretti."

"H-How—"

"Where'd you dispose of the bodies? Teagan and the others from that night?"

Grady frowned at my directness. "We, uh...we've got kindofa deal goin' with a fishing boat Captain. He dumped 'em way out in the bay—too deep to risk a scalloper dredging 'em up."

"...and didn't the detectives say they had Kelley's body?" I asked patiently.

The pieces were all starting to click together, almost faster than I could keep up with. Cops from Beacon Hill, close to where Moretti kept a summer home. One would only hazard to guess he had his hooks in the local police department, and probably some of the local boys here as well. That was how my father and Callum had operated, why not Moretti?

Grady cursed. "Yeah, they did."

I leaned forward and grabbed his arm, trying to telegraph my urgency. "Grady, I know Connor. I know that look in his eyes, the one he gets when he's determined to do something, no matter the cost. Those cops were trying to take us both, but Connor fell on his sword and confessed so they would only take him instead."

Grady' eyes widened. "I knew something was going on! The one looked like he was just itching to pull his gun, and they were both sweatin' bullets ever since they walked through that door. Once Connor confessed, they had no legal reason to bring you in."

I nodded, glad we were finally on the same page.

"Grady, get Alfie up here. Start making the calls, we're going to need everybody for this one. I don't know where to even begin looking for him, and we've already lost precious time."

I didn't even hesitate, pulling up the number. All of our history, all of our differences—none of them mattered now, not when Connor's life was on the line. I pressed the call button, breath stilled as I waited for him to pick up.

"Cass? What's going on?"

"Tommy, I need you. Now."

21

— · —

ALFIE

THE CHEERY SOUND OF a ringing phone bore through my skull as I groggily opened my eyes, my vision blurry and disoriented. Pain throbbed through my body, every nerve ending on fire as if a thousand knives were stabbing me all at once. It took me a moment to fully comprehend where I was - Lady D's, our bar/safe house turned makeshift infirmary.

"Christ," I muttered under my breath, wincing as I attempted to sit up. Involuntarily, my hand flew to my rib cage to steady myself, each breath sawing in and out with excruciating pain.

The ringing continued insistently, and I remembered what woke me. Emilia. I fumbled for my phone for an embarrassingly long moment before I realized that the ringing wasn't coming from my cell phone. It was coming from the landline at Lady D's.

So, not Emilia.

Looking around me, I realized that I couldn't find my phone anywhere. I checked the time on the clock near the couch and cursed. I had only meant to close my eyes for an hour or two, but I'd slept the entire night away.

And still no word from Emilia.

What had happened? With Luca out of the picture--I refused to believe that big tough bastard was dead--there was no way she would have gone through with the rest of our plan. No way. It would be too dangerous. Emilia was strong and stubborn, but she was smart. She wouldn't have risked it.

Would she?

Unbidden, the image of Emilia laid out on her bed, skin pale and eyes closed in a deathlike sleep pushed into my mind. Christ, this plan was so risky--why had I agreed to it? I trusted Cassidy with my life, but my half of the plan had divebombed spectacularly, and if Emilia decided to go through with her end without Luca to help her...

No. I couldn't go down that road.

I needed to figure out what was going on.

Downstairs, the bar blessedly fell silent as the phone stopped ringing, only to pick up again a moment later.

"Will somebody answer the goddamn phone?" I yelled. And, while we were on the subject, where the hell was my phone?

I was still looking for it when Sloane rapped on the doorframe. "We need you downstairs."

"I'm busy." Trying not to panic, I ripped the cushions from the couch, but still no phone. "Get Grady instead."

"That's him on the phone. He says that Connor was just arrested for Teag's murder."

My mind short-circuited. "What? Why? Where's Tommy--"

I finally looked at Sloane, and the question died in my throat. Sloane was one of the most solid people I've ever seen, and she'd never looked this shaken up.

"He was on his way here with Michael when the cops pulled them over. They arrested Tommy, too."

"Skip and Mary?"

"Yep."

Shit. The pieces clicked together, then, slowly but surely, as my brain attempted to process what had happened. It was far too much of a coincidence for the cops to pick them both up within hours of each other. This thing smelled like a setup.

"Where are they now?" I asked. Gasping as my ribs shifted, I clenched my jaw against the pain and pulled on my boots, although tying the damn things nearly killed me. "Has Cohen been in contact?"

Sloane followed me down the hall. "I haven't heard back from him yet. Callum's called everybody back to home base, it's all hands on deck. Grady's driving Cassidy." When I turned at her and frowned, she elaborated. "The police tried to bring her in along with Connor for questioning, but Connor confessed to the murder before they could put cuffs on her."

"Confessed?"

"Let himself be taken, more like. Cassidy was furious," Sloane continued. "Grady said that he did it to make sure they wouldn't take her, too."

"That self-sacrificing idiot," I muttered. I wouldn't blame Cassidy for being livid. I would have done the same thing myself, albeit a little less gracefully.

We finally reached the bottom of the steps that emptied out into the main bar area. Grady had closed the place, waiting for us, and the bar was packed with soldiers, trying to track the incoming leads and information. I managed to push my way through the crowd until I reached the heart of the action where Callum and Michael were holding court.

"Somebody get me the badge numbers of those cops, I want Cohen on the phone with their precinct now," Callum barked at Grady. "And get a tail on them, I don't want either of them within fifty feet of a holding cell."

"You got it, Boss." Grady nodded, gesturing to me. "Alfie."

"Do we have any way of figuring out which precinct took them in?" I asked.

Callum answered. "We have intel that it was Beacon Hill. If they're working with Moretti, then he'll probably have both Connor and Tommy under 24-hour surveillance. Call in your favors with Cohen, we need to get one of our guys on him so he can pay cash under the table to his contacts in the department and get the case records unsealed."

"The first priority is getting them out of holding, with minimal exposure." Michael frowned. "You heard what they tried to pull with Cassidy, those pigs are more crooked than an infield grounder."

"You've got that right," Callum agreed. "Right now, they're working in a vacuum, assuming there's no connection between our two families. It keeps us off their radar, which is how we're going to take them down. And if by chance they show their hand, we can work our way through using Alfie's channels. They might not be as fast as using Cohen, but they'll allow us to save face and get our boys back."

He turned to me. "Alfie, who do you have on the inside? We're gonna need to know who our players are, whether they're Moretti's or not."

Cassidy pushed her way towards us. "We don't have time for that. They're not going to the police station, Moretti already has them--"

"Cassidy, sit down," Michael barked.

"Take it easy on her, will you?" I rounded on Michael. "She's right, we don't have time for this." I was thinking about Emilia, but I was also thinking that Cassidy was probably right.

"Look, sweetheart, there's not a lot we can do for Connor or your brother right now, okay? I promise you we're doing everything we can," Callum said calmly.

"You're not listening! Even before I called you--" she cut herself off with a shake of her head. "You and your egos, can't even hear my brother and Connor are already in a shit situation--"

"Don't be ridiculous--"

"Enough! If the two of you don't take your heads out of your asses long enough to let me talk I will go in there and sort it out myself."

Michael turned to Sloane. "Take her to the back room and get her to calm down."

"Do not treat me like some wilting female." Cassidy rounded on her father, unleashing the full fury of a pregnant mama bear protecting her own. "The same arrogance that causes you to sit around here instead of actually doing something has landed Connor and my brother in some serious fucking trouble, and probably Emilia, as well. If you think I'm going to stand by and just watch, you are sadly mistaken."

Michael narrowed his eyes, but he said nothing. Callum stared at her in disbelief. "Just what exactly do you propose we do, girl?"

There was steel in Cassidy's voice as she replied. "We're going to get my husband and my brother back." She looked at me with the same promise in her eyes. "Emilia, too."

"Leave Emilia to me," I said.

Watching them argue, I'd made a decision. There were too many people involved now, and if I was going to help Emilia, I was going to need to do it alone. A full-scale assault wasn't going to cut it. She was in more danger than any of us realized, and with Luca's fate uncertain, there was nothing to stop her from going through with the rest of the plan. It wasn't in Emilia's nature to simply stay out of the fray.

Especially not when those she loved were in danger.

"Alfie, please," Sloane pleaded, her hands on my shoulders in an attempt to keep me grounded. "We're doing everything we can."

Cassidy and Sloane exchanged a glance, their eyes filled with concern and understanding. I knew they meant well, but it wasn't enough. I needed to see Emilia with my own eyes, to hold her in my arms and ensure her safety.

"Give me your phone," I demanded, my voice hoarse but firm.

Sloane handed me my phone with resignation. "I'll cover for you," she said. "I don't think I can stop you even if I tried."

"Thanks," I muttered, accepting the gesture of trust for what it was – an olive branch. I swiped my thumb across the screen, pulling up the dial pad and punching in her number with trembling fingers. I pressed the phone to my ear, my breath hitching as I waited for the familiar sound of her voice on the other end.

"Come on, Emilia," I whispered, my chest tightening with each ring that echoed through the receiver. The anticipation clawed at my insides, threatening to unravel me completely. "Please pick up."

"What if she doesn't answer?" Sloane asked, her brow furrowed with worry. She was trying to be supportive, but her words felt like a punch to the gut.

"Then I'll keep calling until she does," I snapped back, my frustration boiling over. "She has to be okay. She just has to."

"Alfie, I understand how you feel, but—"

"Shh!" I hissed, cutting her off as the ringing rolled over to voicemail. "She didn't pick up," I gritted out. "I need to find her, Sloane."

"Where are you going?" Sloane called out as I snatched my keys and walked towards the door.

"To do what I should have done a long time ago," I said as I wrenched the front door to Lady D's open. "I'm going to get my girl."

22

— · —

EMILIA

"COME ON, PICK UP. Pick up."

I kept waiting for the familiar sound of Alfie's low, rumbling voice, but my phone just kept ringing. I'd already lost track of how many times I'd called his phone. Wherever he was, it probably wasn't somewhere he had a good cell signal, but just the same I felt my nerves grow more frayed with each unanswered call.

The worst part was, I couldn't even ask Luca to check in on him. Julian still hadn't returned with news.

He knew. He knew that Luca was dead. It was the only explanation for how long he'd been gone. I sent up a prayer, hoping against hope that my best friend had survived, but the longer Julian stayed away, the more my hope ebbed away .

I paced back to the window and looked out. The compound's front gate was locked, and it looked like Lorenzo had tripled the guards. They were stationed every 50 feet, sweeping the entire fence line every 15 minutes. I'd tried to listen in to their radio conversations to see if I could find out what was happening, but I'd only managed to catch snatches. Every single one of them was armed.

No way was I getting out unobserved.

Nothing had changed since I last looked, of course. Everything was hopelessly locked down, and there was no way I was getting past the front gate. Not with Lorenzo having doubled the guard.

"Emilia? What are you doing?"

I spun on my heel at the sound of Sofia's voice, clapping the curtain shut in a futile effort to hide my snooping. "Sofia! What are you doing?"

"What am I doing? What are you doing?" She gestured towards me with the tray in her hands. "I brought you dinner."

"I can't eat now, are you kidding me? Alfie's out there somewhere and Luca is hurt, and--"

"What are you talking about?" Sofia's grip tightened on the tray, and she spoke slowly as if to a child. "Emilia...Alfie...he's--"

"He's not dead," I snapped. I yanked her the rest of the way into the room, ignoring her yelp of surprise when the glass of wine slopped over the rim.

Luca and I had agreed not to bring Sofia in on our plan. It wasn't that she wasn't trustworthy, it was that she was far too impulsive, not to mention young. What we had planned was dangerous and possibly deadly, and Luca had been adamant that she be kept out of it.

Now, however, I had little choice but to let her in. I needed an ally badly.

As I told her about our plan, Sofia's eyes progressively grew wider and wider until they looked in imminent danger of popping right out of her head. When I finished, she was uncharacteristically quiet, a look of soft hurt on her face.

"You were just going to...leave? And not say anything?" I opened my mouth to speak, but she cut me off. "No, it's even worse than that, isn't it? I would've thought you were dead--"

"Sofia, it's not like that--"

"Yes it is! You were going to let me think you were dead. I can't believe you." She stood suddenly. "Were you ever going to tell me, or was that just going to be it? I thought we were friends, Emilia, I--you're like a sister to me."

Sofia's voice broke on the last word, and I felt the sting of guilt all the way to my core. She looked so much younger than she was at that moment, young and so full of hurt that I couldn't help pulling her into a hug. I was so relieved when she softened and leaned into me instead of pulling away.

"Sofia, I'm sorry. I wasn't thinking about anything other than getting away."

"It's all right," she sniffed and pulled away. "I probably would've done the same thing. I'm still mad at you, though."

"And I'm still sorry." I looked around the four walls of the room that had become my prison cell. "Although you're in on it now, whether I like it or not."

Sofia sat on the bed, hugging her legs up to her chest. "What are you going to do? What about--"

A knock on the door startled us both before the key turned in the lock, and the door cracked open.

Sofia's brother Julian was tall and slenderly built, but he moved with the grace of a feral cat. With his dark olive skin and thick wavy hair, it was easy to see the family resemblance. He was more serious than Luca, rarely cracking a smile, but his level-headedness and cool grace evened out Angel's volatile temper, making him a valuable addition to the Moretti capos.

But I could tell just by looking at his face that something was wrong.

I had to swallow twice before I managed to get the words out. "Is Luca alive?"

"He is...for now. But he's badly wounded, and we're not sure if he's going to make it."

The blood drained from my face as I took in the news. "What happened?"

"He caught a ricochet to the face that fractured his skull. The damage was...extensive. They've got him on a ventilator to keep him breathing, but there's no telling when he's going to wake up again, if ever."

"Oh my God." Sofia gasped, her hands flying up to cover her mouth. "Luca."

I nodded, too numb with shock to speak. My knees buckled, and I sank down onto the bed beside Sofia, her arm coming around my shoulders to steady me. Luca had been with me through so much, even before this entire mess had started, and the thought of losing him made my chest ache. I hadn't realized until then how much I had come to rely on him. He wasn't just my best friend, he was like the older brother I'd never had, a steadying, constant presence that I needed in my life.

And he'd gotten hurt trying to help me.

"Can I see him?" Sofia asked. "Can you take me?"

Julian's face softened. "We're on lockdown. I'm sorry."

She shook her head, then buried her head in her hands. I pulled her to my side and stroked her back, fighting back tears myself.

"I'm sorry, ladies," Julian said quietly. "I'll let you know when there's any news."

The door closed behind him, and the finality of it made my stomach twist.

"Emilia, what are we going to do?" Sofia asked, looking at me with fear in her eyes. "If Luca--"

"We have to go."

"I can't just leave Luca," Sofia said. "Not when he's like this. If he wakes up..."

"We can't do anything for him sitting around like this, and I won't be able to find Alfie and help him if we're stuck in this room," I argued. "We need to go."

Sofia chewed her lip. "There's no way I'm getting out of here, and you can't either."

My eyes fell to my bed, to where I'd hidden Luca's syringe beneath the mattress. The one he'd given me after he promised me he'd be with me the whole way. It was still there, nestled safely in its little pocket, the vial of toxin inside.

It was going to be risky, but I didn't have any other choice.

I pulled it from its hiding place and held it up. Sofia's eyes went wide. "What the hell is that?"

"Our way out," I said, my mouth set in a determined line. "But I'm going to need your help."

23

CONNOR

My arms were pulled firmly behind me, the cuffs locking shut with an ominous click.

"It's gonna be okay, Cass. Everything's going to be fine." I stared at my wife's bloodless face, trying my hardest to reassure her despite the lie that sat heavily in my mouth.

At some point during the last twenty minutes, it had dawned on me that while Monroe and Channing may be legitimate detectives from Beacon Hill, they were most certainly dirty. And if they were trying to get Cass and me out from under our security, then they most likely had been paid off by Moretti.

It was brilliant, I had to admit. Bribing a judge and a couple of cops to gain entry, forcibly removing us from our own home.

I realized it as soon as the pair insisted on taking us both in. Channing's hand kept twitching towards his holster, and both men were on edge, even though they had the upper hand. Grady was the only one carrying—I hadn't carried a weapon in my own home since Cassidy's abduction.

But even if I had, there was no way I would have acted on it. No way I would have gotten into a shootout with two cops and risk Cassidy getting hit by a stray bullet.

The tension had built up, thrumming like a live wire. Monroe and Channing were leaving there with somebody, but at least I could make sure Cassidy wasn't going with them.

My stomach had plummeted as I realized it.

This was it. This was the moment. My second chance at redemption—a second chance to keep her safe, permanently, because I knew I would never make it to the precinct. They would take me straight to Moretti.

I could save her from that. I might be walking out that door to my own death, but I would be walking into the same room as Moretti.

And if I was going down, that Italian bastard was coming with me.

I had barely registered their words as the cuffs slid home. False reassurances were uttered, as convincing as I could make them under the circumstances—I had always been a good liar.

But underneath, I was taking my last look. Memorizing her features. The way her hair was shining in the afternoon light. The soft curve of her lips and the precise color of her eyes, wide with shock but still full of so much love for me that it took my breath away.

I drank her in, from top of her hair right down to the firm curve of her belly where our son grew, a son I would never live to see.

And that was okay. I had blood on my hands that would never come clean, and this was as close to heaven as I would ever get.

If my last act on this earth was to keep them both safe, then so be it.

Cass had tried to reach for me, but the detectives blocked her. "I-I'll call Callum, Connor, we'll get ahold of the lawyer. It's going to be okay."

I nodded tightly, not trusting myself to speak further. The detectives started to turn me towards the exit, but at the last moment, Cassidy surged forward, and I almost lost my composure when her lips crashed into mine in a bruising kiss.

"I love you, Cass," I choked, my teeth clenched. "No matter what happens, never forget that. I love you both so much."

"I love you too—"

Monroe grabbed me by the arm and jerked me away from her. The last thing I saw before the detectives dragged me out the door was Cassidy standing there, both hands twisting together while Grady hovered at her elbow.

Then the door shut, and she was lost to me.

Not a word was said as the detectives muscled me past a stunned doorman and into the waiting unmarked cruiser. I watched over my shoulder as our building grew smaller and smaller, until we turned a corner and it was lost from view.

I noted wryly that we were headed north.

"Hate to tell you this, boys, but the precinct is the other way."

"Shut up."

I sighed. "I think we can cut the crap now—we all know you're not taking me in."

Silence from up front. That was okay, though. Now that it was actually happening, I was calm. Calculating my plan, analyzing my options. I was walking straight into the fire now, and if I was going to pull this off, I would need my wits about me.

We drove on for quite some time, and the sun was dipping below the buildings before the cruiser ducked into an alley and pulled to a stop.

My door was opened, and I was pulled from the back. A black Mercedes was parked further down the alley, partially hidden in the shadows.

I didn't recognize the men who stepped out, but this was the North End, so I had little doubt as to who they were. One circled around behind me, and my suspicions were confirmed when the second one spoke.

"Thanks boys, we'll be in touch." He grinned at me. "You're a tough man to get a hold of, McTiernan, but even you aren't untouchable. Moretti has some unfinished business with you."

"Then let's go see him together."

The man just smiled unpleasantly. Too late, I heard swift movement behind me.

Pain rocketed though my skull as the butt of a gun made contact with my temple, and darkness claimed me.

24

— · —

ALFIE

THE STREETS OF BOSTON blurred past my window, a canvas smeared with the golden hues of streetlights and the deep blues of the encroaching night. I tapped the steering wheel, my fingers drumming a nervous rhythm as I navigated through the city's veins. The anticipation and anxiety gnawed at me like a hungry beast, threatening to shred my sanity, and every mile closer to my destination only served to ratchet up the tension coiled within me.

I hadn't been this far north in weeks, but I remembered the route by heart. There was no way I would ever forget, not in a million years. It was ingrained in my DNA, burned into my memory like a scar on my heart.

I wasn't sure what I would find there—if I would even be able to find her—but I had to try. I had to see for myself that she was okay.

The silence in the car was a pressing thing, heavy with my own hammering thoughts until it was shattered by the insistent ring of Sloane's phone.

I glanced down at the screen. Cassidy.

"Hey."

"Where are you?" There was something off in her voice, a tremble that wasn't like her. Cassidy was a rock, unshakable. But now, she sounded like she was one push away from crumbling.

"Headed to Emilia's. Is everything alright?" I asked, even though I knew damn well everything was far from alright. You don't survive in the Irish mob without learning to read the undercurrents of fear in a person's voice. And right now, Cassidy's voice was an undertow threatening to drag me under.

"Alfie, it's... you need to come back to Lady D's—" Her words cut through me, but before she could finish, I interrupted.

"I can't--I'm almost there. I'll call you back once I've seen her, okay?"

The pause on the other end of the line was profound. "Alfie, please, I need you to come back."

"Just tell me what's going on."

She exhaled slowly, a weighted silence that seemed to choke the air itself. "It's Emilia..." Cassidy hesitated, the next words quivered out of her, "She's gone, Alfie."

"Gone?" I shook my head even though she couldn't see it. "You're not making any sense. What do you mean she's--"

"She's dead, Alfie."

Something was wrong with my lungs, the air refusing to go very deep, not quite getting past the pressure building in my chest. "You're wrong. She's fine, she's just...She's not--"

"Her body was found this morning." Her voice was softer now, gentle and quiet, as if she were afraid speaking too loudly would shatter me. "She must have tried to go ahead with our plan on her own, without a safety net. Without someone to help her reverse the effects, the toxin would have been fatal. Or, I don't know, maybe wires got crossed. The shootout in the alley was a mess. Without Luca to verify your safety, without being able to contact you, she might have thought...that you were gone. And it was too much for her to bear."

"No. Emilia wouldn't kill herself. There's some kind of mistake, you don't--" I coughed, tightening my grip on the steering wheel with hands that had suddenly gone numb. Vaguely, I was aware of shaking my head, over and over. "You're *wrong*. You don't understand."

"Alfie, I'm so sorry," Cassidy whispered, her sorrow palpable even through the phone.

"Wrong!" I roared into the phone, the denial a raging beast within me. Emilia couldn't be dead. The idea was absurd, unacceptable. My world tilted, reality fraying at the edges as I fought against the tidal wave of impossibility.

"Alfie, please—"

"Stop," I cut her off, my voice cracking like thin ice beneath heavy boots. "Just stop." My foot pressed harder on the accelerator, the car responding with a surge of power that mirrored the chaotic storm inside me.

"Alfie," Cassidy's voice came through the phone once more, heavy with sorrow. "Lorenzo Moretti himself called Callum. He's declared a vendetta against the McTiernan Clan."

"No. No, no, no."

"It's not safe for you to be driving right now," she continued. "Tell us where you are, we'll send someone to pick you up."

I couldn't, wouldn't believe it. It was a lie. It had to be. Because if it wasn't, then what? Then I was just a man speeding toward a ghost, a memory of something beautiful and untouchable. But as long as there was a shred of doubt, I'd cling to it with bloodied fingers.

"Tell me you're lying," I demanded, the streetlights casting frantic shadows across the interior as I took another corner too fast.

"Listen to me!" Cassidy's voice sharpened with urgency. "Lorenzo has declared war. He blames us. Emilia...she's gone."

My world stopped, a heart-stopping jolt as if I'd hit an unseen wall. "No," I breathed, the single word a denial, a plea, a prayer.

"Alfie, I'm so sorry."

"Stop saying that," I growled. "She's fine. We had a plan, Luca's going to help..."

Except Luca wasn't there.

Was he.

The phone slipped from my fingers and clattered to the floor as I wrenched the wheel, tires screeching.

She couldn't be gone. I wouldn't believe it.

I raced towards the compound, heart pounding. It had to be a lie.

Please God let it be a lie.

But prayers don't stop the relentless march of time, nor do they reverse the irreversible.

The stately wrought iron gates came into view. There was a commotion by the gate, a small crowd gathered, blocking the road. I pulled over as soon as I could, ignoring the horns from the cars I'd cut off. . I pulled up, keeping the car hidden from view as my hands trembled on the wheel, a cold sweat breaking out across my forehead. Light slotted through the mansion's windows, winking cheerily against the encroaching night.

But in front, red and blue lights flashed. An ambulance was parked at the curb, rear doors open.

No.

Taking a few shaky breaths, I stepped out of the car, keeping to the shadows as I approached the ambulance. No sirens pierced the night air; they only use those for the living. The realization hit me like a freight train, but still, I pressed on, fueled by a desperate need to know the truth.

A man in a police uniform was directing a pair of paramedics as they wheeled a gurney towards the waiting ambulance. A white sheet was draped over the body strapped to it, concealing the face of the victim.

It can't be her.

Please God, let it not be her.

I was halfway across the street, moving slowly as if in a dream, when one of the paramedics lifted the sheet to slip an ID bracelet over the victim's wrist.

I couldn't see the face, but I could see the hand. A small, pale thing, the nails painted a glossy pink.

I knew those hands.

No.

The sidewalk tilted. I stumbled, my knees threatening to buckle, the world narrowing to a pinprick. My lungs refused to take in air, my throat constricting as I fought to breathe through a white-hot haze of agony.

I watched as they lifted the body into the back of the ambulance. From the house emerged a slender, miniature version of Emilia, so alike that my heart stopped beating completely for a moment before I recognized the girl as Emilia's younger cousin, Sofia. She was flanked by a taller man who looked enough alike her to be some kind of relation, his arm curled around her shoulders protectively.

Sofia was weeping.

"I'm sorry, Emilia..." Her voice, broken by grief, reached out and latched onto my heart with icy fingers as she placed a trembling hand on the shroud.

That touch, so tender and full of despair, shattered something inside me. My knees betrayed me, folding like a house of cards in a gust of wind. The concrete was unforgiving beneath me, but the physical pain was nothing compared to the maelstrom that tore through my chest.

Gone.

My heart, my everything—gone.

Darkness descended, a grief so profound it stole my breath, but still, I clung to it, a drowning man refusing to let go of the very thing that threatened to drag him under.

Emilia was gone, because I had failed her.

As the cold wind whipped up the street, I couldn't help but think of the last time I'd seen Emilia. Her laughter, her warmth, the way she could make even the darkest situation seem bearable. And now, all that was left was this hollow emptiness where she used to be. God, what she must have gone through those last few minutes. What she must have felt. The images flashed in rapid succession—a life we could have had, moments we should have shared—all torn away in the cruelest twist of fate. I had promised to save her, to be her unexpected knight in ink-stained armor.

But I had failed. We had both become victims of a war neither of us wanted.

She was gone. My Emilia, with her sharp wit and her gentle eyes, who had seen through my facade and touched a part of me no one else had ever reached. She was gone, believing I'd left this world first.

"Emilia," I said again, her name a prayer, a plea, a goodbye. "I should've been there for you," I whispered, my voice trembling under my guilt. "I should've protected you from all of this." But it was too late for apologies, too late for anything. All that remained was the crushing weight of guilt, the knowing that when she needed me most, I wasn't there.

Staggering to my feet, I somehow made my way back to the car, fumbling like a blind man through a whitewash of tears for the door handle. Instead, my ass found the curb. The confirmation of her death hit me; it wasn't a punch—it was a wrecking ball to the gut. My insides hollowed out, leaving behind a gaping chasm where once the spark of hope had flickered.

"Jesus Christ, Emilia..." The words broke, fractured by the sobs that wracked my frame. I pressed my palms into my eyes, trying to hold back the deluge, but the tears came anyway, hot and relentless. They carved tracks down my cheeks, a stark contrast to the blood that had dried on my knuckles.

"Why?" The question hung in the air, absurd and grotesque in its futility. "Why couldn't you have just waited?"

The laughter we'd shared, the way her eyes lit up when she talked about her beloved books, the feel of her skin against mine—all of it was now seared into me as an eternal torment. A life sentence in a world drained of color, of light, without Emilia Russo.

"Fuck!" The word exploded from me, a strangled cry of rage at the cruel twist of fate that had brought us together only to rip us apart.

I punched the side of the car. A sob tore from my throat, raw and primal. I leaned forward, elbows on knees, head cradled in my hands as I struggled to breathe through the onslaught of memories. The last time I saw her, the promise in her smile, the way she said my name—it was all a cruel joke now. A bitter end to a story that should've been written in the stars, not scrawled in blood and tears.

"Never thought I'd pray for anything," I muttered, the irony not lost on me. But if there was any mercy left in this godforsaken world, I prayed that at the end she'd known just how much she meant to me, that she was my beginning and now my end.

I should have been there for her. I should have taken her away from all this.

But the time for regrets was gone, along with Emilia. All that remained now was a burning desire for justice. Lorenzo Moretti would pay for his part in this tragedy – of that, I was certain.

The vibration was a dull sensation against the numbness that had settled over me. It took a moment to register that the insistent buzzing in my hand was Sloane's phone, Cassidy on the other end of a call I didn't want to take. My thumb hovered over the screen, a useless appendage disconnected from a mind that screamed for it not to move. But I answered it anyway.

"Alfie, you need to come back. Now."

"Can't," I rasped out, staring through blurred vision at the Moretti compound. The place where love went to die, and with it, a piece of my soul.

"Alfie, please." Cassidy's voice trembled, mirroring the shivering wreck of a man I'd become. "We need to figure this out together. You can't be alone now."

"Alone?" I scoffed, a bitter laugh escaping my lips. "I've been alone since the moment they took her away from me. The rest... it's just echoes of a life that doesn't exist anymore."

"Damn it, Alfie! This isn't just about you!" Her voice cracked. "This is war. Emilia—"

"Stop!" I shouted into the night, the name like a knife twisting in my gut. "Don't say her name. Don't you dare."

Silence fell between us, a chasm as wide as the one that had opened up inside me. I knew Cassidy cared, in her own way—a way tangled up in duty and shared bloodshed. But this... This was beyond comfort, beyond reason.

"Alfie," she said again, softer this time. "Please."

"Fine," I muttered after an eternity, the word tasting like ash in my mouth. "I'm coming."

"Be careful," she added, but I hardly heard her. My eyes were glued to the place where my world ended, the lights of the ambulance painting everything with strokes of morbid reality.

I cut the call and shoved the phone back into my pocket, rising from the curb with the grace of a marionette whose strings had been snipped. My steps were unsteady, fueled by a grief that staggered under the weight of vengeance. One last look at the Moretti compound, the house that would forever haunt me, and I turned my back on it.

I wouldn't let my grief consume me. Not yet. There were battles yet to fight, enemies to face, and a vendetta declared against my clan.

For Emilia, for the love we shared, for the life we could've had... I would stand and fight.

25

CASSIDY

LADY D's WAS A ZOO.

True to his word, my father had called in all the troops—all of them. I could hear them downstairs. The angry murmurs, the click of magazines sliding home. The scent of the cigarette smoke and the tension, the anger that was palatable even through the closed door. It was like being transported back in time, sheltered in a far-off room with my mother while reality played out just beyond the doorframe.

Upstairs, Callum's office had become my sanctuary. I sat cross-legged on the overstuffed chair, a strangely comfortable position given my belly, and looked out over the city. Watching the twinkling lights. They were almost mesmerizing in their consistency, a never-ending parade of traffic up Bolton Street, centering me and drawing my focus away from the frightening questions that threatened to creep in at the edges.

Wondering where Connor was amongst all those flickering lights. Wondering where he was, because I absolutely refused to believe he was already dead.

Deep breaths. In for four, hold, and out for six, just like Ginny had taught me. Clearing my mind. Allowing the calm—and, hopefully, the solution—to enter.

Sloane hovered in the wings, anxious but unwavering in her support. I felt a new surge of appreciation for her, bringing me the herbal tea Dr. Whittley had recommended and keeping the outside noise to a bare minimum. Speaking calm, soothing words despite her own fears.

Neither of us mentioned Alfie. The man had been a wreck, a broken shell of himself as he stumbled in and collapsed on the sofa. He'd barely spoken a word since, and the pain in his eyes was so tangible that it physically hurt to look at him. To see someone who had always made his way through life with a crooked, mischievous grin on his face and a sarcastic comment or two at the ready reduced to a shadow of himself. Someone who would never laugh again. Never smile.

Emila's death had claimed two souls tonight.

And I was desperately worried the rest of Alfie would follow.

I knew what he was going through, better than most. The way it felt to be ripped apart from the inside out, the bottomless chasm of despair that opened up inside you, threatening to swallow me whole. I'd felt that loss, too, once and I knew it was the kind of pain that never went away.

But as much as my heart went out to Alfie, I couldn't afford to wallow in my own grief. Not when so many lives were on the line.

Not when my husband's life depended on me keeping it together.

Connor. Just thinking his name sent a fresh wave of anxiety through me. I hadn't heard from him since he'd been arrested. Where was he? Was he safe?

I tried to push the worry down, to keep it contained in a little box in the back of my mind, but it wouldn't stay there. It was like an insistent fly, buzzing around my head, reminding me with every beat of my heart that Connor might be gone. That if we didn't act quickly enough, he would be gone.

"Michael—come over here." That was Callum's voice, and even through the closed door, I heard the anger there. The room erupted, and Sloane quickly walked to the door, peering out into the hallway. Something was happening.

"Sloane, what is it?" I asked.

Sloane stood at the doorway for a long moment, listening. "They've got a location on Connor."

"Alive?"

Connor can't be dead. He can't be dead. I can't lose him—

"He's alive. Callum was sent a picture."

"What?"

"Moretti sent a picture of Connor to Callum's phone."

Alarm bells were going off in my head. Every fear was banished as I latched onto that one fact—one that felt all too familiar.

Carefully, I stood and brushed past Sloane. The assembled men parted like the Red Sea before me, startled by my presence. An almost hushed reverence fell over the room as I approached the two bosses.

"Let me see it," I demanded.

"Cassidy, no—you don't want to see this." Callum started to protest, but I snatched the phone from his hand.

It was just as Sloane had said. A picture of Connor. Alive.

He was tied to a chair, duct tape over his mouth, but even with the poor quality of light, I could see the blood running down the side of his face. Someone's hand was fisted in his hair, yanking his head back cruelly to face the camera. My stomach clenched to see him like that, and I had to tighten my grip on the phone to still the tremble that threatened to betray my fear.

It was his eyes—*his eyes*. They blazed with anger. The fiery determination of a man resigned to his fate, and an unspoken promise to take as many of his enemies as he could down with him when he fell. They were a promise, one that he intended to keep.

"W-What about Tommy?" I asked, dreading the answer.

"Nothing. That doesn't mean he's dead," Callum said reassuringly, although by the way Sloane paled, it was obvious she didn't share his optimism. "It just means they know Connor is the bigger bargaining chip."

Not a word was said as I looked down at the phone, but I didn't notice. My gaze had shifted from Connor to the faint outline of lettering behind him. I tried zooming in, but I couldn't make it out.

"It says Malick Processing," Grady said, turning a laptop around so I could see the screen. The image on the phone had been enhanced to show the faded lettering on the wall behind Connor. A couple taps of the keyboard, and he had an entire data sheet pulled up. "It's a meatpacking plant—a slaughterhouse. One that's now owned by one of Moretti's dummy corporations."

I blinked in confusion. "I thought slaughterhouses were banned in the city.

"No," Callum said tersely. "They tried. It looks like Moretti greased some palms and bought them all out—not surprising, it's a very lucrative business if you've got no scruples about sanitation or animal cruelty."

"So do you know where this building is?"

"South and Kneeland, down by the waterfront." He gestured to the men strapping up and checking weaponry. I hadn't even noticed.

My head was spinning. It seemed too easy.

"Wait. Something's not right."

"Cassidy, we'll handle this," Michael said. "There's nothing more for you to do."

"No! It's too easy!" My outburst had the whole room halting, and Sloane reached out to me worriedly. I hated to, but I shook her off. "It's too easy. Grady—how hard was it to render that image to read the sign?"

"Not very."

"Exactly. Why would they position him in front of a sign like that if they didn't want you to know exactly where he was? It's a trap."

Callum stood up now, his hands placating. "Look, just let us handle this. We'll—"

"No!" I took a deep breath, centering myself before I continued. "I was taken as bait—Tegan told me himself. Moretti never intended to make a deal with you, he just wanted to wipe you all out. He was just scared because you had the numbers, so he lured you into a trap. Why would this be any different? He fed you the location, and you're walking right into it!"

My father narrowed his eyes, but I saw he was listening. "She's right, Callum. It doesn't make sense. Moretti has been one step ahead of us this whole time, why would he slip up now?"

"It fits the pattern," Sloane added.

Callum chewed his lip, his gaze intense, but I held my ground. I knew I was right—I knew it—but I needed him to know it too. Finally, he nodded.

"Okay, Cass...okay." He looked over to where Alfie sat at the bar, staring into a recently emptied glass, his face unreadable. He seemed so far away from us, but I knew his mind was working overtime, plotting Moretti's death in a thousand different ways.

Callum saw it, too. "Hey, Doyle. You still have that Russian's number?"

"Misha," Alfie murmured. He carefully set the glass on the bar and turned. "Yeah, I've got his number. You calling in a favor?"

Callum grunted. "Patching up old wounds. Call the Russian, tell him to bring everything he's got. We're gonna light these fuckers up."

My blood ran cold. "What about Connor? He could still be inside."

Michael placed a reassuring hand on my shoulder. "We'll get him out, Cass. Grady's pulling up the old blueprints from the county surveyor's office. We'll know that place inside out and backwards before we move in. Once we know what we're dealing with, we can send in a team to extract them."

I didn't want to wait. I wanted to be in there with the rest of them, tearing the building apart until I found Connor. Until I could feel his arms around me again, safe and sound.

Magazines were loaded and weapons checked, the general noise level increasing as phone calls were made and orders were given. I'd never seen the Clan mobilize like this. They were efficient, almost businesslike as they prepared for battle.

It was strangely comforting.

Sloane was behind the bar, but instead of pouring shots, she was wielding two serious looking guns, checking the weapons with cool, efficient motions before loading them into a holster at the small of her back.

Callum frowned. "What the hell are you doing, Sloane? You're not coming."

"Connor and Tommy are my family." Sloane didn't even look up at him. "Just try to stop me."

The room was eerily quiet, all eyes on the exchange. Callum's face tightened, and I read the indecision playing across it. Finally, he sighed.

"You're not a fighter, Sloane. You're a bartender."

Sloane snorted. "I'm also the daughter of a soldier, and I've been around guns and war my whole life. I'm coming. Besides, you need someone to watch your backs."

But Callum wouldn't be budged. "Absolutely not."

She stared him down. "You can either let me come with you or I'll just follow you there, but either way, I'm going. You can't stop me."

"Somebody needs to stay with Cassidy--"

"I'm going too." I stood up, ignoring the twinge in my lower back as I did. "I may not be good with a gun, but people are going to get hurt. You're going to want a doctor on hand."

"Not one who's one sneeze away from giving birth," Michael said.

I set my medical kit on the bar top. "I've got three weeks left to go. I'll be fine."

"You'll be fine, because you're staying here. Both of you are." Callum finished checking his weapon and handed a vest to Michael. "Are you coming?"

The grin my father gave was like watching a ghost from the past slip over his face. "I'm not dead yet."

I started to protest, but surprisingly, Sloane stopped me with a hand on my arm. She subtly shook her head, but there was a glint in her eye that told me she had no intention of staying behind. She just wasn't going to go head-to-head with Callum over it.

Alfie looked over at us and paused in the act of sliding his own gun into a concealed shoulder holster. He had a strange look on his face.

"We're going to get them back," he said. "Both of them. I promise."

And for the first time since I'd known him, I believed the words coming from his mouth. No more of the usual joking, no flippant remarks. He looked like a man who had just made a personal ultimatum.

I nodded, swallowing past the lump in my throat. "Bring yourself back too, Alfie."

His face was hard as he slipped an ammo magazine into his back pocket. He turned and walked towards the door without saying anything else.

A slow, gathering tension gradually built low in my abdomen, and I inhaled sharply. It felt like a giant hand was slowly, relentlessly squeezing my insides. I leaned into the bar and gripped its edge as the pressure held, then released.

False labor pains. That's all it was. A Braxton Hicks contraction. That's what I told myself as I glanced around the room, making sure no one saw. Everyone was too busy suiting up to notice me.

Except my father.

He buttoned his jacket and stepped over to me. "How are you feeling—do you have everything you need here? Sloane and a couple of guys are going to hang back for protection, but do you want me to call anyone for you?"

My lips twitched up in a bittersweet smile. His concern was heartfelt, even if it was a few months too late. My father had been a nonentity ever since my abduction, and I had all but written that relationship off.

"I'm okay, Dad. Just...try to come back in one piece, yeah?"

In an uncharacteristic display of emotion, he swept me up into an awkward hug. "Anything you need, you let me know."

"Just bring him home to me," I said. "Bring my husband home."

26

CONNOR

SMELL WAS THE FIRST sense that returned to me. The scent of dirt and machinery oil, along with an earthy stench that could only come from livestock living in close quarters. Blood, both old and new, an acrid sharpness that sat heavily over the more pungent, deeper stink of death and decay.

Slowly, I raised my head.

The room swam for a minute before settling out, and it only took a couple seconds to realize I was in a slaughterhouse. A low drain was set into the floor, and hooks hung suspended from a pipe running the length of the room. I supposed I should've been grateful they had tied me to a chair instead of hanging me from one of those hooks.

The drain in the floor was a bit disconcerting, though.

My head throbbed, but I shook it off, craning my aching head around and taking stock of the situation.

There was duct tape over my mouth, and my wrists were bound with the same. Other than the hoard of elephants tap dancing across my skull, I actually didn't feel too bad.

Okay. They didn't kill me yet, and they didn't rough me up too bad, so they must need me alive—for now. Duct tape over my mouth, which means they don't want me screaming or calling out. We must still be in the city, or at least close enough for someone to overhear.

Slowly, I worked at the tape binding my hands. If they'd used zip cuffs or hand cuffs I would've been screwed, but duct tape—that, I could work with.

Time passed. How much, I wasn't sure, but I sat there, working at the tape with a coolly determined focus. I was just starting to get enough leverage to rip a small tear, when they entered.

Frick and frack. One tall, one short. Two nameless henchmen who could've belonged to anyone, and even they couldn't see the irony of the situation as they homed in on me.

"Well, well...look who's awake," the taller one said.

The shorter one with the mean face circled around the chair. I supposed it was meant to be intimidating, but the man looked a little like Joe Pesci, and I stifled a laugh despite the situation.

"Doesn't look so tough to me," the Pesci knock-off said. "Isn't he supposed to be some big name or somethin'?"

"That's Callum McTiernan's nephew, you clown. He and his pals whacked a fair share 'o ours a few months back. Took out Teagan with his bare hands. They say he's got ice in his veins."

Wham!

My head snapped to the side, vision blurring as a fist connected with my injured temple. Blood began to run freely again, but I continued to stare blankly at my captors.

Joe Pesci knock-off swiped a finger-full of blood off my face and laughed. "Nope, looks like regular ol' blood to me." He wiped it harshly across my cheekbone, laughing again.

And on it went. The two taunted me, throwing hits and delighting in seeing a mob boss brought to his knees. I let them—it wasn't like I'd never taken a hit before.

I let them, because while the two played their games, I was busy working at my wrists, loosening the tape and picking at the edge, starting a tear that was getting longer by the minute. I was under no illusions that this would be a clean escape, but if the two of them wanted to sit there and flap their gums at me while I tore through their shoddy restraints, then so be it. A few punches in the face was a small price to pay.

"All right, hold up—we ain't got the picture yet."

"Make sure you get the sign in there, too."

The tall one stepped behind me, and I stopped working at the tape. A rough hand snatched me up by the hair, yanking my head up while the other one took the picture.

So that's it. They weren't going to outright kill me, they were using me as bait. Moretti really was a one-trick pony. It was still no guarantee, but it had bought me a few more precious minutes—minutes in which to free myself and hunt down Moretti himself.

"Got it."

"Good. Send it to the boss—he should be here any minute."

He hit send and tucked the phone back in his pocket with a grin. "That's one for the family album there, McTiernan—your wife's sure gonna love it."

Wham!

———

The second time I woke up was a lot less pleasant than the first.

This time, I way laying on the floor, my cheek pressed to the unwashed tiles. My shoulders hurt from the twisted way I was laying, hands numb, the duct tape renewed and mercilessly tight. Somebody knew what they were doing this time around.

I forced my eyes the rest of the way open, squinting against the dim overhead bulb. My head ached excruciatingly, and I was very glad they'd decided to remove the duct tape covering my mouth, because there was a distinct possibility I might puke. The cold floor felt good against my cheek, and I groaned involuntarily as I waited for the nausea to pass.

"Connor?" Tommy's voice filtered over to me somewhere to my right.

That was one voice I wasn't prepared to hear. With a sinking certainty, Moretti's moves the past few months started to make sense, all an elaborate scheme to take the two biggest players in the McTiernan organization off the board. And, maybe, to use us as leverage.

Abruptly, my plan, such as it was, went out the window. I couldn't risk anything happening to Tommy, even though I knew he would be more than willing to stand by me and take each and every one of these fuckers out, no matter the cost. I was under no illusions, though. Tommy was important, but I was the one Moretti really wanted. I was the one who had broken into his own home, his sanctuary, to kill Teagan and several of his men. Wounded both his sons in that alleyway shootout yesterday. Moretti wasn't going to let that go unanswered, and if I didn't get Tommy out of here, he was going to become collateral damage.

I wasn't going to allow that to happen.

"Yeah, I'm here." I struggled to sit up, but my head swam and I nearly passed out again.

"Jesus, man--don't move. They got you pretty good that second time."

"How long was I out?"

"At least an hour. Maybe more."

I groaned again and leaned my head against the concrete wall, wincing as it jostled the throbbing in my skull. I could hear him shifting around, but I didn't want to turn my head to look. "You okay?"

"Been better. I'm used to taking blows to the head, but I usually get the chance to hit back. I'm looking forward to getting a couple licks in, myself." He grunted, and I felt his hands brush against mine, working at the tape. "Hold still for a sec. I'll get this off."

The tape tore free, and I shook my hands out, feeling the blood flow return with a stinging rush. "Thanks. Now we just need to find a way out of here."

Tommy snorted. "Good luck. This place is a maze of old tunnels and storage rooms."

"Any idea where we are?"

"Somewhere underneath the slaughterhouse. They brought us in through a back entrance, but I couldn't see much before they knocked me out again. They're keeping us here until the bosses arrive. Once they do, they'll probably move us to a more secure location."

"I think I know where we are," I said slowly. "I saw a drain in the floor—that means they use this room for animal processing. If that's the only exit, we're going to need weapons."

"Way ahead of you, brother." Tommy was already on his feet, and I squinted as I finally got a good look at him. He was a mess. His face was bruised, both eyes blackened, his lower lip split and swollen. They hadn't gone easy on him, and I was sure I looked just as bad.

Tommy pulled the grate from the drain and peered down. "We're in luck. We should be able to reach it." He stuck his hand down, reaching for something.

"What's down there?"

"Some kind of tube. I can't quite reach it."

I sat up straighter and squinted down at it. "Here, let me try. I'm taller."

He shuffled back and I reached down. My fingertips brushed the surface of it.

"It's plastic," I said. "Probably a drainage tube for the wash water."

Tommy nodded, then gave a cursory glance at the door. It was shut and locked tight, but we knew we didn't have much time. "Can you get it out?"

"Let me try." I wiggled my fingers, feeling around the edges. It was definitely made of plastic, but it was covered with a thin layer of rust. It was slick, almost greasy, and I was just starting to get a grip on it when I heard the lock rotate.

I stretched my arm to its limit, feeling the socket pop in protest, but I had just closed my fingers around the small bit of jagged plastic when the door opened. I palmed it and sat up, careful not to show any sign of what I'd been doing.

Dominic Moretti stepped inside, flanked by his brother Angel and a tall slender man I didn't recognize. He had a smile on his face like he'd just won the lottery.

"Good afternoon, gentlemen. So nice of you to join us." Dom shrugged off his jacket. "Angel, Julian, get them up on the hooks. I missed my morning workout thanks to these assholes, but I'm sure they'll oblige me. Especially you, big guy."

He grinned at Tommy as Julian re-bound our wrists. Angel kept a gun on us the whole time. This was going to go south quickly if I didn't do something, but I was still feeling woozy from the hits I'd taken and the blood loss.

"Hold him still. I'll do this one."

Angel grabbed me and held my arms behind me. I fought, but he was strong, and I wasn't in any shape to put up a real fight. He shoved me towards a hook suspended from the ceiling. I struggled, careful to keep the jagged bit of plastic concealed in my hands, but the blood was still rushing in my ears, making it hard to focus. Angel grunted in response, pulling me back over to the far wall and slamming my wrists down onto an iron hook. The pain was sharp and sudden, my wrist twisting and bones grinding in protest at the rough treatment.

"Feisty," Dominic commented, stepping further into the room. "Let's see how long that lasts."

"Longer than you think," Tommy interjected, his voice steely.

"Is that so?" Dominic raised an eyebrow before turning to Angel. "Hang this one up, too. Maybe a little one-on-one will loosen his tongue. See how long he can stay conscious once I start cutting."

Tommy struggled. It took a shout from Dominic and three more guards to subdue him, but eventually Angel shoved Tommy forward and hooked his bound hands to another metal hook suspended from the ceiling.

"Now, you two have caused a lot of trouble for my father. So we're going to play a little game, you and me. Don't worry, I won't kill you--yet. Father still wants to talk to you. This is just a little warm up for the final act. So here is how this is going to work," Dominic said conversationally as he selected a knife from the tray "You two are going to tell me everything you know about your precious Clan. And if I don't like what I hear... Well, let's just say things will get very unpleasant, very quickly."

Dominic's grin grew wider as he approached, brandishing the blade. "I think I'm going to start with the little one first. After all, I'm sure you've got a few stories you could share with us, hmmm?"

"Go to hell," I snarled, glaring at him with all the hatred I could muster.

"Wrong answer."

The fist came out of nowhere, connecting with my jaw with such force that I tasted blood. Stars danced behind my eyes, but I refused to cry out. I wouldn't give him the satisfaction.

Julian grabbed Dominic's arm and shoved him back. "That's enough, Dom. This wasn't part of the plan."

"What's the difference?" Angel said. "We're gonna kill them anyway. If you can't handle it, get the hell out."

Julian shook his head and backed towards the door.

Dominic leaned in close, his lips brushing my ear. "You can make this stop any time you want. Just tell me what I need to know. Or you can watch while I take your friend apart. Bit by bit. I'll save his eyes for last—we wouldn't want him to miss out on the show."

I spat blood onto the floor, meeting Dominic's gaze with a defiant stare of my own. "Fuck you."

The grin fell from Dominic's face, and he nodded to Angel. "Make him watch."

27

Emilia

"Emilia...Emilia, come on. Wake up!"

My eyelids fluttered against the harsh fluorescent light that seeped into my consciousness, prying me from the depths of oblivion. God, what had happened? My throat felt like sandpaper and my head throbbed as I blinked open my eyes. I was surrounded by gleaming stainless steel and some serious looking medical equipment. The coldness of metal beneath my fingers sent a shiver up my spine as I tried to lift my head, each movement an agonizing spin of the room around me. The clinical stench of antiseptic filled my nostrils, and for a moment, I couldn't remember why I would be in such a place.

"Emilia, come on. You need to wake up now!" a voice hissed with urgency, piercing the fog in my mind.

I squinted, trying to bring the world into focus. Sofia's pale face hovered over mine, her eyes wide with panic. My cousin, just a girl really, looked out of place in this strange, sterile room.

"Wha—" My throat was dry, every word a struggle. "Sofia?"

Sofia nearly collapsed with relief. "Oh, thank God! I thought I'd messed it up. Are you okay?"

I...wasn't really sure. I felt like I'd been run over by a truck, but when I went to sit up on the metal surface I was laying on, everything seemed to be moving like it should.

Her hands were on my shoulders, helping me to sit up, yet with a tremor that betrayed her fear. "I thought—I thought I'd dosed the second syringe wrong." Her words tumbled out in a rush of anxiety. "God, Emilia, I'm so sorry. You weren't waking up."

"Second syringe? Wh-where are we?" The confusion made my already heavy head pound with renewed intensity. But slowly, pieces began to click into place, memories of our desperate plan creeping back to me.

"Never mind that right now," Sofia replied urgently, her eyes searching mine for any sign of lingering confusion or injury. "Just focus on getting your bearings. Can you sit up?"

With her help, I managed to push myself into a seated position, still feeling unsteady and weak. My thoughts were a chaotic jumble, grasping at straws to make sense of our current situation. Sofia's presence was both reassuring and disconcerting – if she was here, then something must have gone terribly wrong.

She must have caught my look. "You're going to be okay. We just need to get out of here."

My head cleared, and I was finally able to focus and get a good look at my surroundings. Long metal tables with high sides and drains. Refrigerated cubicles built into the wall. The overwhelming antiseptic smell.

"Are we...in the morgue?"

Sofia nodded, her eyes wide. "Dead bodies and everything. This place seriously give me the creeps."

I breathed out, a ghost of a laugh escaping me. It was a grim situation, certainly, but I was still alive, and that was something to cling to. The chill of the basement room crept into my bones, reminding me just how stiff and exhausted I was as I swung my legs off the table.

"Are you sure you should be doing this already?" she asked, concern etched on her face. "You've just woken up from...whatever that was."

"Trust me, I'm not thrilled about it either."

"Okay, but take it slow," Sofia said, her eyes never leaving mine. She finally grasped my arm, steadying me as I sat up fully.

It was then that I realized I was naked beneath the thin sheet covering me. My cheeks flushed with embarrassment, and I pulled the sheet tighter around me. Sofia noticed my discomfort and burst into laughter, a wild, almost hysterical sound that echoed through the sterile room.

"Oh, yeah. You're kind of naked under there, I guess they do that."

"Huh."

"I should probably find you some clothes."

"It would help. I'm catching a draft, here."

"Of all the things to worry about right now," she giggled, tears streaming down her cheeks as she rummaged through a nearby rack of lockers. "Leave it to you to be embarrassed by your own nudity."

"Hey, it's not every day I wake up in a morgue with no clothes on!" I shot back, a reluctant smile tugging at the corners of my mouth. The absurdity of the situation hit us both at once, and our laughter mingled together, the sound bouncing off the cold metal walls.

"Here," Sofia said, wiping away her tears and opening a nearby locker. She pulled out a set of pale blue scrubs and tossed them to me. "These should fit better than that sheet."

I slipped into the scratchy fabric, feeling more human with each piece of clothing that covered my skin. The pants were too long, the top too wide, but none of that mattered.

Sofia watched me, her face pale and drawn, and I felt a stab of guilt. She had risked everything to help me, putting herself in danger by helping me pull off this elaborate scheme. I cupped her cheek, brushing a thumb under her eye. "You look exhausted. I'm so sorry for dragging you into this mess."

"Don't be silly. You're family, Emilia, and family looks out for each other." Her lips curved into a wry smile. "Besides, it was the most excitement I've had in a long time. I deserve an Academy Award for my performance when the paramedics arrived. Everybody completely bought that you had overdosed."

Relief and fear mingled within me at her words. "So, it really happened... That wasn't just a horrible dream?" I asked, trying to wrap my head around the fact that I'd faked my own death.

"Horrible or not, it's our reality now. You're dead." Sofia sighed. "We need to get moving."

Her attempt at humor warmed my heart, but I couldn't shake off the guilt completely. . "You shouldn't have had to do any of this."

"Neither should you," she countered, pulling back from the hug. "Just go find your Irishman and be happy," she said softly. "That's all the repayment I need."

The mention of his name sent a jolt of fear through me, and suddenly everything came flooding back – the threat against my life, the desperate plan we'd concocted, and the knowledge that Alfie might be in danger too.

I drew back, determination burning through my veins like fire. She was right. I had to get to Alfie. But first, we had to get out of this morgue without being seen.

"Stay close," I whispered, my voice barely audible as we reached the door. Sofia's hand brushed against mine, her fingers trembling slightly. It was reassuring to know that she was just as scared as I was – that we were in this together.

I pushed cautiously pushed open the door and peered down the dimly lit corridor. The hospital was eerily quiet, the late-night janitorial staff and night nurses seemingly few and far between. But that didn't mean we could let our guard down.

We crept down the hall, sticking to the shadows. Every flicker of movement had me tensing, expecting armed guards to come around the corner at any moment. But the hall remained deserted, and we made it to the door leading out of the morgue without incident.

Sofia eased it open and poked her head out, scanning the area. "All clear," she whispered. "But we have to hurry. The night shift will be making rounds again soon."

We slipped out of the morgue and into the deserted corridor. My heart pounded as we moved quickly and quietly, sticking close to the wall. We were almost at the main entrance when we heard footsteps approaching.

I grabbed Sofia's arm and pulled her behind a large potted plant, holding my breath as a nurse walked past. She was texting on her phone and didn't notice us, and I breathed a sigh of relief when they turned the corner.

"Let's go." I tugged on Sofia's arm, and we crept towards the stairwell. I didn't dare risk the elevators.

Luckily, the doorways were only keycard protected on the way in, not out. We made our way up the stairs, taking them two at a time. My heart was pounding, and my legs felt like lead, but we had to keep moving.

The stairwell door banged open, and Sofia and I froze, huddled in the shadows. Two security guards entered, talking loudly and laughing. We stood still, hardly daring to breathe, until they disappeared around the corner.

"That was close," Sofia breathed.

I nodded, feeling a bead of sweat roll down my back. "Come on, let's go."

We pushed open the door and stepped out onto the main floor. It was even quieter here, with only a handful of patients and visitors moving through the halls. We walked quickly and purposefully, trying not to draw attention to ourselves.

"Emilia, wait," Sofia said quietly, stopping in her tracks. I turned to see her staring longingly at a nearby door: the entrance to the Intensive Care Unit. My gaze locked onto the bustling room where machines beeped in a cacophony of false vitality. Bright lights and hushed voices seeped from behind the locked doorway. She didn't need to say anything more; I knew exactly what – or rather, who – was on her mind.

"Luca's in there," she whispered, tears welling up in her eyes. I felt my own chest tighten, an all-too-familiar ache clenching my heart.

"I know."

Behind those closed doors, Luca was fighting for his life. Alone. I wanted nothing more than to rush inside and be by his side, to hold his hand and tell him how much he meant to me. But I knew we couldn't risk it – not with so many people around, not when our escape was still so precarious.

Sofia wasn't moving. I tugged at her arm. "We can't. There are too many people."

"But he's right there." Her voice broke. I understood. The agony of leaving him in such a state was tearing at me. Strong, dependable, beautiful Luca, who would've charged headfirst into danger for me. And here I was, skulking away in scrubs.

I gripped my cousin by the shoulders. "Sofia, look at me. Luca is strong. He'll pull through. But if we're caught here, everything we've done will be for nothing."

As true as they were, the words still felt like ash on my tongue. But there wasn't anything else we could do. Our plan, my supposed death, it all hinged on invisibility, on getting to Alfie before anyone realized the truth.

Sofia nodded, wiping away her tears. "Okay."

We moved quickly down the hall, sticking to the shadows. I kept a lookout for security guards, but the place was surprisingly empty.

We finally reached the main entrance. It was eerily quiet. The sliding doors whooshed open, and we stepped outside into the cool night air.

It was strange to think that the world was going on as normal – the city streets bustling with life and activity, the sounds of sirens and car horns filling the air. Our breaths formed wispy clouds in the darkness, and I shivered. I'd never felt more alive than I did right now, standing on the precipice of the rest of my life but not knowing what I'd find at the bottom.

Even if it felt like I had just crawled out of my own grave.

"So what now?" Sofia asked.

"I need to call Alfie. Can I use your phone?"

Sofia handed it over, and I dialed Alfie's number, holding my breath as it rang. He didn't pick up, and I was starting to panic. What if something had happened? What if Moretti's men had already gotten to him?

Damn. Voicemail.

The unease pooling in my belly intensified, and I couldn't shake the feeling that something was terribly wrong. I hung up and handed the phone back to Sofia, my voice barely concealing my growing panic. "He's not answering."

"Maybe he's just not picking up because it's a strange number," she suggested, but I could tell from the worry in her eyes that she wasn't entirely convinced by her own words.

"Let's go to his apartment," I decided, refusing to let myself spiral into despair. "He has to be there."

The cab driver looked at us like we'd lost our minds, and for a second, I was worried he wouldn't let us in. I supposed my bed hair and purloined scrubs lent a certain "just escaped from a mental hospital" look to the situation, and Sofia's tendency to overshare didn't help. Still, he pulled away from the curb, and we headed towards South Boston.

My heart was in my throat as we pulled up to Alfie's building. I had only been here once, back during that sweet in-between time after the raid on the compound, back when we didn't have to hide from Angel's jealousy and Dom's suspicion. Back when I'd believed he was going to be safe, and that our relationship stood a chance.

I took a deep breath, trying to calm the whirlwind of emotions swirling inside me.

"You okay?" Sofia asked quietly.

I nodded, not trusting myself to speak.

We got out of the cab and headed inside. The building was quiet and dark, and I hoped the lack of security was a good sign. We made our way up the stairs and stopped in front of Alfie's door. My heart was pounding, and I felt sick to my stomach as I reached out and knocked.

Nothing.

I tried again, louder this time, but still nothing. I rang the buzzer again and again, pounding on the door for good measure. No movement, no sound, no light seeping under the door. Nothing.

A wave of panic washed over me. Where was Alfie? I pressed my forehead against the cool wood, trying to steady my breathing. Sofia's hand was warm on my shoulder.

"Maybe he's not home."

I shook my head, refusing to give up. "No, he has to be here. I need to see him. I need to know he's okay."

My voice was tight with emotion, and I felt tears pricking the corners of my eyes. Where was he? I leaned heavily against the door, my body suddenly feeling too heavy to carry. The weight of everything that had happened was finally catching up to me.

Sofia rubbed my back, her voice soft and gentle. . "Is there anywhere else he might be?"

I racked my brain, trying to think of any place Alfie had mentioned in our conversations. He never talked about work, so I knew better than to ask him where he was during those times. But he had mentioned one place that was special to him—a bar owned by the Clan.

"He mentioned a bar once... Lady Devine's. He said it was a special place, the only place he really felt at home. That it was a safe place to go." I shook my head, hating the thought of going to a mob-run bar and drawing even more attention to myself, but I knew it was my only chance of finding Alfie.

Sofia quickly googled the location and nodded. "It's just four blocks from here. Let's go."

28

— · —

ALFIE

THE OLD MEATPACKING PLANT loomed like a decaying titan against the night sky, its silhouette jagged and uneven against the backdrop of an indifferent city. A monument to decay and death, with its rusted machinery and broken windows that seemed to stare like hollow eyes. It was bracketed by the disused railroad tracks that trailed off into darkness and the lapping waters of the waterfront—a place caught between two graves.

I sat in the back of the Town Car with Callum and Michael, my gaze fixed on the slaughterhouse's crumbling facade. The air was thick with the smell of rust and ancient blood, a scent that stuck to the back of my throat and refused to let go. Faint sounds of metal creaking under the weight of time echoed through the open window, merging with the distant cries of gulls that sounded too much like wails of the damned. Everything about this place screamed foreboding; it was as if death itself had set up shop and was open for business.

Callum and Michael were uncharacteristically tense. I wondered how long it had been since either of them had seen action. Michael's mouth was a grim slash in his face as he studied the building. Callum kept checking and rechecking his weapon. There was a stillness to the air, a quiet that could only be found when people were waiting for something to happen.

As if summoned by our collective tension, headlights cut through the night, and a car rolled to a stop beside us.

"He's late," Callum grumbled.

Michael chuckled dryly. "You know the Russians. They like to make an entrance."

Misha emerged from the vehicle, flanked by a handful of armed men. He approached with an easy swagger, his smile wide and friendly.

"Callum, Michael," he greeted, extending his hand.

"Misha." Michael took it, his grip firm.

Callum didn't bother to hide the disdain in his voice. "Took you long enough."

It took him a minute, but Callum shook the man's hand. There was a brief power struggle, so subtle you might miss it, but something sharp and cunning flitted across Misha's dark eyes, undercutting the charismatic enthusiasm. Like watching a lion stare down a rhino. Callum's expression left little room for doubt—he had not forgiven the Russians for the double-cross years ago that had killed his son, Aiden. Nor had he forgotten.

But Callum was a pragmatist at heart, and he knew there was no point in holding grudges when there were bigger fish to fry.

"Volkov is glad to bury the hatchet," Misha said in that honey-light accent of his. "No more bad blood, yes?"

"Let's just get this over with," I muttered.

Misha cocked an eyebrow. "I remember you. Where did your sense of humor go, my friend?"

It died with Emilia. I kept the words to myself, though. My patience was wearing thin, and I wanted nothing more than to get inside and find Moretti.

"The Italians just killed someone he loved," Callum said. " We're not the only ones with a score to settle tonight."

Misha's smile faltered. "I am sorry for your loss, my friend."

Loss. As if Emilia was a set of keys I'd misplaced, instead of the woman who owned my soul. I swallowed against the razor blades lodged in my throat and gave a short, sharp nod.

Misha clapped a hand on my shoulder, and I fought the urge to shake it off. Trusting Misha was like cuddling up to a wolf because it had soft fur—foolish at best, deadly at worst. I couldn't shake the feeling that Misha was putting on an act. The man smiled too damn much to be trustworthy. But did it really matter? I had no intention of making it out of this place alive. The only thing driving me now was the need for vengeance – cold, brutal, and final.

The air was thick with the tang of iron and salt from the waterfront as I stood beside the sleek black Town Car, my fingers drumming an impatient tattoo on its cool metal surface. Callum's voice was a distant drone in my ear, blending with Michael's lower timbre and Misha's accented baritone. It all faded into the background like smoke, formless and insubstantial, and I stared at the crumbling brickwork of the slaughterhouse.

This was where it would end. One way or another.

My mind was ensnared by darker musings, by the echo of Emilia's laughter, now silenced forever. I could almost smell her perfume, a haunting blend of jasmine and something uniquely her, laced with the dusty scent of the old books she so loved. The void her absence left was a cavernous wound, gaping and raw, and no amount of bloodshed would ever fill it.

But it might ease the ache for a moment.

"Alfie," Callum said suddenly. "You with us?"

"I'm here." I was numb to everything except my goal. There was only one thing that mattered now, and it was inside that building.

Callum studied me, his gaze hard. "We'll do this together," he said after a long pause. "You'll get your chance, but you have to keep your head. We're not just going in guns blazing. One team goes to the roof, the rest of us will split up and flank the building. Alfie, you're with Michael and these two." He gestured to the Russians standing beside Misha.

I nodded, not bothering to respond. My mind was already made up.

We moved as one, slipping silently through the shadows. The only sound was the faint rasp of breath and the crunch of gravel underfoot. My heart pounded a steady rhythm as we approached the main entrance. The double doors were rusted and weather-worn, hanging loosely from their hinges. A faint light flickered somewhere behind them.

The gun grew heavier with each step closer to the building. My heart thundered curiously despite the detached sense of calm I felt, each pulse pounding heavily in my ears like that useless muscle knew what was happening and was speeding gleefully towards its final beat and Emilia.

But not yet.

First, I had to make sure Connor and Tommy made it out alive.

And then I would kill Angel myself.

One way or another, it would all end tonight.

29

CONNOR

TOMMY SAGGED IN HIS restraints, head bowed and face hidden behind a curtain of blood. I didn't know how much longer he could last.

They'd beaten him mercilessly. Deep bruises on his chest were already blooming, and his shirt was torn and splattered with blood. Dominic stood with a maniacal grin on his face, the knife dripping blood onto the concrete floor. He looked at Tommy dispassionately, like he was just an object to be used and discarded.

We were both hanging by our wrists from meat hooks on the wall, our feet just barely skimming the floor, arms numb under the strain of our own weight. Tommy's body convulsed with each strike, a symphony of pain playing out before me. I closed my eyes, trying to block out the meaty, sickening sounds of flesh thumping against flesh. The metallic smell of blood hung heavy in the air, mingling with the stench of sweat and fear.

Tommy's head snapped to the side, blood and spit flying from his mouth to spatter the concrete wall. His eyes were closed, and I wondered if he was unconscious yet.

I hated to think what would happen when Dominic finally decided he had enough.

"Look at this piece of shit," Dom crowed, grabbing a fistful of Tommy's hair and yanking his head up. Tommy's face was a ruin of bruises and cuts, one eye swollen completely shut. "He's not so mouthy now, is he?"

"Still handsome as ever." He bared his teeth in a bloody grin.

Dom backhanded him so hard Tommy's head snapped back, the meat hooks creaking under the force. I strained again at the duct tape binding my own hands, and Angel kicked me in the side, laughing.

"Maybe you'll learn to hold your tongue after I'm done with your boy here," Dom said, turning back to me with a wolfish grin. He pulled a knife from his belt, the edge glinting under the harsh overhead lights, and ran it down Tommy's cheek almost lovingly.

Tommy didn't even flinch. "Get on with it, then."

Dominic's knife glinted cruelly in the dim light. He seized Tommy's blood-soaked faux hawk, yanking his head back with a viciousness that sent fresh blood running down Tommy's face.

"You're tough, aren't you?" He pressed the tip of his knife against Tommy's throat. "How tough do you think you'll be once I start cutting bits off?

Tommy's pulse thrummed visibly against the sharp blade. A crimson bead blossomed where the edge bit into his flesh, trickling down like a perverse tear.

He spat in Dominic's face.

The room went utterly silent.

Dominic wiped the blood and spit from his face. Quick as a viper, he sank his fist into Tommy's stomach.

I fumbled for the jagged bit of plastic we'd pulled out of the pipe as Tommy sucked air. Dominic was going to fucking kill him if I didn't stop this shit; Tommy never could resist the temptation to goad narcissistic assholes like Dom. Out of the corner of my eye, my friend's head hung limply between his corded arms, but incredibly, the next thing that came out of that crazy bastard's mouth wasn't a curse or an insult.

It was laughter.

Hoarse, deranged laughter that echoed off the walls of the empty slaughterhouse. Dominic drew back, eyes narrowed, and Tommy raised his head to grin at him. His eyes were wild and glassy, filled with a madness that I'd never quite had a chance to appreciate until now. Quickly, I redoubled my efforts on the duct tape, taking advantage of the distraction.

"That the best you've got?" Tommy wheezed. "Why don't you stop pussyfooting around and get on with it, you piece of shit?"

I felt my own pulse quicken as Dom turned his wrathful gaze upon me. The air seemed to thicken, anticipation coiling tight around us. I couldn't feel the bit of plastic in my hands anymore, they were so numb. I just had to hope I wouldn't drop it.

I felt the first layer of duct tape part.

"I think we've been going about this the wrong way, Angel," Dom said quietly. "Tommy here is clearly trained to take a punch. Though, I wonder how much he can endure watching his friend suffer."

Predictable. Asshole.

"Go ahead. I was getting a little bored over here."

"Connor, don't—"

Tommy tried to protest, but Angel silenced him with another vicious blow. "Shut up," he snapped.

Dom dragged the knife down my chest, slicing through fabric and flesh alike. "Going to scream for me, Connor?" he purred, trailing the knife lower.

I stared back at him silently, jaw clenched. He wanted me to break, to beg for mercy, but I wouldn't give him the satisfaction.

The knife bit deeper, and this time I couldn't hold back a grunt of pain. Dom leaned in close, his foul breath hot on my face. "Scream," he whispered.

"Enough, Dominic."

Both Moretti brothers froze at the sound of their father's voice.

"Not to spoil your evening, son, but I would like a word with these two gentlemen before you finish dismantling them."

Dominic glared at me, clearly annoyed. Lorenzo gestured to a few guards who had followed him in, and they dragged in a wooden chair and set it before us. I stared straight ahead blankly, refusing to acknowledge Lorenzo's presence. My wrists were nearly free, but I didn't dare try while there were that many guns trained on us.

"Hello Connor. You're a hard man to track down."

Wham!

It came out of nowhere, a backhand that rocked my body on the hook. I clenched his jaw and rose back up, staring at the man who had ordered my wife's abduction and murder.

"Manners, Connor. You will look at me when I'm speaking, or else I can make this very unpleasant for you."

Lorenzo pulled up a chair, sitting opposite me as if we were two gentlemen sitting down for a cordial drink. Rage burned through my veins, scorching everything in its path, but still, I remained motionless.

Lorenzo sighed. "I'm...disappointed, Connor. Would you like to know why?"

I said nothing.

"I'll take your rudeness as a yes." He leaned forward. "Michael Quinn was a short-sighted fool and a coward. Callum merely lacks ambition. They were too stuck in their old ways, unwilling to embrace the new order and fall into line like everyone else. But you...you were different. You were able to divorce yourself from the petty emotions and do what needed to be done."

He paused thoughtfully. "We could have done great things, you and me. We could've shaped this city. After getting rid of the old guard and assuming control of South Boston, I intended to make you an offer—you could keep control of the Seaport in return for your loyalty to me. This city is at a tipping point, and all it would've taken was a little push, with your help."

"Just one problem with that, old man," Tommy said. "Connor doesn't want anything to do with your fucking city."

Lorenzo glanced over at him and smiled thinly. "Not the silent type, are you? A pity. You're a fighter, I can tell. If you were mine, you'd have made a fine enforcer."

Tommy's eyes were ice, his voice dangerously low. "I'd die before I'd ever work for you."

Lorenzo gave a humorless laugh and turned back to me. "You see, Connor? That's what I mean. Short-sighted. Blinded by emotion. The same could've been said for your wife."

Anger flared, hot and bright. "Don't you dare talk about her."

Lorenzo ignored me. "She was a fighter too, but unlike you, she had ambition. She was always trying to prove herself, to show everyone what a strong woman she was. That's all right. Teagan Kelley was able to put her in her place before you killed him. I'm sure you've found she's much more docile now. You're welcome, by the way."

"You son of a bitch," Tommy spat.

Lorenzo sighed and stood, his gaze never leaving my face. Moretti was starting to get angry, despite all his talk of divorcing emotion.

Good.

"But instead you fell in love with the little slut. Gave up every-thing—for a woman. My men tell me that you've practically become a hermit up there with her, hiding yourself away from the world and grasping at the domestic bliss that you will never have. Not someone like you.

"I heard you got her knocked up. Is that what you thought would happen? That you and the little missus would just live happily ever after? After everything you've done?" He shook his head. "Not in this life. You started this entire plan in motion. Set each of our families at each other's throats, all for a woman. And now, Emilia is dead because of the actions of your man. You took my daughter away from me—my legacy—and now I'm going to take away Callum's. A child for a child."

One of the henchmen pressed a finger to the comms device in his ear and nodded to Lorenzo.

"Just in time. Looks like the cavalry has arrived." He stood, brushing at his suit. "You know, I bet Cassidy will make a pretty widow. I might just pay her a visit after it's over, take her and junior under my wing. That'll be poetic, don't you think?"

"I'm going to kill you."

Lorenzo cocked an eyebrow. "As last words go, not very original." He walked to the gate, pausing as it was opened. "Kill them both. Leave the bodies for their friends to find. Dominic, Angelo, with me."

The rest of the men filed out behind him, leaving Tommy and me alone with the two men from before. The tall one leaned against the wall as the Pesci knock-off pulled his handgun.

He leveled it at my face and pulled the trigger.

30

—·—

EMILIA

"HELLO?" I CALLED OUT tentatively, my voice echoing through the empty bar.

The door of Lady D's creaked open and I slipped inside, Sofia close behind me. The place was dead quiet, not a soul in sight. Unease prickled my skin as we moved through the dark bar, the only sound the scuff of our shoes on the tile floor.

Sofia grabbed my arm. "Em, I don't think anyone's here--"

The sharp click of a hammer being cocked cut her off. I whirled around to see a woman with short, dark hair pointing a gun right at us.

"Who the fuck are you?" she snarled, her eyes darting between us. "And what the hell are you doing in my bar?"

I raised my hands slowly, palms facing her. "We're friends of Alfie Doyle. He's in trouble, I think, and we need your help."

The woman hesitated for a moment, but she didn't lower her gun. "How do you know Alfie?"

"He's my boyfriend. Please, it's a long story, but we need to find him."

"Emilia?" A second figure appeared behind the first, long, strawberry blond hair tumbling over her shoulders.

Although I'd never met Connor's wife, I recognized her from Alfie's stories. Cassidy pushed the barrel of the first woman's gun down, and I noticed that she was very, very pregnant.

"Emilia? Alfie's Emilia?" Cassidy breathed, her eyes wide with shock as they locked onto mine. "But you...We thought..."

"We were told you were dead," the other woman finished inelegantly.

"Sloane."

"Well?" Sloane gestured to where Sofia and I stood frozen. I wouldn't put it past her to pull the gun on us again. "Just what the hell is going on here?"

I knew what she meant without her having to finish. To her, to all of them, I was supposed to be gone, another casualty in this endless war between families and loyalties. Yet here I stood, very much alive, and clearly not an apparition.

My hands came up placatingly. "It's me. I'm here. And I can explain everything."

Sloane narrowed her eyes at me. "Then you better start."

Okay. She was more than a little terrifying.

"Look, I'm okay. Luca was badly hurt and couldn't help me, so Sofia ransacked his room to find the counteragent." I glanced at Sofia, who nodded in agreement. "She helped me go through with the original plan."

Cassidy sank back onto the couch, one hand still resting on her belly as she stared at me with disbelief. "That was...incredibly reckless."

"It doesn't matter now." This wasn't the time for explanations. "We need to find Alfie. Where is he?"

Cassidy and Sloane exchanged troubled glances, and for a moment, it seemed as if neither could find the words to answer my question. The air grew thick with tension, and I felt an icy grip of fear tightening around my chest.

"Please," I begged, unable to hide the desperation in my voice. "Tell me where he is."

Cassidy's expression faltered, the color draining from her cheeks. She seemed momentarily at a loss for words, her gaze darting between Sofia, Sloane, and me. Her face tightened, and I noticed her wince slightly, her hand protectively clutching her pregnant belly.

"Are you alright?" I asked, concern etched on my face.

"Fine," she whispered, her voice strained. "It's just... Braxton Hicks contractions. Nothing to worry about."

I felt for her, I really did, but I didn't have time for this. "Please just tell me where he is."

Cassidy let out a shaky breath, blinking back tears. But her eyes cleared, focusing intently on me. "You don't understand," she rasped. "Alfie...That monster told him..."

"Alfie thinks you're dead, Emilia," Sloane finally spoke up when Cassidy didn't answer. "We all thought you were dead."

Her words struck me like a blow to the chest, leaving me breathless and reeling. My hands shook as I tried to process the implications. If Alfie believed I was gone, what would he do? What desperate measures might he take?

"Where is he?" I asked, my voice barely more than a whisper.

Cassidy found her voice again, though it was filled with an undeniable tremor. "Connor and Tommy were taken to an old slaughterhouse on Moretti property. They're hurting them, using them as bait for the rest of the Clan. Alfie went with Callum and the boys to get them back."

Sloane swore viciously. "What she's trying to say, is Alfie is about to do something very, very stupid."

Stupid. The term was a stark contrast to the calculated risks the men of the McTiernan Clan were known for. The Alfie I knew was reckless at times, yes, but never without purpose, never without some semblance of a plan hidden behind those laughing eyes. But this—this was the act of a man driven by raw emotion, by the unbearable thought of living in a world robbed of light.

"Then we have to stop him," I said, resolve hardening like ice within me. If love had taught me anything, it was that sometimes you had to walk through fire to save the ones who ignited your soul.

Cassidy shook her head. "It's not that simple, Emilia. I want to be there as much as you do, but we can't rush in blindly. The Clan isn't alone in this – we're getting help from the Russians."

"But...that can't be right. Julian told me the Russians are working with Lorenzo."

All three of us turned to stare at Sofia.

"Say that again?" Sloane demanded.

Sofia stood up a little taller under her laser-sharp gaze. "My brother is one of Lorenzo's capos. He's the one who told me about the alliance. Whatever the Russians told you is a lie. They're working for us."

The temperature in the room seemed to drop. Cassidy clenched her jaw, her knuckles white as she breathed deeply, and I wondered just how often those Hicks things were supposed to be happening.

"Then there's no time to waste," she said, her voice wavering slightly but resolute. "We have to go after them."

"Damn straight we do." Sloane had a steely look in her eyes, like she was ready to single-handedly storm the Moretti compound if that's what it took.

She turned to me, her gaze piercing. "Do you know how to use a gun?"

I hesitated for a moment, then nodded.

"Good." She looked at me. "There's extra Sigs from behind the bar. Grab them. And Cassidy? Get the extra ammo from the back room, we're going to want it."

Cassidy obeyed without question, moving surprisingly quickly for a woman in her condition. I admired her strength, even as my heart ached for her. This was not a situation I would want to be in while carrying a baby.

"Are you sure this is a good idea?" Sofia asked, looking at Cassidy's retreating form. "We shouldn't put her in danger."

"She's stronger than she looks." Sloane's voice was firm, unwavering. "And besides, if anybody's hurt, she's the one you're gonna want to have around."

Cassidy tossed a battered medical kit onto the bar top. "Let's go. There's a van in the back we can take. It should be big enough to fit all of us."

Sloane tossed a couple of very serious looking black vests onto the bar next to the medical kit. "Suit up, ladies."

"Oh, Jesus," Sofia muttered.

"We need to be prepared," Sloane said, her voice steely. "None for you, Cassidy. You're staying in the van.

Connor's wife smiled wanly at her. "You know what? I'm not going to fight you on that one."

"There's a first for everything," Sloane said as she strapped on a bullet-proof vest.

I followed suit, feeling the weight of the Kevlar against my chest, a barrier against bullets but not against the terror that clawed at my heart. I couldn't lose Alfie. Not now, not ever. I wouldn't survive it.

Outside, the night air had turned frigid, and my breath curled like smoke in the glow of the streetlights. The parking lot was empty save for a single dark van with tinted windows. It looked like the kind of vehicle that would appear in a horror movie, the one that inevitably drove off at the end with some poor girl's corpse in the back.

Seemed about right.

Sofia pulled open the passenger side door and clambered inside. Sloane got into the driver's seat and adjusted the mirrors and checking the instruments. I slid into the seat beside Sofia, the worn leather creaking under my weight. Cassidy climbed in behind me, but she gasped suddenly, her hand flying to her stomach.

"Cassidy? What's wrong?" I asked.

"It's nothing," she said through gritted teeth. "Just...just a cramp."

I knew she was lying. Her face was pale, her breathing shallow. I'd seen enough women go through childbirth to know that Cassidy was experiencing the early signs of labor. But she was stubbornly insistent that she was fine, and I wasn't about to argue with her. Not when we were about to go charging into a slaughterhouse.

"Emilia, take this," Sloane said, thrusting a pistol into my hands. It was cold and heavy and ugly. I stared down at it, feeling strangely disconnected from the weapon in my hands.

I wasn't a soldier. I was a bookstore owner who was hopelessly in love with an Irishman. But I was willing to do whatever I had to do to save him.

Beside me, Cassidy gasped again. "Fuck," she whispered, clutching her belly.

"Cassidy, what is it?" Sofia asked, concern etched on her face.

"I, um...I might actually be in labor."

"Are you kidding me?" Sloane's voice trembled with worry, her eyes darting between Cassidy and me. "Cass, isn't it too soon?"

"Trust me, I don't want to have this baby in a van any more than you do. I know my limits. I've got time."

"But--"

"Drive, Sloane," Cassidy snapped. "You're out of your mind if you think I'm going to be anywhere else when there's a chance that Connor or Tommy might be hurt. You need me."

Sloane fired up the van and gave her a long look. "You're the doc, so I guess you know best...but that doesn't mean I'm happy about it."

31

— • —

CONNOR

I YANKED DOWN, RIPPING free from the tape and shoving the gun to the side at the last second. It went off, impossibly loud in the cavernous space as the bullet passed inches from my ear.

Beside me, Tommy kicked off the wall and wrapped his legs around the guard closest to him, squeezing his neck mercilessly between his thighs. I grabbed Joe Pesci knock-off in a chokehold and spun. Bullets thudded into his body as I used him as a human shield, firing the dead man's gun until there were two more bodies on the floor, and the chamber was silent once more.

A third thud, and the last guard fell to the floor at Tommy's feet. His neck was broken.

"Fucking took you long enough." Tommy pulled up against the chain he was still hanging from and wrenched his bound hands over the hook. He landed far steadier on his feet than I would have thought.

I searched the bodies until I found a knife, and I sliced through his bonds. "You okay?"

"Please. I've gotten worse in the ring." He jerked his head towards the door. "You know they were probably only expecting two shots."

"Yeah."

I heaved the body of the taller man into the chair, propping him up before dragging the other body out of the way. We both ducked behind the door just as footsteps pounded down the hallway.

Three more men burst through the door, fatally pausing in confusion over the body slumped in the chair. Three shots to the head, and they went down as well.

We moved quickly, snatching up extra magazines and one of their comms devices. The room was full of old machinery, rusty and dusty with disuse, and we crouched behind an ancient-looking carcass hanger.

"We need to find out what's going on," I whispered to Tommy.

He nodded. "I'll take care of it." He grabbed the comms device from my hand and pressed it to his ear, his eyes darting back and forth as he listened to whatever chatter was coming through.

"What's going on?" I hissed.

Tommy grimaced. "Not good. Apparently, they have Callum and the boys pinned down in the warehouse. They're outnumbered, but they've got some Russian mercenaries with them that are giving the Italians trouble."

"They went with the Russians? On this?"

Tommy shrugged. "No accounting for taste."

"Or a desire to be shot in the back."

"Look, if they make it through this, we'll worry about it then," Tommy said, grabbing a spare gun. "Let's just focus on getting out of here and making sure we don't get killed first."

I checked my gun's magazine. "Lorenzo is mine."

"Now's not the time for vengeance, brother."

It wasn't about vengeance. It wasn't even about justice. It wasn't about my ego or my pride or any of that other "not on our turf" macho bullshit that had been spoon-fed down my throat since the day Aiden had died.

It was about keeping Cassidy and my unborn child safe and making sure they would stay that way, whether I was still around or not.

Lorenzo wouldn't stop, no matter what happened here tonight. He would never stop coming after us. I couldn't let them live the rest of their lives looking over their shoulders, wondering when the next bullet in the back might come.

"You're not contemplating something heroic, are you?" Tommy peeked around the door. "Because I'm a little too attached to the idea of being a godfather, so I'd really appreciate it if you didn't do anything stupid."

"Nothing heroic. Just something necessary."

"Fuck."

We moved down the corridor, one shoulder to the wall as we ducked around corners, sweeping room after room. The need for stealth was long gone—by the sound of it, there was quite the shootout going on above us.

There still was need for caution, though. They'd kept us underground in the processing facility, and the place was laid out like a maze. Plenty of spurs and side legs off the main corridor made the situation perfect for an ambush.

I pressed on ahead of Tommy, need making me careless. We reached a corner that branched off in two directions, and I started to move past it before I heard Tommy swear quietly behind me.

Shots rang out just as he yanked me around the corner, peppering the wall behind us.

"You know, we should do this more often," Tommy said conversationally, shoving a new magazine into his gun before returning fire. "I forgot just what a fucking delight you are in a gunfight."

"They're down. Come on."

"Yes, dear."

We ducked through another doorway into a large open area filled with dilapidated pens that must have been used to store the animals. Gunfire lit up the darkness, pinning us down.

"I'm out," Tommy called.

Where the hell did these guys come from? It seemed like not everyone had been taken in by the distraction at the main entrance. A flurry of movement to my right, and I saw Lorenzo being hustled out the back of the room, flanked by his bodyguards. I shot at the retreating figures, ducking back down again as the gunfire intensified.

"What's the plan?" Tommy asked, breathing hard.

I stared at the ground, which was covered in broken glass and other debris from the old processing floor. It was streaked with rusty-looking stains, a macabre trail of breadcrumbs leading into the dark.

I knew what I had to do.

I just didn't like it.

I tossed him my gun. "Cover me."

I sprinted to the nearest animal pen. I flung myself to the ground and slid into the cage, scrambling for cover as Tommy drew their fire.

"Cover me? That's your goddamn plan?" Tommy yelled, ducking behind some old equipment to reload his gun. "Are you trying to get killed?"

"You need ammo!" I shouted back.

I had to get to them, and I couldn't afford to let the guards catch me in the open. I crawled on my belly to the next pen, then the next, trying to be as small a target as possible while using the open spaces to cover the ground as fast as possible.

Tommy swore as he ran dry, dropping his gun and drawing his knife. He launched himself at the nearest guard, sinking his blade into the man's neck in a vicious arc. Blood fountained out from the wound, soaking the guard's shirt as he sagged to the ground.

He rolled to the side, narrowly missing a burst of fire from the other guard. I was too far away to reach them, and even if I could, I had no weapon. Tommy ducked and weaved, keeping close to the guard and forcing him to come in close quarters. He grabbed the man's arm and twisted it, shoving the barrel of the gun against his chest and firing. The body fell to the floor with a wet thud.

We were pinned down. More of Moretti's men had entered the holding area behind us, cutting off our retreat.

One of the men had gone down less than a dozen feet from me, his gun clattering to the dirt. Shots flew over my head, splintering the wood pens around me. My cover wouldn't hold for long. The body was still out of reach, but I tried anyway, snatching my hand back with a curse as bullets kicked up the dirt around me.

I closed my eyes. This was it. I had known that this was the most likely outcome of my decision, but now that it was here, I just felt numb. It was the end of the line—for me, at least, but I was at least going to give Tommy a fighting chance.

I'm sorry, Cass. I could see her face, so clearly it was as if she was standing right in front of him, and all I had to do was reach out and touch her.

I took several deep breaths in preparation for what was to come, and it was with her face in my head that I tensed to move towards the gun and my own end.

"Connor!"

My eyes flew open. Alfie charged into the room like an avenging angel, heedless of the bullets flying around him. I barely got my hands up in time to catch the gun he tossed to me. I moved from a crouch while he covered me, firing blindly around the edge of the pen.

He looked like hell. His eyes were wild, his hair a tangled mess. He was covered in sweat and blood, but I couldn't tell if any of it was his. He turned and looked at me, eyes burning with a savage intensity I'd never seen before.

"Perfect timing." Tommy slid in beside us. "Where the hell did you guys come from?"

It was only then that I noticed that Alfie wasn't alone. Misha was there as well, along with Michael and a handful of the Russians. We made quick work of Moretti's remaining men, and after a few minutes of fierce gunfire, silence reigned in the slaughterhouse.

32

— · —

ALFIE

IN AN UNCHARACTERISTIC DISPLAY of emotion, Tommy swept me up in a bone-crushing bear hug. I winced as his arms squeezed my sore ribs. "Easy, Tom"

He laughed and released me. "Damn glad to see you, man. I was starting to think we were in trouble, there. You okay?"

I was quite sure I looked like absolute shit, but I was grateful he didn't say so. "You?"

They both looked like they'd been worked over by a thresher, but Tommy just shrugged. "Nothing a cold beer and a hot woman won't fix. And speaking of that, let's get the hell out of here."

Connor grabbed Michael's elbow. "Is Cassidy all right? Where is she?"

Michael looked like he'd aged ten years in the last hour. The night had sapped him of his strength, and I was honestly still surprised to see him still upright. "She's back at Lady D's. Sloane's with her," he reassured the younger man. "Still a spitfire, and still a pain in my ass, but she's all right, son."

Connor let out a shaky breath. Nodded. Turned his back on us to check the loadout in the gun he was carrying, but not before I saw his hands tremble and his eyes squeeze shut.

Seeing his relief sent a fresh wave of grief crashing over me. I was happy for him, really I was, but there would be no joyous reunion for me.

I turned away from the scene, trying to swallow down the bitterness rising in my throat. I had tried to focus on finding Connor and Tommy. I hadn't allowed myself to think about anything beyond that. I had never believed in hope—it was for fools and idealists who believed in things like love and friendship—and now that I'd seen it in action, I was glad to be rid of it.

A hand fell on my shoulder. I glanced up to see Tommy standing next to me.

"Are you okay?" he asked.

"I'm fine," I snapped. "Look, we've got to move—Angel is still down here somewhere, I'm not letting him get away. Not this time."

"There's a side entrance for deliveries, he probably made his way there. He's not getting' far—we've got that covered, too. Don't worry, we'll get him." Tommy made a move to take my arm. "C'mon, let's go."

"No!" I jerked back. "I'm not walking' outta here til Angel is dead. You coming, or not?"

The last bit was called over my shoulder as I moved out of the ruined holding area. Tommy cursed and followed, the rest of our motley rescue group on his heels.

Suddenly, Misha pressed his finger to the comms device in his ear. "My men have Lorenzo pinned down at the delivery entrance."

"Let's go."

"Connor, wait—"

Tommy was still calling out to him as he rounded the corner, but the rest of his words were cut off in a deafening roar of gunfire. Moretti and his bodyguards, cut off in their retreat from the delivery entrance.

Something slammed into my shoulder, knocking me back. I staggered, but the impact felt blunted. The vest had caught the slug. I kept moving.

This was bad.

There were just too many of them. We were in the open, exposed. There was nowhere to go but forward, and I had no intention of stopping. I fired at the guards, driving them back and giving Connor a chance to close the gap.

Misha and his men had worked their way over to the side, triangulating their position between us and the Italians. What the hell was he doing? He should be taking out the Italians, not...

Shit. I turned on the Russian as realization dawned. I knew exactly what that bastard was about to do. I opened my mouth to shout, to warn Connor, but it was already too late.

Misha shouted something in Russian, and his men turned, their weapons pointed in the opposite direction.

Towards us.

Moretti's men scrambled to reposition themselves beside the Russians.

The betrayal happened in the blink of an eye, and all I could do was watch.

As Misha and his men turned and opened fire on the Italians.

They never stood a chance. The Italian mobsters tried to retreat, but the Russians were firing from close quarters, their bullets tearing through them like a hot knife through butter. Blood spattered the walls, pooling on the floor as Moretti's men fell one by one.

"Thought you were with them," I called to Misha. "I thought Volkov's interests came first."

The Russian grinned back at me. "Today, Volkov's interest lie elsewhere."

Through the haze of drifting cordite, I saw Connor walking towards something heaped on the floor. I followed him, stepping over the bodies until I was standing right in front of Lorenzo.

Somehow, he was still alive. Not for long, though. The man's pristine suit was stained with crimson, still oozing from at least four bullet wounds.

Connor kicked the gun away and crouched down. "I told you I was going to kill you, Moretti. You never should have gone after my family."

Lorenzo gurgled a laugh. "You really think this ends with me? They are never going to be safe. Not in this life."

"But they will be safe from you." Connor paused, listening to the sound of approaching sirens. The sneer slowly slipped from Moretti's face. "You hear that? That's the sound of your empire crumbling. Your family is decimated, your men are dead, and the police will take the rest. You have nothing. You've lost."

In the end, the man died with a whimper, a look of stunned disbelief on his face.

Connor stared at the body for a few moments before Tommy's hand landed on his shoulder, and he looked up to see Callum and the rest of the Clan rushing towards us.

Tommy glanced at me, and his eyes narrowed as his eyes dropped to my shoulder. Gingerly, he pulled back the edge of my jacket. Blood blossomed, slowly darkening my shirt in a widening circle.

"You're hit."

I fingered the hole in his left shoulder, frowning. "...t-thought it hit the vest..."

"You're not wearing a vest, idiot." Tommy crushed his hand against my shoulder, applying pressure. "It's called shock. Hold still."

"I'm fine."

"The hell you are." He pressed harder, and I grunted in pain. "Dad, we need to get--"

His warning came just as Dom and Angel rounded the corner. Dom's eyes locked on Tommy, pure hatred etched into his features as he drew his gun.

"Tommy, get down!" I shouted, but it was Michael who acted, his shot ringing out almost simultaneously with my warning. Dom's body jerked violently before he hit the ground, dark blood blooming across his designer suit.

Angelo fired wildly in our direction. I saw the flash of muzzle flare and reacted on instinct, tackling Connor out of the path of the bullets. We hit the floor hard, the breath exploding from my lungs. I rolled off Connor and snapped off two shots back at Angelo. One grazed his shoulder, and the second buried itself in his gut, spinning him around and sending his pistol skidding across the floor.

The wail of sirens split the air, distant but rapidly approaching. We had to leave, now. Scrambling to my feet, I turned to grab Connor. He was still down, not moving.

My heart seized. I dropped to my knees beside him, hands frantically searching for the wound. There, on his left side - the dark stain spread rapidly across his shirt. Far, far too much blood.

No. Please, no.

"Connor, hey, look at me," I begged, pressing my hands to the wound in a desperate effort to slow the bleeding. His face had gone pale, his breathing ragged.

"Jesus Christ..." Panic clawed at my throat. "Tommy, help me here!"

Tommy took one look at the wound and cursed. "We need to get him out of here. Give me your jacket."

He tied it as tightly as he could around Connor's midsection. It wasn't great, but it was the best we could do. Together, Tommy and I hoisted him between us, supporting his weight clumsily. Pain ripped through me as my shoulder protested, but I ignored it. Connor dry heaved as we got him upright and turned towards the exit.

The sound of a hammer cocking back stopped us in our tracks. Angelo Moretti swayed on shaky legs, gut shot and dying, his gun pointed unwaveringly at my heart.

"You should've stayed dead, you fucking Irish bastard." He coughed thickly. "You have taken everything from me. But at least I can die knowing I took your little whore from you first."

I saw his finger tighten on the trigger.

Closed my eyes and whispered Emilia's name.

The gunshot was deafening. I flinched instinctively, waiting for the bullet to tear through flesh and bone. But there was no impact. No rushing darkness.

Only silence.

I opened my eyes.

Angel lay crumpled on the ground, a neat round hole in the middle of his forehead, and standing over him was a ghost.

The smoke from Emilia's gun still curled around her fingers like a lover's caress, while Sloane and Sofia stood behind her, staring down at the body on the floor in shock. Emilia lowered the pistol to her side, and I saw her hands tremble, just a little, before she looked up and locked eyes with me.

And then she was running, as fast as her legs could carry her, until she was in my arms and I was holding her, alive, against my chest. My hands tangled in her hair, pulling her lips to mine as I kissed her hard and fierce. She made a small, desperate noise in the back of her throat as she clung to me. I tasted her tears on my tongue as she trembled in my embrace.

Alive. She was alive.

"Emilia...oh, Christ..." I was dimly aware of Sloane and Sofia hovering over us, of Michael's voice calling to Tommy, of sirens approaching in the distance, but all I could focus on was the woman in my arms. "I thought...I-I thought..."

"I know, I know. I'm here," she whispered, pressing her lips to my forehead. "I'm so sorry. I'm so, so sorry."

My knees buckled. Relief and spent adrenaline and blood loss were taking their toll, and Sloane came up beside me and took Connor's weight from my shoulders. The sirens were nearly on top of us. We had run out of time.

"We've got a van parked out by the loading dock," Sloane said. "Cassidy is waiting with her med kit, but we need to move."

Misha stepped forward, flanked by several of his men. "We will take care of this, Callum. Consider our debt paid. Go."

Callum stared at him, hard, but nodded. Then we turned and fled the slaughterhouse, leaving the dead and dying behind us.

33

— • —

EMILIA

I HALF-DRAGGED, HALF-CARRIED ALFIE toward the van. He was getting heavier with every step, his normally lithe body weighing me down. I stumbled towards the waiting van as fast as my legs would carry us, adrenaline pounding at the thought of just how close he'd come to dying – seconds away from Angel pulling that trigger. I had taken a life, but I didn't regret it. I'd do it again if it meant protecting the man I loved.

"Almost there," I said breathlessly. "You're going to be okay."

I tried to reassure him even as panic rose in my chest. Always with a disarming grin or sarcastic remark, Alfie was too quiet and I hauled him towards the van, his head bobbing drunkenly with every step.

"Christ, you're heavier than I thought," I grumbled under my breath, half-joking, trying to lighten the mood. A pained laugh escaped Alfie's lips, but it cut off in a grunt.

The sight of him so vulnerable sent shockwaves through my system. This wasn't the Alfie who laughed too loud or flirted with danger like it was a game. This man in my arms was so much more fragile than I ever imagined he could be.

"Emilia," Alfie rasped, his voice a shadow of its usual carefree lilt. His breaths came out in sharp, ragged pulls, his chest rising and falling unevenly against mine as we moved.

"Shh, don't talk. Save your strength," I murmured, trying to keep the panic from seeping into my voice. "Stay with me."

"Wouldn't dream of leaving you," he rasped, locking his gaze on mine. His eyes held the promise of a thousand stolen moments, a lifetime of love that was still uncertain. And for a moment, I allowed myself to get lost in them.

"Good," I said with a shaky breath, trying to steady my racing heart. "Because I'm not letting you go without a fight."

Cassidy had the back door open and was already waiting for us. We reached the van, and I helped Alfie slide into the open space, settling him against the side.

My hands shook as I pressed them against his wound, trying to slow the bleeding. Alfie hissed in pain, his eyes squeezing shut. Guilt and fear warred within me as I watched him struggle. This was all because of my father, because of the feud between our families. If only—

"Move." Cassidy stiff-armed me out of the way and immediately began assessing the damage. I scooted back, giving her room to work, and she ripped open the shirt to get a better look at the wound. Alfie's body tensed as she poked and prodded the area around the bullet hole, but he remained silent, his jaw clenched tight against the pain. Strands of light auburn hair had fallen limply across her forehead, sweat beading along her hairline as she looked at his wound with practiced eyes.

"Easy--watch his side."

Cassidy's head snapped up at the sound of Sloane's strained voice as she and Tommy hoisted Connor into the van. He looked far worse than Alfie. His shirtfront was soaked with blood, staining the fabric a deep, dark red. I'd never seen anyone look that pale before.

"Through and through, looks like it missed the lung. Keep pressure on it," Cassidy snapped, her doctor's tone cutting through the chaos. She barely glanced at Alfie's shoulder, her focus already shifting to her husband.

I did as told, pressing down on Alfie's wound with all the strength I could muster. His blood was warm and slick under my fingers, and I started to feel lightheaded.

"Hey." Alfie's hand came up to cover mine, his touch gentle despite the pain he must be in. "Look at me, Emilia."

I lifted my gaze to his, tears pricking at my eyes. "I'm so sorry," I whispered.

The corner of his mouth quirked up in a half smile. "Not your fault, sweetheart. None of this is your fault." He squeezed my hand. "Just promise me you'll stay with me. That's all I need."

My vision blurred as tears spilled down my cheeks. I leaned down and pressed a soft kiss to his lips. "Always."

"I need some room here--Sloane, drive!" Cassidy started barking out orders to Tommy. Her voice shook but her hands were steady as she worked to save her husband's life.

I pulled Alfie closer against the side of the van, giving room for Connor's body to be laid out alongside us. Connor lay still, his broad chest rising and falling way too fast, as Cassidy and Tommy worked to stabilize him.

Part of me wanted to go help, to do something instead of just sitting here, helpless. But I couldn't leave Alfie. I kept my hands pressed against his shoulder, murmuring softly to him as the van careened through the streets. His eyes were closed, his breathing shallow. I touched his cheek, willing him to stay conscious. "Alfie. Please, look at me."

His eyes fluttered open, meeting mine. There was pain in his gaze but also warmth. A trembling smile touched his lips. "Still...here. Not getting rid of me that easily."

The engine roared to life, and Sloane jammed the van into gear. We fishtailed out of the parking lot as the lights from the approaching police cars ricochetted crazily off the slaughterhouse's facade.

Cassidy was bent over Connor, her face pale and drawn. She was snapping out orders to Michael and Tommy, trying to stabilize Connor's condition. The front of his shirt was soaked crimson.

My gaze flicked to the floor of the van, bile rising in my throat. So much blood. Too much blood. Alfie's hand covered mine, and I looked back up at him.

"You okay?" His words were slurred, his eyes heavy-lidded.

"I'm fine. Just stay still." My voice trembled, heart thudding wildly.

"Okay," he mumbled, his eyes drifting closed again. His hand started to slip from mine.

"Hey, hey, no closing your eyes." I shook him gently, trying to keep him awake. "Come on, since when have you had a hard time taking your eyes off me?"

"Can't help it," he murmured, his grip on my wrist weakening. "You're just so damn pretty, Emilia Russo. It's like staring into the sun."

"Flattery will get you nowhere when you're bleeding on my dress," I retorted, though my heart swelled at his words.

"Sorry 'bout the dress," he mumbled, the corners of his lips twitching upwards for a split second before pain etched deep lines across his forehead again.

"Focus on breathing, that's an order." My tone was firm, but my insides were quivering. Fear clawed at my throat, making it hard to swallow.

"So...bossy..."

The van jolted over a pothole, sending my heart into my throat as I fought to maintain pressure on Alfie's wound. He winced but remained silent, his gaze never leaving mine.

"Tommy, help me with Connor," Cassidy called out, her voice strained.. Her face was contorted in pain, breaths coming in sharp gasps as she clutched at her swollen belly. The significance hit me like a punch to the gut—Cassidy's labor had progressed much further than we thought.

"Jesus, Cass," Tommy swore, his eyes darting between Connor and his sister. "Are you sure you're okay?"

"No, I'm not okay, but that's not important right now. Just help me!" Cassidy barked through clenched teeth, her voice strained but authoritative. She reached Connor, who lay motionless, and dropped to her knees beside him. Any signs of her own agony were pushed aside; she was a doctor first, a wife second. The transformation was nothing short of miraculous, and I marveled at her strength even as she knelt by her unconscious husband's side.

"Connor, can you hear me?" she asked, her fingers brushing his neck, counting his pulse.

"Is he..."

"Pulse is tachy, he's decompensating." Cassidy tore open his shirt, exposing the bloody mess beneath. The bullet hole was small, but it was pulsing blood. She slapped another wad of gauze on it and rolled him on his side. "No exit wound, but he's hemorrhaging. The bullet punctured the liver."

Beside her, Tommy ripped open the kid. "What can I do?"

"Pack the wound with that gauze, as much as you can, and keep applying pressure. It's going to hurt him, but we've got to get a handle on that bleed."

Cassidy leaned over him, checking his airway and breathing. Her teeth clenched as she endured another contraction, knuckles white until it passed.

"Hang on, Connor." Cassidy's voice wavered as she gently brushed the hair off his forehead. "Don't you fucking give up on me now, do you hear me?"

There was no response, but she continued talking to him anyway, murmuring soft, reassuring words to him as she worked. Alfie's fingers closed around my wrist, watching silently. The scene was so intimate, I almost looked away, an intruder on a private moment.

Cassidy's breathing hitched again, and she groaned in pain. The contractions were coming faster now, and it took longer for her to recover.

Her hands trembled as she fought to stay focused on Connor, but I could see the strain was taking a toll on her.

I moved towards them. "Let me help you."

"No." Her voice was firm. "You stay with Alfie."

"Cassidy, please..." I swallowed hard. "Please, let me help. He'll be okay for a few minutes."

"I've got this." This time, the stethoscope shook in her hands when she applied it to Connor's chest. The grim line of her mouth tightened further, and she moved it lower. For the first time, she looked a little lost. "I can barely hear the heart. Blood pressure's dropping. W-We need to start an IV."

The IV bag appeared in her hands as if conjured from thin air, and Tommy helped her get it started. As she inserted the needle into Connor's arm, her movements were precise, even as her body swayed with the motion of the van.

"Can you tell if he's bleeding internally?" Alfie rasped.

"I...I don't know." Her voice broke, and she ducked her head, trying to hide the tears that threatened to fall. "I-I can't even think right now, I--"

Her words were cut off in a guttural scream as another contraction ripped through her. She bent double, her hands gripping the sides of the van. Tommy caught her in his arms.

"What--are you--it's happening now?" His eyes were wide, realizing his sister was in labor. "But it's too soon."

Cassidy just groaned, trying to crawl back to Connor.

Something snapped in Tommy. "Dad, get back here, and Cassidy, just...just breathe, or something."

"I'm fine--"

"Don't be stubborn."

"Just help me, Tommy!"

"We're almost there," Sloane called from the driver's seat, the tires squealing as she took another corner too sharply.

The van tilted.

Horns blared.

"Hold on!" Michael shouted.

Sofia launched forward to steady Cassidy before she could fall into the side of the van. I'd almost forgotten she was back there with us. She looked stricken, her hands tightening around Cassidy's arms to steady her.

"What can I do?" she asked.

Cassidy shook her head, her teeth gritted. "Get the epi from my bag. He's slipping."

I watched as Cassidy emptied the syringe into his IV, praying that it would be enough to keep him with us until we reached the hospital.

"No, you don't," Cassidy said fiercely. "Don't you dare do this to me, you stubborn Irish asshole."

Amazingly he groaned and briefly came to. He was shaking uncontrollably, each panting breath rasping out of blue-tinged lips as he stirred and blinked.

"Connor?" Cassidy's hands cupped his face, turning it so he could see her. "Connor, look at me."

His chest rose and fell harshly. Cassidy's lips trembled, and she smoothed his hair back from his ashen forehead. I could see in her eyes that she understood how close to death he was, even if she wouldn't accept it. "Please, love, I need you to stay with me. Just a little longer. Please, just hold on."

Tommy wrapped his arms around his sister, holding her up as she bent over in pain. She bit back a scream again, and Tommy gripped her tighter.

Connor's eyes fluttered open. "C-Cass...the baby..."

"I'm here, I'm right here," she reassured him, pressing her lips to his forehead. The light in his eyes had died down to a single glowing ember. She cupped his cheek with her hand. "Stay with me, okay? You've got to meet your son." She hiccupped a watery laugh. "He must be a Mc-Tiernan, because he's already stubbornly deciding to do this on his own schedule."

The faintest ghost of a smile flitted over Connor's lips. "Love...you..."

"I love you, too." Her voice broke on the last word. Tears spilled down her cheeks, landing on his skin like raindrops. "Is breá liom tú, Connor, remember? Always. So please don't leave me."

"I..." His chest rose and fell rapidly. "I'm...sorry, Cass..."

"No. No, don't do this, please."

Connor's eyes rolled in his head as he blinked sluggishly, settling his gaze on Tommy. He raised a bloodstained hand. "Promise..."

"Don't do this shit, brother. You're not dying--you're going to be fine--so don't start asking for promises--"

"Take...care...of them."

Tommy gripped the offered hand, but he clasped Cassidy's around it, instead. "We're gonna take care of each other, okay? We've always done that, right? No promises needed. But I'll help you keep 'em safe if you promise to fight for them."

"Ca...ssidy," Connor managed to choke out, his voice barely audible.

The effort it took for him to speak seemed to sap what little strength he had left. Cassidy curled in her brother's arms as another contraction swept over her. They were coming steadily now, and the only things she seemed to be able to focus on were the labor pains and Connor's bloody hand clasped in hers.

Connor lost consciousness for the last time as the van skidded to a halt outside the hospital's emergency loading area. The back doors flew open, and suddenly we were surrounded by medical personnel.

"Jerome." Cassidy struggled in Tommy's arms, clearly recognizing one of the doctors. "We've got two GSW's, one critical--"

"And you look like you're in labor," Jerome finished.

"Not important right now, just get him in there!"

"Cassidy--"

"Do not fucking argue with me, just help him!" she screamed. Her eyes were wild, frantic.

"Cassidy, you need help, too."

"I know, I know," she trembled. She turned back to Connor, who was being loaded onto a stretcher. "I need to go with him. I have to stay with him, please."

"We'll take good care of him."

"No, no, you don't understand--"

"We'll go with him, Cass." Michael took his daughter carefully by the shoulders and pulled her away from her husband, trying to steer her towards the waiting nurses. "Just let these people help you. Tommy?"

"I've got her, Dad." Tommy wrapped his arm around Cassidy's waist and guided her out of the van. "Come on, Cass, let's get you inside."

"Ma'am?"

I jumped, startled by the hand on my shoulder. A paramedic was gently trying to pull me away from Alfie's side. "We've got him from here."

My chest tightened as they moved to take over. "O-Okay."

Numbly, I allowed myself to be guided out of the van, barely feeling the strong arms that wrapped around my waist as I stumbled over the curb. I didn't even know who it was until I felt the familiar prickle of Sofia's long hair against my cheek.

"It's going to be okay," she whispered.

"But Alfie--" My voice caught in my throat. I couldn't say it, couldn't put words to the horrible dread that was gnawing at my heart. He looked so pale being loaded onto the stretcher that my heart squeezed despite the wavery grin he flashed at me.

"Hey, Emilia..." His voice was hoarse and weak.

I forced a smile, but it wavered, tears rolling down my cheeks. "Hey, you."

"Go with Sofia. I'll see...you soon."

"You'd better."

34

CASSIDY

NEW LIFE. DEATH. TANGLED together in a cruel twist of fate.

Instead of my husband, my brother held me close as I struggled to bring my child into the world, wishing for the first time in my life that I wasn't a doctor. It would be easier to deal with the pain if I didn't know exactly what was happening two floors below me in the trauma bay.

Wishing I could go back in time and alter the path of that bullet.

But there were some things even I couldn't fix. However much I might want to.

All I could do was grit my teeth against the pain.

To hold on just one more second, one more breath, one more heartbeat.

And welcome the new life we had created together.

The bittersweet miracle of it, on a day stained by so much death.

The medical staff swarmed around me as I was transferred onto the delivery bed, their movements efficient but impersonal. They didn't know my husband lay several floors below, fighting for his life. They didn't understand that with every push, with every cry torn from my lips, a part of me was fighting alongside him.

"Complications..."

"...critical condition..."

Fragments of information snatched from the doctors and nurses flurrying around me, all of it tinged with a sense of urgency that at any other time and place would be grounding. Except it had been a very long time since I had been on this end of things.

"Are they...talking about Connor?" I panted, gripping Tommy's hand like a lifeline.

"No, no, focus on your breathing, Cass. He's in good hands," Tommy said firmly. "Connor's a fighter. You know that better than anyone."

He was in good hands. Jerome's hands. Two floors below us, my husband's life was in the hands of my friend and mentor, yet while I understood that on a fundamental level, it didn't make it any easier.

"I should be with him."

"You can't help him right now. Just be here with me, okay?"

Tommy looked decidedly green around the gills, but he refused to leave my side, even when the nurse asked if he wouldn't be more comfortable in the waiting room. He growled over his shoulder at the nurse who was checking my blood pressure. "Just try to make me leave."

She didn't look convinced, but she let it go. "Just keep breathing, Cassidy. The baby's heart rate is very good, you're doing great. Almost there."

I was no stranger to pain, but this... this was something else entirely. I gritted my teeth as another wave of contractions tore through me, the once sterile whiteness of the hospital room now obscured by a haze of agony. My brows furrowed, sweat trickling down the side of my face, as I desperately tried to summon the strength that had carried me thus far.

"It's time to start pushing, Mrs. McTiernan," a nurse said.

Panic flared. It was too soon. Connor wasn't here. I needed him.

"You can do this," Tommy said, squeezing my hand. "I'm right here with you."

I looked into my brother's eyes, seeing nothing but love and strength. He was right. I had to believe we'd all make it through this. Connor would survive. Our son would be born healthy and strong. We were fighters, survivors. Every single one of us.

Time winnowed away to the hollowed-out spaces between the pain, Tommy's hand in mine a warm, constant tether to the real world. He spoke to me in low, soothing tones, but I barely heard him. All I could hear was the roar of my own blood thundering through my veins, and all I could feel was the crushing pressure bearing down on my body.

"Breathe, sweetheart. Breathe with me."

"Stop telling me to fucking breathe."

Tommy choked back a strained laugh. "I don't know what else to do."

"It's not helping."

"Sorry. Sorry, I just--"

"Shut up, Tommy. Please."

"Okay."

"Oh, god," I breathed as another wave of pain washed over me. I knew I was gripping his hand hard enough to leave bruises, but I couldn't pry my fingers loose. "This isn't working, I've got to get up."

"O-Okay."

Alarmed, he looked to the labor nurse, but she just nodded. I was already rolling to me knees, facing the head of the bed. The nurses moved him into a position where he could help me, and I clutched onto his massive shoulders, burying my head against my brother's neck.

"T-Tommy...

"I'm here, Cass. I've got you."

"It hurts, Tommy. It hurts so fucking much."

"You're doing so good, sweetie, so good. Just rest a bit before the next one...I love you so much."

I nodded against him, unable to do much more than pant in his ear.

"Okay, here it comes, another big push...you're got this...c'mon, push with me..."

Time seemed to winnow down to each breath, each heartbeat, each push, everything falling away until it was just the two of us working to bring my son into the world.

"I can see the head now, looks like this little fella's got a full head of hair," the nurse smiled.

"You hear that Cass? Almost there...another big push now..."

And then a tiny, wailing cry broke through the room, and the world seemed to stop.

The most beautiful sound in the world.

The squeaky, ragged cry of a newborn.

My son.

Tommy stared over my shoulder, slack jawed as the nurses maneuvered the tiny, squalling body. Wrinkled and writhing and breathtakingly beautiful, and all he seemed able to do was nod and kiss my forehead as the nurses helped me to turn and lay back, the breath momentarily knocked from his body.

Exhausted, I fell back against the pillows, my body spent but my heart surging with an indescribable love. Tommy released my hand to scrub brusquely at his face, laughing in disbelief as the baby was quickly cleaned and swaddled before being placed in my arms.

"Hello, my beautiful boy," I whispered to the tiny, red-faced infant whose cries softened to curious whimpers upon hearing my voice. His little fingers gripped mine with surprising strength, sparking a fresh wave of tears that cascaded down my cheeks.

Tommy watched the two of us, a mixture of awe and relief on his face.

"Hey, buddy," he said softly, brushing the backs of his knuckles against the baby's cheek. "Welcome to the world."

"He's perfect," I breathed, tracing the curve of his cheek. He snuggled into my touch, his cries quieting even more at the sound of my voice.

"He's a fighter, just like his mama."

I nodded. "And his daddy, too."

A heavy silence hung between us, neither of us wanting to acknowledge the gaping hole that Connor's absence had left in the room. We were both too scared to voice our fears aloud, terrified that speaking them might somehow make them real.

Tommy cleared his throat. "Did you guys pick out a name yet?"

"Aiden," I murmured against my son's downy head. "Aiden McTiernan."

Tommy's lips quirked up in a bittersweet smile. "It's perfect."

"His middle name is Thomas."

My brother stared at me, unblinking, for a long moment. Then he ducked his head, trying to hide the emotion that shone in his eyes. "You named him after..."

I nodded. "We were going to tell you together, but I want you to know now. We'd like you to be his godfather."

Tommy looked stunned. "You want me to...?"

"Of course we do, Tommy. You're his uncle."

"But you know what I am. What I do."

"That's not all you are, Tommy," I said softly. "And it's not all you'll ever be."

"I...I don't know what to say," he murmured, staring down at the baby with wonder.

Aiden yawned, stretching out tiny hands towards his uncle. Tommy grinned, stroking a finger over the baby's head.

"Do you want to hold him?"

"I-I don't know." Tommy backed away. "He's so...little."

"You won't drop him, I promise." I chuckled, seeing his wide-eyed expression.

Tommy edged closer, his eyes wide with awe as I handed Aiden up to him. His hands, usually so steady and sure from years in the ring, trembled visibly as he cradled the newborn. The tough exterior he'd always shown to the world melted away in an instant.

He held the baby close, gazing down at him with naked adoration. "Hello there, little man. I'm your uncle Tommy. I'm going to teach you all kinds of things your mom probably won't approve of, but don't worry, I'll keep you out of trouble."

Aiden snuffled against his chest, tiny fists flailing against the blanket. His voice shook with emotion as he continued. "You're the best thing that's ever happened to this family. We're going to give you the world, little buddy."

"Tommy..." My voice broke, the sight of my brother, this pillar of strength, so openly vulnerable and filled with love—it was a poignant image I knew I would never forget.

"Just wait until you meet your daddy. He's gonna be damn proud of you, Aiden."

He kissed the baby's forehead gently before walking over to where I lay. Tommy's gaze met mine, brimming with unspoken promises and a gratitude too deep for words. He carefully placed my son into my arms, his own hands lingering as if reluctant to let go.

The warmth of my baby against my chest brought a rush of emotions so fierce it nearly overwhelmed me. I looked into his tiny face, his delicate features a blend of Connor and myself, and my heart swelled to the point of bursting.

"Hello, my little warrior," I murmured, my fingertips grazing the soft down of his hair. Each breath he took seemed to stitch together the fragments of my battered soul, filling spaces I hadn't known were empty.

"Thank you, Tommy." I whispered.

He glanced up, eyes shining. "For what?"

"For being you. For always being there when I needed you. Even when I didn't want you to be. I love you, Tommy."

"Hey now," he said gruffly. "None of that mushy stuff. I have a reputation to maintain."

But his smile gave him away. In that moment, I could see the man he was becoming, and it filled me with pride.

In my arms, Aiden was already asleep. I glanced down at him, cradled in my arms, his tiny fingers grasping onto mine with surprising strength. My heart swelled with love and a fierce protectiveness for this little life I had brought into the world. "Tommy, can you see if there's any update on Connor?" I asked, my voice barely more than a whisper as I tried to keep my emotions in check. The thought of my husband fighting for his life just a few floors down sent a wave of fear through me.

"Of course, Cass." Tommy nodded toward the nurse, who immediately understood the urgency behind my request.

"Mrs. McTiernan, your husband was still in surgery the last time we received an update. I'll go check again right away." She gave me an empathetic smile before leaving the room.

"Please." The word came out as a plea, wrapped around the hope that had become so fragile within me.

I closed my eyes and took a deep breath, struggling to reign in the emotional turmoil that threatened to overwhelm me. It wasn't easy, but I managed to find some semblance of control by focusing on the warmth and weight of my son in my arms, drawing on the strength that Tommy exuded beside me.

"Connor's a fighter, Cass. He's going to make it."

"He has to. I can't do this without him." My voice broke on the last word, and I struggled to hold back the tears that burned at the corners of my eyes. Tommy didn't say anything. He just held me in his arms while we waited to hear back from the nurse, the warm bundle of life cradled between us.

After what seemed like a lifetime, the door opened, and the nurse entered, a solemn expression on her face. My heart raced in my chest, and I felt Tommy's grip on my hand tighten as we braced ourselves for the news.

"Mrs. McTiernan..." she began, her voice steady despite the gravity of the situation. "Both your husband and Mr. Doyle made it through surgery. Mr. Doyle is in recovery, and while it was touch and go with your husband, he's stable now and has been moved to the ICU."

A sob ripped through me, raw and unguarded; it was echoed by Tommy's relieved exhale.

Alive.

Connor was alive.

The future, once veiled in shadows, flickered with light—tentative, but persistent.

I knew Tommy expected me to barrage her with questions—what kind of surgery, what were the complications, how long before we can see him—but instead, an unexpected wave of emotion crested over me, pulling me under. Tears sprung from wells I didn't know I had, spilling over my cheeks in torrents.

"Hey, hey..." Tommy's voice was a soothing rumble, his thumb brushing away the tears that streamed down my face. "Cass, look at me."

My brother's face swam into view, his expression etched with concern and something akin to wonder. It was as though he couldn't quite believe that we had been granted this reprieve from the abyss.

"Connor's going to be okay," he murmured, his words a lifeline thrown across the chasm of my fears. "You hear that? He's going to make it."

I nodded, my sobs rendering me incapable of speech. The dam inside me had broken, and all the pent-up worry, the terror of losing Connor, flooded out of me in a deluge of relief.

"Hey, it's okay," Tommy murmured, wrapping one arm around me as I wept. "You're allowed to cry, Cassidy. You've been through hell today, but it's over now."

Tommy's arms tightened around me, strong and steady as a rock. His embrace was warm, solid, and for the first time since I could remember, I felt the role of older brother fit him like a second skin. The tension from the day ebbed away as I cried into his chest, my baby boy still in my arms. For the first time in my life, I felt the comfort of having an older brother who could protect and console me when I needed him the most. He rocked me gently back and forth, the rhythm a soothing balm to my shredded nerves.

"Go ahead and let it go," he murmured. "I've got you."

The tears that streamed down my cheeks were both of joy and exhaustion—rivulets carving paths of release from the torrent of fear that had held me captive. Connor was alive. Our baby was safe. It was almost hard to believe. The sheer magnitude of relief was overwhelming, and for once, I didn't have to be the strong one. Tommy was here, and he was holding me together.

"Tommy, I—" My words faltered, choked by the swell of gratitude.

"Shh, it's okay. Just rest," he soothed, and I felt the gentle pressure of his lips on my forehead.

I clung to him, my fingers twisted in the fabric of his shirt, as the sobs subsided to hitching breaths. The weight of our newborn son in my arms was the only anchor keeping me moored to reality. As my eyes grew heavy with the pull of sleep, I fought to stay awake, afraid that letting go would mean waking to find this peace was just a fleeting dream.

"Sleep, Cass." Tommy murmured, his hand stroking my hair with a tenderness I'd never seen from him before. "I'll hold Aiden for a bit so you can rest."

With a soft sigh, I allowed myself to drift off, trusting that my brother would watch over me and my newborn son. As sleep claimed me, I clung to the belief that Connor would make it through this ordeal too—that our family would be whole once more.

When I stirred again, disoriented by the unfamiliar hospital room, I realized that Tommy had gently taken the baby from my arms. He cradled him with such tenderness, a faraway look in his eyes, like something had fundamentally shifted within him.

Something had shifted in me, too.

My eyelids fluttered open, the sterile scent of the hospital filling my senses before the memories flooded back in—a rush of joy, pain, and gnawing anxiety. I shifted on the bed, a dull ache reminding me of the ordeal my body had just endured. A soft coo drew my eyes to the bassinet where my newborn son lay, swaddled and peaceful.

"Tommy?" My voice was hoarse, more a whisper than a question.

"I'm here, Cass." He emerged from the shadows, a weary smile on his face as he handed me a cup of water. "You've been out for a while. How are you feeling?"

"Like I've been hit by a truck," I admitted with a weak chuckle. "Did they give any more news about Connor?"

Tommy hesitated for a moment before answering, concern etched on his face. "He's still in the ICU, unconscious but stable. Nothing else."

"Can I see him?" I asked urgently, heart pounding.

"Let's get you taken care of first," Tommy suggested, placing a comforting hand on my shoulder. "We've got people watching over him. He won't be alone."

I nodded, biting back a sob. I wanted to be by Connor's side, but I knew Tommy was right—I needed to regain some strength first.

Before I could argue, the door opened, and our father stepped in. Michael McTiernan, always imposing, was even less so now. The lines around his eyes were deeper than I remembered, and there was a new hollowness to his cheeks. Still, he managed to muster a smile when his gaze landed on me.

"Is this a good time?"

"Yes, Dad." I swallowed past the lump in my throat, reaching for his hand. "Please, come in."

His eyes flicked from me to Tommy and back again, searching for signs of distress. Finding none, he exhaled in relief. "How are you feeling?"

"Better now, thank you."

"I came as soon as I heard you'd had the baby," he said. "Sloane and I, we've been taking turns with Connor."

My fingers curled around the blankets. "How is he?"

"Better than expected. It's going to be a tough road, but you married a tough man. He certainly fought hard to stay with you."

"I know." A tear rolled down my cheek. "Thank you, Dad."

He nodded gruffly. Aiden shifted in my arms and yawned, and my father looked down, almost startled to see him there.

"Do you want to see him?" I asked.

A hesitant smile broke across his face as he approached the bedside. He reached out a hand, pausing to ask permission before gently brushing his fingertips over the baby's head.

"What's his name?"

"Aiden. Aiden Thomas McTiernan."

He let out a long breath. "That's a strong name. He'll carry it well."

"I think so, too." I looked up for Tommy, but he'd left the room, sensing we needed a little space.

"You look so much like your mother," he murmured, gazing at the baby with a mixture of sorrow and adoration. "And you've got her strength, too."

"Dad..."

"I know it's been a long time coming, but I want you to know how proud I am of you, Cassidy," he said quietly. "I'm only sorry I haven't said it enough."

I swallowed hard, blinking back the tears that threatened to fall. "It's okay, Dad. I know."

He nodded, a sad smile tugging at the corner of his lips. "When you were born, your mother and I made a promise to each other that we would give you and Tommy the best life possible. And for a while, we did. But after your mother...somewhere along the way, I lost sight of that."

He shook his head, as if trying to clear the ghosts of his past from his mind. "What I'm trying to say, Cass, is that I'm sorry. For all the times I wasn't there, and for all the times I put you through hell because I was too stubborn to change. You deserved better, and I hope you'll give me another chance to be the father you need. To be a grandfather to Aiden."

The sincerity in his words touched me, and I couldn't help the tears that spilled down my cheeks. My father had never been one to openly express his emotions, and hearing him speak so openly now, I felt a surge of love and compassion for him.

"I'd like that, Dad," I whispered.

"Good." He leaned down and brushed a kiss on my forehead. "I'm going to go check in with your Dr. Carter and sit awhile with Connor. I'll be back later to see you again."

"Thanks, Dad. For everything."

"You're welcome, Cassidy." His voice was curiously gruff with emotion as he turned and headed to the door. Tommy met him on the way in, clapping a hand to his back and muttering something in his ear that had my father laugh out, a single, bright bark that made him seem, for a moment, like the man I used to know. The man I always hoped he would become again.

Tommy cocked an eyebrow at me as he settled in the chair by my bedside. "All good?"

I knew he was talking about Dad. "Today is just full of surprises, I guess."

He sighed, scrubbing his hands over his face. "You're telling me."

I glanced up at him, suddenly aware of the lines of exhaustion etched on his face, highlighted by the bruising from the beating he'd taken. Other than a brief trip to the bathroom to wash the blood off his face and arms, he had been by my side for hours. "You look tired. Even your hawk is looking a little wilted."

Tommy snorted. "I'd say you look worse, but I'd be lying. You look.. .radiant. Motherhood suits you."

"That's surprisingly eloquent, coming from you."

"What can I say. It's a day full of surprises."

With a contented sigh, I settled back against the pillows and closed my eyes, little Aiden warm and solid in my arms. The future was bright, and for the first time in a long time, I felt at peace.

35

— . —

ALFIE

THE WORLD WAS A blur when I first cracked open my eyes to an unfamiliar white ceiling. Where the hell am I? My mind churned through a fog of painkillers, trying to piece together the fractured memories of... what? A hospital room materialized around me, sterile and impersonal. The dull thrum of pain pulsated through my entire body, a relentless tide that receded only enough to let me breathe before washing over me again. The steady beep of a heart monitor filtered into my awareness, the pinch of an oxygen line under my nose.

The sound of a hammer cocking back.

Angelo Moretti swayed on shaky legs, gut shot and dying, his gun pointed unwaveringly at my heart.

"You should've stayed dead, you fucking Irish bastard." He coughed thickly. "You have taken everything from me. But at least I can die knowing I took your little whore from you first."

I saw his finger tighten on the trigger.

Closed my eyes and whispered Emilia's name.

I flinched instinctively, but there wasn't any gunshot. Just the sound of the monitor I was hooked up to protesting with an escalating series of beeps, matching the frantic cadence of my racing heart.

Where's Emilia? It wasn't just a dream, it couldn't be. She can't be--

I tried to sit up, to escape this bed, this room, to find her, but a lance of pain shot through my right shoulder, searing and absolute, pinning me down.

"Shh...it's okay. You're all right."

A firm pressure on my chest halted my pathetic attempt to rise, and a cool hand pressed against my fevered skin. I blinked up into Emilia's face, her brown eyes wells of concern and something deeper, something that made my heart lurch with hope.

"Emilia?" My voice broke on her name, the sound rough in my ears. "You're... you're really here?"

"Of course, I'm here." Her cool hand brushed across my forehead, sweeping away the damp strands of hair that clung there. "Where else would I be?"

Her words were both a relief and a gut punch. I'd nearly lost her forever. I let out a shaky breath, and my body uncoiled at her touch. Relief coursed through me, warm and heady, and I turned my face into her palm, seeking the comfort that only she could provide. The pain in my shoulder seemed to subside, just a tad, beneath the weight of her tender caress.

"God, Emilia..." I whispered. My arms ached to pull her close, but I could barely lift my head. "I-I thought..."

"I'm here," she murmured, leaning down to press a soft kiss to my lips. "I'm not going anywhere."

I sank into the sensation of her mouth on mine, warm and sweet as honey. I let the gentle pressure of her lips soothe the jagged edges of my soul, grounding me in the moment. She pulled away too soon, leaving me yearning for more.

"Are you hurt?"

She looked down at me, her eyes glistening with unshed tears. A watery laugh bubbled up from her chest, and she shook her head in disbelief. "You're the one lying in a hospital bed, and you're asking if I'm okay?"

"Can't help it," I replied with a weak smirk.

"Alfie," she sighed, but I saw the appreciation in her warm brown eyes. "I'm fine. Really. Just... don't scare me like that again, okay?"

"Sorry."

"Shh," Emilia hushed me gently, her fingers tracing idle patterns on my arm. "You have nothing to apologize for."

Her fussing was a welcome distraction, smoothing down the sheets, adjusting the oxygen cannula, all the while staying close enough that I could feel the warmth of her skin. My battered heart swelled within its cage, filled to bursting with a love that had weathered storms I once thought insurmountable.

I swallowed hard, my throat parched, but it was the sight of my girl—alive and safe—that quenched a deeper thirst. She looked so damn pretty sitting perched on the edge of the hospital bed, her dark eyes luminous in the dim light. I couldn't resist reaching up to brush a stray lock of hair out of her face, my fingers lingering on the silken strands.

Her fingers tightened around mine, and she leaned forward, her face etched with lines of worry. "Are you in pain?"

"Not really," I lied, not wanting to add to her distress. "Just thirsty."

Emilia sat up immediately. "Of course, I'm so sorry. The nurse left some ice chips before she went to go get the doctor, I can get you those. And I'll ask her to bring you some water too, if you're able to drink."

"Sweetheart, stop fussing," I said gently, though I couldn't help but love how concerned she was for me. It made my battered heart swell to know she cared so deeply. "The ice chips will do fine for now. Come back to me."

She relaxed, settling against my side again. "I just want to make sure you're comfortable," she said. "You went through so much..." Her voice trailed off, and I saw the memories haunting her eyes.

"Hey," I said softly, tilting her chin up. "Look at me. I'm alright. We're both alright. He can't hurt us anymore."

Emilia searched my gaze, as if looking for any hint of uncertainty. But I meant every word. Lorenzo and his sons were gone, and we were finally free.

She let out a shuddering breath, eyes shining with tears. But she nodded.

Emilia carefully scooped some ice chips into a spoon and brought them to my lips. The icy crystals melted on my tongue, washing away the cottony taste of anesthesia. I sucked down another spoonful greedily, and Emilia smiled, her expression softening with relief.

"Better?" she asked.

I nodded, returning her smile. "Much."

I shifted on the bed, trying to ease the dull ache in my shoulder. Emilia frowned, reaching over to adjust the pillow beneath my head. I could smell the sweet scent of her perfume as she leaned in close, her brow furrowed in concentration.

"Thanks," I murmured.

She nodded, her gaze focused on the task at hand. We sat in companionable silence for a few moments, the steady rhythm of the heart monitor and the soft rustle of Emilia's clothes as she shifted beside me the only sounds filling the room. I knew our time alone was limited, and I couldn't help but wish we could stay like this forever – just the two of us, untouchable by the chaos that seemed to follow us wherever we went.

"Alfie," Emilia whispered, breaking the quiet. "What are we going to do now?"

I looked into her eyes, seeing the fear and uncertainty lurking beneath the surface. I squeezed her hand, trying to convey my determination and devotion without words. "We'll figure it out, Em. This is the only thing that matters. Right here."

The door swung open, admitting a middle-aged man with salt-and-pepper hair and kind eyes. A nurse followed closely behind him. Jerome – the doctor Cassidy had spoken so highly of. I'd never met him before, but his reputation preceded him. He strode confidently into the room, exuding an air of authority that was both comforting and reassuring. Sharp, intelligent eyes peered at me over the rim of his glasses.

"Mr. Doyle, it's good to see you awake," he said, typing away at the bedside computer while the nurse busied herself checking my vitals. "I've heard a lot about you from Cassidy. All good things, I assure you."

"Likewise, Doc."

Emilia watched us cautiously, her grip on my hand tightening ever so slightly. Jerome seemed to sense her concern and turned his attention to her.

"Emilia, right?" he asked, already knowing the answer. His tone was brusque yet friendly, putting her at ease. "No need to worry, your man here is in good hands."

His gaze was keen, analytical, yet there was something disarmingly warm about it. It wasn't just his smile, which seemed to come as easily as breathing, but the energy he exuded—a blend of competence and comradery that chipped away at the tension coiling within her.

"Tell me, Doctor," Emilia said, her voice steady now, "how is he really?"

Jerome glanced at the monitors before turning to us, his expression sobering just a fraction. "Well, Alfie, I won't sugarcoat it—you've been luckier than most. The surgery was straightforward. You took a bullet, but it seems fate was on your side."

"Doesn't feel like it," I grumbled, trying to add levity to the throb in my shoulder.

"Could've been worse," Jerome continued. "Shoulders can be messy with all those arteries, nerves, and the lungs nearby. But this bullet, it was a courteous one. Slipped right between the clavicle and shoulder joint, exited cleanly." He made a little 'whoosh' sound, complete with a hand gesture that mimicked the bullet's trajectory. "Aside from bruises and a few minor lacerations, you're in decent shape."

"Decent shape, he says," I echoed, a smirk finding its way onto my lips despite the situation. "Guess I owe someone a thank you card for not aiming better."

"Indeed," Jerome chuckled. "And we've topped off your tank with some premium B positive. You'll be up and terrorizing the streets of Boston in no time."

"Streets might have to wait," I countered, the weight of recent events anchoring me to reality.

"Let's focus on keeping you out of trouble for a while, shall we?" Jerome said, his eyes sparkling with mirth.

"Couldn't agree more," I managed, squeezing Emilia's hand. Her presence was the only painkiller I needed, her touch more healing than any medicine they could pump into my veins. "When can I get out of here?"

He raised an eyebrow. "Anxious to be on your way?"

"Something like that."

"I understand." He checked the monitors, nodding in satisfaction. "If all looks well, I can discharge you tomorrow. But you'll need to take it easy. No strenuous activity or heavy lifting for at least a month."

Emilia nodded solemnly, and I knew she was already mentally planning ways to keep me from overexerting myself. I couldn't help but smile, seeing the protective streak that had come out in her. She was trembling, probably the letdown after all that adrenaline, and I clumsily pulled her into my arms the best I could.

"Hey--come here."

I kept her as tight as my wound would allow, for longer than either of us wanted to think about. It just felt good, needed, to have her safe in my arms again. To kiss her hair and nudge her temple with mine. There was desperation in her grip, and in the fierceness of her lips on mine, but I matched it all. If she had pulled away first, it was doubtful I could've let her go.

I softly nipped at her bottom lip. "Looks like you're stuck with me, sweetheart. It's going to take more than a bullet to get rid of me."

She managed a watery chuckle, and I pulled her closer for another kiss, my fingertips tracing a trail up her neck to cup the back of her head. I savored the taste of her, the sweet tang of her kiss, and the way her body melted against mine.

"I've missed you," she whispered. "So much."

"Not as much as I missed you." I trailed kisses along her jaw, a low growl forming in the back of my throat as I inhaled the soft, delicate scent that was unmistakably her.

"Well," Jerome said loudly. "I can see my presence here is no longer needed. I'll be back in a few hours to check on you, Mr. Doyle. In the meantime--"

"Actually..." I turned to Emilia. "Can you do me a favor? Can you go check on Cassidy and Connor? See how they're doing?"

"Of course," she said without hesitation. "I also wanted to check in with Sofia. She's sitting with Luca right now."

"Please do," I encouraged, feeling a pang of guilt that Luca had been caught up in this chaos because of me.

I watched her leave, my thoughts already racing. We'd survive this, but what came next? How could we ensure our safety, and that of those we loved?

"Was there something else you needed?" Jerome asked.

"Yeah... actually there is."

He glanced at me, his gaze sharpening as he took in my expression. "Something tells me it's not medical advice you're after."

I shook my head.

"Alright," he said cautiously, pulling up a chair beside my bed. "What's on your mind?"

"I need your help."

His eyebrows lifted, curiosity piqued. "What kind of help?"

"Emilia's life—our lives—they're hanging' by a thread." I swallowed hard, the dryness in my throat making each word an effort. "The Morettis think she's dead, and she needs to stay that way. But even with Lorenzo and his sons gone, we're never gonna be safe."

He leaned closer, his professional facade slipping as concern flickered in his eyes. "Go on."

"Jerome," I said, locking eyes with him. "I need you to kill me."

His reaction was immediate, a gobsmacked expression that would've been comical if the situation weren't so dire. "What are you—"

"On paper," I clarified quickly. "I need you to issue a death certificate for me."

"You can't be serious," Jerome protested, shaking his head. "That's –"

"No. Listen." I had already figured it out, and it was so crazy, it just might work. "Here's how it's gonna go. I was the one brought in, not Connor. I was the one with the hole in my liver—hey, how well do you trust those nurses there with you?"

Jerome blinked owlishly. "They're discreet."

"They better be fucking silent. Because tonight, as hard as you tried, your patient still died on the table. Switch the patient records. Discharge

Connor with a healing shoulder wound and assign his record to me.
Make it seem like I died on the operating table from a gunshot wound
to the liver. I want you to write up a death certificate, anything else that
goes with it, make it real believable. I'll make it worth your while."

"Why are you doing this?"

"Because if I don't, I'm gonna end up in your morgue for real. Maybe
my girl, too."

"Alfie, even suggesting this—" Jerome started, shaking his head.

"Please. It's the only way Emilia and I can have a shot at a normal life."

Jerome stared at me for a long moment, his expression unreadable.
The wheels were turning in his head as he weighed the risks and potential
consequences of my proposal.

"Alright," he finally agreed, his shoulders sagging as if the entire world
had settled upon them. "I'll do it. But you two had better make sure you
stay off the radar. If anyone finds out –"

"Trust me," I cut him off, gripping his arm tightly. "We'll disappear
without a trace. You have my word."

Jerome stood, muttering something under his breath about mob de-
generates and how he was getting too old for this. As he walked out,
I sank back into the pillows, closing my eyes against the sting of tears.
For the first time since the nightmare began, hope flickered within me,
a fragile flame against the darkness. I would do anything to protect the
woman I loved, even if it meant giving up my own identity. It was a small
price to pay for a chance at a future together.

The hospital gown hung loose around my shoulders as I ripped the hated thing off and tossed it on the bed. Embarrassingly enough, Emilia had to help me get my shirt over my bandaged shoulder, but it was a vast improvement. The sun cast a warm glow through the windows as I stood by the hospital bed, my heart both heavy and hopeful. With the discharge papers in hand, it was time to face the goodbyes.

"Ready?" Emilia asked, her voice soft and concerned.

"More than ever," I replied, offering her a reassuring smile before we left the room.

Our first stop was Cassidy's, where Connor's wife cradled their newborn son in her arms. The sight of them together – a new life amidst all the chaos – brought a bittersweet ache to my chest. Tommy's knowing nod from the doorway was all it took to confirm he was in, that he got the gist of the death certificate shuffle Jerome and I had cooked up.

"Look at him," Emilia cooed softly as she leaned over to stroke the baby's cheek with the tip of her finger.

"He's perfect, Cass," I said thickly.

Cassidy had shifted baby Aiden into Emilia's arms, and the sight of my girl cradling him close, rocking him gently, stirred something primal and possessive within me. A fierce protectiveness, a yearning to see Emilia holding our own child someday.

I cleared my throat, trying to dislodge the lump that had formed there. "I'm glad you're both doing well. You deserve it."

"Thank you, Alfie," Cassidy replied, her eyes brimming with tears. "For everything."

I nodded, unable to speak, knowing that this might be the last time I would see her. I pulled her into a tight embrace, inhaling the sweet scent of her hair. "You take care of yourself and that little man. And keep Connor out of trouble."

"I'll try." Cassidy took both of our hands. "You two stay safe, alright? And don't be strangers. We'll find a way to keep in touch. Somehow."

"We'll find a way," Emilia promised, squeezing Cassidy's hand before pulling her in for one final hug.

With a final, lingering look at the baby, we left Cassidy's room and made our way to the ICU. The heavy door loomed before us, and I steeled myself for what I knew would be a gut-wrenching sight.

"You okay?" Emilia asked.

I nodded, forcing myself to breathe deeply. I pushed through the door, my heart sinking as I took in the sight of Connor lying motionless in the hospital bed, still unconscious, his breathing still being supported by a ventilator. It was hard to see him like that. I couldn't help but feel a surge of guilt at the sight of him in such a state, knowing that it was my recklessness that had put him here in the first place.

"He looks so... fragile," Emilia said softly, her voice tinged with sadness.

I reached out and took her hand, giving it a reassuring squeeze. "He's tougher than he looks," I said, my gaze never leaving Connor's face.

I took a deep breath and inched closer to his bed. "You dumb fucking bastard."

"Alfie!"

"Always worrying about everybody else," I continued, ignoring Emilia's hushed disapproval. "You've got a son now, a little guy who's gonna need his dad. And Cassidy... she's a rock, but even rocks need something to lean on. You hear me? So you've gotta take care of yourself, too. You need to be here for them."

Connor's chest rose and fell mechanically, oblivious to my words. I could only hope that somehow, he knew we were there, and that we cared.

I sat there longer than I meant to, until Emilia rested her hand gently on my shoulder. "Alfie," she said, her voice thick with emotion. "We need to go."

"I know."

I reached out and squeezed Connor's hand one last time, my throat unbearably tight. "Take care, brother."

Our last stop was Luca.

"Jesus," I muttered under my breath, the sight of him like a punch to the gut.

Emilia gasped, her hand flying to her mouth as tears welled in her eyes. "Luca..."

If I thought Connor looked rough, this was a whole other level. The man who once seemed as unbreakable as stone looked so small and fragile, hooked up to all the machines that were keeping him alive. Half of his face and head were swathed in thick bandages, and what skin was showing had an unhealthy, waxy pallor. The slow beep of the heart monitor was the only indication that he was still hanging on.

"Hey Sofia," I said, swallowing hard. "How is he?"

Sofia was perched on a chair beside his bed, looking like a lost sparrow in the wild nest of medical equipment edging the bed. Her eyes, red-rimmed and swollen, lifted to meet ours as we approached. "He's... he's still in a coma," she said hoarsely. "They don't know when he'll wake up."

Emilia's grip tightened on my hand as she covered her mouth with her other hand, tears welling up in her eyes.

"Doc said he got hit just under the left eye," Sofia explained, her voice wavering. "The bullet must've ricocheted off a brick wall or something, because they found pieces of brick lodged around the wound. They said if it'd been a straight shot, he... he wouldn't have made it."

I winced at her words, knowing that it was my fault Luca was in this situation in the first place. If I hadn't been so careless, so reckless, he would never have gotten hurt. Guilt and shame coiled in my stomach like a snake, threatening to poison my resolve. I took a deep breath and pushed the guilt aside. Now wasn't the time for self-pity.

"He's had two surgeries already. I didn't understand everything they said, some of the medical terms were pretty scary, but he was bleeding into his brain. It sounded bad," Sofia continued, her hands fidgeting in her lap. "The bleeding... they're saying it's stopped, but there could be damage to his brain...and then there's his face..."

"Will he wake up?" Emilia asked the question none of us dared.

Sofia met her cousin's gaze, her own eyes hardening with determination. "He will wake up," she said fiercely. "He has to."

I had to remind myself just how young Sofia actually was. Barely into her twenties and dealing with this. I watched her fuss over Luca, tenderly adjusting his blankets and tidying the wires darting from the thin hospital gown stretched over his broad shoulders. She seemed so grown up all of a sudden, her maturity shining through in the way she cared for him. I couldn't help but wonder if there might be feelings between them, and I hoped so. Luca deserved someone who loved him as fiercely as Sofia did.

"Sofia." I waited until her eyes met mine. "We're going to get out of Boston for a while. But we'll be back. Eventually. I promise you, we'll find a way to make sure he's taken care of."

She nodded, her eyes welling up with tears. "Please. I'll call you...when he wakes up."

I stood, and then wrapped my arms around her. She felt so small and frail in my embrace, a far cry from the brash, wild girl she had been just a few months ago. "Thank you for helping Emilia. You're a good woman, Sofia. You deserve a happy ending."

She gave me a watery smile. "You do, too."

I waited outside the door while Emilia said her goodbyes. When she emerged, her eyes were red-rimmed and swollen from tears, but there was a determination on her face that I hadn't seen before.

"Ready to go?" I asked.

"Ready as I'll ever be," she said softly, a wistful smile tugging at her lips.

We made our way down the hall, hand in hand, and I knew without a doubt that it was the right decision. We would start over somewhere else, away from the violence and corruption that had plagued us for so long. And we wouldn't be gone forever--organized crime has a short lifespan and an even shorter memory.

We'd be back.

Sloane was waiting for us outside the ICU.

"Tommy filled me in on the plan," she said, nodding her head in understanding. "Makes sense, I guess. But I'm gonna miss your crazy ass, Alfie."

I pulled her into a tight hug, cementing our friendship in that embrace. "I'm gonna miss you too, Sloane."

A knowing look passed between us. The kind that only those who've lived life on the flip side of the law can truly understand. We were kin in this chaotic world, bound by secrets and survival.

She hugged Emilia as well, wishing us both well. As we reluctantly pulled away, she handed me her car keys. "Keep it. Callum can buy me a new one."

"Thanks," I murmured, touched by her generosity. I reached into my pocket and pulled out a letter I'd written earlier this morning for Connor. I didn't trust the staff enough to leave it by his bedside, and Sloane needed something to do. "Give this to him when he wakes up, will you?"

"Sure thing," Sloane agreed, tucking the letter into her jacket like she was stowing away something precious.

We stepped out into the cool night air, leaving behind the buzzing fluorescents and antiseptic smells of the hospital. In the quiet darkness, I felt both the weight of what we'd left behind and the lightness of the freedom before us.

The sun rode low in the sky, casting a golden glow over the parking lot. We climbed into the car, a sleek black Mustang that purred like a contented cat under my hands. Fitting for Sloane. My fingers gripped the steering wheel, excitement tempered with adrenaline as I started the engine and let it idle. The city stretched before us, gleaming skyscrapers pierced by ancient church spires under a robin's egg blue sky.

Emilia sighed, a smile curving her lips. "Isn't it a perfect day?"

"It is now," I said, reaching for her hand. Our fingers laced together, and I raised them to brush my mouth over her knuckles.

"It feels like a fairy tale," she said, shaking her head.

"Every fairy tale has its dark forest, babe, but we've walked through ours. Time for the happily ever after part."

She reached over, her fingers tracing the tattoos on my arm. Each one told a story, stories that were now a part of our past. Her touch left trails of fire, stirring that familiar ache that had nothing to do with bullet wounds or bruises.

Are you scared?" Emilia asked, breaking the silence.

"Terrified," I admitted. "Leaving everything behind... it's not just about safety. It's about choosing you, choosing us, over everything I've ever known."

"Me too," she whispered back. "But I choose you, Alfie Doyle. Over and over again."

Her words hit me harder than any bullet. I chose this path. Chose her. It was a conscious decision, a leap into the unknown—a commitment more binding than any vow spoken in a church.

"Emilia..." I started, but she placed a finger on my lips.

"Shh. No more words. Just drive."

"Say no more." I shifted the car into gear. "Daufuskie Island, here we come."

36

CASSIDY

TWO DAYS LATER, CONNOR was moved from the ICU to a regular room. They made me wait until he was settled to see him, but the first chance I got, I made Tommy take me to him.

Tommy was quiet as he wheeled me to Connor's new room. His face was drawn, and I read the worry in his eyes. I knew he felt guilty about the whole thing, but it wasn't his fault. He'd been taken right along with Connor, and if it wasn't for him, my husband might not have made it out alive.

I squirmed in the wheelchair impatiently. "Wheel faster."

"I'm pretty sure there's a speed limit in here, Dr. McTiernan," Tommy replied, but he picked up the pace all the same.

Connor's room was bright and airy, the morning light streaming through the open blinds. The room was much like the one I'd been in after my abduction, except the bed was bigger and Connor wasn't hooked up to nearly as many machines anymore. His eyes were closed, but his chest was rising and falling on its own, and that was all that mattered.

Tommy wheeled me over to the bedside and took Aiden from my arms, waiting with my son out in the hall for a moment. I took Connor's hand in mine, squeezing gently. His eyelids fluttered open, and a slow smile spread across his face when he saw me.

"Cass," he murmured, his voice raspy with sleep.

"Hey, you," I replied, blinking back tears of relief. "I was starting to think you were gonna sleep the whole month away."

His gaze darted around the room, confusion clouding his features. "Where am I?"

"You're in a regular room now," I explained, giving his hand a reassuring squeeze. "They moved you out of the ICU this morning. Do you remember what happened?"

Connor's brow furrowed, as if he was struggling to recall the details. The furrow grew as they came back, then his eyes darted to mine before dropping to my stomach. "The baby..."

"Is fine," I assured him, my voice catching on the lump in my throat. "We're both fine."

He let out a breath, his shoulders sagging with relief. "Thank God."

"You scared me, you know." I bit my lip, trying to hold back the tears that were threatening to spill over.

His expression softened, and he reached out to brush a strand of hair from my face. "I'm sorry, Cass. I didn't mean to."

"I know."

He shifted on the bed and paled severely, his hands fluttering weakly over his chest.

"Careful. You're not exactly operating at a hundred percent yet." I fussed over him, sorting the tangled monitor lines from his IV. "Do you want me to call the nurse?"

"Tired of the bloody nurses poking me. I just want you," he replied, his words slurring with exhaustion.

"Fine, but the moment you start looking too pale, I'm calling them," I replied. I pushed out of the wheelchair and started checking through his charts. "If you think you're going to be sick, or the pain gets too bad, tell me immediately. Secondary hemorrhaging is always a concern after--"

"Yes, Dr. McTiernan." Connor grinned lazily up at me from the pillow. "You know, you're quite sexy when you go all doctor mode."

"Stop your flirting, Mr. McTiernan, or else I will find someone to sedate you." I tried to keep my tone as businesslike as possible, but I couldn't help the rush of heat in my cheeks.

"Should you even be standing right now?"

"Says you. You're the one who's luck to be a--"

Alive.

Connor was damn lucky to be alive. In the back of that van, I thought I'd lost him. I thought I'd never hear his voice again, never feel the warmth of his touch, or the way his lips felt on mine. I thought we'd never have a future together.

But we did.

"Cass? What's wrong?"

I blinked back the tears that threatened to spill over, shaking my head. "Nothing's wrong. Not anymore."

"Hey." His fingers brushed against my leg. "Look at me."

I looked up at him, and his gaze softened, those ocean eyes so full of love and understanding. My throat tightened, and I bit my lip, trying to hold back the wave of emotions that threatened to overwhelm me.

"Come here, Cass," he murmured, gesturing me to him.

I leaned down, careful not to jostle his IV lines, and kissed him gently. His lips were warm and soft, and I could feel him smiling into the kiss. I slipped my hand beneath his hospital gown and settled it over his heart, collecting each precious beat like a miracle.

"God, I love you," he whispered.

"I love you too." I sniffed and gave him a watery smile. "Although if you ever do that to me again, Connor McTiernan, I swear to god, I'll shoot you myself."

He chuckled softly, wincing slightly. "Fair enough."

"Good." I stood up and gave his hand a gentle squeeze before turning to the door. "Now, would you like to meet your son? I love Tommy, but my faith in his babysitting skills at this stage only go so far."

A grin broke out on Connor's face, lighting up his entire expression. "I'd love to."

I smiled and reached for the door, but it swung open before I could even touch the handle. Tommy stepped through, cradling Aiden carefully in his arms.

"Someone's been asking to see his daddy," he said, his gaze darting between me and Connor.

"It's about time," Connor replied, his eyes never leaving our son's scrunched up face.

I helped settle Aiden in Connor's arms, careful of the bandages and wires. Immediately, the baby stopped crying and nuzzled close to the warmth of his skin. Hair as downy soft as peach fuzz and dwarfed by his hand as he gently cupped the baby's head. Something so fragile, so precious, something we had created together.

Then those two little eyes opened and looked at him.

Connor was undone. He looked like nothing would ever be the same. His life had forever changed the moment I'd walked into it, and here, now, looking into our child's eyes for the first time...he looked remade into something new. The start of a new and wonderful chapter in our lives.

"Hey there, little Aiden...I'm you're Da," Connor smiled, kissing the wrinkled little forehead. "And this tough lady right here's your Mum."

I tucked the swaddle cloth tighter around Aiden's tiny body. "He's a few weeks early, but he got a clean bill of health. Eating well, sleeping well..."

"He's perfect, Cass." Connor looked up at me, eyes overbright, and he shook his head. "All by yourself, you did this. I should have been there."

"You're here now. That's all I care about."

He turned his head to kiss me.

I leaned into his side, resting my head on his chest, and watched our son with wonder. I was so lost in the moment, I didn't even notice Tommy slip out of the room.

Connor had an arm around my back, his thumb rubbing gently up and down, soothing me. The other arm cradled Aiden, our baby snug and safe against his chest. His heartbeat thudded reassuringly in my ear, and I breathed a sigh of relief. It seemed like only moments ago, I'd been listening to it struggle to beat. But now, it was strong and steady, a comforting metronome that lulled me to sleep.

"Cassidy?"

"Mmmm?"

"Do you think we'll ever have a normal life?"

The question caught me off guard, and I lifted my head to meet his gaze. "What do you mean?"

"I mean..." He paused, choosing his words carefully. "Will we ever be able to live a normal life? With no more crime, or danger, or violence? Just... us and our family?"

I rested my chin on his shoulder, watching him as he stared down at our son. His gaze was distant, lost in a sea of thoughts and memories, and I knew he was thinking of his parents. Of how they had died.

"I know why you did it, you know. Lie to those crooked cops." I shook my head. "I didn't see it in the moment, but the way you were looking at me—I knew. Big dumb hero."

"I couldn't let them take you again."

"I know." I grabbed a cloth from the nearby table and dabbed at a bit of blood beneath his jawline that had been missed, my hand trembling. Connor took the cloth and set it aside, cradling my face in his hands. Seeing him like this—what he'd done for me, how badly he'd been hurt—it broke something inside me, and this time there was not stopping the tears.

"Shh...no, mo chroí. Please don't cry. I'm okay. I'll be fine. It's over now. It's all over."

Connor drew me into his arms. At first, I resisted, not wanting to hurt him further, but he eventually won out. He laid back against the pillows, cradling me to him as he sighed into my hair.

"I thought I'd never see you again. I thought that was it for me," he whispered.

I knew it. His last words to me had been playing on repeat in my head ever since that door had swung shut. Connor being led away in handcuffs by two crooked cops, and I had been utterly helpless to stop it.

"It wasn't though," I said. And that was the important thing. "You stopped him. You did what had to be done, and you came home to me. And now I'm here with you, Connor, and I am never, ever letting you go."

He shook his head. "Never."

Then his lips were crashing into mine, bruises and cuts be damned. I drank him in, savoring the feel of him once again in my arms. The taste of him, his scent, tainted with the coppery undertone of blood, but that was okay. Connor was alive.

He had fought for me. Laid down his life in order to ensure the safety of his family, but he was *here*. With me. Just as I'd fought to bring him home, and now it was finally over.

"I love you so, so much," he murmured against my lips. His eyelids were starting to grow heavy, and he sighed quietly as he laid back, cradling our son against his chest. "This right here? This is everything. Everything I'll ever want, and everything I'll ever need. I'm done, Cass. I just can't do this anymore."

"What do you mean?"

"I want out—for both of us. Two close calls." He shook his head. "I thought I could keep us safe, time and time again, but look what's happened. I'm tired. So, so tired of all of it. I want to be done. It's not worth it."

I was pretty sure I understood what he was saying, but that was a conversation for later. Connor was blinking heavily, barely able to keep his eyes open.

I tucked into his side, careful to avoid his injuries. Connor nuzzled my cheek, pressing a final kiss there just before he lost the battle with exhaustion, lips still curled in a faint smile as he drifted off to sleep.

I watched him, his face relaxed in a way I hadn't quite seen before. Like a load had been lifted there. Fingers ghosting over his injuries protectively, watching the steady rise and fall of his chest slow and deepen as I thought about what he had said.

Two close calls. For both of us.

Moretti may be dead, but the future was still uncertain. Not knowing how the cards would fall in the wake of the mafia titan's death. We were safe for now, but what happened when the next rival family threatened ours?

Those were thoughts for the morning, though. Instead, I allowed myself to give in to the sleep that was calling, kissing Connor softly on the lips before I settled against him. Between our bodies I felt our son shift in his sleep, and I smiled.

This, right here. This was everything.

37

CONNOR

BY THE END OF the next week, I had become the worst patient my wife had ever seen. She had warned me about pushing myself too hard, but I couldn't help it. The need to see my plan through drove me, and I was determined to make things right. I was healing quickly, but I was still embarrassingly weak. I knew Cassidy worried about my health, but she tried to hide it with her usual feistiness, and I loved her even more for it.

"Connor, are you sure this is wise?" Cassidy asked, looking over the papers in her hands.

"Jerome cleared me. He is your boss, remember?"

"That's not what I meant," she snapped.

I reached out to take her hand. "Cass, please. I'm fine."

She sighed, but I read the worry in her eyes. "Fine, but if you pass out, I am strapping you down to a bed and not letting you up for a month."

"In bed with you for a week? Done. Don't make threats you aren't prepared to follow through on, love," I growled, pulling her in for a kiss.

"Don't you start something you can't finish, McTiernan," she warned, but I could see the blush in her cheeks and the spark in her eyes.

"Is that a challenge?"

"In your condition? Yes."

Fire surged through my veins and straight to my cock. Oh, I fully intended to take her up on that challenge later. I leaned over to kiss her, but Aiden interrupted us with a squawk of displeasure.

"Come on, little man," I said, scooping him up. "Let's go home."

We made our way to the waiting car, where Tommy was already waiting for us. He helped Cassidy and Aiden into the back seat while I got in the front. He knew better than to treat me like an invalid.

"Where to?" he asked. "The penthouse, or..."

"The summer house." I grinned, seeing Cassidy's surprised look. "Sloane and Michael went ahead and got things ready for us. They've got a room ready for Aiden and everything."

"But all the baby stuff--"

"All the baby stuff. It's all taken care of."

I hated that our lives had been in such a turmoil that Cassidy hadn't had a chance to take care of that herself. Nesting, or whatever the hell they called it. A normal pregnancy.

I couldn't give her back that, but I could give her a shot at a normal life.

Cassidy was still asleep when I woke the next morning. Dawn was just beginning to peek through the curtains, and when I craned my neck to look at the time, I saw with no surprise that we had slept the entire day, straight through the night.

my wife for a moment, still in utter amazement that I was with her, safe and sound in my arms. Drinking in the sight of her, bridging the gap between this moment and what I had been sure were his last look, just a couple days ago.

I took a shuddering breath, closing my eyes and nuzzling Cassidy's hair as silent tears fell. I could easily lose myself in the downward spiral of what had been taken and what more could have been lost, and I clutched her to me like a lifeline. Grounding myself in the warmth of her skin and the feel of her body pressed against mine.

If it wasn't for that touch, I wasn't sure that I would have believed she was real. In my experience, the things that seemed too good to be true often were, but this right here, what I held in my arms—this was real. She was mine and I was hers, the soft breathing from the crib in the corner reminding me of the life we'd brought into the world together.

My family.

A few days after I'd been moved from the ICU, Sloane showed up with a letter from Alfie. It hurt, not being able to say goodbye to a friend who had become my brother in every way that mattered, but I understood it. Alfie was doing what he had to do to protect his family, and I had to let him go. I would see him again.

His letter said everything I was already thinking, but it was still good to hear it from someone else. Someone who had just as much to lose as I did. His words were the final push, setting a plan in motion I had been subconsciously forming ever since my brush with death. Ever since I almost lost Cassidy, and most certainly ever since our son Aiden was born.

Nothing was ever going to take from my family ever again. I was going to make sure of it.

Although it physically pained me to do so, I carefully crawled out of bed with a final, lingering kiss to Cassidy's forehead. There was something I had to do first, and if I let myself stay there with her like I wanted to, I might never get up.

I walked into the closet, pulling out one of my suits. I knew the conversation I was about to have could be conducted just as well in the tee shirt and sweats I was wearing, but I put the suit on anyway. I wasn't a moody teenager slinking into my uncle's office anymore, begging to be allowed to go to college. No. This was a conversation between two businessmen—between the Clan Chief and his Warlord—and I would conduct myself as such.

I clenched my teeth as I fumbled with the tie. My entire body ached, each bruise and cut singing out in protest at every movement, and my abdomen was positively screaming. I ignored the pain meds Cassidy had left me and opted for a couple ibuprofen instead—I wanted a clear head for what was to come.

Callum was already up, staring thoughtfully out at the water, abandoned coffee cup still in his hand. He seemed to have aged a decade in the past few weeks. Sloane, Michael, and Tommy had spent the night after a little impromptu welcome home party for us, and I had told Callum that I had something important to discuss first thing this morning.

If he was surprised to see me up and about, he didn't show it, instead gesturing vaguely to the chair opposite him.

"You're up early," he said. "Shouldn't you be resting? You look like death warmed over."

"There's something I've got to take care of."

Callum looked me for a long moment. "Well, before you get started, take a look at that." He gestured to the newspaper onto the coffee table, stabbing a finger at the headline in triumph. "That should put a smile on your face."

I leaned forward in my chair. *Lorenzo Moretti Dead*, the headline proclaimed, *Slain Boston Businessman Revealed to be Mafia Kingpin*.

Further down was another story.

Former North Boston CEO's Estate and Business Assets Seized as Evidence: Criminal Investigation into Moretti Holdings Begins Next Week.

"They're saying he was shot by his own men—a conflict within the family. Tragic, isn't it?" Callum said with a grin of his own. "It's all falling down like a house of cards, everything Moretti built. It's all gone."

I stared at the headlines without really seeing them. Enough to put a smile on my face? No. Maybe once, but not now. Looking at them gave me a dark sense of satisfaction, but mostly...mostly, they just made me feel tired. All the way down to my bones.

"Long time coming," Callum said. "Too long. A lot of wheels are in motion, now that he's gone, and we need to strike while the iron's hot. I spoke with Michael this morning, and he agreed we should concede the territory but hang on to Moretti's buyers. He thinks we could sway them to our side..."

"Callum."

"Now, it's not gonna be easy, but Lorenzo crossed a line going after family members, especially women, and that's not going to sit well with them. I've already had Tommy reach out to our contacts up there, and they've agreed to a meet."

"Callum."

He either wasn't listening to me, or he was choosing not to. "I know it's going to take you a few days to get back on your feet properly, but as soon as your able to, I want you to sit down with them, and see who else—"

"Callum. I want out."

Callum's mouth snapped shut. I hadn't raised my voice, but my tone and the look on my face was one of deadly seriousness, one I knew my uncle understood all too well. Slowly, he sat back and leveled a gaze at me.

"You want out."

I smoothed the newspaper flat as if that caress could impart the weight of those headlines, a weight I was getting damn tired of carrying. "I'm done. With all of it. The guns, the money, the killing—every aspect of this. What we do. I'm done with it."

When he said nothing, I continued. "Cassidy and I are going to move out of the Penthouse and into our own place. I'm going to get a job—an honest job—and we're going to live free and clear of all of this. I'm done."

Callum still didn't say anything, but I could see by the muscle ticking in his jaw that he was upset. The minutes continued to stretch on in silence, and I finally got fed up.

"What—you have nothing to say?"

"What would you like me to say?" Callum said evenly. "My nephew tells me that he's decided to walk out on his family, and—"

"Walk out on my family? I never said anything about that!" I was starting to get angry now. "This business? What we do? Yes. I'm walking away from that. But I never said I was walking away from my family. Never."

I felt my blood heat as I leaned forward, staring my uncle down. I had never squared off with him about a decision like this, not since Aiden died, and then I had practically rolled right over. I was not about to roll over now.

"You told me once that a man is worth nothing if he can't protect the people he loves. Well, I love Cassidy. She's my wife. She's the mother of my child, and that's what I'm trying to keep safe."

Callum sighed and looked at me sadly. "Safe? Do you really think it's going to be as easy as just walking away? You still have enemies. You still have ties to this family whether you like it or not, just like Cassidy has to hers. No matter how far you try to push it away, it could always drag you back."

"I know." I swallowed thickly. "I know. But I can protect them a hell of a lot better standing on the shore rather than wading hip deep in the muck like I have been. I left half my liver and any desire to pursue this kind of life on that operating table, and my wife gave birth to our son with my blood on her hands. If that isn't a wakeup call, I don't know what is. This is not a perfect solution, but it's a better way to live. It's what we want, and it's what we need. I'm not asking for your permission, Callum. I'm telling you what we decided."

Callum sat back. I read the disappointment and resignation in his eyes, but I also saw an equal measure of respect. He sighed heavily. "This doesn't exactly come as a surprise. Tommy told me where your head was at after Cassidy's abduction, and with a baby on the way and everything that went down the past few weeks..."

Callum cleared his throat and shuffled the papers around his desk, frowning. To the casual observer he looked every bit the cold, polished businessman, but I saw right through it. I knew where to look, knew his tells enough to see the true feelings lying just beneath. It was a move I had perfected myself, one that had gotten me into a lot of heartache in the beginning with Cassidy.

"Callum, talk to me."

"Truth is, I'm thinking of stepping down myself. I'm not getting any younger, you know."

I frowned. "Why? Is this about what happened to me? Because if it is—"

"No, no. It's not that." He shook his head. "It's just...I've been doing this for so long, and I've seen so much, done so much. And the last few months...I fumbled the ball. Big time. It's only because of you and Tommy that we all made it through this. And it's made me realize that maybe it's time to pass the torch. I can't carry this weight forever, and the business needs fresh eyes. Younger minds. This is the natural order of things, Connor. You should know that better than anyone. One generation follows another, and so on and so forth. It's the way of things."

I swallowed hard. "Who?"

He grinned, a genuine smile. "Tommy, of course. Who else would it be?"

"God help us all," I muttered, but I felt a wave of relief. "When?"

"As soon as we can get things settled here. We'll have to lay low for a while. There's going to be an investigation into Moretti, and we have to keep our heads down." He sighed heavily. "I know you want to get out, Connor, and I'm not going to try to stop you. In fact..."

Callum opened a drawer and pulled out an ancient rolodex. He thumbed through it a minute and pulled out a card, staring at the raised lettering before handing it over.

"Mikey is an old friend. A friend, mind you, not a business associate. Tommy told me about the security system you set up at the penthouse, and I checked it out myself. You did a good job—it was professional." Callum cleared his throat. "Mikey owns a security company. Installations, evaluations, that sort of thing. You give him a call, show him what you did there at the penthouse, and I'm sure he'd be more than happy to take you on."

I bit the inside of my cheek against the swell of emotion. Callum continued. "It's not going to be easy, starting over—"

"Neither is living like this. But it's what we want."

"Fair enough." Callum stood up. "Well, it that's all—"

"Callum. I'm sorry."

Callum froze. His jaw worked for a moment, and he slowly sank back into his chair, shoulders slumping like he'd just let go of something heavy and tiresome.

"Don't be," he said quietly. "You almost lost everything. Twice. I understand why you're doing this, even if wish it hadn't come to this."

"You know, Da isn't here to back me up, but he always spoke highly of you. I'm sure he'd be okay with you filling in for him," my lips twitched, suppressing a smile. "I fully expect you to fulfill all grandfatherly duties. That means baby holding and story time, Sunday afternoon couch cushion forts and weekends in the park playing ball."

"I wasn't any good at any of that as a father."

"Yeah?" I shrugged. "Well, you got a fresh start of it now. We both do. Grandpa."

"Jesus, how did I get so old?"

We stood. Callum held out his hand, and I rolled my eyes, pulling him in for a hug. The old mobster stiffened for only a moment before he relaxed, even going so far as to hug me back, and when we parted the old man's eyes were suspiciously red.

"You should go back to bed...get some rest. That wound looks like it's giving you some grief."

"I think I will. Eight in the morning and I'm already wore out."

"Wait until "junior" starts teething—you don't know what tired is."

I laughed. "Any advice?"

Callum thought a minute. "Just love him...listen to him. He's gonna have two stubborn, headstrong parents, so I imagine he'll be a little bullheaded himself. Guide him, but...just let him be the man he wants to be."

Don't make the same mistake I did. The words were there, even if they weren't said. "I'll keep that in mind," I said hoarsely.

Callum nodded and turned back to the window. "You're a good man, Connor. You're gonna be a great father."

"No hard feelings, then?"

He sighed but shook his head. "You've given me a headache and a bit of a mess to sort through, but no. If this is what you want, what's going to make you both happy..."

"It is."

"...then it's worth it."

<hr>

Cassidy was awake when I got back to the room, and I halted in the doorway, the sight of her momentarily stealing the breath from my lungs.

She was curled up in the overstuffed chair by the window, reading. The early morning light caught in her hair, illuminating the soft curves beneath her dressing gown with an ethereal radiance that had me all but melting into a little puddle on the floor. Just when I thought I couldn't fall more in love with her...

I crouched down next to her, whispering the ghost of a kiss to the soft spot just behind her ear. Another one, even softer along the angle of her jaw, grazing my lips up her skin until I found hers.

"Morning, beautiful."

Cassidy hummed. "Morning. You're up early."

"I talked to Callum...I didn't want to wait."

"How'd it go?"

"It's done." I took both of her hands in mine, but her smile faltered a bit.

"Connor, are you sure this is what you want? You're not just doing it for me?"

"I'm doing this for us. All of us. You, me, and this little guy right over here." I glanced over to where Aiden lay sleeping, and I interlaced our fingers. "This. This is what I want. And this is how I get to keep it."

"And you'll be happy? Just living a normal life?"

"Cass, I'm so damn happy right now I feel like my heart's gonna burst. That's how I always feel around you." I shook my head. "I don't know what I did to deserve someone like you, but I am never letting you go."

"Good, because I'm never letting you go either." She grabbed my tie and pulled me close into a sizzling kiss, one that left me with a dizziness that had nothing to do with the bandages around my chest. "Come back to bed with me, you still look tired."

I playfully bit her lip as I went back for seconds. "Love, you don't have to tell me twice."

38

Epilogue - Emilia

The chime over the door tinkled its last for the day as I ushered out the final stragglers from my coffee shop slash bookshop slash plant shop. Because, apparently, that was a thing.

"Take care, Mrs. Henderson," I called out, waving to the elderly lady who spent every afternoon curled up in the corner with a new smutty romance novel. Good for her.

"See you tomorrow, Emily dear!" she called, brandishing her book at me. "Tell that man of yours not to work so hard. He could learn a thing or two about romance from these books!"

I laughed, shaking my head as the door closed behind her. If she only knew.

I filed away the last of my receipts and breathed in the scent of sun-warmed paper and leather bindings, listening to the quiet tick of the old grandfather clock in the corner.

My little bookshop was cozy and intimate, mismatched bookshelves and chairs and tables scattered about haphazardly. The air was heavy with the scent of espresso and salt carried in on a breeze that whispered through the open windows. The shop itself was a haven of tranquility, all warm woods and soft cushions, walls lined with books that ranged from tattered paperbacks to leather-bound classics. It was a mosaic of my soul, peaceful and inviting, a stark contrast to the steel and shadows of my former life. It was everything my old shop had been and more, a sanctuary of knowledge and escape, of words and worlds. Of second chances and new beginnings.

Of hope.

As I wiped down the counter, my thoughts drifted to how much my life had changed since escaping the confines of Lorenzo Moretti's gilded cage. Alfie and I now shared a small home on the beach, our sanctuary away from the dangers of Boston's criminal underworld. He ran charter boats, his laughter and easy smile brightening even the stormiest days. Most importantly, we felt safe.

How different my life was now. I gazed out the window at the sailboats bobbing in the harbor, a smile curling my lips. No more fear, no more violence. Just peace, and love.

Alfie and I had built a life together here on this little island, away from the crime and corruption of Boston. He ran fishing charters during the day, and at night we curled up together in our little beach house, listening to the waves lap at the shore. Alfie had put his heart into fixing it up, painting the walls in shades of sunrise and seafoam. Even I had learned to swing a hammer, disastrous as that was at first, but it was our own blood, sweat and tears that had reaped something honest and true. Our bedroom window opened to the ocean, where the sound of waves was a lullaby, and the salty breeze was our blanket. With Alfie, I felt a safety I'd never known—a safety not born of guards or guns, but of love and laughter.

So much has changed in the last six months.

Connor and Cassidy had been down to see us a few months ago. The Feds investigating Agent Halliwell's murder had dropped the case due to lack of evidence, so they were free to travel again. Connor had completely healed from his injuries, and he was working in private security, now. Apparently, he had a big glowing recommendation from Callum McTiernan, and he jumped at the chance. With Cassidy still working full time, and a child, their lives were somewhat chaotic but it seemed like both of them were happy.

Most importantly, it was something they had chosen for themselves. Cassidy had switched from trauma to internal medicine, so her hours were more regular and not as stressful. Their son, Aiden, was thriving and proving himself a little scamp already, especially since he had the entire family wrapped around his finger.

Alfie told me that Callum McTiernan had stepped down, naming Tommy as his successor. I hadn't met him more than a handful of times, but I had a hard time reconciling him into any leadership role. If I had heard it from anyone else, I might not have believed it, but Alfie said Callum had a way of assessing someone's capability. The idea of the big, tattooed, faux hawked hellion as a Clan Chief was mind boggling. When I asked Alfie about it, he just laughed, saying that Sloane would keep him in line.

Whatever that meant.

I set a cup of coffee to brew while I closed out the register. Locked the front door and flipped the sign to "Closed." There was a back door to my new coffee shop slash bookshop slash plant shop, but I rarely used it.

Here, Alfie always came in the front door.

I checked the clock. He'd be getting off work, soon. I hustled through my closing routine, anticipation bubbling pleasantly over what was to come tonight. As I worked, I thought back to what had been left of my family.

After nearly two months in a coma, Luca woke up.

It was rocky at first. He'd lost the use of his left eye. Chronic headaches, anomic aphasia, and tremors. He'd undergone two reconstructive surgeries to repair the damage to his face, but with time and therapy, he was expected to make a full recovery.

What wasn't known was what effect losing his place in the organization would have on him. Not the power or money—not so much losing something he enjoyed—but the loss of the family. Me. The guilt of leaving him there in that hospital bed, fighting for his life after sacrificing it willingly for me and Alfie never left me.

I couldn't suppress a small smile as I thought of Sofia, her voice animated over the line, recounting the latest tête-à-tête with Luca. "He's so damn stubborn, Emilia," she'd huff, exasperation laced with something softer, something tender. "I'm just trying to help."

"Luca doesn't stand a chance against you," I had teased, picturing her petite frame standing ground against his brooding presence.

"Nobody does," she'd shot back, laughing.

I often wondered if there was more brewing beneath their playful bickering. Sofia was a constant by his side, a surprising pillar in his convalescence. Their calls were peppered with arguments and laughter in equal measure—Luca's gruff admonishments met with Sofia's irreverent retorts. It was a dance they seemed to have perfected, one where steps of frustration and care somehow fell into a harmonious rhythm. And while part of me feared for her young heart, another hoped for healing in whatever form it might take—for both of them.

But Luca was a fighter. A stubborn, loyal, fiercely protective fighter, and he would be all right. A smile tugged at my lips as I remembered the phone call I'd had with them both last week. Sofia had been at Luca's side every step of the way, fussing over him constantly despite his surliness. He'd grumbled about her ceaseless hovering, but I wondered if there wasn't something blossoming between them.

The thought warmed me. After everything we'd endured, we all deserved to find love...and if anyone could temper Luca's brooding nature, it was Sofia.

I hadn't heard anything else about the family. The Moretti Empire had crumbled in the wake of Lorenzo's death. I wasn't sorry he was gone. I was glad Connor killed him, after every horrible thing he'd done. Julian was still in North Boston, working, but Sofia hadn't mentioned much about who had filled the void left by Lorenzo.

I was glad I didn't have to worry about it anymore. I only worried for Sofia and Luca's sake.

Two strong hands closed around my hips, and I was pulled back into a hard chest. Alfie's lips brushed the sensitive spot behind my ear, sending a shiver of pleasure down my spine. "Hello, beautiful," he murmured, nuzzling my neck.

I leaned back into him, breathing in the scent of sun, sea, and sweat after his shift on the boats. "Hello, sailor," I murmured, turning to capture his mouth with mine. His lips were warm and soft, and he tasted like sunshine and salt.

"Have any trouble this afternoon?" He'd been stopping by most days to check in, but his question was more out of an old habit.

"No, just the usual gang of elderly bookworms and sunburnt tourists," I said, craning my neck for another kiss. "The tourists are pretty predictable."

"And the old salts?" he asked, his lips dragging up my neck.

"They have their fingers in every pie going. Mrs. Henderson read aloud from her scandalous romance book, but it made for a busy afternoon."

Alfie snorted. "I'm sure that went over well. Is she always like that?"

"She's eccentric but sweet." I turned to run my hands along his broad shoulders. He was still tense from the day, and I kneaded the knots away as he melted into my touch. "You look tired."

"It was a busy day." He turned and took one of my hands and pressed a kiss to the inside of my wrist, then brought my palm to rest over his heart. "And you, my love, are overdue for a distraction."

Alfie curled his arm around my waist and tugged me against him. I slid my arms around his neck, linking my fingers together, and breathed in his scent as his lips nipped their way down my neck. "Mmmm, is that so? What did you have in mind?"

"Well, for starters, I could kiss you until you can't think straight."

His warm breath sent a delicious shudder through me, and I tilted my chin up to meet his mouth with mine.

We started slow and soft, tender kisses exploring and tasting and savoring, but Alfie quickly deepened the kiss, driving me wild. He bit my bottom lip gently, drawing a soft moan from my lips. He caught my moan, teasing it from me and swallowing it down, his tongue sliding against mine in silken strokes.

"You know, I've always had a thing for checkout counters," he said, eyeballing the cash register. The mention of the first time we'd been intimate sent a thrill through me. He curled his fingers around my hip. "Do you remember that night, Emilia?"

Heat licked up my skin. Oh, I remembered. Heat filled my belly and spread through my limbs, curling deep. I nodded, running my fingers over his broad shoulders.

"That was the night I knew you were the one."

"Oh?" I feigned innocence. "Was it because of how amazing my oral skills are?"

"No." He took my hand and placed it on his chest, right over his heart. The rhythmic beat was strong and steady under my fingertips, and something warm unfurled inside of me. "It was because when I touched you, I felt..." Alfie trailed off, struggling to find the words. Finally, he looked at me and cupped my cheek with his palm, gazing deeply into my eyes. "I felt like I had come home."

My eyes filled with tears. I turned my head to kiss the inside of his wrist, meeting his gaze unflinchingly.

His other hand came up to tuck a strand of hair behind my ear, then cupped my cheek as well. My pulse quickened as his thumb brushed against my lip, as soft and warm as a breath.

"That night," he continued, his voice husky, "was the night I realized how much I loved you."

"And when I told you to leave?" I asked, my stomach fluttering at the fire in his gaze.

"It tore my heart out of my chest." His thumb stroked over my cheekbone, his lips curling in a dangerous smile. "But I was always yours. We both knew it wouldn't be for long. And the thought of returning to you..."

He shuddered in a breath and leaned close, his lips grazing my ear. "It broke me and remade me all over again."

I leaned into his warmth, feeling the hard planes of his body press against me. His hands splayed across my back, fingers finding the skin exposed by my loose sundress and trailing over the curve of my spine. A delicious shiver coursed through me and I arched my back, pressing against him.

He lifted me onto the counter and kissed me deeply, stealing my breath with hot, drugging kisses. "You brought me to my knees," he murmured. "You always have, and you always will."

Alfie fell to his knees between my thighs.

"Alfie, we're in my shop..." I protested weakly, but my words dissolved into a moan as his tongue traced the edge of my panties.

"I want you right here, right now, on this counter." His voice was dark and low, and it sent a wave of heat through my core. "I want to taste you, Emilia, and I don't want to wait another minute."

I couldn't argue with that, and I surrendered to his touch.

He pushed my sundress up around my hips and hooked his fingers into the waistband of my panties. His breath was warm on my skin, and I shivered with anticipation as he pulled them off and tossed them aside.

He nudged my thighs apart and dipped his head to press a kiss to my inner thigh. "I want to hear you," he said, nipping my skin gently. "I want everyone in town to hear you scream my name."

Before I could reply, his tongue traced across me. I gasped, and my fingers curled around the edge of the counter as he licked and teased me mercilessly. His tongue swirled over my clit and I cried out, arching my back to chase the feeling.

He groaned against me, and the vibration sent a wave of pleasure through me. "God, you taste good," he growled. One finger, then two slid inside me as he stroked me in a deep, aching rhythm. He chuckled, the vibration of his laughter sending a surge of pleasure through me. "You're so wet for me. What do you want?"

I could barely breathe. "You," I panted. "I want you."

"You have me."

"I want more."

His eyes darkened, and he pushed my legs further apart. "I can give you more," he whispered. "But only if you ask me nicely."

My head fell back as he circled my clit with his tongue. "Please."

"Please what?" His tongue flicked against me.

"Please. I want to feel you inside me."

"Yes." He stood and leaned over me, his mouth capturing mine. I could taste myself on his tongue as he kissed me deeply, fiercely, and my whole body trembled with need for him.

Alfie tugged me to the edge of the counter so that I was pressed against him. The hard length of him strained against his jeans, and I reached between us to pop the button open and free him. I wrapped my fingers around him, stroking him with firm, slow strokes. He groaned, his eyes darkening with lust as I ran my thumb over the sensitive tip, spreading the wetness down his shaft.

"Emilia..."

I guided him to me. "I need you," I whispered, and he slid into me.

We both moaned as he filled me.

He kissed me, hard and deep, our bodies moving together in a rhythm as old as time. I buried my face in his shoulder as his hands found my hips and guided me to match his thrusts.

"Harder," I begged, raking my fingers down his back. He groaned, fingers digging into my hips as he pushed deeper.

I threw my head back as pleasure surged through me. Alfie's teeth grazed my neck, and he rocked into me, his hips driving into me with relentless, agonizing precision.

"I love you, Emilia," he said, and his voice was husky and raw.

I cried out as he drove into me again and again, and I felt the orgasm building in my core. "Alfie..."

He leaned down, kissing me fiercely. "Come for me," he growled.

My breath caught in my throat. His hand slipped between us to tease my clit, and pleasure surged through me. I clung to him as the orgasm crested, white-hot bliss exploding inside me, and Alfie's name fell from my lips.

He came hard, groaning as his hips slammed against mine. We stayed like that for a moment, breathing each other's air as we both trembled with aftershocks of pleasure.

I stroked his cheek, my heart swelling as I gazed up at him. "I love you, too, you know." I whispered.

He grinned. "Well, thank God for that, or this would be a hell of an awkward moment."

I laughed and kissed him deeply, wrapping my legs around his waist to pull him close. I felt him harden against me, and I couldn't help but grin.

"Again?" he teased. "Aren't you tired, yet?"

I shook my head. "Never."

Fate, however, intervened in the form of my cellphone ringing on the counter. I bit back a moan, reaching for the phone. Cassidy. They'd landed and were on their way to the island.

"We have to stop," I panted, pushing at Alfie's shoulders. He rose up on his elbows, eyes glazed and lips kiss swollen. "Cassidy and Connor are almost here."

Understanding dawned, followed swiftly by a wry disappointment. Alfie sighed, rolling off me and onto his back.

"Perfect timing," Alfie teased, his grin never faltering even as he reached for me again, hungry for another taste.

"Uh-uh," I giggled, sidestepping his advance while deftly snatching his pants from where they lay crumpled on a nearby chair. With an exaggerated swing, I tossed them at him. "You, Mr. Soon-to-be-Married-Man, don't want to be late to your own wedding."

"Fine, fine," he grumbled, pulling on his pants and buttoning them up. "But don't think this is over," he added with a devilish grin.

I stood on the screened porch of our little home on the beach, watching Sloane and Cassidy fuss over my gown and hair. The sun was starting to set, casting golden hues across the sand and turning the water into an endless expanse of shimmering light. It was perfect – everything I had ever dreamed of. I thought about the summer nights spent here with my parents, and how they were now just a bittersweet memory.

The sun was sinking toward the horizon, its golden light filtering through the screens of the porch. I stood before the full-length mirror, admiring my reflection.

"Emilia, are you even listening?" Sloane's voice snapped me out of my reverie.

"Sorry, I got lost in thought," I confessed, blushing slightly. "What did you say?"

"Your hair," Cassidy replied, gently pulling a strand into place. "Do you want it up or down?"

"Down," I decided, wanting to feel the soft caress of my dark curls on my bare shoulders. "And maybe a few braids intertwined with flowers."

"Perfect," Sloane beamed, getting to work on the intricate design. As they styled my hair and added the finishing touches to my gown, a sense of peace washed over me. I knew Alfie was waiting at the end of the aisle, surrounded by friends who had become our family.

"Everything's perfect," Cassidy agreed, her smile soft and reassuring. "Alfie is going to lose his mind when he sees you."

"Let's hope he keeps it together long enough to say, 'I do,'" I joked, but my heart fluttered at the thought of seeing him waiting for me at the end of the aisle. The man who had become my anchor, my unexpected port in the storm that was my former life.

"Trust me," Sloane chimed in, her confidence unshakeable, "that man is more ready than anyone I've ever seen. He's been out there pacing the sand like a caged animal since noon."

As the sun began to dip below the horizon, casting a warm, golden glow over the sand, I stepped out onto the screen porch. Connor stood by the railing, his muscular arms cradling baby Aiden while he cooed softly. As he noticed my approach, he gently passed Aiden into Cassidy's waiting hands.

"Ready, Emilia?" he asked, offering me his arm.

"More than ready," I replied, looping my arm through his and feeling that familiar surge of love for this ragtag group that had become my family.

"Before we go any further," Connor said gruffly, tucking a wayward lock of hair behind my ear, "I have some strict instructions on how to handle a hellion like Alfie."

"Please, do tell," I chuckled, raising an eyebrow in mock seriousness.

"First rule: never let him win at poker. It'll only feed his ego. Second, always keep his favorite whiskey on hand – it'll make him more agreeable when you need a favor," he winked.

"Got it," I laughed, the joy bubbling up inside me. "Anything else?"

"Last but not least, always remind him how lucky he is to have you, because he truly is, Emilia."

"Thank you, Connor," I whispered, touched by his words. Together, we made our way towards the edge of the beach, where rows of chairs faced the ocean, and a makeshift altar waited beneath a canopy of fairy lights. The music swelled around us, signaling the start of the ceremony.

But just as we were about to step onto the sand, Connor stopped, a strange smile playing on his lips.

"Wait," I said, my voice wavering with confusion. "What's wrong? Why are we stopping?"

"Emilia," he murmured, his eyes twinkling, "while I would be honored to walk you down the aisle, there's someone here who's a bit more qualified for the job."

"What do you mean?" I asked, my confusion growing as he took a step back.

Just then, I saw a tall, dark-haired figure approaching from the tree line, and my breath caught in my throat.

Luca.

"Hey, kid," he said, his voice a soothing balm even as it cracked with emotion. The left side of his face was a tapestry of scars, brutal and unforgiving, yet they did nothing to diminish the handsome warmth of his smile.

He'd lost weight, making his cheekbones more prominent, and his hair was much shorter than I remembered – they'd had to shave it the hospital. His once-vibrant eyes, such a unique shade of dark brown were now mismatched, the left now a milky grey, leaving an ache deep within me.

"Thought you couldn't travel," I managed to say, my voice trembling as much as my hands.

"Emilia," he replied, reaching out to gently wipe away my tears with a tenderness that belied the ruggedness of his appearance. "I wouldn't miss this for the world."

"Thank you," I managed, choking back a sob. "Thank you for being here."

"Always," he replied, offering me his arm. I took it gratefully, feeling the familiar warmth and strength beneath my fingertips.

His touch steadied me as he offered his arm, an anchor in the swirl of emotions threatening to sweep me away. Together, we stepped forward onto the soft, white sand. The music enveloped us, a sweet serenade that seemed to bless each step we took. Luca's gait was slower than I remembered, a slight unsteadiness to his movements, but there was an undeniable strength that radiated from him.

"Never thought I'd see the day," he joked weakly, trying to lighten the mood as we made our way down the aisle lined with the smiling faces of those we loved. Neither of us had forgotten that kiss in my bookstore, Luca's unrequited feelings splashed messily across the pages of our history.

"Neither did I," I confessed, feeling the weight of the moment settle around us.

As we reached the end of the aisle where Alfie waited, looking every bit the roguish hero with his dark red curls and inked skin, I saw the promise of our future reflected in his eyes.

"Take good care of her, lover boy," Luca gruffly admonished Alfie, his voice infused with the protective edge I knew so well. It was more than a request; it was the passing of a torch, from one guardian to another.

"Always," Alfie promised, his gaze never leaving mine.

With one last nod, Luca released me to Alfie's care and took his seat next to Sofia, who reached out to squeeze his hand in silent support.

The sun dipped below the horizon, casting a warm golden glow over the beach as the preacher spoke. My heart pounded in my chest, all my fears and insecurities washed away by the love I saw in Alfie's eyes. He held my hands in his, his tattoos a beautiful contrast against my skin, and I couldn't help but think how perfectly we fit together.

"Alfie, do you take Emilia to be your lawfully wedded wife, to have and to hold, for better or for worse, for richer or for poorer, in sickness and in health, until death do you part?" the preacher asked, his voice gentle and strong.

"I do," Alfie replied without hesitation, his gaze never leaving mine.

"Emilia, do you take Alfie to be your lawfully wedded husband, to have and to hold, for better or for worse, for richer or for poorer, in sickness and in health, until death do you part?"

I swallowed hard, tears welling in my eyes as I whispered, "I do."

"Please exchange rings as a symbol of your commitment to one another," the preacher instructed.

As Alfie slid the wedding ring onto my finger, it nestled perfectly beside the thread ring he had given me months ago. The significance of both bands brought a fresh wave of emotion, making it difficult to breathe. With a tender smile, Alfie leaned down and pressed his lips to mine. Our first kiss as husband and wife was everything I had ever imagined – passionate, loving, and full of promise.

"By the power vested in me, I now pronounce you husband and wife. You may kiss the bride," the preacher announced, though we were already lost in each other's embrace.

"Congratulations, Mrs. Doyle," Alfie murmured against my ear, causing a shiver to run down my spine.

"Thank you, Mr. Doyle," I replied, my voice choked with happiness. "I love you."

"Forever and always, Emilia."

And as the sun disappeared completely, the afterparty began in full swing. Surrounded by our family and friends, we all laughed, danced, and celebrated together. Alfie led me onto the dance floor for our first dance as husband and wife, holding me close as we swayed to the music.

"Can you believe we made it here?" I asked him, resting my head on his shoulder.

"Never doubted it for a second," he lied dutifully, kissing the top of my head.

Across the dance floor, Callum and Michael took turns holding baby Aiden while Connor and Cassidy danced together, their love for each other evident in every movement. I watched as Alfie tried to coax Tommy into dancing with Sloane, but he just grumbled something under his breath and retreated to the bar, leaving Sloane glaring after him.

For the first time in my life, I felt like I truly belonged. In the arms of my husband, surrounded by people who loved me, I knew that this was where I was meant to be. And as the night wore on, our laughter and joy echoed across the beach, a testament to the incredible journey that had led us all here – together.

Much later, I padded out onto the sand. The warm sea breeze carried the melody of laughter and music from the wedding reception as I made my way over to Luca and Sofia, who were sitting at a table near the edge of the beach. Their faces were illuminated by the glow of the tiki torches that lined the sand, casting dancing shadows on their features.

"Hey, you two," I greeted them, taking a seat next to Sofia and tucking her into my arm. "I can't believe you're here. I'm so happy to see you."

"You'd have to drag this one away with a pack of wild horses," she said, grinning brightly at Luca. "He's talked of nothing for the last two months. 'Sofia, do you think she'll like my hair? Should I wear the blue suit, or the grey? Do you think I should shave?'"

Luca scowled. "You were the one asking me for advice on shoes and what dress to wear, princess. I'd say it goes both ways."

"Don't mind him," Sofia said, leaning into me conspiratorially, "he's just grumpy because he hasn't had a drink yet."

"No, I'm grumpy because you won't let me have a drink yet," Luca muttered, the corners of his mouth twitching up slightly as he watched Sofia.

"Meds, remember?" Sofia shot back. "Not for a few more weeks."

I took Sofia's hand in mine. "How are you holding up?" I asked her. "Things were so chaotic last time we spoke."

"I'm okay. It's been an adjustment, but I'm managing," Sofia said, smiling wanly.

I sensed there was more to it than that. "How's Julian?"

Sofia looked away. "It's been a while since I've heard from him. He's still with the family, but he's keeping his head down."

There was something in her tone that made me wonder if she had tried to reach out to him. "I'm sorry, Sofia. I know how much you care about him."

She smiled sadly. "That's just it, isn't it? Love can be so complicated sometimes, especially when the people involved are in such different places. He's still tangled up with the Family, and probably always will be. You wouldn't believe how many people showed up at Angelo and Lorenzo's funerals – it was overwhelming. I think something big is in the works."

My stomach tightened at the mention of the Moretti family. "What about Dominic?" I asked cautiously.

Sofia shook her head, her lips quirking into a wry smile. "Funny thing, they never found his body at the slaughterhouse."

"Really?" I frowned, my mind racing with the implications of that revelation. But I pushed those thoughts aside; tonight was a night for celebration and love, not dwelling on the past. "I'm sure it's nothing."

"Maybe. I hope so," she replied, but her voice sounded doubtful. Then, she brightened. "I've moved out of the compound, though. A little place in Charlestown. I'm trying to make a new start, you know? A fresh start away from the Family."

"That's great," I replied, genuinely happy for her. "You deserve some peace and happiness, Sofia."

Luca's expression softened as he looked at Sofia, and I wondered if he didn't feel the same way. It was hard to miss the way he looked at her, or the way his gaze lingered a moment too long on her lips.

"What about you, Luca?" I asked, trying to break the sudden tension between them. "How's the rehab going?"

Luca shrugged. "It's going. Still got a long way to go, but I'm getting there," he said, his expression tightening again.

I knew that he had a long road ahead of him, and that his recovery would be a process of ups and downs. But as I watched him interact with Sofia, I couldn't help but hope that maybe one day he would find the happiness he deserved.

"I'm proud of you, Luca. You're doing great," I told him, and he smiled.

"Thanks, kid. That means a lot."

Luca grew tired quickly as the evening wore on. He and Sofia exchanged a look before he nodded, giving me a small smile. "We should head out, Emilia. Long day tomorrow, and I'm a bit slower these days."

"Of course," I said, hugging them both tightly. "Thank you for being here. It means the world to me."

"Take care of yourself, Emilia," Luca whispered in my ear, his voice thick with emotion.

"Always," I promised, giving him one last embrace before they left.

I found myself back in Alfie's arms, swaying gently to a tune that spoke of endless summer nights. The revelry around us began to wind down, the crowd thinning as people murmured their goodbyes and disappeared into the dark.

"Ready to call it a night?" Alfie's voice was husky, sending shivers across my skin.

"Definitely," I replied, a cheeky smile playing on my lips. "I'm ready for bed."

"Alright, let me take you there." With that, Alfie swept me up into his strong arms, carrying me towards our home as laughter bubbled up from within me.

"What are you doing?" I managed between giggles.

"Patience, Mrs. Doyle," he chided playfully, the smirk evident in his voice. But then he stopped, and I followed his gaze.

A bonfire roared on the beach, casting dancing shadows onto the sand. Next to it, a hammock was slung between two palm trees, swaying gently in the evening breeze. Before us was an echo of my past, a tender memory brought to life under the watchful eyes of the moon and stars.

"Alfie..." I breathed, speechless as he set me down on the sand. "You did this for me?"

"Of course," he grinned, holding me close. "I wanted tonight to be as special as you are."

"Thank you," I whispered, my heart swelling with love for this incredible man who had somehow become mine. I wrapped my arms around him, pressing a tender kiss to his lips. "I love you, Alfie."

He set me down gently, hands lingering at my waist as he leaned in close, his breath hot on my ear. "I've never done it in a hammock, but I'm sure I'll get the hang of it once I get my sea legs." His words were a playful challenge, his green eyes twinkling with mischief.

I reached up, threading my fingers through the curls that fell into his eyes, and pulled him down to me. Our lips met in a kiss that held the fiery passion of the bonfire and the depth of the ocean that surrounded us. "I love you," I murmured against his mouth, tasting the salt and sweetness of our new beginning.

"I love you more," he replied, his voice a deep rumble that vibrated through me.

We nestled into the hammock together, bodies entwined as we watched the flames dance. The world around us faded away—there was only Alfie and me, our hearts beating as one, wrapped in each other's arms. We swayed gently, lulled by the rhythm of the tide, the warmth of the fire warding off the chill of the night.

And there, curled up under the canopy of stars, I knew we had found our sanctuary—a place where love conquered all, where we could be safe from the shadows of our past. In this sacred space, nothing else mattered but the steady thrum of our hearts and the promise of forever whispered by the wind.

39

— • —

Epilogue - Cassidy

"Sweetheart." A kiss to my temple, and I felt the couch dip as Connor sat next to me. "Hey—wake up."

"Sorry," you mumbled, blearily looking up at him. "How long was I asleep?"

"Not long, and I'd let you keep napping, but...your Dad's here."

That got me up. "What?"

Connor was chewing the inside of his cheek, picking up on my mood. "He just buzzed the intercom, he said he wanted to talk with you if that was okay. I asked him to wait."

"Yeah. Yeah, send him up. It's okay."

I rubbed my eyes, rolling up to a sitting position as I tried to straighten my clothes nervously, hoping that I didn't have pillow marks on my face. Dodging the moving boxes strewn about the penthouse, we both made our way to the door, and with a final deferring glance at me, Connor opened it.

"Dad. Hi."

"Hi, Cassidy. I hope it's not a bad time."

"N-No. It's fine. Come in."

My father walked past me and into the kitchen, carrying a large box. Connor's eyebrows raised and he looked at me, but I just shrugged.

"You need any help with that, Michael?" Connor asked.

"No. Thank you, though," he said, setting it on the kitchen island. He seemed uncharacteristically nervous, fidgeting as he removed his coat. "Actually, I was wondering if I might have a word with my daughter."

Behind him, Connor rose up protectively, but I held up a hand. "Yeah. Sure."

Connor looked at me questioningly but let it go. He still resented the way my father had treated me in the beginning. The relationship between the two of us was still rocky and uncertain, but we were both trying, and he understood that.

He squeezed my hand as he passed, pressing a kiss to my cheek. "I'll be in the office if you need anything, okay?"

"Okay, Connor. Thank you."

The door to the office shut, and for a long while you both stood there awkwardly.

"Connor looks well."

"Yeah, retirement suits him."

"Good. That's good." Michael rocked back and forth on his feet, one hand reaching blindly up to pick at a corner of the box. "You're looking well too...I'm glad to see you both back on your feet."

"What's in the box, Dad?"

I cut to the chase, tired of the small talk, and my father pursed his lips.

"Some of your old baby things...and some of Rosaleen's things from when she was pregnant. I thought that you should have them."

Wordlessly, I went over to the box and peered inside. A few of my old stuffed animals and toys, some children's books. A baby blanket that I remembered had been knitted by my grandmother. A very old baby scale and several well-worn booties, as well as a rattle I suspected might have belonged to one of my parents.

And there at the bottom was my baby book.

Paging through it felt like my heart was being squeezed in a vice, but the pain was bittersweet. Photographs of my mother, her face shining with radiant expectation as she carried me, the joyful looks on both my parent's faces as they held me for the first time. Little notes jotted in the margins here and there. Little anecdotes, what my favorite foods were, when I got my first tooth and what my first word was. The difficulties and joys of pregnancy and her changing life as a new mother, thoughts and hopes for her daughter.

I wasn't sure at what point the tears had started, but they fell in earnest now. "I miss her so much."

"I miss her too."

Michael moved to sit next to me, and this time I didn't move away. "I miss the way things were, Dad. Before, when we were happy. I miss you both."

"I know. I'm sorry. I'm sorry for how it's been between us, and the blame falls entirely on my shoulders. You were hurting just as much as I was, and I wasn't there for you, either time you needed me. I can't go back and change that. It can't be undone."

When he finally looked at me, I was surprised to see the tears in his eyes as well. "I almost lost you like I lost your mother, and it...it messed with my head badly. I know that's no excuse, I can only imagine how it was for you. I'm so sorry I wasn't there for you after...after..."

His gaze drifted down to the puckered scars on my hand and wrist, and the words died in his throat. Suddenly I was struck by how old he looked. For all his power and wealth, he was now practically alone, guilt eating him alive.

I closed my eyes. The old grudges had all but faded for me, and as much as his lack of presence the past few months hurt, I understood it. He was a broken man, and I could either perpetuate this cycle of blame and loathing, or I could try to salvage what was left of our relationship.

"Dad, no." I took his hand, holding it tightly. "I don't want to go back to that place. All this ugliness between us? I want it to be over. I want to start over. I'm tired of all the bullshit and the fighting. I want my son to grow up knowing his grandfather, and I'm willing to put it behind me if you are. Mom wouldn't have wanted us to fight like this."

A watery laugh. "She would've kicked both our asses, and then made us hug it out."

"Under threat of violence."

Michael slowly closed the baby book. "I didn't bring this over today to try to work my way back into your life, now that you're moving on from all this. I really just wanted you to have these things."

"I know, Dad. I meant it, though. I want to start over. Okay?"

"Okay."

We both leaned into the hug at the same time, emotions spilling over and overruling any remaining reservations. It was as if we'd been pulled together by an invisible force, and for a moment, I could almost see my mother smiling down at us both.

***

Long after my father had left, I sat there paging through the book, heedless of the tears that hadn't stopped falling since I'd opened it again.

"Cass?" Connor was at my side in an instant, eyes liquid with concern. "What happened? Are you all right?"

I nodded, hiccupping as he pulled me into his arms. Connor looked down at what was laying in my lap, and he froze. "Is this..."

"My baby book. It's almost like a diary my mom kept while she was pregnant and then after I was born."

Connor picked up one of the photographs. In it was a fuzzy headed girl with her face frozen in a delighted squeal as she reached for the woman holding her, a woman about my age with precisely the same color hair. A slow smile spread across his face.

"He's trying, Connor, and I want to give him a chance. I'm tired of all the anger."

Connor reverently placed the photo back in the book. "I am too. It's a turn of the page for all of us, I think, and if this is what you want, then I'm behind you one hundred percent."

"Thank you. It's not gonna be easy, but it's what I need."

Connor gently cupped my face, smoothing away my tears before he kissed me. His mouth was sweet and warm against mine, and it was only a few minutes before the kisses led to something deeper and more insistent. Connor moaned, shifting on the couch as he felt all his blood drain south.

"I swear," he panted as I kissed down the length of his throat, "I wasn't pushing for it to go...this way."

I was equally breathless, gently closing the book and setting it on the table before I climbed into his lap. "Mister, I am a mess of hormones right now. I might be crying one minute, but all you've got to do is bat those baby blues at me and I want you naked."

Connor laughed, high and breathless as I started unbuttoning his shirt. "I'm not complaining, love. One look from you and I'm a goner. You can have me anytime you want."

My eyes flashed. Grabbing him by the hand, I led him towards the bedroom, shutting the door firmly behind me.

"Sloane just texted, she's on her way over."

Connor was leaning in the doorway to the nursery, already dressed in his suit and tie and looking good enough to eat. My breath caught just at the sight of him, and he bit his lip, color rising high in his cheeks as I undressed him with my eyes.

"Steamin' Christ, you're the only woman in the world that can make me blush like a schoolboy just by lookin' at me," he said, though the way he was looking at me left little doubt as to what sinful thoughts were currently running through his mind.

"Bashful's a good look on you," I teased. "Especially when you do that scrunchie nose thing—yep, there it is."

Connor huffed and tilted my chin up so he could kiss me, his lips curling into a smile as he felt his son's hands grab at his face. "Sorry little guy, not paying you enough attention? Why don't you come to Da and let your Mum get ready for her big date."

I carefully handed both baby and burp cloth over to Connor, who expertly shifted Aiden against his shoulder, rubbing soft circles on his back until he coaxed out a burp.

"Thank you—I think he needs to be changed, though, too."

Connor made a face as he agreed. "I'll give you one thing, little man, you're regular. Go on, sweetheart, I've got this."

One final kiss, and I walked across the hall to the master bedroom, reveling in the thought of a night out with Connor. It wasn't as if the two of us hadn't been able to go out together—on the contrary, Aiden never lacked for enthusiastic babysitters. Tonight was different though. Tonight was special.

It was our anniversary.

A little smile was on my face as I put on my dress and did my hair and makeup. Heels slipped on and perfume applied. I felt happy and alive and deliciously sexy, but above all, I felt loved.

And who would have thought, all those months ago. Standing there at the altar with a complete stranger, a shadow from my memories. Even then, he had opened his heart to me, offering up all of the warmth and love and safety he had to give.

"Cassidy Quinn. I know this union isn't ideal and it's not what you wanted, but that doesn't change the fact that we're both standing up here before God and half the population of Boston."

"From this day forward, I give you my heart, and I promise to love you and protect you. I promise to be faithful to you and to make you happy. I promise to be your equal in all things, during the good times and the bad, for the rest of our lives."

"With this ring I seal these promises to you, my darling wife."

"Love? You okay?"

I hadn't heard him come in behind me. For a minute, all I could do was stare at him. This man I loved more than life itself.

"More than okay. I'm perfect." I stood and wrapped my arms around him. "Where's Aiden?"

"Sloane's got him. She and Tommy just walked in." Connor held me at arm's length, looking me up and down. "You are...a vision. Even now, you take my breath away. How'd I get so lucky?"

"Funny, I was thinking the same thing. I can't believe it's been one year."

"Been a hell of a year."

I nodded. "I wouldn't go so far as to say I'd repeat any of it, but...it got us where we are now, and there is nowhere I'd rather be. I love you, Connor."

"I love you too, sweetheart."

Connor hummed as I kissed him, lips parted as I drank him in. Every shudder and every sigh, my hands fisted in the lapels of his suit while his roved down over my waist, settling on my rear before he pulled back breathlessly.

"Careful now," I laughed. "You're gonna make a mess of me before we even get to the restaurant."

"Lass, you are gonna be the death of me," he groaned. "We've got a whole night ahead of us and all I can think about is how to get you out of that dress. At the same time, though, I just want to sit back and look at you, you're so beautiful. Pretty as a picture."

Connor frowned. "One thing missing, though..."

From the inside of his suitcoat, he pulled out a small, flat box. Black with a gold fabric bow.

"Connor, you didn't have to—"

"Trust me. I did."

I opened the box, and I understood.

It was my mother's necklace. The one my father had given her the day I was born, the one she had never taken off. Of all the things I remembered most about her—her scent, the sound of her laugh, her smile—that necklace always stood out in my memory.

Of course, it wasn't the same necklace. It couldn't be. The original had been lost years ago on the fateful night we had lost her. It had never been found, and seeing it again brought a wave of emotion.

"Connor...Connor, I—" I sniffed and looked up at him in surprise. "How did you—"

Connor looked at me, his face solemn. "Recreated from old photographs. Michael helped me with the details, and we found a jeweler that was able to reconstruct it. Except this one has Aiden's birthstone instead of yours."

"Oh, Connor..."

He drew me close as I furiously blinked back tears. "You know I'd give you the world if I could. I'd bring her back if I could. Anything for you," he whispered. "I know how much you miss her and I thought, maybe, having this would help you to feel closer to her."

And it did. Connor fastened the clasp, lightly kissing the back of my neck as I watched in the mirror. Just seeing it again felt like coming full circle, Rosaleen there to guide me through my journey as a wife and mother with the same strength and grace that she had.

"It's perfect, Connor, it's...I don't even have words. Thank you."

Eyes blown wide, the thin ring of blue dazzling in intensity as he gently tipped my face up to meet his. "I never knew what a hole I had in my life until you filled it. How lost I was, until you were there, brightening everything you touched. There were so many times this past year when I felt like...like I had caught a shooting star by the tail, and as hard as I tried to hold onto it, it just kept slipping through my fingers.

"And now, standing here with you in my arms, in the home that we made together, watching you with our son...I'm the luckiest man in the world." He shook his head, a crooked, besotted smile of disbelief on his lips. "Happy anniversary, mo chroí."

The night was perfect. I felt like we were dating again, holding hands, walking down the sidewalk towards the river. Stealing kisses under the stars and the city lights, as carefree as any two lovers can be.

"I hate that we missed out on this," Connor said.

"What—the dating?"

"Yeah. We're kind of doing it backwards...Everything was so jammed up in the beginning, I wish I'd had the chance to woo you properly."

I laughed. "Woo me? Connor McTiernan, you sound like a romance novelist."

"Whatever it's called. You deserve it."

I pulled him to a stop. "You remember what you said up at the front of that church? Maine? Picking flowers for me every morning, cooking for me, playing piano for me? Whispering sweet nothings—in Gaelic, no less?"

"Mo chroí...Is breá liom tú" Connor grinned. "I'll tell you I love you in every language I can."

I gently brushed my thumb along his jaw. "And then later, even when we had our ups and downs, you never gave up. You reached out to my friends, the things you did for me...you were even willing to let me go. To let me decide, just because you didn't want me to feel trapped. You wanted me to be happy."

I shook my head. "Connor, you've been wooing me since the second we met, and you've never stopped. Your first words to me knocked me off my feet, and I've been falling for you ever since. Is breá liom tú, Connor."

He looked down at me, eyes shining with all the love I knew he held for me in his heart.

"Is breá liom tú."

Much later that night, after Connor and I had fallen into an exhausted but blissful sleep, limbs tangled and bodies still shining with the afterglow of our lovemaking, I crept out of bed. A tender, lingering kiss to

Connor's forehead, smiling when he didn't even so much as twitch, he was sleeping so heavily.

I padded across the hall to our son's bedroom.

Aiden slept like Connor. Heavily, which was a blessing in itself, arms thrown wide. He wrinkled his nose as I smoothed a light hand over his fuzzy little head, lips twitching as he sleep nursed.

Satisfied that he was neither in need of a change or a feeding, I padded into the kitchen to get a glass of water. Everything silent and still. Loved etched in every corner of the little apartment, the soft light from the city that never sleeps filtering though the blinds and throwing everything into a dreamlike haze.

This. This right here—this was our life now. Our world. A year ago I could never have imagined being this happy, this at peace with myself and my role in life. I still had my work, but this—my family—it meant everything.

Connor blinked sleepily as I slid back into bed. "Everything good, love?"

If it wasn't me making the nightly rounds, then it was him, both of us sharing the same incessant need to ensure the security of the little world we had created. The caretaker and the protector.

"All quiet, he's sound asleep."

"Good. C'mere."

Connor tugged me back into his arms and was asleep again with a soft sigh. I curled into him, fingers ghosting over the scars on his chest and settling over his heart as sleep claimed me as well.

The future was still uncertain and would always be. It was something we had both accepted. It was okay. As scary as the prospect of the unknown might be, it was also what made life worth living. It was what had led us to where we were now.

And there was nowhere else we would rather be.

THEIR STORY ISN'T OVER YET...

Click here for a FREE exclusive bonus epilogue from Connor and Cassidy – five years later!

———

Want to read Alfie and Emilia's story from the beginning? Click Here for a FREE copy of *SAINT – A MCTIERNAN CLAN NOVELLA.*

———

Look for the series to wrap up in *Brutal Empire* – Tommy and Sloane's story, available NOW!

BOSTON IS BURNING

The McTiernans have taken back South Boston, with Tommy Quinn as their newly-appointed Clan Chief. But heavy lies the head that wears the crown—infighting and disillusion have left Tommy struggling to keep the family united. The only person he seems to have on his side is the woman he's been secretly carrying a torch for, Sloane McTiernan.

Bullets or whiskey—Sloane dispenses whatever her boys need. Bartending at the family pub has left her no stranger to heartbreak, but she's still got Tommy, her friend and confidant, the man she turns to when it becomes too difficult to plaster on a flirty smile. But when an old enemy returns seeking revenge against Tommy, Sloane realizes her feelings for the Irishman run far deeper than she was prepared to admit.

Enemies are around every corner.

Their backs are to the wall.

And this time, Sloane must decide just how far she's willing to go for love...even if it means burning it all to the ground.

AVAILABLE NOW

AUTHOR'S NOTE

Thank you so much for reading! I hope you enjoyed *Cruel Empire*—for me, this was where the series really got fun for me to write, all the ins and outs of the interconnected relationships and bringing everything together in one, huge climax. The angst level was high on this one! Journeying along with these characters and seeing them through to the resolutions they all deserved was so satisfying, but it's not over yet! You'll see more from Connor and Cassidy in the final book in the McTiernan Clan Trilogy, *Brutal Empire*, and well as a cameo from Alfie and Emilia. *Brutal Empire* in now available, and focuses on Tommy and Sloane, with appearances from the rest of the McTiernan family as we bring the series to a close.

I have big things planned for an expansion series, so stay tuned—a trilogy featuring the Moretti Family AND a trilogy featuring the mysterious Volkov Bratva are in the works, as well as a couple related stand-alone novels. Keep in touch with me on Instagram, my website, and, of course, the best source of bookish news, my newsletter.

If you enjoyed reading this book, please consider leaving a review. Reviews are fuel for my writing machine, and they help spread the word to new readers.

Thank you for reading!

About the Author

AJ Fallow writes dark, gritty contemporary romances featuring strong heroines and morally grey heroes. Her works contain strong themes, steamy romance scenes, and graphic violence. Please check the trigger warnings for each individual book, AJ's works are not intended for readers under 18.

AJ has been previously published under several pen names in romance, fantasy, paranormal, and horror genres. She is currently pursuing her MFA from Southern New Hampshire University, and lives with her family in Maine.

You can find her on social media @author_ajfallow

and on her website at www.authorajfallow.com

Subscribe to AJ Fallow's newsletter HERE

www.ingramcontent.com/pod-product-compliance
Lightning Source LLC
Chambersburg PA
CBHW051513250626
47156CB00001B/74